PRAISE FOR

The Rhetoric of Death

"Amazing . . . Ms. Rock takes you back to fascinating and dangerous seventeenth-century Paris so well that I suspect her of being a time-traveler who's been there."

—Ariana Franklin, national bestselling author of *Mistress of the Art of Death*

"Rich with telling detail and a deep feeling for time and place."

—Margaret Frazer, national bestselling author of *The Witch's Tale*

"Rock skillfully builds her suspense plot, all the while incorporating splendid detail of seventeenth-century Parisian monastic and street life and the relationship between church and Crown, along with the intricate political and religious conflicts of the era. She proves herself a promising new talent by creating this powerful, absorbing, complex, and thoroughly satisfying novel."

—*Historical Novels Review* (editor's choice)

"[A] superb historical debut . . . With an experienced writer's ease, Rock incorporates details of the political issues of the day into a suspenseful story line. Fans of Brother Cadfael, another military man turned priest sleuth, will be pleased."

—*Publishers Weekly* (starred review)

"Rich with historical detail . . . meticulously researched. [Rock] captures a city and time that is lively, dangerous, and politically charged, and makes it sing. . . . [Her] fine eye for historic detail and well-drawn characters will continue to engage readers."

—*Kirkus Reviews* (starred review)

continued . . .

"Rock brings firsthand knowledge of dance, choreography, acting, police investigation, and teaching to what is hopefully the beginning of a mystery series . . . [A] fascinating historical mystery . . . Plenty of derring-do and boyish mischief sprinkled into the plot make this a fun read, and Charles's thought-provoking struggles as he questions his vocation lend added depth. A fine counterpart to S. J. Parris's suspenseful historical mystery novel, *Heresy*, which dramatizes religious strife in an earlier era, and similar in theme to P. D. James's *Death in Holy Orders*, Rock's novel boasts a style all its own and is sure to satisfy those eager for a great new historical mystery." —*Booklist* (starred review)

"Rock is an exciting new discovery. Her plotting holds your interest, her characters are real, and her attention to details of the time period is extraordinary. Highly recommended for fans of historical thrillers and readers who enjoy Ellis Peters, Edward Marston, and Ariana Franklin." —*Library Journal* (starred review)

Berkley titles by Judith Rock

THE RHETORIC OF DEATH
THE ELOQUENCE OF BLOOD

The Eloquence of Blood

Judith Rock

BERKLEY BOOKS, NEW YORK

THE BERKLEY PUBLISHING GROUP
Published by the Penguin Group
Penguin Group (USA) Inc.
375 Hudson Street, New York, New York 10014, USA
Penguin Group (Canada), 90 Eglinton Avenue East, Suite 700, Toronto, Ontario M4P 2Y3, Canada
(a division of Pearson Penguin Canada Inc.)
Penguin Books Ltd., 80 Strand, London WC2R 0RL, England
Penguin Group Ireland, 25 St. Stephen's Green, Dublin 2, Ireland (a division of Penguin Books Ltd.)
Penguin Group (Australia), 250 Camberwell Road, Camberwell, Victoria 3124, Australia
(a division of Pearson Australia Group Pty. Ltd.)
Penguin Books India Pvt. Ltd., 11 Community Centre, Panchsheel Park, New Delhi—110 017, India
Penguin Group (NZ), 67 Apollo Drive, Rosedale, Auckland 0632, New Zealand
(a division of Pearson New Zealand Ltd.)
Penguin Books (South Africa) (Pty.) Ltd., 24 Sturdee Avenue, Rosebank, Johannesburg 2196,
South Africa

Penguin Books Ltd., Registered Offices: 80 Strand, London WC2R 0RL, England

This book is an original publication of The Berkley Publishing Group.

This is a work of fiction. Names, characters, places, and incidents either are the product of the author's imagination or are used fictitiously, and any resemblance to actual persons, living or dead, business establishments, events, or locales is entirely coincidental. The publisher does not have any control over and does not assume any responsibility for author or third-party websites or their content.

PRINTING HISTORY
Berkley trade paperback edition / September 2011

Library of Congress Cataloging-in-Publication Data

Rock, Judith.
  The eloquence of blood / Judith Rock.
     p.   cm.
  ISBN 978-0-425-24297-1
1. Collège Louis-le-Grand (Paris, France)—Fiction.   2. Jesuits—Fiction.   3. Young women—Crimes against—Fiction.   4. Murder—Investigation—Fiction.   5. France—History—17th century—Fiction.
I. Title.
  PS3618.O3543E56 2011
  813'.6—dc22   2011014289

PRINTED IN THE UNITED STATES OF AMERICA

10 9 8 7 6 5 4 3 2 1

For John Padberg, S.J.
Charles's godfather
Fountain of knowledge about all things Jesuit
And best of all, friend

ACKNOWLEDGMENTS

Though writing is solitary work, it takes many people to create a book. Heartfelt thanks to all of them: Patricia Ranum and John Padberg, S.J., historians who helped with research and set me straight on many seventeenth-century questions; my hawkeyed team of readers who vetted the manuscript-in-progress: Lydia Veliko, Damaris Rowland (my incomparable agent), John Padberg, and my husband, Jay, who also created the map of Paris; Shannon Jamieson Vazquez (my incomparable editor), who takes what I think is a finished manuscript, finds the holes, and fixes them. Any errors that remain are mine alone.

And thanks especially to all who read *The Rhetoric of Death*, Charles's first adventure, and told me they wanted more!

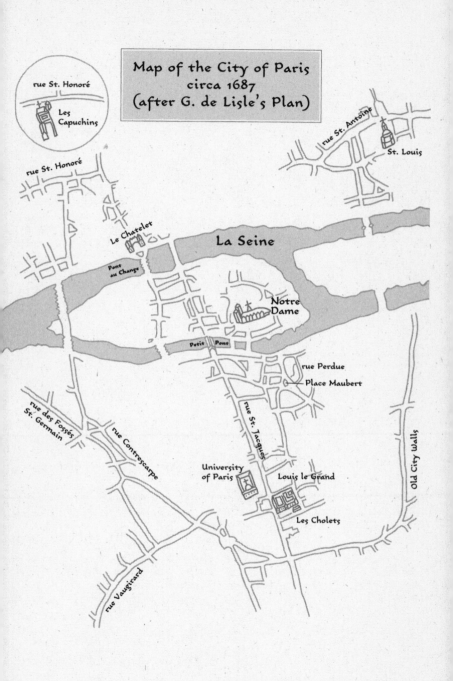

Map of the City of Paris
circa 1687
(after G. de Lisle's Plan)

rue St. Honoré

Les
Capuchins

rue St. Honoré

rue St. Antoine

St. Louis

Le Chatelet

La Seine

Pont
au Change

Notre
Dame

Petit Pont

rue Perdue

Place Maubert

rue des Fossés
St. Germain

rue Contrescarpe

rue St. Jacques

Old City Walls

University
of Paris

Louis le Grand

Les Cholets

rue Vaugirard

Chapter 1

CHRISTMAS EVE 1686

Under a sky the gray of slushy puddles, the afternoon was fading to an early dusk. Silence lay like a glaze of ice over the college of Louis le Grand and its motley façade of stone, plaster, and brick, its honeycomb of courtyards, its slate-roofed towers and gables. Then a door banged open and a flood of boys poured into the Cour d'honneur, the school's vast main courtyard, followed by two black-cloaked Jesuits. Most of the students started warming games of chase, but two fourteen-year-olds, trailed by a younger boy, sped to the chapel.

"I somehow doubt that those three have been struck by an urge to prayer," Maître Charles du Luc said dryly to his companion. "Shall I go and see?"

Père Thomas Damiot nodded, laughing. "I think you will find them searching diligently for an *answer* to prayer."

Huddling into his cloak, Charles crossed the windy courtyard to the always-open chapel door and stopped unnoticed on the threshold. A little way inside, the three boys were gathered around the stone clamshell that held holy water.

"It's frozen!" one of the older boys said jubilantly. "Oh, thank the Blessed Virgin!" He bent his knee hurriedly toward the altar and crossed himself.

But the other was poking a skeptical finger at the skim of ice on the water. "It's not frozen enough."

The first speaker turned and stared at the shattered ice skim. "Oh, Venus's bosoms!"

Round-eyed at the daring oath and shivering so hard his teeth chattered, the smallest boy stood on tiptoe to peer into the shell. "*Quid—quem—*um—" Giving up trying to speak Latin, as the older boys were doing and the college rules required, he whispered in French, "When *is* it frozen enough?"

Allowances being admissible for the as yet un-Latined, the oath swearer descended to French. "When you can skate on it. Then we stay indoors for recreation."

"Skate on that?" The little one stared in bewilderment at the holy water. "How?"

"Figure of speech, dunce!"

"He hasn't had rhetoric," the other fourteen-year-old said mildly. "And anyway, what you said *isn't* a figure of speech." He frowned. "Is it?"

"Who cares? It's Christmas vacation! Come on, race you!"

Deciding that he hadn't heard the oath, Charles swallowed his laughter, stepped quickly aside from the doorway, and pretended to study the complex set of sundials on the tallest tower. A pointless exercise under the cloud blanket, but he was well aware that students expected professors to do pointless things. The older boys ran past him with barely a glance. The little one plodded after them, absorbed in pulling his wide-brimmed hat down over his ears, and went to join a game of tag.

"I take it their prayer is still unanswered," Damiot said, joining Charles.

"Is that the rule? They can't stay indoors until the holy water freezes solid?"

"Certainly it is the rule. Ah, there they are." Damiot nodded toward the pair of courtyard proctors arriving to oversee this first recreation for students spending the Christmas break in the college. "Now we can go. And we'd better make speed to St. Louis, or Père Pinette will have our heads."

"Who is Père Pinette?"

"Rector of the Professed House—our house near the church of St. Louis. For fully professed Jesuits who work in Paris but aren't connected with Louis le Grand." Damiot started toward the vaulted stone passage leading from the Cour d'honneur to the street. "Our Père Pinette takes ceremony as seriously as a general takes battle."

"Well, it is the Prince of Condé's ceremony," Charles said, following him into the dank, echoing passage, "and he *was* France's greatest general." He caught up with Damiot and lowered his voice. "I know we're all deeply honored that the Condé has left us—um—part of himself, him being a Prince of the Blood. But I confess that dead royalty leaving their hearts and entrails and so on to churches and monasteries has always seemed to me a little bizarre. Why is it done?"

Damiot looked at Charles as though he'd asked why the sun rose. "Because it's always been done." He shrugged. "Surely it's obvious. A man's heart is the most important earthly part of him, so to leave that to a monastery or a church is to confer a very great honor."

"Yes, I suppose I can see that. About what the heart means." Charles assumed a puzzled frown. "But what does it mean if he leaves you his—um—bowels and so on?"

Damiot's mouth twitched. "Fortunately, the Condé left us

only his heart, so restrain your thirst for knowledge. Seriously, Maître du Luc, a royal personage gives an incomparable gift when he leaves his heart in the keeping of those who will pray for his soul and honor his life. Such a gift is a mark of the greatest honor and can only enhance the reputation of the community chosen. Which is another reason we *cannot* be late."

Charles forced his numb feet to move faster. "I'll be frozen to death before we get there, so it won't matter if I'm late."

"Don't be so dramatic, it's not really cold at all for Christmas Eve. You should have been here last year."

"Dear Virgin of Sorrows," Charles muttered under his breath, reaching under his cloak to rub the old war wound in his left shoulder, which minded the weather even more than the rest of him did.

This winter was his first in Paris and he was hating the cold. He tried to remind himself that this was only Paris, and they were only going to the church of St. Louis across the river, not setting out over snowy wastes for a frozen Jesuit mission in New France. Nevertheless, Charles suspected that if the devil appeared out of the street passage's chill shadows and offered him sunbaked warmth in trade for his soul, he'd have a sharp spiritual struggle on his hands. Not that winter wasn't cold in his native south of France. It snowed there, too, but less, and at least the sun showed itself. This endless northern gray threatened to sink deeper into his soul than the cold had sunk into his bones. But when he'd made the mistake of saying so, his fellow Jesuits had only laughed and told him darkly to wait until January.

The sniffling lay brother who had drawn the day's duty as porter opened the narrow postern door and let them out into the rue St. Jacques. Wind whipping merrily up from the Seine hit them full in the face.

"If you're so warm, Père Damiot," Charles said through his chattering teeth, "you can give me your cloak!"

"That was Saint Martin who gave away his cloak, Maître du Luc, not our blessed Saint Ignatius." Damiot grinned at Charles. "Besides, I am a priest, and you are a lowly scholastic." Charles, though a teacher, was still in what was called the scholastic phase of the long Jesuit training, still studying as well as teaching, and years from priesthood and final vows. Which was why his title was *maître*, which meant master, and not *père*, Father. "So if there is any cloak-giving," Damiot said, in the pious tones of a novice seeing himself in line for the papal throne, "it should go the other way. For the good of your soul, of course."

Happily trading mild barbs, they went down St. Geneviève's hill. Charles, twenty-eight, with wide shoulders and his Norman mother's thick, straw-colored hair, was taller than most Frenchmen. But the thin, dark, thirty-five-year-old Damiot was only half a head shorter and their long strides matched well enough. Their love of words and the stage also matched, Charles being a rhetoric teacher and producer of college ballets, and Damiot being the author of this year's holiday farce—for Louis le Grand Jesuits only—to be done the day after Christmas.

The rich smell of roasting chestnuts sweetened the air around them and they caught an occasional flare of warmth from the street vendors' small fires. Though the rue St. Jacques was the Latin Quarter's main street, it was emptier than usual. Many students from the University of Paris and the quarter's teeming colleges—secondary schools for boys from ten to twenty or so—had left for the holidays. A handful of servants were hurrying home from the Petit Marché, the market a little up the hill beyond the college. Tools on their shoulders, men working on an old College of Les Cholets building that now belonged to the

Jesuits were heading for the warmth of taverns. Charles saw one of them—likely a master carpenter, given his better clothes—break away from his fellows and make for the Necessity Man, who stood in the shadow of a gateway. The Necessity Man saw him coming and held out an old theatre mask from his assortment. The carpenter put it on, and the Necessity Man took off his voluminous cloak and held it up while his customer settled himself on a large bucket. Then he wrapped the cloak around both man and bucket and turned his back, leaving his masked customer to answer nature's call in disguise, if not in privacy.

A clattering of wheels and the ring of horseshoes on stone made Charles and Damiot leap aside and press themselves against a wall, the rue St. Jacques being wide enough for two carriages to pass and not much more.

"I am battling the sin of envy, Maître du Luc," Damiot shouted in Charles's ear, as carriages hurtled in opposite directions.

"Why?" Charles shouted back.

"Because our Louis le Grand *confrères* who teach theology and philosophy have nine days for their Christmas break. Their classes don't start again until the second of January."

They started walking again, brushing at the mud the carriage wheels had thrown onto their cloaks.

"While you," Damiot went on, "a martyr to rhetoric, and I, even more of a martyr to grammar, have a bare four days." He cast his eyes up at the unprepossessing heavens. "Why, oh ye saints and fates, was I set on Lady Grammar's stony way instead of the easy path of Lady Philosophy?"

"Lady Philosophy probably decided not to trust your slippery way with words. As for your sense of injustice, it's the twenty-fourth and our vacation started at noon. We have till the morrow of Holy Innocents, the twenty-ninth. That's four and a half days. Five and a half till we teach, since the morrow of Holy Innocents is a Sunday, which means our classes start again on Monday the thirtieth."

"Oh, don't split hairs, that's the worst of you rhetoricians. Just imagine the peace if we could send them all home, rhetoric and grammar classes along with theology and philosophy. Think about it, no boys in the college till after the Feast of the Circumcision!" January first, the Feast of the Circumcision, commemorated the ritual circumcising of the baby Jesus eight days after his birth. "With a few more days added to the break," Damiot went on, "most of them could go home or to some relative nearby."

"The thought has its points," Charles said dryly. "But it would still be a bit rushed to send the boys from Poland and China home and back again by January second."

"Yes, all right. But as things are now, there's hardly even time for Père Jouvancy to take a group of them down to the school's country house at Gentilly." Père Joseph Jouvancy, the renowned senior rhetoric professor, oversaw Charles's work in the college, both his teaching and his ballet production.

Charles shuddered. "He told me they'll walk to Gentilly after Mass tomorrow. As cold as it is! A great Christmas treat, he called it. He can't wait. Unbelievable."

"Gentilly is a bare few miles away, but even that little *promenade* will be rushed, because they'll walk back again on Holy Innocents." The Feast of the Holy Innocents on December twenty-eighth commemorated King Herod's massacre of boy babies when he tried to find and kill the newborn Jesus.

"But, *mon père*, we tell them that keeping them on college property protects them from worldly temptations. Are you denying that argument?" Charles's eyes were wide and blue with feigned dismay.

"Logic." Damiot snorted in disgust. "That's the other worst thing about you rhetoricians. Besides that, nothing could protect some of our—oof!" He ducked as the wind blew a clot of snow off a gargoyle leering down at them from the church of Saint-Séverin. "I'll tell you one thing, sending them home would save the school money. Judging from the belt tightening we've been doing lately, surely that would be welcome."

Charles grunted agreement. "I've heard we have a bequest coming, though."

"So I've heard, too. If it's true, it's not before time—I never want to see another bowl of bean pottage! On the other hand," Damiot added ruefully, "Saint Ignatius did say we should live like the poor."

"Saint Ignatius *was* a saint, after all . . ."

They melted into the gloom of the Petit Châtelet, the fortress entrance of the bridge called the Petit Pont, at the end of the rue St. Jacques. When they emerged onto the bridge, its tall stone houses somewhat sheltered them from the wind. But the bridge road was all too short. On the Right Bank, the wind seemed to blow even colder than on the Left, and they grabbed their wide-brimmed, flat-crowned black hats and gave up talking in favor of simply getting where they were going.

The church of St. Louis, just beyond St. Catherine's well on the rue St. Antoine, was an Italian oratorio of a building in pale stone. As they started up the church steps, the setting sun burned a rent in the clouds and stained the columned front with red. The door beneath the pediment's big gold and blue clock burst open and Père Jean Pinette, rector of the Jesuit Professed House beside the church, came out onto the porch. Impatience was visible in every line of him. Charles bit his lip to keep his countenance, thinking that Pinette's pale bony face and red-rimmed eyes made him look like an evil-tempered rabbit. His nose even twitched as it started to drip in the cold air.

"Get inside, you're late." Pinette swiped at his nose and stared in the direction Charles and Damiot had come from. "At last, thank the Blessed Virgin!" The sound of running feet behind them made Charles and Damiot turn to see a long-legged novice flying toward the steps, red cheeked from the cold.

"They are coming, Père Pinette!"

"Walk decently! Go and get the torches. I don't know how you'll keep them alight in this wind, but see that you do!"

Pinette chivied Charles and Damiot into the church, where three hundred other shivering Jesuits stood facing the door. They represented the three Paris houses of the Society of Jesus: the Professed House here beside St. Louis, the college of Louis le Grand, and the Paris Novice House. Charles and Damiot, last to arrive from Louis le Grand, started meekly toward the back row, but Pinette hissed, "No time!" and pushed them into the row just inside the doors. As they fumbled under their cloaks for their three-pronged ceremonial hats called *bonnets*, Pinette's voice boomed through the nave.

"Nearly here, be ready!"

The gathered Jesuits stopped hugging themselves for warmth, straightened their *bonnets*, and stood as though carved from black stone. Like soldiers, Charles thought, ducking aside to put his outdoor hat and Damiot's out of the way behind a statue of St. Ignatius. Ignatius, ex-soldier and courtier, founder of the Society of Jesus, had thought of his Jesuits as stalwart and obedient soldiers. That was part of what had attracted Charles, an ex-soldier himself, to the Society. After seven years, though, the soldier image was no longer one of the things he cherished about being a Jesuit. And obedience was his greatest stumbling block.

With a rueful quirk of his wide mobile mouth, Charles resumed his place in this soldierly gathering of men to honor France's greatest general, the Prince of Condé, who had died on December eleventh. The Great Condé, as he was called, Louis II of Bourbon, was a soul newly reclaimed for Holy Church after a lifetime of freethinking apostasy. Because Jesuits had helped return him to the fold, he had left them the great gift they were assembled to receive. This was only the ceremonial reception of the gift, though. Its interment in the wall behind the high altar would be in April, to give time for the writing of new music for the funeral Mass and the creation of elaborate church decor for the occasion.

The Professed House rector raked a last sharp look over his troops and barked, "Doors!"

Novices hauled the church's great doors open wide, and Pinette went out to stand at the edge of the porch. The first row of Jesuits filed out past him and stood one on the end of each step. Charles was on the bottom step in the wind's path, holding his *bonnet* on with one hand. Damiot was just above him. From the alley at the side of the church, four novices came with flaring, spitting torches. Two stopped at street level and two climbed to stand wide apart just below Pinette.

The sound of slowly rolling carriage wheels, the rattle of harness, and the slow beat of scores of hooves drew all eyes to the west. Along the street, people hurrying to get out of the early-evening cold stopped and crossed themselves, and the men took off their hats. Black and slow under the last slash of crimson in the clouds of Christmas Eve's sunset, the Great Condé's procession came. The first riders passed St. Catherine's well, a score of black-caparisoned horses carrying noblemen so blackly clad they were only white faces in the dusk. Behind them rolled two black-plumed carriages, the first with the heraldic arms of the Bishop of Autun, the second with those of the Prince of Condé. Behind the carriages rode yet more men-at-arms. The first carriage drew

up at the church steps and a lackey sprang down to lower the carriage step and open the door. Two clerics emerged and together
helped a slow-moving mass of sable and silver to descend. The
Bishop of Autun stood stiffly upright and straightened his mitre
as one of his attendants pulled the episcopal crozier from the carriage. The second carriage disgorged three more clerics, one of
them bearing a small box of pale gold. They paced gravely to
their bishop, and the box bearer set his burden on the bishop's
upturned, black-gloved palms.

The bishop mounted the stairs, one cleric going before him
with his crozier, the other four coming behind. Jewels on the
gleaming box flashed red, blue, and green in the torchlight. Père
Pinette bowed deeply to the bishop and kissed his ring. In clouds
of silver frost, the bishop spoke and Pinette replied. Then Pinette
received the box, which held the Great Condé's mummified heart,
and the bishop gave his blessing. From their places on the steps
and inside the church, the Jesuits began a sonorous Te Deum. The
bishop descended majestically down the church steps, back to his
carriage.

"*Allez, allez, mon cher évêque,*" Charles thought toward the bishop
behind his singing. "Achieve your carriage and get us out of this
wind, or you'll send us all to join the Condé before our time!"

But the bishop, warm in his sable, knew good liturgical theatre
when he met it, and he paced solemnly on. When the episcopal
posterior finally disappeared and the carriage door was shut, Pinette turned with equal majesty and bore the box into St. Louis,
toward the gated altar where it would stay until its April interment
behind the high altar. Still singing, the Jesuits who had stood on
the steps followed him in double file, trying not to shove each
other to get out of the wind. Those in the nave parted neatly
before Pinette and his burden, allowed those who had been out-

side to pass, then closed behind them in procession toward the gated side altar bright with wax candles and covered with cloth of gold.

The twinkling box had almost reached its temporary resting place among the side altar's blazing candles when a man reared, bellowing, out of the shadows. He launched himself at Pinette, the singing shattered into chaos, and the box went bouncing end over end into the darkness, clanging on the stone floor like an out-of-tune bell.

Charles lunged for the attacker, saw that Damiot and others were already grabbing him, and instead changed course to go after the box. He prayed that it hadn't broken open. Or, if it had, that he wouldn't step on its contents. His first prayer went unanswered. A faint whiff of death overlaid with spices led him toward the side wall. A fast-thinking novice brought a torch, whose light showed them the box lying open on its side. A little way beyond the gleam of its sapphires and rubies lay a misshapen thing the size of a large apple, tightly wrapped in dull gold silk. As Charles bent to pick it up, the attacker broke partly free of his captors and limped a few steps toward the box. He was old, wild haired, and dirty, and his seamed face was twisted with hatred.

"Your box is full of nothing!" he screamed, pointing a shaking finger at the lump in Charles's hand. "That's no human heart! That's a cold clod of filth; the thrice-damned Prince of Condé *had* no heart!"

In the stunned silence that closed around the words, a dark, slender young man—almost a boy still—threw himself to his knees in front of the Professed House rector. His brown breeches and coat were worn, and his hands were blue with cold as he clutched at Pinette's cassock.

"*Mon père*, I beg you, forgive him, let him go! He is old and his brains are weak, he does not know what he does!"

"He does violence and blasphemy!" Pinette jerked his cassock skirt out of the youth's fingers. His hard stare shifted from the young man to the old one. "Who is he? What are the two of you doing here?"

"He is no one, I swear it!" The boy was shaking with fear. "We only—we only came inside because we were cold, *mon père*."

The stone walls caught and magnified the frightened whisper. "Cold, cold, cold . . ." Pinette seemed to be choking on what he wanted to say. A muscle jumped in his jaw and his lips were a thin bloodless line. Charles hoped he would remember that Jesus' mother had also been poor and sought refuge from the cold one Christmas Eve . . .

"Get out," Pinette said through his teeth. "Stay out. If I find either of you here again, I will turn you over to the *commissaire*. Go!"

The youth scrambled to his feet, and Damiot and another Jesuit escorted him and the muttering old man to the nearest door. The old man twisted in their hands and looked back, his eyes glittering with rage.

"Hypocrite!" He spat at Pinette, barely missing Damiot. "You're like him, priest, coldhearted as the devils in hell! You'll be dead and rot like him, too!"

Pinette turned a deaf ear, drew himself up, and faced his men. "Arrange yourselves!"

The lines re-formed. Charles put the swaddled heart back into its lead-lined nest, closed the lid on it, and bore it as decorously as he could to Pinette. Pinette took it, they bowed to each other, and someone started the Te Deum again. Exchanging silent, sidelong looks, the singing Jesuits paced the rest of the short distance. Reverently, Pinette carried the silver gilt box through the open gate of the candlelit side altar and placed it on the glowing cloth of gold. After prayers of thanksgiving and a dismissal blessing, the Jesuits bowed and went silently out of the church to the duties and joys of Christmas. But when they reached the walkway to the Professed House and the steps of St. Louis, the air grew sibilant with outraged whispers about the disrupted ceremony. Inside the church, the sacristan locked the altar gate, pocketed the key, and hurried to contribute his own morsel to the indignant talk, leaving the heart of the Great Condé, Prince of the Blood, to await the spring and its final resting place.

Chapter 2

The Feast of Christmas passed in Masses, a modest but welcome feast, and equally welcome rest. When the five o'clock rising bell clanged through the winter darkness the next morning, it pulled Charles from dreams of home and warmth. He forced himself out of bed, shivering in his long white linen shirt and the black knee-length underpants and stockings he'd taken to wearing night and day in the cold. He felt his way into his shoes, easy to do in the dark since they had no right and left, and twitched his woolen cassock down from its old-fashioned hanging rail. Thrusting his arms into its narrow sleeves, he pulled it on over his underclothes and tied the black cloth belt around his waist in the regulation knot. By feel, he pulled a narrow edge of shirt cuff and neckband to show white at neck and sleeve against the cassock's black, retrieved his cloak from its night duty as an extra blanket, and draped it around his shoulders. Then he knelt at his prie-dieu for the required hour of meditation.

He said the Hours of Our Lady, added prayers for particular people, and finished, as always, with fervent prayers for the safety and well-being of his Huguenot cousin Pernelle and her little girl

Lucie, living now in Geneva. Some of his brother Jesuits might have censored his prayers for Protestants—called Huguenots in France—unless he was praying for their conversion. But St. Ignatius had founded the Society of Jesus "to help souls," and Charles sheltered his prayers under that wide rubric. When he reached his "amen," he rose resolutely from the prie-dieu, refusing to stay there with the images of Pernelle that rose in his mind. It being still too dark to see the little painting of the Virgin and Child on the wall in front of him, he took his candle into the passageway. Listening to the faint morning sounds from other chambers, he lit the candle from the night lantern on the stair landing and hurried back to his own door, shielding the spark of warmth with his hand.

His chamber and tiny adjoining study were on the third floor of Louis le Grand's main building, whose tall double doors were the college's public entrance. The ground floor, which also housed the most important administrative offices, offered a few traces of elegance with its carpets and paintings, but Charles's rooms were anything but stylish. The white walls were roughly plastered and the low ceiling was crossed with massive beams. Besides the prie-dieu and his little painting of the Virgin and Child, Charles's sleeping chamber held a narrow uncurtained bed with a painted crucifix at its foot, a single chair without a cushion, and an old-fashioned, age-blackened wooden chest. Everything in the chest, except for his two extra shirts, was black: an extra pair of underpants, two extra pairs of stockings, a skullcap, and a pair of breeches for wearing under his cassock when activities like riding or directing ballet rehearsals threatened modesty.

The work of scholastics differed, and Charles spent more time as assistant rhetoric teacher than he did studying. Rhetoric was the art of communication, and because Jesuits believed that the body should be as eloquent in the service of God and virtue as the voice, rhetoric teachers produced plays and ballets in which their students acted and danced.

The only other things in Charles's sleeping chamber were two hooks beside the hanging rail, and two niches in the thick plaster walls. The hooks held his two black hats. The flat-crowned, wide-brimmed one was his outdoor hat, and the brimless *bonnet* with its three corners, or points, was usually worn only indoors, on ceremonial occasions like the one for the Condé on Christmas Eve. The niche over the clothing chest held several books, and the one at the foot of his bed held his mother's New Year's gift, a small Pietà—the Virgin cradling her dead Son—carved in black stone. Eventually, it would be put where others could see it, but for now, he was allowed to keep it in his chamber.

In the study, another painted crucifix hung over a large scarred table that served as Charles's desk. The chair had a hard red seat cushion, and a small frayed piece of brown rug kept his feet off the cold wood floor. Like most rooms in the college, chamber and study were unheated. The rector and a few others sometimes had a brazier in chamber or office, but only the kitchens, the infirmary, the fathers' small refectory, and the common warming room—the calefactory—had fireplaces. There were also fire-places in a few large chambers in the student court, but those were strictly reserved for noble or very wealthy boys. Otherwise, the assumption was that a cold and solitary body made for warm devotions, and that in large gathering places, so many bodies crowded together made heat enough.

Shivering in spite of his cloak, Charles broke the skim of ice on the water that had stood overnight in a tall copper jug. One of his eccentricities was that he liked to be clean. To most people, "clean" meant wearing a clean white linen shirt or *chemise*. But to Charles, it meant using water—even soap. Though he had to admit that he was washing less in this winter weather. Last summer, when he'd first come here, lay brothers had brought water to his chambers most mornings, sometimes even warm water, but this autumn, the rector had stopped that small luxury. Money was unexpectedly short, and the lay brothers—who cleaned, cooked, marketed, ran the infirmary, and also took care of many of the college's mundane interactions with the outside world— were spread thinner because no new brothers could be accepted until college finances improved.

Charles wiped his teeth with a linen rag dipped in the little pot of tooth cleaner he kept. He didn't shave, because his confessor had taken his shaving mirror and ordered him to go to the college barber like everyone else. Charles missed the mirror. Not from vanity—he didn't mind going stubble-jawed half the time, nor did he want to look at himself. But the little mirror's greenish glass had made everything look mysteriously under water, and he'd found that being reminded of mystery, even in the mundane act of shaving, had been a good part of the day's beginning.

He started toward the window to open the wooden shutters, then wondered if leaving them closed might keep his rooms warmer. Telling himself that was exactly as likely as the miracle of loaves and fishes happening in the refectory and replacing the omnipresent bean pottage, he opened them in case the sun shone, put on the skullcap he'd gotten permission to wear for warmth, and went to Mass.

Unlike Benedictines, members of the Society of Jesus were not cloistered and did not pray the canonical hours together. Besides each day's solitary hour of meditation, they gathered for Mass before scattering to the day's duties, and twice during the day took time for an *examen*, the examination of conscience.

After five months in the college, Charles no longer got lost on his way to the chapel, or tripped over the way's odd steps and sudden turnings, even in the early-morning dark. The original college buildings had been part of a private *hôtel,* or townhouse. But in the century and a quarter since the Society of Jesus acquired the property, the old buildings had been reconfigured again and again to accommodate the growing number of students and teachers, and these upper floors were haphazard mazes of small chambers, studies, an occasional cramped salon, dead-end passages, and low doorways. He hurried through narrow passageways, around corners, up and down inconsequential steps waiting like traps, and finally down a last steep flight of stairs to a small door set into a corner.

The door opened into Louis le Grand's main chapel, long and high ceilinged. Charles stopped for a moment, as he always did, under the small false dome where the aisles crossed, and looked up at the well-fed angels in their blue sky, reaching down to struggling mortals. He could barely see them as yet in the dim light, but knowing they were there was enough. The side altars, too, were swathed in shadow, and the gallery and its colored glass windows were black. He went to his usual place on one of the backless wooden benches, knelt on the stone floor, and bowed his head onto his clasped hands. All around him, heels tapped over stone, and cassocks, cloaks, and coats rustled as Jesuits, students, and a scattering of people from the neighborhood, especially men who belonged to the college confraternities, arrived and settled. Then the Mass began and Charles gave himself up to the mystery of God.

After a breakfast of bread, a little cheese, and leftover soup, eaten standing in the fathers' refectory and as near the fireplace as possible, Charles walked back through the archway between the fathers' courtyard and the students' court, thinking about the day before him. His first task was calling on Monsieur Edmé Callot, an elderly member of Louis le Grand's bourgeois Congregation of the Ste. Vierge. These Congregations of the Holy Virgin, based in Jesuit houses and colleges all over Europe, were social groups promoting spiritual formation and charity among men and boys. Besides Louis le Grand's four student Congregations, two for *pensionnaires*, boarders, and two for *externes*, nonboarders, there were also two Congregations for men, one for bourgeois and another for artisans. Charles was in charge of almsgiving in the older *pensionnaires'* Congregation, and he also helped with the bourgeois group, which his friend Père Thomas Damiot served as priest. This morning's call was a courtesy offering of Christmas greetings, accompanied by a plea to M. Callot for a contribution to the bourgeois Congregation's alms budget.

Charles's spirits rose as he emerged from the students' court into the Cour d'honneur and crunched across its gravel to the street passage. The air was sharp in the nose, but through the bare branches of trees scattered along the court's edges, the sky showed a thin blue in the growing light. The surprising promise of sunshine made the short walk to the Place Maubert a pleasant assignment. Scholastics were not supposed to leave the college alone without special permission, and his companion this morning was Maître Louis Richaud, whom he knew slightly and who was visiting a member of the artisans' Congregation.

Richaud was waiting in the passage. A scholastic like Charles, he was lean and quick moving, with perpetually watchful black eyes. Unlike Charles, he was not a teacher, but a *cubiculaire*, who helped provision the private student chambers and the small dormitories for the less well-born and wealthy boys, and also supervised students. Students in Jesuit colleges were rarely left alone, especially boarding students, most of whom were the scions of rich and influential families.

Charles and Richaud greeted each other, and the porter let them out into the shadowed street.

"My man lives just off the Place Maubert," Charles said, as

they started down the hill. "In the rue Perdue, I'm told, at the Sign of Three Ducks. And yours?"

"He's a tallow chandler, well off for his kind, I think. His shop is on the west side of the Place. Where the gallows used to stand, he says."

Richaud sounded almost regretful that the gibbet was gone, but Charles shuddered. He'd seen too many corpses in the army, including too many poor souls left hanging for the birds.

Though the Christmas festival lasted until the Feast of the Epiphany on January sixth, working people couldn't afford to stop work for so many holidays in a row, and the street was fairly busy. A carter bawled encouragement to his horse pulling a load of cured skins up the hill for the bookbinders along the rue St. Jacques. Cheaply cured skins, Charles thought, as the smell from the cart hit his nose. Farther along, at the corner of the Benedictine Hôtel de Cluny's property, a clutch of tonsured, black-robed monks argued with three fishwives who had blocked most of the small side street with a temporary stall. The oldest woman was giving as good as she got, and swinging a large fish by its tail in wider and wider arcs. Charles grinned at Richaud.

"Looks to me like she's warming up her arm to use that fish on someone," he said, surprising Richaud into what Charles sensed was rare laughter. On impulse, Charles said, "Are you coming to our Christmas farce tonight?"

Richaud's mouth tightened angrily and he walked a little faster.

Charles eyed him. "*A Farce of Monks*, I mean. By Père Damiot. It's good, very funny, you'll like it."

"I doubt it. But I have to go."

"Have to? What do you mean? Every group of Jesuits puts on an in-house farce of some kind at Christmas! Surely you go every year?"

"No." The negative fell like a stone at Charles's feet. "But this year my confessor, Père Dainville, has ordered me to go. He thinks I dwell too much on sin." Richaud sniffed disdainfully, making his disagreement clear.

How like Père Dainville, Charles thought, smiling to himself. The old man was his confessor, too. Though he seemed frail, he was as implacable as a wall in demanding truth from his penitents. But once he had it, he was compassion itself in setting penances. He was also inventive at finding ways to puncture the self-absorption that guilt so easily bred. During these last months, Charles had had the hard but comforting experience of just how inventive Dainville could be.

The next turning to the right, and the second to the left, brought them out in the long, Y-shaped Place Maubert. Its stone houses were well kept: some set back behind tall, solid wooden gates, others with doors opening onto the street. Some had been rebuilt in a more modern style, with brick and stone, but one still showed timbering, and another was old enough to have a corner finished with a small, round tower capped with blue slate. Most of the houses had ground-floor shops with garish signs. There was an enormous red-brown boot, a loaf of golden bread the size of a carriage wheel, and a towering candle with an orange flame as long as Charles's arm. The painted tumble of chops and trotters and tongues on the butcher's sign was so realistic, it made his stomach growl.

"I'll be over there," Richaud said, pointing to the candle.

"Can you wait there for me, if my business takes longer than yours?"

"Of course. The chandler loves to talk. *Bon chance* with your Monsieur Callot."

"Good luck to you, too, with your chandler."

Circling around servants and housewives gossiping and filling pots and jugs at the fountain in the middle of the cobbled Place, Charles angled south, looking for the rue Perdue. It turned out to be hardly wider than a footpath, and he wondered as he started along it if it was called Lost Street because of its size. Its houses, whose doors opened directly onto the street, were also smaller and looked less prosperous than those on the Place. He found three ducks carved in stone over a door just beyond the lane's sharp turn. The door was opened by a gangling serving man tugging at the sleeves of his tight gray jacket, as if that would make them long enough.

"Bonjour," Charles said, "I am Maître du Luc. I would like to see Monsieur Callot, if I may."

Still pulling at his sleeves, the servant nodded and stood back from the door. Charles walked into a small antechamber with a worn but handsomely patterned black-and-red stone floor. An oak staircase rose on the right, against dingy plastered walls. The manservant disappeared through a doorway opposite the street door, leaving Charles at the foot of the stairs, listening to violin music, thumps, and loud laughter from the floor above.

Minutes went by. In a pause in the music, Charles heard the manservant arguing heatedly with someone. The voices seemed to come from beyond the door the servant had gone through, and wondering how long he was going to be left waiting, Charles opened the door cautiously and looked in. The bed with faded green curtains, the ragged cushioned chair, and cooking utensils scattered around the cold hearth told him this was a lodger's chamber—not surprising, since Parisians of all ranks rented out any extra foot of space, especially on ground floors or in attics. The voices came from beyond a door straight across the room.

"Oh, blessed saints," a woman said impatiently, "he doesn't care, so why should we?"

Quick light steps approached and Charles withdrew his head

just in time. An exasperated maidservant walked through the lodger's chamber, tucking stray black curls under her white coif. Her gray woolen skirt and bodice were old, but better fitting than the young footman's jacket. Ignoring Charles, she hurried up the stairs and into the room the music was coming from. And almost immediately backed out of it, as a man burst onto the landing.

"Maître du Luc!" M. Edmé Callot, bent and brittle and in his seventies, leaned precariously over the wooden stair railing, his long, high dressed chestnut wig threatening to slip off his bald head and land at Charles's feet. "Welcome, *maître!* Come up, come up and be at home!"

The maid hovering behind Callot threw up her hands and bustled back down the stairs, this time rolling her eyes at Charles as she passed him.

Charles gave her a rueful smile and started up to the landing. "*Bonjour*, Monsieur Callot," he said as he climbed. "I have come to wish you a blessed Christmas season. And to have perhaps some talk about the Congregation of the Sainte Vierge."

"Good, excellent!"

Callot wove his way back toward the music. Charles sighed and followed. But he was hardly through the door of the small salon when a young woman leaped at him. Her full red lips were smiling and her lemon-colored skirt was bouncing on the small hoops supporting its inverted cone shape. He jumped backward. She pirouetted without missing a beat and struck out toward the salon windows in a series of simple but prettily done *chassées*. A young dancing master bowing a little pocket violin beside the fireplace nodded at her enthusiastically and redoubled his efforts.

"Ha! She almost had you, *maître!*" M. Callot was convulsed with mirth. In a parody of the girl's *chassées*, he sidled to Charles and smote him on the shoulder. "Christmas, *maître*, make the most of it!"

From the fumes accompanying Callot's words, and the glass and bottle on a table near the fire, Charles gathered that the old man had already been making the most of it, with the help of the distilled spirits called *eau de vie*. This was definitely a new view of the quiet, pious elder whom Charles had glimpsed at gatherings of the bourgeois Congregation.

"May we talk somewhere a little quieter, *monsieur*?" Charles said, raising his voice to be heard over the music. "About the Congregation."

"No, no, stay and dance! I know you can dance, I saw your Louis le Grand show in August! That *Labors of Hercules* was a good ballet, though why you bother with those godforsaken Latin tragedies, the sweet Virgin only knows. Ah, me, I would dearly like to dance Hercules . . ." He posed unsteadily in fourth position, his right arm straight out as though he held a sword. As the girl danced past him, her feet flickering in swift *pas de bourrées*, he lunged, swiping the imaginary sword left and right, overbalanced, and fell into her arms. Laughing, she stopped and pushed him back onto his feet. The dancing master stopped playing and glowered.

"Oh, no you don't, uncle," the girl admonished, one capable-looking hand spread on Callot's chest to hold him at arm's length. "No more Christmas kisses." She glanced at Charles, shrugged a wry shoulder, and dipped the best curtsy she could in the circumstances. She was perhaps nineteen or twenty, Charles thought, robust and auburn haired, a little too broad-faced for conventional beauty, but her tip-tilted nose and slightly down-slanting brown eyes were appealing. Her mouth, which Charles saw now was naturally red, looked as though it nearly always smiled. And her body—Charles lowered his eyes and firmly refused to consider her body.

"She calls me uncle to make me feel younger, but in fact she is my all-too-lovely great-niece," Callot was saying. He waved his hand airily between the girl and Charles. "Maître du Luc, Mademoiselle Isabel Brion." Then he stepped back from her and grinned at the scowling dancing master. "And that is her very devoted *maître de danse*, Monsieur Germain Morel."

Monsieur, Charles noted, which meant that the dancing master was just beginning in his profession and had not been at it long enough to be called by the more honorable title of *maître*, given not only to Jesuit scholastics but to many positions in French society. With a visible effort, Morel composed his face and managed a civil bow to Charles.

"Come now, *mon cher* Monsieur Morel," Callot laughed, "it's Christmas, we must make the most of it!"

"Hush, uncle, I fear you have already made the most of it," Mlle Brion chided. "I think today you put *eau de vie* even in your morning chocolate!" She turned to the red-faced dancing master. "Do forgive us, *monsieur*," she said sweetly. "Shall I try it once more?"

"Of course! By all means!" The young man's face cleared and he set his violin on a chest against the tapestry-covered wall. "But first, *mademoiselle*, allow me to correct your *pas de bourrée*."

With a dazzling smile, Isabel Brion presented herself in front of him. Morel began to demonstrate, dancing in a circle around her so that she could see the step from every angle. Charles, only half listening to Callot rambling on about Hercules, watched with pleasure. The young teacher might be a beginner, but he was good, very good. Slender and supple, of middle height, wearing his own chestnut hair cut several inches above his shoulders, he had grace and speed, and his technique was perfect. Morel stopped beside

Mlle Brion and resumed the pose from which the step began. She studied his well-muscled, stockinged legs, his tautly poised torso, his graceful arms, as though they were Holy Writ, and copied his stance almost exactly. But somehow, her right arm, in its ruffled sleeve that showed her round, firm forearm was just enough wrong that he had to stretch his own arm around her to make the correction. Color flooded their faces and they gazed earnestly at each other. Somehow, Morel forgot to withdraw his arm from around her shoulders.

Charles turned to Callot to hide his smile, wondering what the girl's father would do if he walked into the salon and hoping he wouldn't. Callot was still practicing unsteady sword thrusts and mumbling a running commentary on his own performance.

Charles watched him for a moment and said, "I think, *monsieur*, that I should return another day. I wish you—"

He broke off as the front door opened and shut and voices rose. Callot turned anxiously toward the landing, and the dancing master and Mlle Brion moved apart.

"*Mademoiselle*," a deep voice rumbled, "I beg you, calm yourself. It will all come right, I assure you. And now—"

"But if we *cannot* find it?" It was a girl's voice, shaking with emotion. "I will have nothing, Monsieur Brion, what will happen to me? No one will want me without money!"

"*Ma chère*, you forget your faithful Gilles. My son may seem shy in his suit, but I assure you, his heart is yours. But now that you are coming to live in my house, you will have more time to learn that he loves you."

"No, Monsieur Brion," the girl said with sudden spirit. "You are very good, but I have told you that I want to stay in my mother's house. I want to be where she was."

"Now, *ma petite*, do not start on that again. You are a minor and must do as I, your guardian, tell you. You will enjoy living with my Isabel, will you not? And as I say, you will come to know Gilles better."

With an anxious look at Morel, Isabel Brion ran out onto the landing. *"Papa,"* she called down, "didn't you find it?"

"We will, *ma chère* Isabel," her father called back. "We will! This is only a little setback. I have brought Martine to you to amuse. I am going again to the Châtelet to search. Some disgracefully careless clerk has brought us to this pass, but we will find what we need, never fear, no reason in the world to fear. I don't know what the Châtelet has come to, it is disgraceful . . ." The front door opened and shut again, cutting off the stream of words, and feet ran lightly up the stairs.

Frankly curious, Charles moved so that he could see the landing. A weeping girl pushed back her wide black hood and threw herself into Isabel Brion's open arms. She was so small she hardly reached the other girl's chin.

Isabel led her into the salon and sat her down in one of the high-backed chairs beside the fire. Murmuring comfort, she untied the girl's cloak, a heavy black *manteau*, and pushed it gently back to reveal a front-laced, stiffened bodice and skirt of fine black wool, trimmed with lace like black spiderweb. Callot hurried to his bottle and half filled the glass beside it. Morel came hesitantly forward and bowed to the newcomer.

"Bonjour, Monsieur Morel!" The girl's voice was high and sweet. She wiped her tears with a matching spiderweb handkerchief and glanced from the young man to her friend. "I am so happy to see you here, *monsieur,"* she said, smiling a little.

Callot returned and went awkwardly down on one creaking knee beside the chair. "This will do you good, *ma petite."* He put the glass into her hand.

Charles was trying not to stare. From her little low-heeled, bronze leather mourning shoes to her black taffeta coif, the girl was breathtaking. Her bright hazel eyes were enormous, her lashes thick and dark. Her brows slanted like little wings. Her skin was milky, and the sun coming through the salon windows made a golden aureole around the ringlets showing under the coif. But even with such beauty, Charles knew that she was right to be afraid for herself if she was without family or finances. Beauty without money was rarely enough, marriage being nearly always made for social or financial advancement, and preferably both. For most people, building up the family fortune was the eleventh commandment.

The girl handed the glass back to Callot. "You are very kind, *monsieur*."

"Ah, *ma belle* Martine, if I were forty years younger, I would be kinder still." He opened his eyes wide at her, and she laughed in spite of herself.

"Even if—" She looked down and bit her lip. "—if I have no money?"

Callot smote himself on the chest. "On my honor, I would be your faithful knight until the *bon Dieu*'s stars fall from the sky!"

They both laughed and she touched him playfully on his withered cheek. Mlle Brion, who had perched on the arm of the chair, shook her head impatiently and leaned closer to her friend.

"But, Martine, if you *would* only marry Gilles, as my father so earnestly wishes you to, you would be safe forever. And we would be sisters!"

Callot snorted. "Gilles. Much use that one would be as a husband."

Martine turned her head away. "You know that my mother did not wish me to marry your brother, Isabel," she said softly. "I would be your sister with all my heart, but my mother saw that—well, that Gilles and I would not suit each other."

"Oh, I know Gilles is not exciting," the other girl cajoled.

"But—" She shrugged expressively. "How many husbands are exciting?"

The dismay on the dancing master's face made Charles clear his throat in an effort not to laugh. Callot laughed heartily.

Isabel blushed and stood up, seeming suddenly to remember her manners. "Maître du Luc, forgive me for my discourtesy. This is my dearest friend, Mademoiselle Martine Mynette. The *bon Dieu* is testing her sorely. As you see, she is in mourning. Her mother, whom we all loved, had been ill for many months, and she died just over a week ago. Martine has no other family, and my father is now her guardian. The trouble is that the paper that assured Martine's inheritance—drawn up many years ago by my father, who is a notary—is lost. He is trying every day to find it. But so far, he has not and we are very worried."

Charles frowned in confusion. "But surely children must *always* inherit something of the family fortune?"

Martine Mynette glanced at her friend and drew herself up in her chair.

Isabel Brion said quickly, "Children of the blood always inherit, yes." The two friends exchanged another glance. "But Mademoiselle Mynette is an adopted daughter, *maître*."

Charles looked from one to the other, even more confused. "I thought adoption was not legal here in the north. In the south it is, where we still follow Roman law, but—"

Sudden fire flashed in Martine Mynette's eyes. "Some of our judges say adoption is not legal, but they are stupid, because people do it all the time. You have only to go to a notary like Monsieur Brion and promise to raise and care for the adopted child as though it were your own. And if the notary draws up for you what is called a *donation entre vifs*, you can give the child whatever you wish. Even if there are blood relatives, they cannot take away what the *donation* gives you. But the *donation* Monsieur Brion helped my mother make cannot be found." Her lips quivered and she put a hand to her mouth.

Feeling increasingly at sea, Charles said, "I have never known a lone woman to adopt a child."

Both young women looked at him disapprovingly.

"Of course a woman can adopt a child on her own," Isabel Brion said. "Spinsters and widows without children have done it for ages. Even married women, though they must have their husband's permission. My father often draws up such papers, though he does say women seem to do it less often now. But it is still perfectly possible. The trouble is that Martine's mother's copy of the *donation* is gone from their house, and my father found that mice had nested in his ledger for that month. And the stupid Châtelet clerks cannot find the original."

"I see." Charles offered an arm to M. Callot, who was struggling up from his chivalric pose beside the chair.

"Oof! I thank you, *maître*. The knight would suffer all for his lady, though his knees greatly object." Either the effects of the *eau de vie* had somewhat worn off or Callot was covering them for Martine Mynette's benefit. He gazed sorrowfully at the girl. "I will bet anything you like, *maître*, on any game you like, that my lazy, useless nephew never even took that original *donation* to the Châtelet!"

Isabel shook her head angrily. "Of course he did, Uncle Callot, that's only your *eau de vie* talking. Some clerk has put the paper in the wrong place, that's all. The point is, what are we going to do? Shall I come and help you search again, Martine?"

"I have looked and looked in the house," the girl said, shaking her head hopelessly. "I've done little else since the morning my mother died." She looked at Charles. "As Isabel said, she died on St. Gatien's Day, exactly a week before Christmas. The *donation* was not where she'd always kept it, but I was sure I would find it when Monsieur Brion had the inventory done just a few days later. You know how the inventory clerks go through everything. But it has disappeared."

"Where did you expect to find it, *mademoiselle?*" Charles asked, and then felt himself blushing at his naked curiosity. "Forgive me, I have no reason to—"

"I am glad to tell you. My mother hid her copy for safety behind a painting of Saint Elizabeth in her oratory, a little alcove in her chamber. She fixed it to the back of the painting with glue—you can still see a spot of glue where it was attached. But one night, a few days before she died, she told me to go and get it for her, she wanted to hold it in her hands and know that I would be safe when she was gone. I went to get it, but it wasn't there. I thought she must have moved it and forgotten. I never doubted I would be able to find it. But—" She shook her head and gazed sadly into the fire. "My mother had terrible pain in her breast, and the poppy syrup they gave her made her confused." Her voice dropped to a whisper. "I sat with her every night toward the end. By then, even the syrup didn't help. I could do nothing for her."

No one spoke, and the only sound was the crackling fire.

"Come," Isabel Brion said briskly. She pulled her friend to her feet. "Let me get my cloak and we will go and search one more time. Two are always better than one." She smiled at the dancing master. "And perhaps Monsieur Morel will be so kind as to escort us to your house? It is barely a step, Monsieur Morel, just to the Place Maubert, at the Sign of the Rose."

"I am entirely at your service, *mesdemoiselles!*" Morel grabbed his hat from the chest and stowed the little violin in a deep pocket inside his wide-skirted coat.

Charles said he would walk as far as the Place with them, and

Callot made as if to come, too, but his great-niece firmly refused him and he wandered sadly back to his bottle.

The little party went out into the thin sunshine, the two girls walking arm in arm and talking earnestly. Once, Martine Mynette laughed and looked archly at Morel, and Isabel Brion blushed crimson. Morel walked beside Isabel, studiously seeing and hearing nothing. Charles was silent, admiring the Mynette girl's teasing attention to her friend's romance, even as she herself faced disaster. His heart ached for the grieving girl, and he hoped that she had proof that she was the orphan of legitimately married and respectable parents, which she surely was, since Mademoiselle Anne Mynette had adopted her as her heir. And since Henri Brion wanted her as a wife for his son. People made an inflexible distinction between the orphans of respectable married parents and those nameless foundlings left on the street. The children were received in different institutions and faced vastly different fates. The best a foundling could hope for was to be taken in and raised as a servant, or sometimes as a future apprentice. Without the *donation*, and if she couldn't prove her parentage to strangers, Martine would have very little chance of a good marriage. Her future could well be bleak indeed, if she went on resisting her guardian and his unexciting son.

When the little party reached the Mynette house at the Sign of the Rose, a substantial stone house with gates in a stone arch protecting its cobbled court, Charles made his polite farewells. But he was frowning as he started back across the Place to the chandler's shop. How could a notary—and a guardian—lose track of such an important document?

Chapter 3

The early darkness had fallen. The long chamber in Louis le Grand above the older *pensionnaires'* refectory, called the *salle des actes*, was full of laughing professors and lay brothers crowded shoulder to shoulder on benches. On the small stage at the chamber's east end, *A Farce of Monks*, this year's strictly in-house comedy, was galloping to its conclusion. These private, Jesuits-only farces were a Christmas tradition in the Society of Jesus, a wise chance to poke fun at each other, puncture overblown solemnities, and generally let off steam. From the stage, Charles saw that even the college rector was smiling, something he'd rarely done in recent months. Maître Richaud, on the other hand, sitting farther back in the crowd, looked as though devils with pitchforks were prodding him from every side.

Charles, playing Brother Infirmarian, was waving a clyster—an outsize enema syringe—at a bug-eyed patient.

"But *mon père*," Charles caroled, "it is for your own good!"

"No, no, I beg you!" The patient keeping his back to the wall and his eyes on the clyster was the college's real infirmarian, the lay brother Frère Brunet. "I tell you I am well," he gabbled at Charles, "it is a miracle, there is no need for your medicines."

"They are often like this when they see my clyster," Charles said cheerfully over his shoulder to the audience. "But, never fear, this will clear his head as well as his bowels!"

The audience roared and wiped its streaming eyes on sleeves and cassock skirts so as not to miss anything onstage. Charles pounced on his patient. Brunet yelped, picked up the skirts of his brown monk's habit, and fled through a doorway in the scenery. Charles followed, and the shouts and pleas from offstage convulsed the audience anew. He came back dancing an intricate little *gigue* of triumph and tossed the empty clyster aside. Brunet popped out of the exit and lumbered downstage to address the audience.

"*Mes frères*, I have a grudge to state, a bone to pick! This *gigue*-hopping brother is a mere scholastic, is he not?"

Knowing what was coming, the audience called back, "The merest of scholastics, yes!"

Brunet nodded soberly. "And the *end* of a scholastic is . . . ?"

"To be kicked!" the audience roared, and Brunet proceeded to follow their instructions.

Charles picked himself up from an elaborate fall and bowed deeply to Brunet while rubbing his posterior and grimacing at the audience. Then the two of them opened the door of a large cupboard standing onstage, revealing a tall wooden barrel.

"How do you fare, Brother Cellarer?" Charles shouted, addressing himself to the pair of square-toed black shoes sticking up from the barrel. He turned to the audience. "What do you think, *mes pères et mes frères*? If Brother Cellarer promises never to water our wine again, shall we pull him out?"

Shouts of "Yes!" and "No!" drowned each other.

"Come and help me, then!"

That was the cue for a half dozen Jesuits to leap onto the stage. They pulled the red-faced and realistically dripping mathematics professor playing Brother Cellarer out of the barrel and set him on his feet. He swore by Bacchus, classical god of the grape, never to so much as mention water in the same breath with wine, and everyone onstage joined in what began as a *gigue* and ended as a hilarious rout. Père Montville, former assistant rector and now the newly appointed college principal, provided the accompaniment, sawing joyously on a squawking violin.

Then Père Damiot, the farce's beaming author, walked downstage to speak the verse epilogue. His rich voice filled the chamber and the audience quieted to listen.

> *Now, Fathers and Brothers, a mirror we've held*
> *to the high and the low, what was hidden's revealed.*
> *Now nothing's concealed. Let's give thanks for the season,*
> *for laughter and reason, for our house and each other,*
> *both Fathers and Brothers!*

There was long applause and more laughter, and then lay brothers began clearing away the benches and setting out jugs of wine and trays of refreshments along one side of the chamber. The cast and Damiot left by the door through which Charles had chased Frère Brunet and shed the brown monks' robes they'd worn over their Jesuit cassocks.

Straight-faced, Charles said to Damiot, "Think they liked it at all?"

"No. They were only laughing at your left-footed dancing."

They grinned at each other and went back to the noisy chamber in search of wine and food. Carrying cone-shaped glasses and small sweet cakes shaped like the animals at the Christmas manger, they made their way through a barrage of teasing and compliments to a relatively quiet corner.

"To your immortal prose," Charles said, raising his glass to Damiot.

"To your two left feet," Damiot replied.

They drank and looked sadly at the pale reddish wine in their glasses.

"Watered," Charles said.

"Very. But I suppose we're lucky it's not straight river water."

Charles drank again. The stuff was, at least, discernibly wine. "Why do you suppose our finances are suddenly so bad?"

"Cash is scarce." Damiot tended to know these things, because his father was a wealthy merchant goldsmith. "All those fleeing Huguenots have drained us of so much money and skill. I continually ask myself how heretics can be such good businessmen." He shrugged. "Even gold itself is scarce. Silver, too."

"Surely that is not the Huguenots' fault." Charles knew more than a little about the French Protestants called Huguenots, some of his own family in the south being counted among them.

Damiot drank and scowled at his glass. "In any case, the New World mines aren't producing like they used to. Or Spain is keeping it all, who knows? What anyone with two thoughts to rub together does know is that war against the Augsburg Alliance countries is inevitable, and war always means new taxes. And what will a new war do to trade? Prices will no doubt go up. And if the next few grain harvests are not good—" He shrugged. "I imagine that those who have something put aside are keeping it."

"Too bad our king is more concerned with war and glory than with the well-being of his own realm and people," Charles said grimly.

Damiot's eyes widened, and he glanced around to see who might be close by. "That's fascinatingly close to treason. I don't think I heard that."

"But I said it," Charles muttered. "And it's not treason, it's reason."

"Here." Damiot shoved an ox-shaped cake into his friend's hand. "You can't talk with your mouth full." They gave their attention to eating and drinking. In the rumble of talk around them, Charles caught the words of two priests.

". . . but *I* heard," the older one said eagerly, "that a demon nearly carried away the reliquary!"

"No, no, just some deranged old beggar, probably an old soldier with a grudge against the Condé. Trying to steal the box and sell it, I imagine."

"But Père Pinette would have had a mere mortal—beggar, soldier, what have you—arrested! Explain that!"

A burst of laughter from somewhere covered his companion's response. Charles shook his head and swallowed the last of his cakes.

"I suppose," he said to Damiot, "that our rector looks so happy tonight because of this rumored bequest."

"The prospect of no more bean pottage in the refectory is enough to make anyone look happy."

Charles sighed in mock despair. "And there was I, hoping that Père Le Picart was smiling because he liked my performance."

"Don't be ridiculous. It was my script he was liking!"

"In fact, it was all of those," a light dry voice said behind them.

They turned and bowed to Père Jacques Le Picart, rector of Louis le Grand. The lean and wiry son of a Norman farmer, Le Picart ruled his college with shrewd justice and a warm heart. His cool gray gaze often saw more than a man wanted seen, as Charles had learned last summer when his vocation had hung in the balance.

Le Picart smiled at Damiot. "I greatly enjoyed your play, *mon père*. And your performance," he said, turning to Charles. "In fact, I was marveling that you joined us and not the Opera," he added with gentle mockery.

Charles bowed his thanks, wondering if Le Picart realized how seriously he'd once thought of choosing the stage—in spite of what that choice would have cost him in parental fury. But then the musket ball tore through his shoulder at the battle of St. Omer, leaving permanent damage and changing everything. The loss of his stage dream had been his gain, in the end, because it had shown him what he really wanted. Though he rarely said it aloud, his deepest wish was to come as close to God as a man could. But he wanted to do it in God's good world, not behind cloister walls. That desire had led him to the Society of Jesus and the teaching of Latin rhetoric. Which had, in God's odd economy, restored dance to him.

"I wish Père Jouvancy were here," Le Picart said. "He would have been very pleased with you both."

Charles said, "He brings the boys back from Gentilly on Sunday?"

"Yes." Le Picart sipped his wine in silence and then raised an ironic eyebrow at Charles. "As I have already said, Maître du Luc, you were perfectly correct, I was also smiling tonight over the welcome bequest coming to us. *Le bon Dieu* and all the saints must be growing weary of my unceasing thanks."

"Can you tell us who the bequest comes from?" Damiot said diffidently.

"From the family of one of our own, Père Christophe Mynette, who taught here until his death many years ago. Before Christmas, a week or two back, Frère Brunet went to the apothecary in the Place Maubert to replenish his stock of medicines. The apothecary mentioned that Père Mynette's niece, the last Mynette relative, had died. May God receive her soul."

Le Picart and Père Damiot crossed themselves, but Charles stood motionless, staring at the rector.

"Did you say Mynette, *mon père?*"

"He did," Damiot said. "I remember old Père Mynette, poor soul. My father knew him. I was still in the Novice House here in Paris, and there was a terrible epidemic of the little pox. It took Père Mynette among the first. Understandable, since he must have been eighty or so."

"With the passing of Père Mynette's niece, Anne Mynette, the Mynette family dies out," the rector said. "Otherwise, of course, the family fortune could not come to us."

"*Mon père,*" Charles began reluctantly, but the rector talked over him.

"Monsieur Simon Mynette, who was Père Mynette's younger brother, was a well-off lawyer, and always very proud of his older brother's Jesuit vocation. Jesuits, of course, cannot personally inherit money, but Monsieur Simon Mynette promised that after his daughter Anne's death, the Mynette money would come to the college in Père Christophe Mynette's honor. Anne Mynette, you see, never married and there were no other relatives. No, I lie. I believe there was one other, but he went out to the New World and died there. We have, of course, very carefully kept Monsieur Simon Mynette's notarized letter explaining all that and laying out what we can expect. I have summoned the notary who drew it up, but he has not yet answered me."

Charles tried again. "Is Mynette a common name?"

Damiot and Le Picart looked at him in surprise.

"Common enough, I suppose," the rector said. "Why?"

"Because this morning, when I called on Monsieur Callot from the bourgeois Congregation of the Sainte Vierge, I met a young woman with that surname. Her Christian name is Martine, and she is a friend of Monsieur Callot's great-niece. This

Martine Mynette is an adopted child, and the woman who adopted her, one Anne Mynette, died recently. The girl is distraught because the *donation entre vifs*, by which her mother left her the Mynette fortune, cannot be found."

The rector looked as though someone had slapped him. "And where does this girl live?" he said, when he could get words out.

"In the Place Maubert, at the Sign of the Rose."

"That was Simon Mynette's house." Le Picart drained his wineglass and stared narrow-eyed at the wall, as though unpleasant sums were written on the plaster. "This *donation*—did the girl say who drew it up? And when?"

"She didn't say when. Monsieur Callot's nephew drew it up, a notary whose surname is Brion, I don't know his Christian name."

Le Picart's face darkened with anger. "Brion? The notary who witnessed and sealed our letter from Simon Mynette promising us the bequest was Monsieur Henri Brion. He lived near the Place. There cannot be two notaries there called Brion. Why in God's name did the man not tell us about the *donation*? That is inexcusable! And his behavior since Mademoiselle Anne Mynette died is also inexcusable. I have sent him message after message, and he sends polite nothing-saying messages back, but he does not come to tell me how things stand with the money."

"But *mon père*," Damiot said, spreading his arms and sloshing wine onto the floor. "Maître du Luc has said that the *donation* is lost. Which one must feel is only just, if this Anne Mynette really flouted her father's wishes so brazenly by adopting an orphan, a child of some other blood, and trying to give it the Mynette fortune. I feel strongly that one should not be allowed to do that with a family *patrimoine*."

"How can you say this loss is just?" Charles shot back, stung on Martine Mynette's behalf. "Plainly, Mademoiselle Anne

Mynette came to have other wishes about the money after her father and her Jesuit uncle were dead. And why shouldn't she? I think you must not have sisters, *mon père*."

Damiot blinked. "Sisters? No. What does that have to do with it? What matters is that the paper is lost. So where is our difficulty? There is no impediment in the way of the bequest."

Le Picart frowned at Damiot but said nothing. Charles could almost see his thoughts moving behind his eyes.

"Maître du Luc," the rector said, "you know Monsieur Callot. I want you to go back to him tomorrow morning—and go alone; I don't want word of this getting out yet. For the sake of absolute certainty, find out the name of this deceased Anne Mynette's father and whether she had a Jesuit uncle. Then find out when this alleged *donation* was made. When I am certain of those facts, I will confront our elusive notary Henri Brion."

"Exactly," Damiot said, nodding vigorously. "*Alleged* is exactly the word! Do we really believe that the Châtelet clerks are so careless as to lose a *donation entre vifs*?"

"I believe they are all too human, Père Damiot." The rector fixed him with a hard gray stare. "Like all of us. Are you saying we should simply disregard this Mynette girl and her claim? Assuming she can substantiate it. Are you so eager to be done with bean pottage that you would not choke on fraud? Until we know whether there was a *donation*—and if there was, that it is truly lost—we will do nothing."

"No, *mon père*, but if—"

"We will not defraud the girl, don't even think it. More than that, don't tempt me to it!" The rector rubbed a hand over his face. "Because God knows, the money means a great deal to us. A dozen more scholarships for promising boys from poor families. Finishing repairs to the old college of Les Cholets building we've bought for more classrooms. A doubled alms budget for the student Congregations of the Sainte Vierge. And, yes, we would eat less bean pottage. And if this money does *not* come to us, not only will those things not happen, the figures in the bursar's ledger will force me to raise rents on houses we own. And the tenants cannot afford it." Le Picart looked grimly at Charles. "Report to me the moment you return tomorrow." Then his face softened a little and he said, "I wish this happy evening had ended more cheerfully. I thank you both again for the pleasure you gave to us." He gave Damiot the ghost of a smile. "I should tell you that I, too, loathe bean pottage."

Chapter 4

Charles went early to the Place Maubert, walking through skiffs of snow fallen in the night and under a lowering sky that promised more. Turning off the rue St. Jacques, he just managed to dodge a vinegar seller pushing his low, single-wheeled handcart to a house door, where a pretty young servant waited with her wicker-wrapped jug. As the curly-haired vendor took her jug to fill from his spigoted barrel, she dimpled and spoke teasingly to him, and he laughed and teased her back.

The hair straying from under her starched white coif was nearly as fair as Martine Mynette's. Charles hoped fervently that Martine Mynette would find her *donation*. Or that she could at least prove that she was a legitimately born orphan. He wondered why her adopted mother had never married and had children of her own. A woman with family wealth would almost certainly have had marriage offers, unless there was something direly wrong with her. How could her father have been so sure that she wouldn't marry after his death? If she had, and had borne children, his promise to the Jesuits would have been meaningless. By law, no one could will a *patrimoine* away from blood relatives.

But Anne Mynette hadn't married. So now, if her adopted

daughter's *donation* wasn't found, and the girl went on refusing the Brion son, her guardian could make life difficult indeed for her. Without the *donation*, even entering a convent would be difficult for her, since most convents required dowries. And even with a dowry, the better ones wouldn't have her at all unless she could prove that she'd been orphaned, not abandoned. The chance of a gently reared girl like Martine descending to the shame of domestic service was unthinkable. Charles had awakened in the night worrying about her. Something about the girl's aloneness touched an answering aloneness in himself. Though his own present loneliness came from his own choice not to marry and have children, it companioned him these days like a sad ghost. Not that he was alone in the world—he had legions of Jesuit brothers and also living blood relatives: his mother, sisters, a brother, and more cousins than he could count.

His cousin Pernelle, in Geneva, haunted too many of his restless nights. Most du Lucs were Catholic, but Pernelle, his second cousin and first love, was a Huguenot. The king's recent decree making Huguenots outlaws had unleashed havoc all over France, and last summer, against the laws of king and church, Charles had helped Pernelle escape the king's soldiers. Charles took his faith and his Jesuit vows very seriously. But blood was blood, and even more than that, he believed with all his heart that the beginning and end of God was love. Which made cruelty in the name of religion the worst kind of blasphemy. But helping Pernelle had rekindled both his old love for her and his vocational doubts.

At the end of the summer, he'd made an eight-day retreat with other Jesuit scholastics, and at the end of it he had renewed his first-level vows of poverty, chastity, and obedience, publicly reaffirming his vocation. The autumn had been a time of willing penance for the vows he had broken. It had also been a time full of the grieving that comes with deep choice. It was grief without the scourge of regret, thank God; but nonetheless, Martine Mynette touched the sorest place in his heart.

As Charles started across the bustling Place Maubert to the rue Perdue, he saw a small crowd gathered outside the open gates of the Sign of the Rose. He stopped and stared, and then broke into a run.

"What's happened?" he asked urgently of the first person he reached.

The man, a baker by his apron and baglike cap, turned, his mouth open to answer, but when he saw Charles, his mouth closed with a snap and he turned away. A woman next to him glared at Charles.

"Listen to that one," she muttered to her neighbor. "Pretending he doesn't know what's happened, but that's them all over. Hypocrites, all of them."

Charles, pushing through the crowd into the court, hardly heard her. An aproned apprentice took his arm. "Don't pay attention to them," he said in Charles's ear. "The *commissaire* just went in—that's all anyone knows."

Charles nodded and made his way to the house door, which stood open, and was inside, staring at what lay on the antechamber floor, before the *sergent* standing guard could stop him.

"Here, *mon père*," the *sergent* growled, "stay out, there's been murder here!"

Then he saw the stricken look on Charles's face and stepped aside. Like someone in an evil dream, Charles crossed the antechamber to the foot of the stone staircase. Martine Mynette's face was turned away, her silvergilt hair spilling from its little black coif. The blood from the wound in her neck hardly showed on her black gown. But blood stood in pools on the stone-tiled floor around her. A weeping woman knelt beside Martine. A hand gripped Charles's shoulder, and Charles pulled roughly away, thinking it was the *sergent*.

"Pray for her, *maître*," M. Callot quavered. He was as sober as a gravestone, but he reached for Charles's arm as though he might fall. "Pray for all of us. Who would do this to little Martine?"

Charles, beyond speech, shook his head.

Callot tightened his grip. "Pray, *maître!*"

From somewhere, Charles dredged up the opening words of the prayers for the dead, and Callot joined him. When they finished the familiar, steadying words, Charles's brain was working again. He realized that the weeping woman kneeling beside Martine was Isabel Brion.

"Did you and Mademoiselle Brion find Mademoiselle Mynette's body?" Charles asked.

"We came to see how she was, after being so upset yesterday. The girls still hadn't found Martine's paper, of course. Nor did my lazy, useless nephew, so far as I know—I haven't seen him yet today, he's probably still sleeping. And when I get my hands on him—dear Blessed Virgin, if I'd known what was happening here—no servants but a kitchen boy and that drunken maid. I tell you, Henri is as guilty of her death as anyone, the miser! If she'd been properly looked after, this wouldn't have happened, how could it? If Martine had only told us how things were, we would have taken her in. But as you heard, she didn't want to come to us because of Gilles. I see now that Henri let this household fall apart to try to force her to come and live with us. Because he didn't want to spend any of the Mynette money on this house and its servants!" The old man was shaking with fury. "And the servants certainly knew the *donation* was missing." He sighed. "In fairness to my unspeakable nephew, I should have known they'd start leaving as soon as they heard that. What can you expect—they knew they'd be out on the street soon enough if the paper wasn't found, so they went looking for more secure places." Callot shook his head and breathed hard to steady himself. When he could speak again, he said more quietly, "When Isabel and I arrived here, Martine's maid was screaming. She'd just come down and found her. The idiot woman reeks of wine." Callot wiped his eyes and jerked his head at an alcove to the right of the stairs. "I sent the kitchen boy for the *commissaire*."

The *sergent* stood at the alcove's entrance now, and beyond him was a tall man in a *commissaire*'s long black legal robe and black hat. A clerk scribbled at his side, taking down the testimony of a sobbing woman in a smoke-blue skirt.

"The *commissaire* is still questioning the sot of a maid," Callot muttered. "Much good that will be to him. Dear God, who would do this?"

Charles patted the old man's arm and went to Isabel Brion. Seeing that she was kneeling in blood, he pulled her gently to her feet. She looked up at him, her face drowned in tears.

"Maître du Luc? How could this happen? Poor Martine, she never harmed anyone!" She covered her face with her hands.

With his arm around her for fear she would fall, Charles led her to a carved bench against the wall and settled her on it. Then, hoping his face showed nothing of the storm of pity and anger that raged inside him, he went back to Martine's body and bent over it. The barest of touches told him that while the front of the bodice was soaked in blood, the skirt was hardly stained. He leaned closer, studying the ragged rip in the right side of the young woman's neck. Swiftly, closing his ears to Mlle Brion's gasp of surprise, he raised Martine's upper body so he could see her back. There was blood there, but it could as easily be from the blood pooled on the floor as from another wound. But that would not be sure until the body was undressed. There was, at least, no other visible wound. Charles started looking for the blade. A small knife, he thought, but deadly sharp. If the blade hadn't ripped open the great artery, the wound in her neck would have been much too small to kill her. He combed the floor and the staircase, looked under the bench, but found nothing. There were blood splashes, though, on the plaster wall nearest her body, which made Charles think that the murderer had almost certainly been splashed himself. Even so, the man had been self-possessed enough to take the weapon away with him. Charles leaned down and touched Martine's hand. It was cooling—she would cool quickly on the cold floor—but some of her body's warmth was still there. Not long, then. She had been alive to see the morning, if not the light. He went to the open house door and looked at the elaborate lock. Then he saw the iron key, as long as his hand, hanging beside the door. He went back to Isabel.

"Mademoiselle, did the maid have to unlock the door to let you in?"

She hesitated. "No, she didn't. When we heard her scream, my uncle pushed on the door and it opened."

Charles nodded. "Another question, *mademoiselle*. Did Martine Mynette's mother have an uncle who was a Jesuit?"

"Oh. Yes, she did. But he died a long time ago. Before Martine and I were even born, I think. I remember my father saying that he was a teacher at Louis le Grand."

It was the answer he'd expected. "Thank you, *mademoiselle*. Shall I find your great-uncle and ask him to take you home?"

"No. No, I thank you, but I want to stay here. Martine was my dearest friend. When they will let us, I will help the maid do the last things for her."

Charles had to swallow before he could speak. "You are a

good friend to her. I will pray for you and for Mademoiselle Mynette. If you will allow it, I will come tomorrow to see you and Monsieur Callot."

She nodded, and he took his leave of her. He went to where Martine lay and looked once more at her still face. Then he left the house, deaf to the growl of angry talk as he passed the crowd around the gate. He walked quickly, numb with grief for this girl he'd met only yesterday, blackly full of anger at whoever had destroyed her. Before he reached the college, snow came. It settled on his shoulders, stuck to his eyelashes, and half blinded him. It comforted him, silencing the streets and seeming to shroud the houses in cold white mourning.

Chapter 5

"Dead?" Père Le Picart looked up from his desk. "Dear Blessed Virgin," he whispered. And then, "God forgive me."

It was Charles's turn to stare. Then he understood. The girl had been the unexpected and unwelcome obstacle between the college and the Mynette fortune. Which the college badly needed. Le Picart had no doubt been trying not to think about—let alone hope for—the only two things that would remove the obstacle: failure to find the lost *donation entre vifs*, or the girl's death.

Le Picart let his held breath go. "How did she die? Some sudden illness?"

"Sudden, yes. But no illness." In spite of the rector's small fire and the worn red-and-green carpet on the floor, Charles huddled deeper into his cloak, cold to the bone, though not from the snow. He took a deep breath. "She was stabbed." He crossed himself.

Le Picart did likewise, his eyes wide with horror. "Ah, no! May God receive her soul," he whispered.

"I should also tell you it is definite that Martine Mynette's adopted mother was the Anne Mynette you spoke of," Charles added.

Le Picart looked down at his clasped hands, braced on the desk as though for an ordeal. "The police were there?"

"The local *commissaire* and a *sergent*, yes."

"Do they suspect someone?"

"I don't know, *mon père*." Charles sighed. "I was crossing the Place on my way to the Brion house when I saw a crowd outside the gate of the Mynette house. I went in, and the *commissaire* was questioning a maid. From what I learned, it's obvious how the killer got in. The house door was not locked or barred when the maid found the girl's body."

"A thief, perhaps, and she interrupted him?"

"Perhaps."

For a long moment, the only sound was snow against the window. Listening to its soft patting at the glass, like some small creature wanting in, Charles tried to think how to say what he had to say.

A log broke in the fireplace and the rector straightened in his chair. "Whoever it was, we must find him."

Charles looked half fearfully at Le Picart, wondering if the man had read his mind. "Yes, *mon père*. We must." He realized too late the fervor in his voice.

"I wonder if our reasons for thinking so are the same," the rector said cautiously.

Charles looked at the window and the gray snow light. "Martine Mynette had no family," he said carefully. "There is no one to see that justice is done for her."

"There is Lieutenant-Général La Reynie and his police."

Charles said nothing.

"I think that more than just this girl's murder is wringing your heart. Was she beautiful?"

"I want to see her killer found. Is that wrong?"

"That depends on who is speaking—the bodily man grieved for a beautiful young girl, or the Jesuit caring for a human soul."

To Charles's dismay, he felt blood rising to his face. He bowed his head, thinking that it might well take him the rest of his life to sort the one from the other.

"Don't bother to dissemble, Maître du Luc, I don't have time for it. Outrage is useful in getting at facts. But if you want to see clearly the facts you find, you will have to call some degree of dispassion to your aid," Le Picart said. "Our need to find this girl's killer is more urgent than you probably realize. If the man who killed Martine Mynette is not found, the Society of Jesus will be accused of her death."

Charles's head came up and he suddenly remembered the angry muttering in the crowd outside the Mynette house. "Because now the Mynette money will come to us?"

"Yes. And even more because smoldering hostility to the Society is never very far below the surface in Paris. Parisians never forget anything, and all they need is a small spark to light the past into flame."

"And Martine Mynette's death is more than a small spark," Charles said flatly.

Le Picart nodded wearily. "Again yes. And why? Because no one here will ever forget our poor Jean Châtel and his attack on King Henry." Nearly a hundred years ago, a former Jesuit student named Jean Châtel, a deranged and rabidly fanatical Catholic, had tried to kill King Henry IV, a Huguenot who had converted to Catholicism in order to claim the throne. Châtel had been executed and his family house razed. One of his Jesuit teachers had been hanged and burned at the stake. The Society of Jesus had been banished from the realm for years.

"Feeling against us has grown again." Anger flashed in the rector's eyes. "Largely because our enemies fan the political flames, twisting all the facts and accusing us of being only the pope's men and not the king's."

"We are far from innocent of misdeeds," Charles said soberly, thinking of the Jesuit role in the Huguenots' plight. "But our first loyalty *is* to the pope and the church. Isn't it?"

"Yes. But we are also loyal to the king." Le Picart picked up a quill from the tray at his elbow and smoothed the feather barbs as though quieting himself. "Why is it that human beings so rarely see that two things can be true at once?" He pointed the quill's nib at Charles. "The world is changing. The pope's power shrinks as the power of kings and states grows. And so those who want us gone—especially the Gallicans in France's *Parlements*, who want no foreign influence in France—whisper that we are plotting to regain power for His Holiness. What the hypocrites really want is our power and property for themselves. So they say we are not Gallican enough, not French enough, for these enlightened times. And if, on top of that, people begin whispering that we killed Mademoiselle Mynette, or had her killed, to get her money, all these angers and hatreds will flare into a conflagration." He threw the pen down. "And before it ends, people will no doubt believe that we also stole the girl's *donation entre vifs*, and probably poisoned her mother into the bargain. Dear Blessed Virgin, I wish with all my heart the girl had not been killed! For her sake, God knows, but also for ours."

"What are we going to do? If I may ask, *mon père*."

"What I should do is tell you to go about your lowly scholastic business." The rector shook his head, almost angrily. "But you proved last summer that you have some skill in picking apart this sort of coil. So. Let us see if you can put your personal feelings about this girl aside and act not for yourself, but for the Society. Will you do that?"

"With all my heart, *mon père*!" Seeing Le Picart's skeptical expression, Charles added hastily, "I mean—that is—to the best of my ability, I will. God helping me."

"Good. You have worked a little with Lieutenant-Général La

Reynie, and he respects you. I want you to watch the police investigation during these next few days and keep me informed." Le Picart's eyes narrowed, and there was unmistakable warning in his gaze. "As I did last summer, I give you permission to go and come as you will, unaccompanied. But you will not take advantage of that or neglect your college responsibilities."

"So I will continue to assist in Père Pallu's morning rhetoric class as well as work with Père Jouvancy on the February performance?"

The rector considered for a moment. "If this task I am giving you lasts beyond the beginning of the rhetoric and grammar classes on Monday, I will tell Père Pallu that you will be absent for a time. But you will continue working on the February performance with Père Jouvancy. If a few assignments take longer in Père Pallu's class, that is a small matter. But the performance date is set and cannot be altered. Père Jouvancy needs you at every rehearsal. Meanwhile, you have today, tomorrow, and Sunday to do what I am asking. I want you to discover and tell me everything possible about what the police uncover. Facts won't stop the mudslinging, but facts will help me decide what actions to take. Or not take. For my part," he went on grimly, "I am going to get from our idiot notary Monsieur Henri Brion everything he knows about this affair, if I have to go through his sluggish brain with a soup ladle. Before you returned, I sent a lay brother with a message demanding Brion's presence immediately after dinner. With the girl's death, he should at least be more willing to speak to me freely about this *donation*. After I hear what he has to tell, I will send a report to Père La Chaise at Versailles."

"And he will speak to the king for us?" The Jesuit Père La Chaise was King Louis's confessor.

"If need be, yes."

A flurry of knocking came suddenly at the door.

Startled, Le Picart called, "Come!"

Two lay brothers entered, the older one holding the younger by the arm. The younger man, wrapped in a snow-spattered cloak, had a swiftly blackening eye. His bloodied hand was pressed to the side of his face. Le Picart rose from his chair and hurried around the desk.

"Frère Guiscard, what has happened to you?"

Charles recognized the older brother as Frère Martin, who often served as postern keeper.

"I would have taken him to Frère Brunet, *mon père*," Martin said, "but I thought you ought to hear this as soon as might be."

"I went to the Brion house, *mon père*, as you told me to," Guiscard said, wincing as he talked. "Monsieur Brion was out and no one seemed to know when he'd be home. So I left your message for him and started back. As I was crossing the Place Maubert, two men came at me. They started throwing fists and yelling about Jesuits and saying I'd killed some girl! Crazy, they seemed, *mon père!*"

"Let me see the side of your face."

Guiscard let his hand drop and Charles, who had also stood up, saw that the brother's cheek was badly cut and bruised. Le Picart picked up Guiscard's hands and turned them over, revealing equally bloody knuckles.

"I couldn't let them beat me to a *pâté, mon père*," Guiscard said reasonably. "Since I hadn't done any of what they said."

"Have Frère Brunet see to your hands as well as your face. Did you know the two men?"

Guiscard shook his head. "I think one was an apprentice, but the other was older. I didn't know them."

"Did anyone else see what happened?"

"I don't know, *mon père*. It was snowing hard and when I got clear, I ran."

Le Picart nodded. "I am glad your hurts are no worse, *mon frère*. Frère Martin, please see him to the infirmary."

When the lay brothers were gone, Le Picart sank into his chair again, pressed clasped hands against his lips, and closed his eyes, shaking his head slightly. Charles sat down and waited, not sure whether the rector was praying or simply deploring what had happened.

"So it has started." Le Picart let his hands drop and looked up. "And as soon as the shorter vacation is over and we have day students coming and going in the streets, it's going to get worse. Much worse." He glanced at the black, one-handed clock on the side table. "If Henri Brion does not come to me this afternoon, you will have to find him and bring him here."

"Shall I go to the Châtelet now, *mon père*? He may well be there searching for the *donation*, if he doesn't yet know that Mademoiselle Mynette is dead. He was not at home this morning, and both his daughter and his uncle said they had not seen him yet today."

"Yes, go there. We will pursue our legal claim to this money, and I must speak with him about how to proceed without further inflaming rumor and gossip. And after he tells me that, he is also going to tell me why he kept knowledge of this *donation* from us."

Charles stood up, bowed, and went to the door. Then he turned back, frowning. "How did they know?"

"What?"

"The men who attacked Frère Guiscard must have known that we stand to get the Mynette *patrimoine*. Why else would they link a Jesuit to Martine Mynette's murder? So how did they know that the money now comes to us?"

They looked at each other in silence.

Le Picart said slowly, "I have spoken of the bequest to no one outside the Society. No one at all beyond the college except my superior, our Provincial. Have you?"

"Only to you and Père Damiot, *mon père*."

"Very well. Go now, I want a report from you before midday. Meanwhile, I will discover who has spread our affairs abroad."

Charles went, glad he had to face only the weather and not Le Picart's inquiry.

Chapter 6

Hunched against the snow falling around him, Charles crossed the Petit Pont and most of the Île de la Cité, and then veered right to cross the Pont au Change to the Châtelet. In the old days, money changers had had their *banques*, or benches, on this bridge. And how ironic, Charles found himself thinking, that the money changers' bridge led to a prison and law courts. Where money seemed so often to lead, mortals being unable to do without it, and so often unable to do honestly with it.

In spite of the snow, he slowed as he came to the triangular islet of houses at the north end of the bridge, where the roadway split into a Y. He squinted against the snowflakes, looking up at the larger than life-size bronze statues of the royal family crowning the south-facing point of the triangle, the child Louis XIV standing between his parents, Louis XIII and Anne of Austria. Another family not without its problems, he thought, brushing snow off his eyelashes, and taking the left-hand branch of the Y around the triangle, the way that led into the Place du Châtelet. The looming old Châtelet had been the city's northern gate when all of Paris was contained on the Île de la Cité, just as the Petit Châtelet on the Left Bank had been its southern gate and was still the entrance to the Petit Pont.

Charles had a glimpse of thick walls, round stone towers, and conical blue roofs as he crossed the Place, and then the torch-flaring darkness of an arched passage swallowed him into the ancient fortress. He came out onto the roadway dividing the Châtelet's prison from its law courts. He'd been there once before, but at night, and now, in daylight, he was shocked by how dilapidated the buildings were. Fallen stones and broken roof tiles lay along the road, and a little way ahead was what looked like half a fallen wall. He'd heard Jesuits arguing over whether Julius Caesar had built the Châtelet, which certainly seemed possible, since the Romans had built a town where Paris now stood. But even if it hadn't been Caesar who built it, the crumbling fortress was unimaginably old.

Inside, though, the modern love of litigation pursued its tortuous path. Christmas season though it was, a few clerks came and went in the echoing stone-vaulted anteroom, and two lawyers in voluminous curling wigs and silky black robes with ribbons on their sleeves stood arguing loudly, while their clients glowered at each other. Charles had grown up listening to his father's diatribes about these new men. They had bought their posts from the king, just as notaries like Monsieur Brion had. But notaries occupied the lowest rungs of the legal ladder and ranked only as *bourgeoisie de Paris*. These lawyers and judges, wealthy and with University law degrees, were the modern *noblesse de la robe*—so called because of their long, beribboned gowns—and they considered themselves every bit as noble as the old *noblesse de l'epée*, the nobility of the sword. Which, of course, outraged the old sword families. Mostly, Charles suspected, because the new nobles of the robe were far richer than many of the old nobility, who had lost their money along with their ancient military function. Hereditary nobles could still buy royal military commissions, though, as Charles's father—a very minor noble—had done for him when he'd insisted on soldiering. But even there, there was less and less place for the old ways. The army Charles had fought in had been the minister of war's increasingly reorganized, state-run army, no longer the old motley collection of lords and their men-at-arms, and their shifting allegiances.

Charles spotted a clerk sitting at a table beside a wide archway in the far wall, but as he started toward him, the man sprang up, grabbed a ledger, and turned toward the arch.

"Monsieur," Charles called, "one little moment of your time, I beg you."

The clerk swung around, not so much stopping as hovering, and regarded Charles across the ledger. "What is it, *mon père?*"

Charles had mostly given up trying to explain to laymen that, though he looked like a fully professed Jesuit, he was only a scholastic and not yet a *"père."*

"I am seeking a notary, one Monsieur Henri Brion."

"Brion?" The little man's heels came to rest on the floor and he shifted the ledger to one arm. "Haven't seen him. Notaries are usually wall to wall here, and even today I can find you one, a much better one if—"

"No, I thank you, *monsieur*, it is Monsieur Brion I need."

"Then your best chance is the coffeehouses. Try The Saracen's Nose. Just beyond the other end of the Pont au Change."

The clerk had risen onto his toes again, poised for flight, and Charles put out a hand to stop him. "When did you see Monsieur Brion here last? I was told he has been here daily, searching for a document."

"Him? Hah! That one's never here, *mon père*. Can't remember when I saw him last. And I see most who come in, my *bureau* is just there." He pointed at the big littered table. "How they expect me to work in such a dismal excuse for an office, I couldn't say.

Ah, well. We're the law here, things aren't supposed to make sense!" With another bark of laughter to mark his joke, he shot through the arched door.

Charles, grim-faced, made for the outer door. So Brion had lied to Martine. If, of course, the clerk was telling the truth and hadn't simply failed to notice Brion. But the man's obviously low opinion of the notary matched old Callot's, and Charles saw no reason not to accept it. Seething with anger, he went back through the passage and across the Place to the bridge, walking so fast he nearly missed The Saracen's Nose. It was the run-down ground floor of a house with a timber lower story. Its old window glass was thick and grimy, and the whole building seemed to be leaning tiredly toward the river. Inside, tallow candles reeked, firelight flickered, and the ceiling was black with smoke. A half dozen men were ranged on benches at two long trestle tables with small coffee bowls in front of them, but the sounds from a back room made it clear that coffee was not the Saracen's primary business. The clatter of dice, the whirring of shuffled cards, anguished cries, and raucous laughter announced high-stakes gambling. Taking off his clerical hat to make himself somewhat less noticeable, Charles slid into the shadows and along the walls, scanning the benches for someone who looked like he might be Brion, but not finding any candidates. When he reached the back room's closed door, he pushed it open and called affably, "Henri Brion?"

Most of the men didn't even look up. "Not here," someone yelled back, shaking his dice.

Standing slightly aside from the door, Charles yelled back, "Seen him?"

Heads shook and a few men glanced vaguely toward the door. "Not today."

Charles slid back along the walls, but now the stout woman who had been behind the counter was coming toward him, watching him narrowly. Charles put his hat on, smiling benignly, sketched a cross in the air, and left her staring after him as he let himself out again into the snow.

He crossed the Île, making for the rue Perdue. The snow was slacking, but it was ankle deep and the footing had grown even more treacherous. By the time he reached the Place Maubert, his shoes were soaked. Remembering what had happened to the lay brother a few hours ago, he crossed the Place warily, watching the doorways. But few people were out, and he reached the Brion house without incident. The same awkward footman answered the door, still trying to pull his faded sleeves down to meet his wrist bones and seeming even more uneasy than he had yesterday.

"Oh. My lady is not—that is—no one is—"

"I have come to see your master," Charles said.

"Oh. No, he—I mean, I already told your lay brother who came earlier. My master is not here."

"Yes," Charles said, thinking about that brother's cut and bruised face, "I know you told Frère Guiscard. When is Monsieur Brion likely to return?"

The footman shook his head, looking everywhere but at Charles. "He—ah—went out—very early. No one has—but we're not supposed—I mean, we never—I don't know!" He jerked a bow and closed the door in Charles's face.

Charles raised a fist to knock again, then shrugged and started back toward the Place, wondering how many coffeehouses there were in Paris, and how many he would have to search before he found Brion. Enough, probably, that he should warn Père Le Picart not to count on seeing Brion this afternoon.

The snow had stopped. Apprentices were beginning to sweep the paving stones in front of shops, and a few shivering maids with pitchers and jugs were picking their way to the Place's fountain. A church bell struck the hour. Charles was counting the

strokes, thinking he was going to be late for dinner, when someone hissed behind him. He swung around and a glaring apprentice raised his broom like a shield.

"There may be snow serpents somewhere," Charles drawled,
knowing even as he said it that the boy was not going to laugh.
"But there are none in Paris. Speak."

The boy backed away, but his glare lost none of its malev-
olence.

Charles sighed. "Hear me, *mon ami*. I, too, am grieving for
Mademoiselle Martine Mynette. You would do better to pray for
her soul than make witless accusations."

"Not so witless! Convenient for you she's dead, now you'll get
the Mynette money!"

"The money will go by law where it is supposed to go."
Charles advanced on the boy. "Who is spreading this slander
about Jesuits?"

Swinging the broom wildly at Charles, the boy ducked into a
baker's shop and slammed the door. Charles turned away, sick at
heart. Who *was* spreading this anti-Jesuit slander?

From what he'd been told, the University of Paris was usually
the first answer when that question had to be asked. But this
poison seemed to be spreading from the Place Maubert, not the
rue St. Jacques. Jansenists were always a possibility, and there
were no doubt Jansenists among the artisans of the Place Maubert. The Jansenists, though Catholics, were so strict and sober
minded they seemed more Protestant than the Protestants, and
they thoroughly disapproved of the more tolerant and worldly
Jesuits. Such an incendiary word *worldly* could be. Yet the world
was where everyone lived, even those in monasteries and Jesuit
houses. As far as Charles could see, that included even saints,
because when mystical ecstasies ended, where else was there to
come back to? For beings of spirit and flesh, the world then was

inescapable, as long as life lasted. And if God was *not* to be found in the world He had made, then where? Absorbed in his theological argument, Charles turned down a narrow lane, hoping to cut a little distance from his walk to the college. Jesuits were called worldly because—at their best, anyway—they used whatever seemed good and innocent in God's world to help people toward God. But what could be wrong with that? He shook his head in exasperation. Of course, distinguishing between good-and-worldly on the one hand, and sinful-and-worldly on the other, involved thinking. And how many people chose to think, rather than enjoy pleasantly horrified and self-righteous feelings?

Charles stumbled over a loose paving stone, skinned his hand against a wall trying to recover his balance, and swore aloud. No one was in sight—just as well, considering his worldly swearing—but he had the sudden sense that the air around him was listening intently. His scalp tingled. The Silence had not visited him in a long time. During the autumn, he'd longed for the comfort of it, but it had not come. The secret Charles kept even from his confessor was that he'd become a Jesuit because he wanted to come as close to God as a man could, wanted to reach God's heart. And wanted to do that while solidly rooted in God's good world, not from behind cloister walls. In his hunger for the Silence, he'd promised himself that if it ever visited him again, he would fall on his knees—on his face, even—in utter gratitude, no matter where it found him. Instead, he did what he usually did when it came. He argued. Which was just as well, considering that he was standing in snow to his ankles.

How could You allow Martine's death? he demanded. *Why? She was so young. She was innocent, good, beautiful.*

The air itself seemed to bite back at him. *No one young and innocent and good ever dies?*

This was murder, Charles flung silently back.

For a long moment, nothing moved at all. Then the air seemed to sigh. *I know something of blood*, the Silence said.

Chastened, Charles bowed his head. *Yes. But Your blood was for healing. What can be worth this girl's death?*

Worth? the Silence said. *Life and death are a bargain?*

Not a bargain, Charles thought back. *But does death mean nothing?*

A small cold wind breathed along the lane. *Nothing is wasted*, the Silence said. And added, *Unless you waste it.* And was gone.

Charles stumbled out of the lane, breathing as though he'd been running and wondering why he'd longed so desperately for the Silence to come back when it only gave him answers he didn't want.

Chapter 7

When Charles reached Louis le Grand, he took his turn at overseeing dinner for the *pensionnaires* and their tutors who hadn't gone to the country house in Gentilly. During the holidays, the fully professed Jesuits usually ate separately, in the fathers' refectory, leaving the scholastics like Charles to take turns overseeing student meals. It was a small group, and both younger and older boys ate together in the older *pensionnaires'* dining hall. Today's dinner, for which Charles had little appetite, was a savory mutton *gallimaufrée*. A half dozen braziers had been brought in as an extra holiday treat, though in the vast room, no one sitting more than a few feet from one felt any warmth. But at least their orange glow was pleasant to see on a dark, snowy day and made the ceiling's faded gold stars shine between its dark beams.

When dinner was over and the refectory empty, Charles went to Père Le Picart and told him what he'd learned at the Châtelet and the Brion house. The rector demurred at the idea of Charles scouring the city's coffeehouses and reluctantly decided to give the notary one more day to appear on his own.

"I have thought of something else I could do this afternoon in regard to this, *mon père*, if you permit," Charles said. "I keep thinking about the classes beginning on Monday and all that will then be upon us."

"What do you want to do?"

"I would like to talk to Maître Richaud. He went with me to the Place Maubert yesterday to call on a chandler from the artisans' Congregation of the Sainte Vierge. He may have heard something about the Mynette household, or about Henri Brion."

"That is well thought." Le Picart frowned briefly. "I believe—yes, I am sure you will find him just now in the first house on the right in the student court, in the bedding closet."

Startled—not for the first time—at Le Picart's minute knowledge of who was doing what in his domain, Charles went through the Cour d'honneur and through an archway into the next courtyard to the north, the student court. The bedding closet was a small, windowless room on the ground floor, where sheets and blankets were kept in old wooden chests and newer cupboards with tall doors. Maître Richaud was indeed there, muttering to himself with his nose nearly touching a heavy linen sheet.

"Holes? How am I supposed to see holes in pitch dark?" He lifted the sheet higher and turned slightly toward the open door.

"You could light a candle," Charles said mildly from the doorway. "Unless, of course, you *prefer* to curse the darkness . . ." A strong scent of lavender and wormwood, specifics against moths—and probably also unwelcome to nesting mice—came from a chest whose lid stood open.

"We're told to save candles." Richaud looked up irritably. "Oh. It's you. Well, stand out of the light, if you can call it that." He went back to examining the sheet.

"Want help?"

Richaud grunted, and Charles pulled a sheet from the open chest. "The other morning, when we went to the Place Maubert," Charles began, "did you—"

"Look at this! The entire middle is gone! What do they do, stick swords through them?"

"Can't it be mended?"

"Oh, I suppose so." Richaud threw the sheet into a pile on the floor and picked up another. "What about the Place Maubert?"

"While you were with your chandler," Charles said patiently, "did you hear any talk about the Brion family on the rue Perdue? Or about a Mademoiselle Martine Mynette?"

"The one who's dead?"

"So you know that. How?"

"Probably everyone in the college knows it. Once the porter at the postern door hears, everyone knows. Of course, I don't listen to gossip," Richaud added repressively, and nodded with satisfaction—whether at the sheet he held or his own upright-ness, Charles couldn't tell.

Keeping a firm grip on himself, Charles said mildly, "If some-one gossiped beside you—in the chandler's shop on the Place Maubert, say—how could you help hearing it?"

"You're the one who went to the Brion house, Maître du Luc. And they knew the Mynette girl, so I heard, and knew her very well. Why are you asking me about these people?"

Charles cast his eyes up, glad of the dim light. "Because gos-sip and what people say of themselves and their closest friends are not often the same thing. And because I've been directed to ask, if that salves your conscience."

Richaud's eyes slid sideways toward Charles. "What kind of gossip?" He dropped another sheet onto the pile and picked up a stack of neatly folded sheets.

"Any kind," Charles said, stifling the urge to tear a strip off a discarded sheet and strangle Richaud with it.

"Well . . . I did hear something." Richaud dumped his stack of sheets into the open chest. "About the Brion son," he said, straightening. "Gilles, he's called."

Charles nodded encouragingly.

"He hated that Mynette girl. Because his father was making him court her and he didn't want to, he wants to be a monk."

"A monk?" Charles said in surprise. Well, that explained a lot.

"But his father won't give him an endowment to take to the monastery," Richaud said. "Refused to give him anything at all unless he married the girl, who was supposed to get a lot of money after her mother died."

"Oh?" Charles tried to keep his tone even. "Who told you this?"

"The chandler's apprentice."

Charles went on studying the sheet in his hands and considered what Richaud had just said about Isabel's brother. Was it a motive for murder? An argument could be made either way. On the one hand, Martine would probably have had no qualms about opening the door to Gilles Brion. So he would have had easy entrance to the house if he wanted to kill her. But on the other hand, though Gilles might well have killed Martine in sudden desperation, his father would almost certainly try to force some other heiress on him. So what would taking such a terrible risk gain him in the end? Most people had few choices about their lives beyond what their parents chose for them. Even when they came of age, defying parental choice usually meant losing not only the means to live, but the social connections necessary to get on in the world. Parental will and family gain ruled everything.

Charles wondered if the neighborhood police *commissaire* knew about young Brion's forced courtship of Martine. Probably, if even the neighborhood apprentices knew. But it wasn't something to leave to chance.

"Thank you, *maître*." Charles thrust his bed sheet at Richaud and made for the street passage, leaving Richaud complaining loudly that he could at least have folded the sheet first.

But before Charles reached the postern, he was overtaken by

a small crowd of teenage boys escorted by their tutors. The boys were all helping to carry a deep basket full of dark round loaves and piles of clothing.

"It's time, *maître!*" one of them said excitedly.

Charles had forgotten completely about overseeing the distribution of alms by these representatives of the older *pensionnaires'* Congregation of the Ste. Vierge. With an effort, he swallowed his frustration at the delay in seeing the police *commissaire* and in finding Lieutenant-Général La Reynie, for whom no detail of policing the city was too small and who might be anywhere in Paris. Charles dismissed the escorting tutors and followed the boys into the main building's anteroom, where the big double doors opened directly onto the street. The boys brought a heavy walnut table from the neighboring *grand salon*, placed it before the doors, and piled the loaves and clothing on it. Then Charles drew them together to pray for God's poor and ask the Holy Virgin to increase mercy and generosity in their own hearts. At the "amen," two boys pulled the doors open to the snowy street. Everyone knew that alms were given out on Friday afternoons, but no one approached until the doors stood open. Charles pulled his cloak more tightly closed, wondering aloud if the weather might keep people away, but the boys all shook their heads.

"No, *maître*," Walter Connor said. Connor was one of Charles's rhetoric students and dancers, and the journey to his home in Ireland was too long for the short holiday. "The worse the weather, the more they need. They'll come."

He had hardly finished speaking before three ragged men and a woman appeared at the doors, as though they'd conjured themselves from the air. Charles stepped forward, greeted and blessed them, nodded at the students, and stood back. His role now was to see that the boys distributed the alms courteously and evenhandedly, intervening only if there was need.

The crowd of beggars grew quickly. Connor and three other boys handed out loaves, and the rest offered the worn but serviceable clothing and shoes from the store they'd brought with them. One of the boys held out a long *manteau* of soft brown wool, hardly worn, to a thin, pockmarked woman. She snatched it from him and held it against her chest, stroking the cloth, wide-eyed at her good fortune. Watching her, Charles thought of the young butcher in the artisans' Congregation who had given it. Knowing that the man's wife had recently died in childbirth and that he had other small children to provide for, Charles had urged him to sell it to the secondhand clothing dealers. But the butcher had pushed it into Charles's arms, saying brokenly that it was his wife's and that she had always been tenderhearted to the poor.

Charles's thoughts jumped from that death to Martine's. Forcing aside his memory of her lifeless body on the blood-fouled floor, he told himself that even if the drunken maid had not left the house door open, only forgotten to bar it, it was possible that someone had a key, honestly or by stealth. Gilles Brion, for example, could easily have come by a key. His father, as the family notary and the girl's guardian, surely had a key. Charles took a mental step back and reconsidered the elder Brion. Whom no one admitted to seeing since yesterday. Who had apparently lied about searching for the lost *donation* at the Châtelet. But why would Henri Brion lie about searching for the *donation*? He had forced his son to court the girl for the Mynette money. Why would he intentionally conceal the document that ensured that the money would come to her? And if the *donation* was not found, presumably the Jesuits would get the money. Which was the last thing Henri Brion would want. Those thoughts led Charles back to the younger Brion. If Gilles had killed Martine, what would he do next? Had Henri Brion vanished because he knew his son had killed her and was busy helping him get out of France, busy working out a pretext for the boy's sudden absence? But would Henri Brion try to save his son if the boy had killed the pretty goose and lost the family's chance at the golden egg? A son—an only son, as far as Charles knew—was a son, though. For some men, nothing mattered more than that.

"I don't want that, give me that thicker one, the green one there, you bloated whelp, hand it over!"

Charles came abruptly back to the almsgiving and was at the doors before the angry demand reached its end. A bearded old man leaning on a stick had flung a brown coat onto the table and was grabbing for a green one held by one of the younger students. The boy had backed away from the shouting beggar and was looking anxiously at Charles.

"Calm yourself, *monsieur*." Charles took the coat from the boy. "And have some respect for the Virgin's alms. We are glad to give you this coat, no need to grab for it."

The man glowered at him, his eyes hollow under straggling gray brows. "No need to grab from them with money and feasts on their table every day? Them with their golden boxes, while other men starve in the street!"

Golden boxes? Charles peered more closely at the dirty seamed face and recognized the man who had attacked the Condé's reliquary on Christmas Eve. He looked for the young companion who had seemed to be the old man's keeper, but didn't see him.

"That box is not ours to sell, *monsieur*. We must do with it what its giver asked. What is your name?"

The man froze like a wary animal. Then his sinewy hand shot out and snatched the green coat, and he limped away with surprising speed. The boys began to murmur indignantly, but Charles hushed them.

"Do you think men always control their fate?" he asked reprovingly, and reminded them of all the things that could bring an ordinary man to begging. Sin, surely, but also simple ill luck, sickness of body or mind, all the misfortunes that crushed a man as though he were a flea. No matter how much the flea might pray, some impious voice said in Charles's mind. Then a clutch of women surrounded by crying, shivering children pushed their way to the front of the crowd, and for the next half hour, he and the boys were too busy for thinking.

By the time the store of alms was gone, the final blessing given, and the great doors shut, the short winter afternoon was already beginning to fade. The boys put the walnut table back in the *salon* and gathered around Charles. He led them in prayers of thanksgiving to the Virgin, finished with an Ave, and dismissed them to their waiting tutors. Before anyone else could want him for something, he was through the postern and on his way to the Place Maubert police *commissaire* and the rue Perdue.

The *commissaire* was not at home. His *sergent*, of course, had no idea where Lieutenant-Général La Reynie might be found. Henri Brion was still not at home, either. The maidservant took him up to the *salon*, where Mlle Brion and M. Callot rose from their chairs on either side of the fire to greet him. Isabel Brion was dressed in black now. Her eyes were red and her face tired and drawn. She looked a different creature from the rosy, exuberant girl Charles had met the day before. Callot was sober and nearly as subdued as his great-niece. He placed a cushioned and fringed chair for Charles between the other chairs, and they all sat quietly until Charles broke the silence.

"Monsieur Callot, your servant says that Monsieur Henri Brion is not yet at home."

"No. He is not."

"Where do you suppose he is?"

"Nowhere I care to mention before my great-niece."

Charles decided that he would have to leave finding the elder Brion to Lieutenant-Général La Reynie, but before he could ask about Gilles, Isabel Brion spoke.

"Martine is to be buried on Monday morning, *maître*. Her funeral Mass will be at Saint-Nicolas du Chardonnet, do you know it? It is just a little south of the Place. Will you—oh—but no, forgive me—" She colored and looked away, and Charles thought he knew why.

"I know what is being said about her death, *mademoiselle*," he said gently. "But if my rector permits, I will be there."

M. Callot spoke from the flickering shadows on Charles's other side. "And that which is being said, *maître*, do you swear it is false?"

His great-niece gasped. "Uncle Callot! Be quiet! Of course it is false, you have only to look at him to know he tells the truth!"

"I am not a young girl, Isabel, to have my mind made up by a handsome face."

Charles felt himself go as red as the flames in the fireplace. Thankful for the room's dimness, he turned toward Callot. "I assure you, *monsieur*," he said evenly, "the Society of Jesus had nothing whatever to do with Mademoiselle Mynette's death. You well know that there are always those ready to accuse us of any ill thing that happens."

Callot grunted. "But money is money. A significant sum of money, which more than a few would do much to have."

"Including your nephew, I understand."

The old man bridled at Charles's riposte. "So you've learned more about the unhappy courtship my nephew forced on his son? Ah, well, it is true enough."

Charles decided that bluntness was the fastest way to what he needed. "How much did young Monsieur Brion dislike being forced into courtship?"

"He didn't kill her! He would never kill anyone!" Isabel Brion shook her head so hard that one of her pearl earrings fell into her lap. "He was obeying my father. Although I would dearly have loved having Martine as my sister, I begged my father and begged him to stop forcing Gilles, but he—he—oh, may God forgive him, my father is so greedy!" Trying to hold in tears, she rose and went to the small mirror beside the fireplace to replace her earring.

"Is your father in such urgent need of money, *mademoiselle*? And where is he, does he know of Mademoiselle Mynette's death?" Charles ventured.

"I don't know where he is. Or whether he knows she is dead. He is the master here and comes and goes as he will." She sighed. "As for money, who is not in need of more?" She turned from the mirror and wiped her eyes with a tiny black linen handkerchief. "But to get it, my father has made Gilles desperately unhappy. He wants to be a monk. And my father will never let him."

"Having his religious vocation thwarted could make a man very angry," Charles said quietly. "Where is your brother, *mademoiselle*?"

Too late, she saw the danger of what she said. "Gilles is across the river with the Capuchins, where he always is!" she flung at Charles. "Go and see, if you don't believe me!"

"Ah, it seems you are no longer so handsome, *maître*," Callot murmured.

"Mademoiselle," Charles said, "someone viciously murdered your friend and must be discovered. At any cost. No one is beyond suspicion."

"What about me, then?" she demanded.

Charles started to say that she could hardly have a reason to wish her friend dead but then held his tongue. For all he knew, she might have some motivation, though he couldn't imagine what it would be. "Where were you, then, *mademoiselle*, when she was killed?"

"Here," Isabel Brion said hopelessly, all the fight suddenly gone out of her. "Asleep, I suppose. Then I went to her house with Uncle Callot and she was dead." She turned to the fire, wiping her eyes. "Oh, Blessed Virgin, I wish I had been with her to keep her safe. Or that she had come to us, as my father wished!"

"Can anyone swear that you were here asleep?" Charles pressed her, thinking that he might as well do the thing thoroughly.

She spun around in surprise, realizing that he was taking her seriously. "My maid. She sleeps in my chamber."

Not necessarily proof, but Charles let it go. He could not believe in Isabel Brion as her friend's killer. Though not believing is hardly the same thing as knowing, the ruthlessly blunt part of himself pointed out. He turned to Callot. "And you, *monsieur*?"

"The same. Asleep. Though with no one to swear to it. I have no valet. But you have only to look at me to know that I have not the strength to do what was done."

Charles was not sure he believed that, either, but Callot seemed as unlikely a killer as his great-niece. Beyond the salon windows, the December dusk was closing in and the corners of the room were filling with shadows. Charles shifted in his chair, knowing he should leave. "What about Mademoiselle Mynette's maid, the one who found her?"

"Renée? Oh, she's too lazy to kill anyone," Isabel Brion said dismissively. "And from the smell of her, she'd drunk herself to sleep the night before. She's a good enough woman, though, good-tempered, and she'd been with the Mynettes for a long time."

"I see. Well, it grows late and I must take my leave, *mademoiselle*, *monsieur*." Charles got to his feet. "When Monsieur Henri Brion comes home, I beg you—"

The salon door opened, and Charles turned eagerly, thinking that the notary had at last returned, but it was a much younger man who stood hesitating on the threshold.

"Gilles!"

Isabel rushed to embrace her brother, but Callot remained sitting by the fire, eyeing his great-nephew.

"I'm so glad you've come home," she cried. She looked over her shoulder. "Oh, I beg your pardon," she said to Charles, and stepped away from her brother. "Maître du Luc, may I present my brother, Monsieur Gilles Brion?"

The young man turned his wary, slightly open-mouthed stare on Charles, and his sister made an exasperated noise.

"Gilles?"

Her voice prodded him into an awkward bow, and Charles inclined his head in return. Gilles Brion stood barely as tall as his sister, small boned and delicate. He seemed younger than Isabel, though Charles didn't know his age. His elaborate light brown wig dwarfed his sallow face. Finely embroidered lace frothed at the neck and cuffs of his ash-brown broadcloth coat, and the heels on his water-spotted but well-made shoes were unnecessarily high. Without them, he probably wouldn't even reach the tip of his sister's nose.

Poor Martine, Charles thought, before he could stop himself. *Or, perhaps, poor Capuchins . . .*

Mlle Brion laid a hand on Gilles's arm. "We have been talking about Martine." Her eyes searched his face. "You may not know, Gilles, but she—she is dead. Someone killed her."

"Dead?" Young Brion—it was hard not to think of him as a boy, though he must be in his twenties—was suddenly radiant. His eyes shone and he clasped his hands to his breast. Seeing the look on his sister's face, he let his hands fall and tried for a suitably shocked countenance.

"That is terrible, Isabel. But how can she be—" He shook his head in seeming confusion. "Who would kill Martine?" His eyes went from face to face. Everyone was watching him intently, and no one answered him. The blood drained from his cheeks, leaving his eyes dark as caves. "Who, Isabel?" He clutched her hand. "Have they found him? If they have not found him, the *commissaire* will say it was me!"

"Was it?" Charles said pleasantly.

Gilles caught his breath, suddenly as red as he'd been pale, and his jaw set with anger. "How dare you say that!"

So, Charles thought, *not quite as limp as he seems.* "I was only startled by your own words, *monsieur*. Why would anyone think you killed her? Where were you early this morning?"

"That is none of your concern, *maître*," Gilles said through stiff lips.

Charles rose from the chair and advanced on him. "I met Mademoiselle Mynette just yesterday, Monsieur Brion. This morning I saw her lying in her blood. Finding a murderer is every man's concern. So I repeat, where were you early this morning?"

Brion flinched. "Here, of course. Before dawn, I mean. Asleep. Like everyone else. Then I went to the Capuchins for Prime."

"I understood that you were paying court to Mademoiselle Martine Mynette?"

"No! I mean—yes. But only because—" Brion stared at Charles like a hunted animal. "My father forced me," he said defiantly. "She was a good girl. She—but I didn't want her! I don't want any girl; I want to be a monk." His shoulders slumped and he sighed hopelessly. "Everyone knew it, and now the *commissaire* will think I killed her. Blessed saints, alive she was a stone around my neck, and dead she will pull me down to hell! God knows, I am sorry she is dead, but I had nothing to do with it!"

Callot finally spoke. "So go and tell your monks they can have you now. Quickly, before your father finds you another heiress. And before the police *commissaire* comes for you."

Brion looked in panic at the windows. "Is he coming?"

Callot rolled his eyes. "Can I see through walls? How do I know? He was here earlier and I told him you were off praying."

Isabel Brion looked at Callot suspiciously. "Was he really here, uncle? Why did you not tell us?"

Callot smiled blandly. "Our good *commissaire* was not worried. He knows he will not need to hunt your brother through the taverns." He looked the boy up and down. "And certainly not through the usual brothels, more's the pity."

"God forgive you." Brion's eyes filled with tears and his voice quivered. "If I were as old as you, I would have more care for my immortal soul."

"You will not need to, when you are as old as I, Gilles. Your frightened little soul will long since have left your unused body and be flapping around God's ears like a mosquito, whining its little prayers."

The old man's attack was so full of acid that it took Charles's breath away. For the first time, Charles felt some sympathy for Gilles Brion. But if the young man thought that the Capuchins were going to coddle his overweening self-love, he was, from what Charles knew of Capuchins, in for an unpleasantly surprising novitiate. If he ever got even that far.

Both the young Brions were staring furiously at Callot. The boy's mouth was still trembling but the girl looked as though, had Charles not been there, the *commissaire* might have had two murders on his hands. Gilles Brion finally blundered out of the salon, and his sister followed him. Charles and Callot listened to their footsteps on the stairs. The murmur of their voices rose and fell in the foyer until, upon a dismayed cry from Mlle Brion, the house door opened and closed. Then they heard her on the stairs again and saw her hurry past the salon door and climb to the floor above. She was crying as though her heart would break.

Callot sighed heavily. "I apologize for Gilles. As they say, dress a spindly bush in lace and fine cloth, it looks like a man. Undress it, it is nothing but a bush."

"Still, you love him, don't you?" Charles said, standing by the fire. "Even though you nearly flayed him alive just now."

"You have a very hearing ear. God help me, of course I love him, I have to love him, he's my niece's son, though she was worth a dozen of him. And a dozen of his father, too. But Gilles made me ill just now, the way he talked about Martine. That precious girl is dead, and he thinks only of himself."

"Do you think he killed her?"

Callot spat into the fire. "Of course not. No matter how much he whined about her—can you imagine complaining about marrying that delectable girl?—he is not stupid enough to have killed her. But I tell you, if he says one more selfish word about her, I may kill him!"

Chapter 8

Outside, the cold was deepening and it was full dark. The street lanterns were lit, but the little rue Perdue had few of them, and Charles had to pick his way carefully over patches of ice. As he went, he admonished himself for his contempt toward Gilles Brion's claim to a religious vocation. Any Jesuit should know better. "There are very few people," St. Ignatius had written, "who realize what God would make of them if they abandoned themselves into His hands, and let themselves be formed by His grace."

But, Charles told himself, even if he had no right to judge Gilles Brion's vocation, he had every right to find out if the young man had committed murder. And if he had, to bring justice on him. On the whole, though, Charles doubted that he had, simply because he couldn't imagine Gilles taking such decisive action. He wondered, though, why Mlle Brion had been crying after talking to her brother alone. She was worried, exhausted, grieving, all of that. But she'd left the salon dry-eyed and angry. What had her brother said to reduce her to such despairing tears?

Ahead of Charles, shouts and singing spilled from a tavern. *La Queue du Cheval's* sign showed plump brown equine hindquarters, with a long yellow tail sporting a bow of blue ribbon. The Horse's Tail was doing a good Friday night business, crowded with Parisians celebrating the holidays. In spite of the cold, the door was open, and as Charles got nearer, he caught the words of the song the patrons were bellowing.

> *"Elle était riche, elle est morte*
> *Les Jésuites dansent sur son corps.*
> *Elle est perdue, pour ainsi dire,*
> *Les Jésuites pour enrichir!"*

His first furious reaction was to start for the tavern door, but his second was less stupid and he kept walking, repeating the gist of the song under his breath. "She was rich, she is dead," the drinkers were bawling, "the Jesuits are dancing on her corpse. She is lost—so to speak—to make the Jesuits richer!" Though cautiously not saying it outright, the song was claiming that Jesuits had killed Martine or connived at her death. And with a clever little slam at the Society's commitment to dance—something enemies frequently criticized—thrown in for good measure.

Behind him, men were coming out of the tavern, and Charles moved close to a house wall, as far into shadow as he could, and stood listening and watching.

"So let's take pots and bells and sing it under their windows, the greedy bastards!" someone said, to a chorus of enthusiastic agreement. "Treacherous to France, that's what they are," someone else said drunkenly. "Always after power and gold for the pope." That got angry muttering, which swelled into shouts of, "Let's serenade them, then, let's go!"

But they only reeled around the corner of the tavern, fumbling with their breeches so they could water the tavern wall.

Charles walked on and got back to the college and the fathers' refectory with time enough before supper to wait for Père Le Picart in the passage outside the door. Tonight it was someone else's turn to supervise the students' supper, so Charles ate with the other Jesuits. When Le Picart arrived, Charles told him about the elder Brion's continued elusiveness and the younger Brion's connection to Martine. Then, reluctantly, he recounted the song being sung in The Horse's Tail. Grim-faced, Le Picart nodded and dismissed him to sit with the other scholastics. Grace was said and Charles greeted the others at his table. Then, avoiding as much conversation as he politely could, he ate his way steadily through a stew of salted fish followed by dried apples. He was more grateful for the crackling fire in the great hooded fireplace than for what was on his plate, but too worried about Martine Mynette's murder and the poisonous tavern song to pay much attention to either. When the final grace was said, he escaped and went to his chamber—cold, but blessedly quiet and even more blessedly private.

In spite of the chill, he opened a shutter and looked out at the street. The night was windless and the street lanterns hung motionless from their long iron hooks on the sides of buildings. When he'd arrived last summer, the lanterns had hung from chains stretched across the street, but during the autumn the chains had been taken down and the hooks put in place, making it easier to lower and raise the lanterns to replace the two-pound candles they burned. The candles would burn till after midnight, casting gold-tinged shadows on the ground and picking out the ruffles of snow lying along window ledges and the tops of walls. Across the rue St. Jacques, the windows of most of the University houses were dark, but that would change soon, as scholars and professors returned for the start of new classes. On Sunday, Père Jouvancy would return, and he and Charles would begin working in earnest on the theatre performance scheduled for mid-February. *And then it will be Lent*, Charles thought, with an inward sigh. A holy season with much to offer mind and spirit, but one the body perpetually dreaded. Fasting was no longer as strict as in times past, but it was strict enough. And would likely be even more so in the refectory this year. Especially if the Mynette fortune went elsewhere.

Charles closed the shutter and went to his prie-dieu. In truth, he didn't care where the money went. Or most of him didn't care. Or at least not very much . . . Though, besides better fare in the refectories, a half dozen new costumes were needed for February's performance. And Père Jouvancy had already been talking about new scenery before he left for the holidays. Charles set his candle in the wall holder above the prie-dieu and knelt, pulling his cloak tighter around him. He clasped his hands and gazed at the little painting of the Virgin and Child on the wall in front of him.

"Forgive me for coveting the money," he said softly. "In my heart, I try not to want it. But in my mind, I covet it for what needs doing." He forbore mentioning what his body wanted to see on the dinner plate.

Mary, smiling gravely, cuddled the dimpled baby on her lap and gazed back at Charles. Her gown was a rich blue and she wore a thin gold necklace. The polished wooden bench she sat on was cushioned in red and there were rose-red curtains at her open, leaded window. A silver vase of lilies stood on the mantel, and a silver pitcher and basin and linen towel waited on a small table, ready for the baby's bath.

"Not a poor room," Charles said to her, and flinched at his accusing tone. Though what he said was true; his own room was far poorer. But God's mother didn't need the discipline and sacrifice of poverty, he chided himself. Bitter sacrifice awaited her when the fat laughing baby she held grew up. The painter had surrounded Mary with beauty and luxury to honor her. Honor mattered, of course, but money bought far more basic gifts. Like safety, especially for women like poor little Martine Mynette, who had been rightly terrified should her lost *donation* not be found.

"If the Garden of Eden were now," Charles told Mary, "the serpent wouldn't bother with an apple; he'd offer Eve a handful of gold. And who, in these days, would blame her for taking it?"

Beyond the shuttered window, the bells began to ring for Compline, their untuned clanging growing across the city. Something about their clashing notes comforted Charles, reminding him that he didn't have to fit things perfectly together. He only had to pray.

Though as a scholastic he wasn't required to say the offices, he began a psalm. He was praying, "I will bless the Lord who gives me counsel; my heart teaches me night after night . . ." when something smashed against his window, a shutter banged open, and glass shattered musically on the floor. Charles jumped to his feet, shivering in the flood of freezing air. Keeping as much as he could to the side of the window, he looked down into the street. A half dozen men, maybe more—they were moving so fast he couldn't tell exactly how many there were—launched another hail of stones at the building. Across the street, a group of shadowy singing figures cheered them on from the open door of a University house. "*. . . elle est perdue, pour ainsi dire, les Jésuites pour enricher!*"

Charles ran from the room and took the stairs down three at a time, ignoring opening doors and questions behind him. Then someone else was running and overtook him.

"What is it?" Père Damiot said as they reached the bottom of the stairs. "I heard glass breaking."

"Some men throwing stones. Come on."

In the street passage, Charles grabbed a key from the porter's room, opened the postern a little, and stood still and hidden, watching. Damiot was at his shoulder. There were only five attackers. The bystanders across the street were cheering loudly as two men did something in front of the big double doors. Two more were farther down the façade, prying up loose cobbles to throw at windows. The fifth was standing a dozen feet from the postern, his back to Charles, glancing up and down the street, looking out for the watch, most likely.

Charles slid into the street, Damiot silent behind him. Praying they wouldn't slip in the rutted snow, Charles closed on the man whose back was turned. Before he was aware, Charles and Damiot had him by the arms and were walking him swiftly to the postern. The man started to yell, but his captors jerked his arms up behind his back and he grunted and shut his mouth. But the men across the street saw what was happening and cried a warning to the other attackers, who fled toward the river. As the bystanders surged across the rue St. Jacques, shouting threats, Charles and Damiot pulled their captive through the postern door. Charles slammed it and turned the key. Fists pounded on the door's planking and voices demanded the man's release. These were definitely students, Charles thought, hearing their swearing—too inventive and polished for anyone else.

"Stretch your arms straight out against the wall and keep them there," Charles told the captive as he and Damiot shoved the man against the stones.

"Going to crucify me?"

"Don't blaspheme," Damiot snapped. "Who set you to this?"

The man licked his lips. "No one," he said sullenly, breathing a miasma of *eau de vie* into the air. "I think for myself. I know who murdered that girl." He was short and thickset, dressed in a workman's rough brown coat and breeches, with unkempt black hair and a battered felt hat.

"Excellent," Charles said briskly. "We'll take you to our police *commissaire*, and you can tell him who the killer is. And then we'll explain to him how you and your *confrères* have been 'thinking for yourselves' this evening."

The flickering night lantern suspended halfway along the passage roof showed the hot anger in the man's eyes. What bothered Charles, though, was that the eyes held no fear. And they should have. Did the *peuple menu*, the ordinary people, dislike the Society of Jesus so much? Did they truly think it had so little power and influence these days? Where was the respect it usually commanded?

The flurry of fists on the postern grew louder. As it began to bounce in its frame, the door from the main building burst open and Père Montville, the new principal, stormed into the passage.

"Bring the rector, Maître du Luc," Montville ordered. "His windows face the courtyard and I doubt he has heard this rough music."

Running feet sent echoes along the passage's vaulted roof, and a young and very large lay brother skidded to a stop beside Charles.

"Don't move," Charles told his captive. "Not a muscle." He stepped cautiously back from the man and glanced from the enormous brother, whose eyes were shining with illicit battle lust, to Damiot.

"Our friend here surely has a knife somewhere. Which, just as surely, he knows better than to use on clerics. But if he moves even the slightest fraction of the length of your thumb, grab his arms, both of you, shove him down, and sit on him."

Charles turned and ran for the passage door. When he reached Le Picart's rooms, he knocked softly. The fewer people who got up and followed them, the better, at least for now.

"*Mon père,*" he said, with his mouth against the space between the side of the door and the frame, "come, you are needed."

The door opened almost at once, as though Le Picart had

been waiting for Charles's summons, waiting for trouble. As soon as he saw Charles's face, he reached back into the room for his cloak.

Charles told him what was happening as they walked. They were nearly at the side door to the passage when wood splintered and furious yelling echoed off the passage walls. Le Picart tried to push past, but Charles unceremoniously stopped him.

"Wait!" He opened the side door just enough to see into the passage. Damiot and Montville and several lay brothers were trying to shove the intruders back though the ruined postern, all of them tripping and stumbling over the remains of the door as they fought. Their captive was nowhere to be seen. As far as Charles could tell, the only weapons in use were feet and fists. He stepped into the passage, bent swiftly, and grabbed two long, sharp staves of splintered wood.

"Here!" He thrust one into the rector's hands. "Stay beside me, *mon père*, use your weapon, and we'll part the waters."

Le Picart nodded grimly and hefted the stave of wood, trying its weight and balance. Shoulder to shoulder, they surged into the passage. "*In nomine Patrie, Filios, et Spiritu Sanctu*," the rector thundered, and they advanced on the fray. The lay brothers and Montville, who were getting the worst of the fight, looked over their shoulders and renewed their efforts. With sudden inspiration, Charles began declaiming Psalm fifty-three.

> "*Deus . . . salvum me fac . . .*
> *Quoniam alieni insurrexit adverum me*
> *et fortes quaesierunt animam mean . . . averte mala inimicis meis*
> *Et in veritate tua disperde illos!*"

Damiot fought his way to Charles's unprotected side, and he and the rector made the litany bounce off the stone walls.

*"Defend my cause, for haughty men have risen up against me
and fierce men seek my life . . .
Turn back the evil upon my foes,
in your faithfulness, destroy them!"*

Charles and Le Picart swept their improvised weapons in unison from side to side, as though sweeping uncleanness out of the air itself. Whether it was the sharply pointed wood cleaving the air or the echoing church Latin that made the intruders retreat, retreat they did. Within moments, there was nothing but the sound of running feet. The victors exchanged furtive glances, wiped their streaming faces, and tried to catch their breath.

"Amen!" Damiot said with relish.

"So be it!" Le Picart responded liturgically and with equal fervor. He dropped his piece of wood and went out to inspect the damage.

Snow was starting to fall. The others followed him along the college façade, stepping over broken glass, looking up at shattered windows. Le Picart was the first to see the doors. He stopped as though frozen between one step and the next, and the others stopped behind him, craning their necks. In the light of the nearest street lantern, they saw what else the attackers had done. Scrawled across the doors in charcoal letters two feet high was a single word: *MEURTRIERS.*

Murderers.

Chapter 9

The rector refused to let Charles go for the nearest police *commissaire.*

"I will pursue my own questions first," he said flatly to Charles and the others gathered around him. "The fewer who know, the less talk. More of our lay brothers will have to know because work must be done tonight. But otherwise, none of you will speak of this. To anyone. Now, before anything else, are any of you injured?"

Most had only a few bruises. The two lay brothers bleeding from cuts, Le Picart sent Frère Brunet to the infirmary, along with one whose shoulder had been pulled out of joint. Then he set the rest of the lay brothers to cleaning up the damage, and told them to wake others to help them sweep up the glass in the street, scrub the ugly accusation from the big doors, and guard the postern entrance while a temporary door was constructed and set in place. All before first light.

"I will arrange for new window glass in the morning," Père Montville said grimly. "It's going to be hellishly expensive. Meanwhile, we'll cover the windows with canvas."

"The canvas over the windows will be noticed, *mon père*," Charles said. "No matter how silent we are, there will be questions and talk."

"There is already talk. I will ask my own questions first," Le Picart repeated.

Charles bowed and held silent. When canvas for his window had been found and Le Picart had dismissed him, he returned to his freezing chamber, covered the window as best he could, and went to bed. But the violence of the night kept him long awake. The attack had deepened his anger over Martine's death, she who had been so defenseless, and when he finally slept, he dreamed about her.

When Saturday morning came, he prayed for her soul, but his angry certainty that the rector's attempt to cover up the attack was going to make things worse distracted him from his prayers and made them worth little. When Mass and breakfast were over and the dull gray light was growing, he made his way to the hastily constructed new postern, thinking as he entered the passage that at least the sharp smell of raw wood was an improvement on the usual winter smell of cold dank stone. Before he reached the door, a clamor of voices sounded outside and, to his surprise, the porter opened the postern to let in Père Joseph Jouvancy and a flock of red-cheeked, bright-eyed boys with their tutors. Jouvancy hailed his assistant rhetoric teacher.

"Maître du Luc, well met! I want to see you; come back inside with me one little moment."

He waved the boys and tutors through the main building's side door. Charles laughed to himself as the college's two shivering Chinese students, usually the essence of politeness, outmaneuvered the rest to get inside first. Jouvancy and Charles followed at the rear, skirting the crush of boys handing swords to a lay brother in the little chamber off the anteroom and receiving in exchange wooden tokens bearing their names. Students whose social rank entitled them to the sword were allowed to wear it when they left the college, but all weapons were strictly forbidden inside the school walls. Jouvancy led Charles through the *grand salon* and up a staircase to his office, talking nonstop, like the Seine in flood.

". . . which, of course, made it even more glorious at Gentilly than it usually is, *maître*," the handsome little priest was saying happily as he sank into the chair behind his desk. Jouvancy was somewhere in his forties, with the tireless energy of a squirrel. "Snow!" He threw out both beautifully expressive hands as though to catch falling flakes. "One of the *bon Dieu's* most beautiful gifts, especially in the quiet of the country. And Gentilly is still very quiet, you know, even though it's so near Paris. Our chateau flourishes and the flocks seem well. But speaking of snow, do you know that it was all I could do to make those Chinese boys walk back to Paris with us? They tell me they hate the snow, can you believe it? They say it only snows on mountains in their part of China. I tell you, coaxing them away from the fireplace this morning was like trying to tell mice they don't like cheese!"

"How peculiar," Charles said straight-faced, as Jouvancy paused for breath. "Imagine liking warmth. But I thought you were not returning until tomorrow, *mon père.*"

Jouvancy gestured dramatically at the pewter sky outside the office window. "The old woman who keeps our dairy there is a weather prophetess, the best for leagues around, they say. She told me it would surely snow again tonight, and most likely snow hard. So I thought it better to get the boys back to the college now."

Charles frowned at the window and hoped the elderly dairy maid was right about the new snow's timing. Slogging through a heavy snowfall any sooner would make all he had to do take even longer. He needed to find out if the elder M. Brion had returned home. And where the younger M. Brion was. And he had to find Lieutenant-Général La Reynie, or at least find out from the police *commissaire* if anything new had been learned about Martine's murder.

Jouvancy was still talking. ". . . so I wanted to see you to ask if you have heard from Monsieur Charpentier. About whether his music for February is finished."

"No, *mon père*, I've heard nothing."

Jouvancy tsked with impatience. "Musicians! They are as bad as builders, always of a lingering humor! Well, we will live in hope. *Celsus Martyr*, our spoken Latin tragedy, is only three acts instead of five. Monsieur Charpentier's French *Celse*, the musical tragedy, has five acts. Though it is longer, it is still the *intermèdes* for the spoken tragedy. But it will have far more singing than dancing, which will make your job easier. We still need all the time we can get for rehearsing, though!"

Charles thought privately that the short spoken tragedy was going to seem like *intermèdes* for the long musical tragedy. They would certainly need all the time for rehearsal they could get, since—dances or not—he would have to oversee much of the musical tragedy's staging. "And will the performance be on the same stage where we did Père Damiot's farce, *mon père*?"

"In winter, there is nowhere else. Was his *Farce of Monks* well received?"

By the end of Charles's retelling, Jouvancy was laughing nearly as hard as the audience had.

"Ah, Maître du Luc, I wish I had seen you chasing Frère Brunet with that clyster! I often wish we could risk more comedy here. But public comedy is such a vexed question." He frowned and shook his head. "All comedy is a vexed question when one is dealing with young people."

"Do you disapprove of comedy, then, *mon père?*"

"Oh, in most cases, yes, I do! Because the young are so easily led astray, you understand. And so much comedy in public theatres is frankly scurrilous." He looked furtively at the door and lowered his voice. "I must admit, though, that I dearly love some of Molière's pieces—I once saw the incomparable *Gentilhomme* and laughed myself silly at poor Monsieur Jourdain! Our little Molière sometimes went too far, I admit," Jouvancy said affectionately. The great playwright had once been a day student at Louis le Grand, back when he was only little Jacques Poquelin, the upholsterer's son. "A genius, though. And cut off in his prime, poor man."

Interested in Jouvancy's opinion, Charles ventured, "Do you think, then, that the church is too severe on actors?"

"In truth, I do! Excommunicating them, as happens too often, only drives them farther away from virtue, yet as we prove regularly in our colleges, the theatre can be an excellent school for virtue. If only actors would use it as that, there is no reason they should be denied the sacraments any more than dancers— and the church certainly does not excommunicate dancers!"

Charles laughed a little cynically. "If it did, it would have to excommunicate half the nobility of France! Not to mention the king."

"Well, Louis does not dance himself anymore, but yes. Speaking of dancers, who are you going to cast in the musical tragedy?"

"Walter Connor, I think. And Armand Beauclaire, who in spite of his directional difficulty is an excellent dancer."

"But poor Maître Beauchamps," Jouvancy said, his lively face a mask of mendacious concern. "Do you want to be answerable for the results if our dear dancing master has, yet again, to teach Beauclaire the difference between right and left?" Pierre Beauchamps, probably the greatest dancing master alive, was dance director of the Paris Opera and also Louis le Grand's ballet master. And an indispensable thorn in the rhetoric master's side. "There might well be murder done, *maître!*"

Murder. Charles winced, seeing in his mind the word scrawled on the college doors—innocent of the slander now after the lay brothers' long and hardworking night. Unbidden, his mind also showed him Martine, lying dead as he'd last seen her. Jouvancy, oblivious, had risen to hunt along his bookshelf for something. He looked up as someone tapped at the door.

"Come!"

A lay brother stuck his head into the room. "Your pardon, *mon père.* There's a Monsieur Germain Morel to see Maître du Luc." He looked at Charles. "In the anteroom by the main doors."

Startled, Charles looked at Jouvancy for permission to leave, wondering uneasily what Mlle Isabel Brion's dancing master could want.

"Yes, yes, very well, go." The rhetoric master sat down again, leafing through his leather-bound costume book. "We will talk again before all this madness starts."

"Thank you, *mon père.*" Charles rose. "Please tell Monsieur Morel I am coming," he said to the lay brother, who withdrew and clattered down the stairs.

Charles left the chamber quietly and hurried down behind him. Before he reached the anteroom at the bottom of the curving stone staircase, Morel was bowing, words tumbling out of his mouth.

"Forgive me for troubling you, Maître du Luc. But Mademoiselle Brion begged me to come." Morel was sweating in spite of the cold and seemed hardly able to catch his breath. "Because—" He gulped air. "Monsieur Brion is dead!"

Charles stared in confusion. "Her brother? Or do you mean her father?"

"Monsieur Henri Brion. A *sergent* of police came to tell Mademoiselle Brion that her father had been found murdered!"

Charles tried to think past his surprise. Lying awake during the night, he'd wondered whether, for some unguessed-at reason, it was Henri Brion, and not his son, who had killed Martine and fled, which would explain why no one had seen him since her death was discovered. But if that was true, why would he be suddenly dead himself? "Who found him, Monsieur Morel? Where?"

"I don't know who found him. His body was—is—in a ditch very near the rue Perdue. The ditch is behind some old houses near the Place Maubert. Can you go there with me, *maître*? Isabel—Mademoiselle Brion, I mean—wants you to pray for him. And she says"—color rose in Morel's face—"she says you will know what to do."

"I am sure that you will know quite well what to do yourself," Charles said diplomatically. "But of course I will come." He gathered his cloak around him and led the way to the postern door, thinking irreverently that it would take a papal bull to keep him away.

When he and Morel reached the Place Maubert, Morel led the way across it and down the small street that ran past the Mynette garden's side gate.

"This is a back way to Henri Brion's own house," Morel said. "I think he must have been on his way home when he was attacked."

The small street crossed a larger one and became an alley between old timbered houses. At the mouth of the alley stood a huddle of talking, eager-faced women. Servants, most of them looked to be, but the one at the center of the group was a wood seller resting the legs of her heavy carrying frame on the ground. She nodded to Charles. "They said you'd be coming, *mon père*. It's down the alley, in the ditch."

Charles thanked her, and he and Morel hurried between the

houses to a snowy ditch that had perhaps once been a streambed and was ending its life as an illegal neighborhood midden. Two men stood in the ditch with their backs to the path. Charles didn't know the man in workaday brown, but the one in the plumed hat and long black wig he knew all too well, even from behind.

Giving thanks for the cold for once, because it lessened the ditch's stench, Charles picked his way down the snowy slope, Morel behind him. Morel arrived at the bottom with his dignity intact, but Charles stepped on something nastily soft under the snow and slid precipitously, saved from falling flat only by a long arm and a lace-cuffed iron grip.

"*Bonjour*, Maître du Luc. I thought you might be arriving." A spark of warmth flickered in Nicolas de La Reynie's dark eyes, and a corner of his mouth turned up beneath the moustache arching like a gray half moon above his lips. La Reynie was not a young man. But he was a commanding presence, tall and strong and powerfully built.

"And I am glad to find you here, *mon lieutenant-général*," Charles said. "And not only because you saved my poor bones, if not my dignity."

He didn't bother asking why La Reynie had been expecting him. Or why the *lieutenant-général* of the Paris police had come himself to stand in this noisome ditch. The man knew more than anyone except God about what happened in the city, and probably knew it faster. He would certainly know of Martine Mynette's murder and no doubt knew quite well that Henri Brion had been her notary. And that the Mynette money would now come to the Society of Jesus. Pressed unwillingly into La Reynie's service last summer, Charles had quickly learned that nothing was beneath the *lieutenant-général*'s attention.

The other corner of La Reynie's mouth lifted. "Dignity? Oh, Jesuits have dignity to spare, I find. Though no more bones than the rest of us. And perhaps, just now, no more money? At least, not yet."

Charles smiled affably. La Reynie was not the only one who could play verbal games. "Certainly not more money, *monsieur*, since we take a vow of poverty."

La Reynie gave him a small ironic bow and presented his *sergent*, the man in brown breeches and coat, lean and hard bitten. Charles, in turn, presented Morel, who eyed La Reynie warily. The four of them turned their attention to the most recent dead creature to be thrown into the ditch.

Charles crossed himself and the others followed suit. Henri Brion's frost-glazed dark eyes stared past them at the sky. Charles looked at his dead face, recalling that although he had heard the man's voice, he had never seen him until now. He was somehow surprised to see how much Brion looked like his daughter, robust and wide-faced, and how little he resembled the small frail Gilles.

"I have heard that our corpse was a notary and had worked for your college," La Reynie said.

"Yes. And you no doubt also know that he was Mademoiselle Mynette's notary. And her guardian. I know his family slightly, but I had never met him. How was he killed?" Charles asked.

"Stabbed in the back. To the heart. We found him lying on his face and turned him to have a look at his other side. There's little blood on the ground around him, because his clothes are good thick cloth and his shirt and coat soaked up most of it."

Morel flinched. Charles said nothing, again seeing Martine Mynette lying in a sea of red. But that blood was let by a little blade, not the long knife needed to pierce a heart.

Charles said, "Then you don't think he was killed elsewhere and moved here?"

La Reynie shook his head. "I see no reason yet to think so. Though I wonder how he ended in this ditch."

"He must have been on his way home." Morel swallowed hard. "He lives in the rue Perdue, very near here."

"Ah." La Reynie nodded consideringly.

"Do you have any thought about how long he's been dead?" Charles said. "I know that in cold like this, it's very hard to tell. But it may help you to know that his family has not seen him since at least Thursday evening."

"That may help indeed." La Reynie eyed the body. "And there was snow off and on yesterday and through the night, and snow mostly covered the body when we found it. And that bush screens it. The body wasn't immediately obvious."

In silence, they looked down at the dead man. A sense of futility assailed Charles. Brion had been described to him as greedy and unsuccessful at his work. He'd seemed somehow negligible, even in his own household. Unfortunately, he had not seemed negligible to his killer. If he had, murder would not have been necessary. But no human soul was negligible. Charles began the prayers for the dead, and the other men bowed their heads.

When the prayers were finished, there was a moment of sober quiet and then the *sergent* folded his arms over his chest and said, as though continuing an argument Charles had interrupted, "I still say the beggars would have found him yesterday, if he'd been here." Seeing Charles's questioning look, he explained, "Beggars search the ditches for anything usable. They would have had that cloak and everything else off him and he'd be mother naked."

Charles frowned. "They'd search even a midden like this?"

The *sergent's* eyes widened in disbelief at the naive question. "Beggars would search your chamber pot and lick your empty plate, *mon père*, if they thought there might be anything they could sell."

Charles took the rebuke to his naiveté in silence, wondering why he'd asked such a stupid question when he'd seen firsthand the half-ruined part of the old Louvre palace, which destitute Parisians had made into a warren of fetid living quarters.

La Reynie nodded toward the muddy path. "The woman with the load of wood there met a beggar, a woman called Reine, coming out of the alley this morning with a good beaver hat. Reine told her she'd found it on a dead man in the ditch and named him as Henri Brion."

"Could she have killed him?" Charles said.

"No. The *sergent* just told you beggars scour all the ditches. But Reine told the other woman that she didn't go on her rounds yesterday because she wasn't well. And Reine's scavenging places aren't often bothered by other beggars. After Reine found the body, the woman selling wood sent one of her friends to the police post and the *sergent* came. And he sent for me." Police posts, called *barrières*, were scattered across the city and were usually the fastest way of appealing to the law.

The *sergent* said, "We both know old Reine. She begs outside coffeehouses, and says she often saw this Henri Brion at Procope's."

"But she didn't see him there or at any of the other coffee-houses on Friday," La Reynie added. "Which is another reason why I think he was already dead and lying here yesterday."

"*Messieurs!* A small word!" A canvas-aproned man came slithering into the ditch, pulling a sullen, white-faced boy of thirteen or so after him. "This parsnip-brained apprentice of mine has something to tell you that may be about your body here."

La Reynie scrutinized them both. "And who are you, *monsieur*?"

"I am Michel Bernard, *mon lieutenant-général*. Oh, yes, I know you, all Paris knows you. I am a carpenter." Raising a work-hardened hand in a fingerless glove, the man pointed at an old house backing on the ditch. "We're working on that house there. My wife just inherited it and she wants to rent it out for good money." He rubbed his hands together and blew on his exposed fingers. "I'll start after the Epiphany, I told her, but no, I must start now, why should we lose money, she says, so here I am freezing my"——he suddenly registered Charles's presence——"my immortal soul off while she sits by the fire at home. But you may be sure that body's been there awhile."

"And why is that?"

"Go on, tell him!" The carpenter pulled his apprentice forward. "I've been leaving him in the house at night to keep out the beggars while it's empty." He poked the boy hard in the ribs. "Talk!"

"I heard people running," the boy mumbled, staring wide-eyed at the body. "On Friday morning before light. I heard one of them yell out." He shut his mouth, and his lips trembled.

His master prodded him again. "Well, go on! Tell the rest."

"Then, when I came down here to piss after I got up——Friday morning, I mean——he——it——was here. But I was afraid to say anything. I thought if I did, you'd think I killed him. I didn't, I don't know him, I never saw him before, as the *bon Dieu* sees me!"

Everyone gazed speculatively at the boy. Tears began to trickle down his cheeks and he fell on his knees in the snow.

"I swear it, *messieurs!*"

La Reynie sighed. "Unfortunately, I believe you. But the next time you find a body, for God's sake tell someone if you don't want to be suspected. Where can I find you both if I need you again?" he asked the carpenter.

"My workshop's at the sign of the Magdalene, rue Clopin, *mon lieutenant-général.*"

"Thank you. You may go. Both of you." La Reynie dismissed them. When they had clambered out of the ditch, the boy still crying and his master berating him, La Reynie turned to Charles and the *sergent.* "Well. If the apprentice is telling the truth, we have good reason to think that Monsieur Brion was killed before dawn on Friday morning and has lain here ever since. A popular time for murder in this *quartier*, it seems. Your Mademoiselle Martine Mynette and her notary, both murdered on the same day."

Charles said, "You think the two are related?"

"A child would think they are related." La Reynie walked over to Morel, who was still staring disconsolately at Henri Brion's body. "May I ask why you are here, *monsieur?*" he said pleasantly.

Startled, the dancing master tore his eyes from the body and bowed. Graceful, Charles noted, even in a midden beside a corpse.

"As Maître du Luc told you, I am a friend of—of the Brion family. One of your men came to tell Mademoiselle Brion of her father's death, and she sent me to find out what happened."

La Reynie nodded slowly. "And you brought our friend Maître du Luc. Mademoiselle Brion is fortunate in her champions. I had understood that she also has a brother. Perhaps I am misinformed?"

"Her brother was not at home, *mon lieutenant-général.*"

"And where is he?" La Reynie and the *sergent* exchanged a look.

Warned by the new quality in their attention, Morel's eyes went to Charles in silent appeal.

"You will probably find Monsieur Gilles Brion at the Capuchin monastery across the river," Charles said. "He hopes to be a monk."

"And cannot be interrupted at his prayers even for his father's death? A devout young man," La Reynie murmured, making it clear that he would have that whole story from someone and soon. His gaze settled on Charles. "What do you know about this, Maître du Luc? You did not come here only to pray."

"No," Charles agreed, returning the gaze. "I came to find out about Monsieur Brion's death. As I told you, I was already wondering where he was, since no one seems to have seen him since Thursday evening." Charles sorted rapidly through what he wanted and did not want to say. "Monsieur La Reynie, you said you knew that Henri Brion was Martine Mynette's guardian. You may not know that she was adopted. Her adoptive mother died a week or so before Christmas and the *donation entre vifs*, drawn up some years ago by Henri Brion to ensure that the girl would get the mother's considerable property, has been lost. There is no other family to inherit."

La Reynie smiled. "But there are Jesuits."

Charles let that pass. "Monsieur Brion claimed to be searching for the original of the adopted girl's *donation* at the Châtelet, where he long ago registered the document. But it seems he was not."

"Was not?" La Reynie echoed.

Morel was frowning angrily at both of them.

"A clerk there told me that Monsieur Henri Brion has not been seen at the Châtelet recently."

La Reynie studied Charles. "What else?"

"Nothing," Morel said, before Charles could answer.

"No?" The *lieutenant-général* smiled genially at Morel. "I see. Since you are Mademoiselle Brion's representative, *monsieur*, will you go and tell her that after we have taken her father to the Châtelet and examined him for other wounds or anything else his body might tell us about his death, I will have him brought to his house?"

"I—she—" Morel chewed his lip. "Monsieur, this Mademoiselle Mynette of whom you have been speaking was Mademoiselle Brion's dearest friend and she is grieving terribly for her. It is too much to expect her to see her father's body, after what has been done to him!"

Charles put a hand on the young man's shoulder. "It will be a shock to her, yes. But do you not think that, even so, she will want to do the last offices for her father?"

"But wasn't he a member of one of your confraternities? Couldn't they see to him?"

"His uncle, Monsieur Callot, is a member of the Congregation of the Sainte Vierge, but Monsieur Brion was not. Forgive me, Monsieur Morel, but I wonder if you are not thinking too little of Mademoiselle Brion's courage. That is an easy mistake to make with women. I have known Mademoiselle Brion a very short time, but I suspect she has more than enough courage—and love—for this new ordeal."

Reluctantly, Morel nodded. "Yes, she has courage. And she loved her father. In spite of his faults."

La Reynie said kindly, "Monsieur, please do me the favor of going now and telling her to expect her father's body this afternoon. I will see that he is conveyed to her with all respect. She will be grateful for your coming now with my message, because she will have preparations to make."

Morel hesitated and looked at Charles. "You will come with me, *maître?*"

"I have another matter to discuss with Maître du Luc," La Reynie said smoothly. "Better not wait for him. For Mademoiselle Brion's sake." He gestured courteously toward the street.

With a last warning look at Charles, the dancing master went. When he was out of hearing, La Reynie said, "His reason for protecting the Brion daughter is obvious, but I also noticed that when the Brion son was mentioned, Monsieur Morel didn't want us to talk about him. Is this son already a novice?"

"No, his father did not approve of his wish."

"Ah. Did they quarrel over it? Could the son have killed him?"

"Yes to both. But I've met him and I don't think he has the stomach for it."

"Monsieur Morel was trying so hard to keep us from discussing him, I can only think he disagrees."

"He is trying to save Mademoiselle Brion from more grief. As I would like to do, too. What he didn't want you to know is that her brother has been quarreling with his father over more than religious vocation. His father was forcing him to court Martine Mynette for her money and he, of course, didn't want to marry."

"And now the unwelcome bride and the implacable father are both dead. Even a would-be monk may strike back if you push him too far. But how does this *donation* fit into that convenient picture—I would think Monsieur Henri Brion would have searched for it very diligently indeed. Why marry his son to a failed heiress? Which makes what the Châtelet clerk told you more than a little odd. Who is this clerk?"

"I don't know his name," Charles said absently, as his thoughts about Gilles Brion shifted suddenly. It was hard to see the young man as a killer. But a thief? Henri Brion indeed had no reason to want the *donation* lost, since he wanted the Mynette money. But Gilles Brion had an urgent reason. And he would have had opportunities to steal it, frequenting the Mynette house as a suitor. If the document disappeared permanently, so would the reason for the marriage. But Gilles Brion did not have his father's access to the Châtelet records, so how could he also have stolen the original? Had he realized that he could not hope to get his hands on the original document and decided that killing his father was the only way to put an end to his difficulties?

La Reynie had turned to his *sergent*. "Leave the wood seller and her friends to guard the path, and get men to take the body to the Châtelet. And then to the Brion house. Which is where, Maître du Luc?"

"Off the Place Maubert in the rue Perdue, at the Sign of Three Ducks."

La Reynie nodded his thanks. "But before you do any of that," he said to the *sergent*, "send a man to watch the Capuchin house on the rue St. Honoré. If any young layman comes out or goes in, stop him. You are looking for Gilles Brion. What does he look like, Maître du Luc?"

"Small, frail looking, brown hair. He wore embroidered linen the only time I saw him. And high heels on his shoes."

"And if you find him, hold him there at the monastery until I come—tell him only that I need to speak with him."

"Yes, *mon lieutenant-général.*" He climbed quickly up the slope and disappeared into the alley.

"Now," La Reynie said, "as we climb out of here, *maître*, tell me the rest of the reason you are concerning yourself in this."

"As you obviously know, the Jesuit college stands to get the Mynette money. Simon Mynette, the father of the murdered girl's adoptive mother, promised the money to the college when his daughter was gone, because there was no other family left. But that was before the adoption and the *donation entre vifs*. Now that Martine Mynette has been murdered, rumor is growing that Jesuits connived at her death to have the inheritance. I met Mademoiselle Mynette at the Brion house the day before she died. Père Le Picart has asked me to find out what I can about her death to help quell the rumors that are flying. Unless Henri Brion's killer is found quickly, this death is going to make them fly even faster."

La Reynie nodded, and they made their way in silence up the narrow path between the old houses. The gathered women, quiet now, were still standing in the rutted little dirt street.

"*Mesdames*," La Reynie said, sweeping off his white-plumed hat, "where might I find Reine now?"

The women traded looks and the eldest said, "Probably at The Procope, *monsieur.*"

"I thank you. And my thanks to you especially, *madame*," he added to the wood seller, "for sending to the *barrière* for the ser-

gent. He is going to ask you and your friends to keep people from the path here for a short while. I hope you will oblige him."

To Charles's surprise, these poor, lowborn women did not curtsy to La Reynie. They simply nodded regally, and La Reynie nodded respectfully in return and replaced his hat.

"I find it interesting," he said, as he and Charles walked away, "that men mostly ignore each other until someone's honor is threatened. But women! They ignore nothing and so they know everything that goes on in a *quartier*. I could not do my job without them."

Charles murmured acknowledgment, but his thoughts were across the river. "Are you going to the Capuchins to look for Gilles Brion?"

"Not yet. If young Brion killed his father and fled, he is gone. If he is still at his prayers, the *sergent* will find him easily enough. We are going to Procope's coffeehouse."

The thought of hot fragrant coffee nearly brought tears to Charles's eyes. But Jesuits did not go to coffeehouses and La Reynie knew it.

"That is a wickedly tempting suggestion, *mon lieutenant-général*. You know I cannot sit in a coffeehouse."

"The Society of Jesus forbids tobacco, not coffee. If the head of the Paris police compels you to sit in a coffeehouse, you can sit there. Two sets of eyes and ears are better than one." He smiled a little. "Even if the one is me."

Chapter 10

Procope's coffeehouse was in the rue des Fossés St. Germain, west of Louis le Grand and near where the old wall curved north to meet the river. The rue des Fossés was part of the ongoing effort to free Paris from its walls and make it a modern, open city. The old, towered stone walls were being slowly leveled and the defensive ditches on either side filled in to make wide, somewhat raised promenades planted with trees. On the Right Bank, the walls had come down quickly, but on this side of the river progress was slow, as progress always seemed to be on the Left Bank.

Francesco Procopio dei Coltelli's coffeehouse was a world away from the ditch where Henri Brion's body lay. Charles expected to see the beggar woman called Reine sitting at its door, but no one was there and La Reynie led the way inside. Everything about Procope's had the glitter of success. Its walls were hung with tapestry, paintings, and even a mirror. Graceful chandeliers with crystal pendants hung from the ceiling, banishing the morning's grayness. Well-dressed men sat at round tables, sipping coffee from bowl-like cups. Many were absorbed in books and news sheets, while others played cards or talked and argued in low voices. An enormous brass kettle with a spigot warmed at the front of the fireplace, and a waiter dressed *à la Arménien*, in a red-

and-gold turban and a long embroidered robe, moved through the room, refilling cups from a long-spouted silver pot.

A woman of fifty or so, in a high-necked gown of sober black, collected the money and kept watch over the proceedings from a half-walled counter near the fireplace. Her eyes widened as she recognized Lieutenant-Général La Reynie, and she hurried out of her little fortress, her tall white *fontange* headdress quivering like the erected crest of a startled bird. At the clattering of her low heels on the diamond-patterned floor tiles, a dozen men looked up to see who had come in and a ripple of silence followed her across the room. With a disapproving glance at Charles, she curtsied to La Reynie.

"You are welcome to The Procope, *monsieur*."

"Thank you, *madame*." La Reynie smiled widely. "May I take it from your welcome that we no longer have a quarrel about your closing time?"

Her lips smiled back, but her small black eyes were cold as she said, "Naturally we have no quarrel. You will find, if you stay so long, that we close and lock our door at six, exactly as required. Would you care to sit by the fire, *monsieur*? There is a table there."

Charles waited for La Reynie to explain that they were there on business, but the *lieutenant-général* only looked questioningly at him, as if a table by the fire or not were the extent of his worries on earth.

"That would be a great gift, *madame*," Charles said sincerely.

Eyes followed them as the woman led the way to a warm corner hung with red-and-blue tapestry. She beckoned the waiter to them, curtsied again, and returned stiff-backed to her post. The turbaned and gowned young waiter had liquid dark eyes and a scattering of pockmarks. He bowed elaborately.

"What is your pleasure, *messieurs*? I can offer you coffee of the best, or chocolate in the Spanish style, or spiced *limonade*. Or one of our frozen waters, since you are sitting so warmly. We have anise, orange, cinnamon flower, frangipani, and barley. And our cakes and wafers are the freshest and most toothsome in Paris!"

La Reynie ordered coffee and cakes for two, and the waiter sped gracefully away.

"What about the beggar?"

"Wait. We'll watch a little first. The word will be out that the body has been found. We may not be the only ones wanting to speak to Reine."

"Ah." To keep up the appearance of polite, nothing-saying talk, Charles said, "I know Signore Procopio is Sicilian. Are the rest of them Sicilian, too?"

"Yes, mostly. Procopio's relations. It's always a good idea to employ relations, because you can pay them nothing. Very Italian." La Reynie grinned. "Also very French." He raised his eyebrows slightly at Charles. "And now let us survey our fellows. When our coffee comes, we will enjoy it like tired men glad to be silent and listen to others talk. Before we move on to other things."

As Charles let his gaze wander the room, he realized that no pipes were in evidence. "No tobacco here?" he whispered, surprised.

La Reynie shook his head. "No. In some others, but not here. I don't think the French will ever hide themselves in a reeking fog of tobacco smoke as the English do. Also, Procopio welcomes women—escorted, of course—and women will not come if the air is foul."

This morning, though, there were only men at Procope's.

"Recognize anyone?" La Reynie asked softly.

Charles shook his head. "Do you?"

La Reynie looked surprised, for once. "Of course I do, I recognize half of them. For what that's worth. Probably not much.

Most of our fellow idlers have probably done nothing worse than lie to their wives and refuse to pay their tailors."

The coffee arrived, along with small almond-flavored cakes. Charles had drunk coffee before, but not often. He breathed in its fragrance and drank deeply, sighing with pleasure as he set his cup down and thinking that this was worth penance. He picked up a cake and went back to watching the room. Most of the interest in the newcomers had subsided. Aside from two or three men eyeing them and leaning toward each other as they talked, their presence didn't seem to be much bothering anyone. La Reynie took off his cloak and turned his chair so that he could stretch his black-stockinged legs in front of him. He sipped his coffee contentedly, seemingly oblivious of everything else.

Charles ate a cake and scanned the wall across from them without moving his head. The instinct that had kept him alive during the Spanish Netherlands war was telling him they were being watched, and too intently. From the barely open door, he guessed, which probably led to the kitchen. Seeming to study a shelf above the door that was lined with glowing copper pots graduated in size like a fertile man's family, Charles murmured to La Reynie, "Someone beyond that door across the room is very interested in us."

"Ah. Yes, I see, very nice." La Reynie nodded appreciatively at the pots. "One would like to see them at close range."

"One would. Shall we pay a visit to the kitchen?"

"We were already going to. That's where Reine will be, if she's here. But we should go now, before our interested friend disappears. The necessity is through there, anyway. After you, *maître*."

"You are too courteous, *monsieur*."

Charles drained his coffee bowl and set it down. Rising, he walked casually toward the slightly open door. It shut with a snap. He told himself that even in these times, most people would not do a cleric serious damage. Whatever the truth of that, the invulnerable feeling coffee seemed to give him was rising into his head, and he pushed the door open harder than he meant to. It slammed against the wall and bounced back into his hand. Which told him that the watcher was not behind the door.

"I beg your pardon," he said genially, and stepped into the kitchen.

An aproned man squatting beside the fireplace with a long-handled fork in his hand stared at him and went back to poking a roasting chicken. A frowning woman of thirty-five or so stood at the central table, kneading dough. But Charles still had the feeling that someone was watching him. Sensing La Reynie at his back, he let go of the door and stepped farther into the kitchen.

"The necessity, *monsieur*, if you please?" he asked the man at the fireplace.

"In the yard." He gestured with his fork.

"You first, *maître*." La Reynie moved up beside Charles. *See who's out there*, his eyes added.

As Charles crossed the room, shadows moved in a corner. He tilted his head slightly toward the movement and kept going.

Behind him, La Reynie circled toward the corner, chatting affably to the cook and the woman. Charles went out into the cluttered back court, stopping the outer door's swing so he could hear what went on in the kitchen. He surveyed the yard. A man unloading barrels from a cart and rolling them across the snow-edged cobbles and down a ramp to the cellar paid him no attention. Charles looked swiftly into the privy beside the kitchen door, found it empty, and went back inside.

La Reynie, holding a rusted iron candlestick with a tallow candle in it, was standing in front of the corner where the shadows had moved. The man with the fork had dragged a stool in front of the fire and set a carafe full of dark wine beside it. He was sipping from a large glassful as he kept loving watch over his chicken. The woman at the table had stopped kneading her dough and was scowling at La Reynie.

Drifting toward the corner, Charles put himself between her and the *lieutenant-général*.

". . . then when and where did you last see him?" La Reynie was saying, still looking into the corner.

"Thursday evening. Here." The voice was a woman's, old but still melodic, like a cracked viol that could make you imagine its past glory.

"At what time?"

"He left just before the absurd hour you force Monsieur Procope to close, *mon cher*." The woman's laughter played suddenly up and down the scale. "Come, Nicolas, it is not the old days, you cannot herd people into their houses at dark, like they were cows."

Mon cher? Nicolas? Charles shifted, trying to see the woman, and waiting for La Reynie to put her scathingly in her place.

But he didn't. He laughed. "That never did work well, did it? As you know better than any of us, Reine."

The woman laughed deep in her throat. "Curfews were never worth a cabbage, and the ones who made them were the worst at keeping them. You certainly were."

Bewildered by the easy familiarity, Charles moved again, trying to see La Reynie's face without interrupting him. The *lieutenant-général* was smiling a little, looking with affection at the hunched figure in the corner. The woman was sitting on a low stool, working at something held in her lap. The frayed gold embroidery on her tattered velvet underskirt caught the candlelight, and her scarlet taffeta bodice had alien yellow sleeves. Her patched black overskirt was so threadbare it hardly needed to be open in the front to display the underskirt's gold thread. Ragged saffron lace was wrapped around her withered neck, and a turban of stained blue satin, intricately wrapped with more of the saffron lace, covered her hair. Charles wondered if her parents had named her Queen, or if that had come later. In her bizarre way, she looked regal enough.

"Back to business, Reine," La Reynie said. "Why did Henri Brion leave Procope's before closing?"

"Why *do* men leave, Nicolas? Because they have somewhere more important to go." She lifted her gaze suddenly. Her face was a maze of lines, and Charles thought she was at least sixty. But her vividly green eyes were as young as new beech leaves.

"Please," La Reynie said softly. "I need to know."

"Then know that he left with two men. Not willingly, I thought. But he went. They walked him out the door between them, pretending he was drunk—he wasn't—and then they took hold of his arms and he had no choice at all."

"Where were you, to see this?"

"Outside. By the door."

"You were begging."

"Yes, Nicolas, begging. Looking cold and pathetic and making a nice bit for my supper. Not as much as I used to make, of course. But still needing the charity of men in order to eat. But isn't that the fate of women?"

"Did you recognize the men who took Brion? Or hear what they said? Where they were taking him?"

Reine bent over her lap again, and Charles saw that she had a small knife and was working carefully at a piece of wood.

"I don't know where they took him. They walked toward the river. One man I knew. Monsieur Claude Bizeul, a goldsmith."

La Reynie said sharply, "A goldsmith? Are you sure?"

The old woman didn't speak, seeming absorbed in her carving, and to Charles's surprise, La Reynie waited patiently.

"Oh, yes, Nicolas, I am very sure," she said at last, still not looking up. "Claude Bizeul is white haired now, but he has kept his figure admirably. His companion I've seen here before, but I don't know his name. He is a younger man, dark haired. Taller."

"And they went toward the river? You're sure?"

"Of course I'm sure."

"Where does this Monsieur Bizeul live?"

Her hand stilled. "I will have to think on that."

"Think well, Reine." But he didn't press her. Instead, he turned to the woman kneading dough. "Did you see any of this, Renée? Do you know these men?"

She shook her head and reached up to tighten the white linen kerchief she wore over her brown hair, fumbling with the knot at the nape of her neck. "I was back here, how could I see them?" she said, returning to her kneading as if she had her enemies under her hands.

"You were not, you were still at your Martine's house," the cook said laconically, without looking around.

The woman flung her head up and spat over her shoulder, "What if I was? Who cares where I was?"

La Reynie glanced at Reine, listening intently from her corner, then turned back to Renée. "Ah, yes, you worked in the Mynette house," he said to the younger woman, making it a statement, not a question. "How could I have forgotten that?" His tone made it clear to Charles, at least, that he had not forgotten for a moment.

Renée leaned on her fists in the dough, her breath coming short. "Yes, I worked there. And if I could find the animal who murdered her, I would tear his throat out. Whoever he is, he came there to kill her. Don't bother thinking he was some ordinary thief she interrupted as he was about his black business. Your *commissaire* made me search the whole house and nothing was taken. Nothing!"

Flames leaped as a log broke in the fireplace, and Charles saw that Renée's eyes were the same vivid green as the old woman's. Her face, though, was round and plain, while the old woman had bones a duchess would pine for. Charles suddenly remembered where he'd seen Renée's smoke-blue skirt, good-quality wool, much better than a kitchen servant would have.

"You were Mademoiselle Mynette's maid," he said, moving so that she could see him. "I had a glimpse of you yesterday morning at the Mynette house, when the *commissaire* was questioning you."

La Reynie nodded at Charles and stepped a little aside. Taking his cue, Charles said courteously, "I am Maître du Luc. I know the Brion family. Before you found Mademoiselle Mynette yesterday morning, did you hear anything unusual, anyone in the street, or at the door?"

Suddenly shamefaced, Renée shrugged and looked away, biting her lip. Charles remembered M. Callot saying angrily that the maid had been the worse for drink when she found Martine.

"I think you did hear something," Charles said, watching her.

She turned back to him, her eyes glistening with tears. "I heard—I thought I heard—someone call up to her from the street. But I didn't get up to see." Her voice dropped to a whisper. "I was heavy with sleep."

"With drink," the cook said laconically from the fireside. He upended his glass and refilled it.

"Hush, Giuseppe," the old woman said sharply. "Let her be!"

"And being understandably tired the night before from all your work—I've heard that the other Mynette servants had already left—perhaps you forgot to lock and bar the street door?" Charles read the answer in her sullen face. "You were alone in the house with Mademoiselle Mynette, were you not?"

"Except for the boy who turned the spit in the kitchen and

laid the fires. The others went like rats from a foundered ship. They knew that paper she needed was gone, and if she didn't get it back, how would she pay them?"

"Did any leave with pay owing to them?"

"No! She had her faults, but she would have fasted to a bone before she let any go unpaid."

Charles was sure that Martine Mynette would have done exactly that. "But grudges can still be held unfairly. Who were the servants who left?"

Renée's eyes, suddenly calculating, went from Charles to La Reynie.

"There was Paul Saglio. The footman. My young mistress turned him out when her mother was ill. She wouldn't tell me exactly why, but it wasn't hard to guess. Monsieur Saglio was much too free with his hands," she said resentfully. "With Mademoiselle Martine's mother lying ill, he thought there was no one to protect her." Her eyes flashed and she picked up a knife lying beside the bread board and shook it at Charles. "If I'd seen him, I would have made him a capon, you may be sure of that. And he would never have bothered another woman!"

Charles regarded her thoughtfully. "So you are saying that this Paul Saglio likely went away angry at Mademoiselle Martine. Where did he go?"

"Vaugirard, most likely. He always said he knew someone there who could get him a better place, if he wanted it."

Then it shouldn't be hard to find him, Charles thought. The village of Vaugirard was only a few miles south of Paris. "Did anyone else leave with a grudge?"

"The gardener, maybe. Tito he's called." Renée glanced at Reine and said, "He left in the autumn. And good riddance."

"Why?"

"He was a liar."

A rustling came from the corner. "You've told me he was just soft-witted, Renée," the old woman said reprovingly.

"That, too. He was always saying people took things from him. What did he own? Nothing. What would anyone take from him? Anyway, he left."

"Why did he leave? And what is his surname?"

Renée dealt her dough a hard slap and turned it over. "He's Tito La Rue. Late one night at the start of November, I found him opening Mademoiselle Martine's bedchamber door. Mademoiselle Anne was already ill, but not yet so desperately ill. She'd fallen asleep and Mademoiselle Martine had gone to bed, too. I was just going to my own bed when I saw him. I chased him downstairs and outside, and he spent the night in the garden shed. When I told Mademoiselle Anne the next day, that was the end of him."

"Was he angry at being dismissed?"

She snorted. "No, he wept and pleaded with Mademoiselle Anne to let him stay. Even if he is soft-witted, he's a man and he knew what he was doing!"

"Where did he go?"

She shrugged and shook her head. "Who knows? If you want to know about all the servants, there was also the cook, Thérèse, her name is. After Mademoiselle Martine's mother grew ill, Thérèse started taking things. Little things, but worth something. But she is an excellent cook, so Mademoiselle Martine only warned her. And locked the jewelry and silver away. Thérèse pretended to be very insulted and went home to her mother in St. Denis. To sell what she'd stolen." Renée pummeled her dough.

Servants could be punished severely for attempting assault on a mistress or for stealing. Tito and Thérèse had gotten off lightly and would have known it, would have had every reason to be grateful. Mentally dismissing the light-fingered cook along with the lusty gardener, Charles said, "So only Paul Saglio seemed truly angry at Mademoiselle Martine Mynette. Yet the others left. All except you."

"I'm loyal, me." Muttering under her breath, Renée wiped her hands on her apron and went to the fire, where she plucked the cook's glass from his hand and drained it. Without a word, the cook took it from her and filled it again. Renée stalked back to her dough.

Well, Charles thought, loyal or not, there was little need to ask why she'd stayed with Martine Mynette. And little need to wonder if she might have killed her young mistress herself. Why would she destroy the soft nest she'd found for herself? In a disintegrating household, Renée would have been well fed and free to drink herself to sleep every night under a good roof, with no one the wiser. Charles looked questioningly at La Reynie, who shook his head slightly and glanced toward the door into the coffeehouse. They thanked the women and the cook and took their leave, but before they reached the door, Reine called out, "Nicolas, you will find Monsieur Bizeul the goldsmith at the Sign of Two Angels, on the rue Christine."

La Reynie walked back to where she sat. "What else do you know about him?"

She looked up from her carving and smiled, revealing missing and blackened teeth. "Much that was of use to me. Nothing that would be of use to you."

La Reynie moved closer to her, and Charles saw coins glint in the firelight. Then Charles followed him back to the front room and the counter where the Sicilian woman was busy over her accounts.

"On Thursday, *madame*," La Reynie said, "not long before you closed, three men were here together. Monsieur Claude Bizeul the goldsmith, Monsieur Henri Brion the notary, and another man. Do you remember them?"

Her black eyes were opaque, her face expressionless. "No, *monsieur*."

"Surely you are more noticing of your customers than that, *madame*."

"They gave me no reason to notice them."

La Reynie leaned closer. "Then tell me what you did not notice, *madame*. Because one of them, Monsieur Henri Brion, is dead. As I am certain you already know."

Dislike flared in her face and was as quickly gone. "Of course I know. Old Reine told me. But it's nothing to do with Procope's. And how can I tell you what I did not see?"

The *lieutenant-général* gave her his teeth-baring smile. "Easily, if you wish Procope's to remain in business, *madame*."

She breathed in slowly, her nostrils white and pinched. "Perhaps I remember them slightly. The dead man was here often and so is Monsieur Bizeul. The third, the younger one, I had not seen before. That is the truth, as the Virgin sees me. They argued, but not so I could hear what they said. In his anger, Monsieur Brion spilled his coffee onto the floor. Monsieur Bizeul said to me that Monsieur Brion was drunk. The two pulled Monsieur Brion to his feet, apologized to me for his discourtesy, and the three of them left. That is all."

A small hissing sound made Charles look toward the fireplace. The waiter who had served them earlier rolled his eyes at the woman and shook his head. As though bored with waiting for La Reynie, Charles wandered toward the street door. The waiter grabbed a broom and energetically swept his way to the door.

"I heard your talk with her, *mon père*, I cannot help it. She is lying." He glanced at the woman behind the counter and pulled a towel from the waist of his breeches. Flourishing it across the seat of a chair, he said, "The little notary did not spill the coffee. The young companion, the one she did not name, he pushed it off the table, and they blamed the notary to make him leave. You understand?"

Charles nodded. "Who was the young companion, *mon ami*?"

"Alas, I do not know him. But the notary, he did not want to go! He pulled from them, he cursed them, but they forced him. They repeated that he was drunk and apologized for him." The waiter's eyes were as round as the coffee bowls, and his jet eyebrows were halfway up his pockmarked forehead. "But they were very angry with him. And now Reine says he is dead."

"Luigi!" The woman's voice was furious. "To your work!"

The waiter made an eloquent face at Charles and scurried away. Charles smiled vaguely at several men who had watched the exchange and went casually into the street. When La Reynie joined him, Charles told him what the waiter had said.

"So the spilled coffee was an excuse for taking Brion out of here," the *lieutenant-général* said grimly. "And he has not been seen, so far as we know, by anyone else since he was taken out of here. Why a respectable goldsmith would have a hand in killing him is hard to imagine. But I am going to the *barrière* for the *sergent*, and he and I are going to call on Monsieur Bizeul and see what story he cares to tell."

"And me? Am I dismissed?"

Le Reynie's mouth twitched. "I am only *lieutenant-général* of Paris. If memory serves, I have not been entirely successful at telling you what to do."

Before Charles could answer that, a loud and untuneful voice made them turn toward the end of the street. A street vendor, the

frayed and wilting brim of his plumed hat at a rakish angle, his
arms full of printed sheets, was walking toward them, singing:

> *"Elle était riche, elle est morte*
> *Les Jésuites dansent sur son corps.*
> *Elle est perdue, pour ainsi dire,*
> *Les Jésuites pour enrichir!"*

Chapter 11

Charles started toward the singer, but La Reynie put out a hand and stopped him. The singer, seeing Charles, grinned and redoubled his efforts, flourishing his song sheets at house windows as he bellowed out the words. An upper casement opened, and a woman shouted down that he should leave a sheet on her doorstep. As she tossed him a coin, two grinning men came out of a shop to buy copies. Charles seethed but held where he was. La Reynie leaned on his walking stick and watched. The singer kept coming. Then he saw La Reynie, shut his mouth abruptly, and disappeared into an opening between houses. Charles hurried to the place where he'd turned and found a tiny alley snaking into shadows.

"Don't be an idiot," La Reynie said behind him. "Anyone could be waiting for you down there. Or for me. I am even more unpopular than you are."

"The man is inciting violence! Men have already—" Charles swallowed the end of his words, belatedly remembering the rector's order not to talk about the attack on Louis le Grand.

La Reynie cocked an interested eyebrow, but contented himself with saying, "When one broadside seller is peddling a scurrilous song, you may be sure that two dozen others are doing the same across the city. You look like you've heard that song before."

"Last night. As I passed a tavern called The Horse's Tail, near the Place Maubert. If you let them go on singing the thing all over Paris, Jesuits will not be able to go out into the streets! Nor will our students, and most of our classes for day students are about to start."

"*Maître.*" La Reynie sighed. "Even in Provence and Languedoc, you must have had broadside sellers. If the songs are seditious, I imprison the sellers and try to find the printers. But these people are like fleas; who can be rid of them? And this song does not even mention the king. Yes, it stirs up the people and I will try to find out the source. But surely you know that the only thing that will stop it is catching the Mynette girl's killer. And Henri Brion's killer, because, as you have already implied, Henri Brion is going to be the song's next verse unless the killer is quickly found. And now, before I look for the would-be monk, who seems to stick to his Capuchins like a leech and is probably the least likely of my suspects to disappear, I am going to visit Monsieur Bizeul the goldsmith." He smiled ominously. "I regulate the guilds, you know. If he is innocent, he will tell me what he knows rather than provoke me. If not—I will provoke him. As for you, go back to the college by the main streets. And shut your ears to insults. Your soldier's training will not serve you against a crowd, nor will a reputation for street brawling improve things for the Society of Jesus."

"That sounds suspiciously like an order."

"Does it?" La Reynie laughed softly as he bowed. "Then God go with you as you obey it."

"Wait, *mon lieutenant-général*—what about Paul Saglio?"

"Saglio?" The *lieutenant-général* looked momentarily blank. "Yes, Saglio." He sighed and shook his head. "Do you have any idea how many men I do not have? When I find someone to send to Vaugirard, I will send him."

On his way back toward the college, no one challenged

Charles, but he felt as though accusing eyes watched him from every doorway, as though everyone he passed were about to start singing the tavern song. He walked along the rue des Fossés, looking out at the Faubourg St. Jacques, the suburb that had grown up south of the walls. The Faubourg was thick with recent monastic foundations, built solidly of stone, with ample land around them. Beyond the gray lace of winter trees lay the walled precincts of the Feuillantines, Ursulines, and Daughters of Mary, their frozen gardens bare and empty. The great dome of Val de Grace, the Benedictine house beloved by Louis XIV's mother, rose above the convent walls like a sugared Christmas cake.

New private houses of gleaming stone were scattered along the road among the religious foundations, but not far beyond them, the countryside still spread itself. Soon, Charles told himself, plowing would start in the barren fields, fruit trees would blossom, the sun would come back. And, please God, his own heaviness of spirit would lighten. In truth, though, he wasn't sure. He'd chosen clearly and from his heart to remain a Jesuit. But his grief for what he hadn't chosen had been ripped wide open by Martine Mynette's murder, by her loss of the future she should have had. *Nothing is wasted*, the Silence had said—not death, not grief—*unless you waste it.* Was this renewed grief of his meant to drive him to find her killer? Was that what the Silence had meant?

He waited, very still on the windswept roadway, hoping the Silence would answer him. And caught his breath, wondering if the white horse galloping along a path beside a snowy field, its rider's black cloak flying, the man's streaming hair black as a crow's feather in the gray light, might be a sign. He watched them out of sight, but the Silence held its peace and the horse and rider only left him yearning to ride in the wind's teeth and leave grief behind.

Charles was nearly at the college when he saw a huddle of

beggars in the street ahead of him, outside the church of St. Étienne des Grès. A halting voice came from their midst, and he realized that someone was reading aloud. A man hushed a chattering woman, who hit him and started pushing her way out of the huddle. The reader's voice grew louder. *"Elle était riche, elle est morte, les Jésuites dansent sur son corps . . ."*

Bursting from the group nearly in Charles's path, the woman who'd been hushed screeched, "Here's one, here's a Jesuit vulture! But he can't eat us, we've no gold for his guts!"

The others turned and Charles saw that the reader was the young man who'd pleaded for the old beggar on Christmas Eve. When he saw Charles, his eyes grew round with fear and he dropped the sheet of paper and backed away. Some of the beggars started singing the words of the tavern song, but the old man who'd attacked the Condé's reliquary limped close to Charles, thrust his head forward, and squinted at him.

"Shut your mouths," he yelled over his shoulder. "This deathbird gives good alms, he gave me this coat."

Charles picked up the broadsheet from the cobbles and smiled reassuringly at the reader.

"Where did you get this, *mon ami?*"

The young man ran. Seeming to catch his fear, the others ran, too, and the old man limped after them, yelling at them to stop and cursing them for idiots. They rounded the corner of St. Étienne des Grès and Charles followed them, wondering suddenly where they sheltered. But in the scant moments it took him to reach the side street that ran in front of the college of Les Cholets, they disappeared. He turned back to the rue St. Jacques, studying the broadsheet as he went. This sheet, at least, still had only the one verse, which was somewhat reassuring. No printer's name, of course—no one would put his name to an effort to stir up unrest and disturb the city's peace.

As Charles neared the postern door, a shop sign on the college façade creaked in a burst of wind. Charles looked up. The sign's crusty, golden loaf of bread made him smile, thinking of the LeClercs, the family of bakers who rented the shop and its living quarters. Mme LeClerc and her small daughter Marie-Ange had taken him to their hearts when he arrived last summer, helping him when he'd sorely needed it. The family should soon be back in Paris from their Christmas visit to M. LeClerc's brother in the nearby village of Gonesse.

His spirits lightened a little by that thought, Charles went to the rector's office, where he found Père Le Picart sitting by the fireplace, his breviary in his hand.

"I see news in your face, Maître du Luc," Le Picart said. "Please, sit."

Charles took the chair on the other side of the hearth and loosened his cloak. "News indeed, *mon père*. Henri Brion is dead. Stabbed to the heart."

Le Picart crossed himself. "Brion? Dear God. So that is why the poor man never came to see me?"

"I don't know how long he's been dead. A beggar found him in a midden ditch near the Place Maubert. Someone came from the Brion house to tell me, and I'm just back from seeing the body."

"May God receive his soul. This is the last thing I expected! Certainly the last thing we needed. Of course," he added dryly, "poor Monsieur Brion hardly needed it, either. Were the police there? Is there any thought of who killed him? Or why?"

"Lieutenant-Général La Reynie was there. He has gone to question a goldsmith called Bizeul who, according to one of The Procope's waiters, took Brion forcibly out of the coffeehouse on Thursday night. The waiter and a woman who was begging at the coffeehouse door say that this Bizeul and another man pretended that Brion was drunk, but he wasn't. And since then, no one seems to have seen Brion alive."

Le Picart frowned thoughtfully. "A notary may come to know financial secrets, after all."

"True. Though family secrets are often more deadly."

"So you don't suspect this goldsmith?"

"He must be suspected, if it is true that he took Henri Brion forcibly out of the coffeehouse. But I can imagine no reason for him to have killed the girl. I cannot help but think that there is only one killer. Martine Mynette and Brion were both stabbed. Their lives were joined in family friendship as well as in the *dona-tion entre vifs* transaction. For both to die on the same day is too much coincidence."

"I agree. So who had reason to kill them both?"

"The most obvious answer is Henri Brion's son, Gilles," Charles said reluctantly. "His father was trying to force him into a marriage with the Mynette girl. And if he killed only the girl, his father would surely have tried to force him to court another heiress. But from the little I've seen of Gilles Brion, I simply can-not imagine him as a killer."

"Anyone may be tempted to kill. And until we find the person who *has* been so tempted," Le Picart said grimly, "the connec-tions between the two victims mean that Brion's death will be laid at our door along with Martine Mynette's."

They were both quiet under the weight of that certainty. The dim light through the small window's greenish glass made the rector's face look even more tired and drawn than it was.

The quiet was broken by a knock at the door. The rector gave permission to enter and a lay brother came in, holding out a folded piece of paper.

"This was left with the porter, *mon père*. For Père Damiot." He handed the folded paper to Le Picart, bowed, clasped his hands against his apron skirt, and composed himself to wait.

"Please excuse me, Maître du Luc." Le Picart opened the letter and scanned the page. Like the older religious orders, the Society of Jesus required that any letter sent to or written by a Jesuit be read by a superior. When he finished reading, he stared open-mouthed at the page in his hand. "Unbelievable," he breathed. Still looking at the letter, he said to the lay brother, "*Mon frère*, bring Père Damiot to me, please."

The brother bowed and went out.

"Well," Le Picart said, looking up. He seemed more at a loss for words than Charles had ever seen him. "Well. This suggests that your initial impression of Gilles Brion may be correct, *maître*. But we must wait until Père Damiot has read this, since it is written to him."

"Of course, *mon père*."

"A goldsmith," Le Picart murmured to himself, thoughtfully tapping a finger on the letter in his lap. "Very likely."

Charles folded his hands tightly in his lap to keep himself from snatching the letter and devouring it.

"*Mon père*," he said after a moment, both to take his mind off the letter and also because he needed to relieve his conscience, "after Monsieur La Reynie finished examining Brion's body, he asked me to go with him to talk to the people at Procope's. I went. I sat with him and drank coffee. I felt it was part of doing the task you've set me. But—well—it is a coffeehouse."

The rector sighed. "Maître du Luc." He sounded as though he were talking to a sixteen-year-old novice. "I am not aware that Rome has condemned coffee." He smiled at Charles. "Rather the contrary, if gossip serves."

"Oh, yes?" Charles was momentarily diverted by the thought

of His Holiness in papal tiara, sipping coffee in some Roman Procope's.

"You are pursuing these questions at my express order, *maître*. Where the questions take you, you will go. I charge you only to remember that Monsieur La Reynie pursues his own interests first and last."

A flurry of knocking came at the door, and Père Damiot was inside almost before Le Picart could bid him enter. His thin, olive-skinned face was alight with curiosity.

"Yes, *mon père*? A letter for me?"

The rector waited serenely until Damiot remembered the required *reverence* to his superior. Then Charles rose and offered his chair to Damiot who, as a priest, was his superior.

"*Bonjour, maître,*" Damiot said hurriedly. "Thank you. With your permission, *mon père*?"

Le Picart nodded and Damiot sat. Charles's mouth twitched. Damiot was looking at the letter in Le Picart's hand the way Charles's boyhood beagle had watched meat roasting in the kitchen fireplace.

"From your esteemed father, *mon père*," the rector said, holding the letter out. "Read it here, please; it touches on what Maître du Luc and I were discussing."

"Yes, *mon père*." Damiot glanced at Charles and then was absorbed in reading. Fortunately, the letter was short. Incomprehensibly, before Damiot reached the end of it, he was laughing. Eyes dancing with mirth, he looked at Le Picart. "Incredible! Have you ever heard anything to match this, *mon père*?"

"Certainly nothing financial," the rector said dryly. He turned to Charles, who was utterly at sea. "We will tell you shortly what is entertaining Père Damiot, *maître*, but first you need to know that his esteemed father is a merchant goldsmith and a member of the Six Corps."

"I do know from Père Damiot that his father is a goldsmith, *mon père*—but, what is the Six Corps?"

Damiot looked at Charles in disbelief.

The rector said kindly, "The association of Paris's six most influential guilds."

"My father is head of the goldsmiths' guild." Damiot looked questioningly at Le Picart, who nodded at him to continue. "It is like this, *maître*. This morning, my father heard something that closely concerns Monsieur Henri Brion. He had already heard about the Mynette bequest coming to us—I think everyone in Paris has heard of it by now." Damiot looked apologetically at Le Picart. "I hope I did not speak out of turn, *mon père*, but when my father visited me yesterday, he asked me if we had sure proof of Monsieur Simon Mynette's intention, and I told him we had Simon Mynette's letter, notarized by Monsieur Henri Brion."

"Continue," Le Picart said noncommittally.

"Well, now my father has written to me because he is worried that news that has just reached him about Monsieur Brion may somehow touch us—because of the Mynette property, you understand. Are you with me, Maître du Luc?"

"Barely."

He leaned almost gleefully toward Charles. "What has come to light is a scheme for smuggling silver through customs. It was just uncovered at the port in Brest. This scheme has been traced to Paris, and rumor has it that our Monsieur Henri Brion is its creator."

Le Picart lifted his hand slightly to pause Damiot. "What you do not know, Père Damiot, is that Henri Brion left Procope's coffeehouse on Thursday evening with a goldsmith named Bizeul and another man. Those who saw him go say he didn't go willingly. And this morning Henri Brion was found dead."

"No!" Damiot looked incredulously from the rector to Charles. "Is this certain?"

Charles nodded. "I saw his body."

"Well, I can easily imagine," Damiot said, hastily crossing himself, "that Brion's investors may have been tempted to kill him over losing so much money because this smuggling scheme has failed. But I know Monsieur Bizeul and I cannot imagine he would do murder."

"Why not?" the rector said sharply.

"Many reasons, *mon père*. My father has known Monsieur Bizeul longer than I have been alive. And Monsieur Bizeul is a senior member of our bourgeois Congregation of the Sainte Vierge. As both my father's son and the priest in charge of that Congregation, I have had many dealings with Bizeul. If he is not as upright and devout as I have supposed, I am badly deceived." His face changed suddenly. "Though it is true that he recently dowered his last daughter very generously. Overgenerously, some said. Oh, dear."

"Go back a little," Charles said. "What is the role of investors in this scheme?"

"*Ma foi!* Do you understand nothing about money?"

"I'm noble, remember? We never understand anything about money. That's why we don't have any."

A snort of laughter escaped Le Picart.

Damiot rolled his eyes. "You're only minor nobility. Listen. Notaries are the middlemen in French investment schemes. We, unlike the English, have not seen fit to have a national bank, so notaries like Monsieur Brion bring together those who have money and those who need it. A notary has to know not only where money is, but who wants it and who will pay for it. And that includes things that can be turned into money, one way and another. Especially things like silver."

"Which brings us to the details of Henri Brion's scheme," Le Picart said.

Damiot's eyes were brimming with laughter. "So let me set the scene. The silver might not have been discovered, you know, Maître du Luc, except for the drunk. And the handcart, of course."

Deadpan, Charles said back, "Ah, yes, it always *is* a drunk, isn't it? The handcart, though, figures less often." And waited to see how much of a comic script Damiot was going to make up right there in the rector's office.

The rector shifted warningly in his chair.

"Yes, well," Damiot said quickly, "it seems a drunk dock workman ran the wheel of his cart into the end of a barrel lying on its side on the dock. The barrel was one of fifty full of chocolate from Mexico. The barrel's bottom split and chocolate seeds—beans, whatever you call them—spilled out. As the drunk tried to push them back in, he felt something hard in the barrel and pulled it out. It was a pretty little bar of silver, thickly wrapped in wool. All fifty barrels turned out to be salted with these small silver bars."

"But wouldn't the weight of the silver in the barrel give the whole thing away?" Charles said, frowning.

"That's why the bars were so small. And there weren't many of them, maybe a half dozen to each barrel. But a fifty-barrel shipment of chocolate would net you enough silver—on which you'd paid only the customs charge for chocolate—to make it worthwhile."

"Reprehensible. I'm shocked." Charles tried to stifle his grin. He might be from the south, but he was enough of a Frenchman to enjoy a story of tax evasion. "Henri Brion thought of this? That surprises me, after all I've heard of him."

"My father says the customs people think he did. And that now Monsieur Henri Brion's investors are out a great deal of money."

"Because the investors financed the shipment," Charles said, finally understanding.

"Habes," Damiot said, classroom Latin for "you have it." "And though what they would have paid Henri Brion for being allowed into the potential profit was far less than they would normally pay for silver, it was still too much to simply lose."

"Not to mention facing prosecution for smuggling," Le Picart said. "A substantial enough motive for murder, if Brion refused to give them their money back. Or if they feared he would try to lighten his own penalty by giving up their names to the authorities."

So much, Charles thought, for his certainty that there was only one killer. "Does your father say if Monsieur La Reynie knows about this?"

Shaking his head, Damiot started to say something, but the rector, whose thoughts were going in other directions, forestalled him.

"Could this scheme of Henri Brion's have given him—Brion, I mean—a reason to kill Martine Mynette? Could he have stolen money from her and used it to promote this smuggling? While her mother was ill, perhaps?"

"I don't know. I suppose it's possible. But it isn't clear yet which of them died first."

Damiot was looking from Charles to the rector and frowning. "The police are keeping us so well informed?"

Le Picart said, "For our own protection, we are following their efforts regarding both murders. You know that people are accusing us of involvement in Martine Mynette's murder. People are going to say the same about Monsieur Brion's murder, too, until the real killer is found. Have you not heard the song already in the streets? I heard it yesterday."

Damiot shook his head. "I have not been out the last few days."

"I have a copy," Charles said, suddenly remembering. He brought out the broadsheet and handed it to Le Picart. "Still only the one verse, thank all the saints. A beggar was reading it to his *confrères*, but when he saw me, he dropped it and ran."

Le Picart glanced at the sheet and passed it to Damiot.

Damiot read it and grimaced. "Not bad. Though I could do better," He said it lightly, but his dark eyes were worried as he handed the paper back. "I wonder," he said slowly, "whether my father could help us."

The rector studied him. "How?"

"He knows all the rich merchants in the city. If Monsieur Brion found his investors by trawling The Six Corps, my father could probably find out whom he caught besides Monsieur Bizeul. Assuming he did catch Monsieur Bizeul, of course."

"Yes, write to him," Le Picart said. "Ask if he knows who the investors are. Casually, as though you are only curious." He smiled slightly. "As though you are indulging in a little worldly gossip. I feel sure you could do that convincingly."

"I can only try, *mon père*," Damiot said modestly.

"*Mon père*," Charles said to Le Picart, "Martine Mynette's funeral is on Monday morning, at Saint-Nicolas du Chardonnet. Mademoiselle Isabel Brion has asked me to attend. It would be a good way to listen to what's being said on the Place. It's possible that someone in another house heard or saw whoever came to the Mynette house just before Martine was killed."

The rector pursed his lips and shook his head. "I think your presence at the funeral would be too incendiary. Go, but wait outside for Mademoiselle Brion. When she comes out of the church, offer to escort her to her house. You can watch and listen as people leave the church and as you walk. I will tell the senior priest at Saint-Nicolas that you will be there—he is well disposed toward us and can speak a word from the pulpit to calm difficulties. And Maître du Luc, I want you to write a note to Lieutenant-Général La Reynie about Henri Brion's silver scheme, on the chance that the news has not yet reached him. You do not need to show it to me, but have someone take it right away."

Damiot's eyebrows rose at Charles's familiarity with the head of the police, but he asked no questions. "And I will write a message to my father as you ask, *mon père*," he said, "before I immerse myself again in preparations for Monday's classes." He sighed. "Though I could recite the venerable *Nouveaux Principes* grammar textbook in my sleep."

"Unfortunately, the goal is for your students to be able to recite it in *their* sleep," Le Picart said, laughing. "You are excused, *mon père*. And you, too, *maître*. You must also have preparations to make. And so do I. I am still putting the final touches on our New Year's Day celebration of King Louis's recovery from his recent surgery."

Charles groaned inwardly, having forgotten about the celebration since he wasn't directly involved. Having a long list of grievances against the constantly lauded Louis XIV, he wondered if staying on the heels of the police could be made into an excuse for absenting himself.

But Damiot said enthusiastically, "I would be only too glad to write a little something for the occasion, *mon père*. Such a delicate assignment, considering the kind of surgery . . ."

Charles choked back laughter. The surgery had been for an anal fistula, and what Damiot could make of that did not bear thinking about, at least not in the rector's presence.

Le Picart smiled blandly. "I think we will not trouble you, Père Damiot. Just write the message to your father."

Damiot acquiesced gracefully, and he and Charles bowed themselves out of the office.

When they were far enough away, Damiot said gleefully, "Too bad, that livret would have been my masterwork!"

"That livret would have been your ticket to life as an over-age apprentice to some crabbed goldsmith," Charles said through smothered laughter.

"Yes, not worth it, after all my efforts to avoid that very thing. Ah, well, back to work. First the note to my father and then the wretched *Nouveaux Principes* again." Humming under his breath, Damiot loped upstairs to his study.

Charles went into an alcove off the big reception salon, where writing materials were kept. Assembling paper and a quill, he quickly wrote his note to La Reynie and found a lay brother to take it to the *lieutenant-général* at the goldsmith Bizeul's house, or if La Reynie was no longer there, on to the Châtelet.

That done, Charles decided to go to the stage in the *salle des actes*, over the refectory. The Christmas farce, private and very quickly put together, had used no scenery. The February performance would have scenery, though not the elaborate stage machinery of the summer show, and taking time now to begin considering what would be needed would save time later. He went out the back door of the main building into the Cour d'honneur. Snow was falling again. And with it, somehow, the cold weight of loss and death settled on him. He went heavy-footed into the silent refectory building and up the elaborately curved staircase. In the empty *salle des actes*, he stopped at one of the long, small-paned windows and stared bleakly out at the snow, hating its cold, dead white and the wet black and gray that were all the color left to the miserable world. A sudden flurry of swirling black and the sound of laughter nearly made him jump, as seven or eight half-grown boys in their long scholars' gowns burst from the student court into the Cour d'honneur. They stood with their faces lifted, catching flakes on their tongues. Then they grabbed hands and began whirling in a circle, black gowns flying, a spinning, laughing hieroglyph on the white page of the courtyard. Eased somehow, Charles murmured his thanks for the small visitation of joy and walked on toward the bare stage.

Chapter 12

After a Sunday spent coping with returning boarding students in the rhetoric and grammar classes, and futile waiting for a reply from Lieutenant-Général La Reynie about the goldsmith Bizeul and Henri Brion's silver smuggling, Charles was glad for the arrival of Monday. Though it also brought Martine Mynette's funeral and found him standing in the midmorning cold outside Saint-Nicolas du Chardonnet, waiting for the funeral Mass to end. Père Le Picart had sent word to the priest at Saint-Nicolas that Charles would be waiting to escort Isabel Brion to her house after the Mass.

Charles stood like a mournful black sentinel beside the church doors. Père Jouvancy's weather prophet had proved all too accurate. The last two nights' snowfall had made the city a pattern of thick white on the grays and blacks of walls and streets and trees, and the opaque sky threatened more snow. Charles watched a milling group of paupers gathering, waiting to follow Mlle Mynette's coffin. He suspected that Isabel's great-uncle Callot had hired these customary mourners, giving them their cheap black garments, candles, and a few coins to attend Martine's coffin to its burial.

As the hired mourners talked among themselves, Charles heard them murmuring Martine Mynette's name. He asked a woman near him if she'd known Mlle Mynette, and a score of voices rose. Of course, they said, Mlle Mynette had never forgotten them. She'd sent food and necessities to anyone in trouble, especially orphans, and women in childbed.

With a tight throat, Charles blessed them. Then people began to come out of the church, and the paupers drifted toward the door at the side of the church to meet Martine Mynette's coffin. Charles stepped back, close to the wall, to watch unnoticed for Isabel.

She was quick to emerge, followed by her awkward manservant. She saw Charles before he could speak and pushed her black veil back. Her eyes were red with weeping, her warm coloring turned almost sallow.

"The priest told Uncle Callot that you would be here to see me home. Uncle Callot and my brother are going on to the burial. And Monsieur Morel, too." A faint blush warmed her skin as she named the dancing master. "I felt that I could not go. I should, but—" She lifted her small gloved hands and let them fall.

"You bear a heavy burden of grief, *mademoiselle*, no need to try yourself harder." Charles offered her his arm to help her down the steps slippery with patches of ice. "Please allow me to say how very sorry I am about your father's death. Especially coming in the way it did, and so soon after the death of your friend."

She nodded silently, pulling her veil down over her face, and took delicate hold of his proffered arm. "To tell you the truth, *maître*, I feel Martine's death even more than my father's. Which I know is very wrong of me."

"Mademoiselle Mynette shared much with you. Fathers do not often do that," Charles said, as they reached the bottom of the stairs and set off toward the rue Perdue, followed closely by the servant.

Ruefully, she shook her head. "Poor Papa, always busy with a new scheme for growing rich."

"Yes?" Charles was watching her closely now, wondering if she knew about the silver.

She tried to laugh. "In truth, more money would be welcome in our house. Papa spent too much money on things like our clothes. But he often spent nothing where he should have spent something. You see how our servants are dressed." She sighed. "He was kind to me, though," she went on, "and he tried to be kind to Martine. I wish he hadn't been trying to make her live with us, though. She hated that."

As they walked, a few people scowled at Charles and one called insults from a distance. Mlle Brion seemed not to hear, but Charles memorized the hostile faces and made sure no one came too close. When a passing couple slipped and fell briefly against him, he was poised to defend Mlle Brion and himself before he registered the couple's apologies. He caught himself just in time, joined in the little flurry of politeness, and everyone walked on. This kind of overquick reaction to threat, even when there was none, had plagued him since the army. It was sometimes useful, but more often embarrassing.

They arrived without further incident at the Sign of Three Ducks, and Mlle Brion crossed the threshold with a sigh of relief.

"Please bring wine to the little salon, Bon," she said to the servant, as he followed them in and shut the door. Pushing her veil back again, she turned to Charles. "My father's coffin is in the large salon. My maid is there, too; someone is always with him. If you will sit with me in the little room across the landing, *maître*, I have something to tell you."

"With pleasure, *mademoiselle*." Charles stood aside and then followed her up the stairs.

The door of the salon where the Brions had received him before was open, and he saw that the room had been turned into a mourning chamber. The shutters were closed and the walls hung with black. In the center of the room, candles burned around the open coffin resting on trestles. The maid sat in a chair against the wall, rubbing at her eyes as though she'd been roused from dozing.

"Will you come in with me, *maître*?" Mlle Brion asked hesitantly.

Charles bowed his acquiescence and they went to stand beside the coffin. Isabel rested her hand on her father's chest and bowed her head. Helped to greater feeling for the dead man by his resemblance to his daughter, Charles prayed for him and then gazed at his still face. *Where did you go from Procope's?* he asked silently. Did one of your unhappy investors come at you with the knife? Or did you die looking into the face of your even more unhappy son?

Isabel Brion stirred and sighed, and Charles made the sign of the cross over the coffin. They went out onto the landing, where the manservant had just arrived, balancing two glasses on a tray.

"There's only the local wine left," he said, thrusting the tray at Mlle Brion as if he expected her to take it.

She frowned repressively at him. "No need to describe the wine, Bon, what I asked for will do very well. Take it in, please, and put it on the little table." She rolled her eyes at Charles and dropped her voice. "He is only seventeen and very raw, but he means well. He was all we could afford when our old Albin left us."

"Willingness to learn is everything," Charles said politely.

Bon sidled out of the little salon and stumbled down the stairs, looking over his shoulder at them, and they went in. Charles, as a Jesuit scholastic, should not have been alone with a woman, especially a young woman. And the young woman should not have been alone with him. But both of them had much to say, Charles told himself, and none of it threatened their virtue. The window's light was welcome, but the little salon had no fireplace and the chill struck through Charles's cloak and cassock. Several chairs were set against the walls. Two of them flanked the carpet-covered table where the servant had put the tray.

"Please sit." She went to the table and gestured Charles toward the cushioned and fringed chair on its other side. When they were both seated, she stripped her black gloves from her hands and Charles sniffed appreciatively at the scent of jasmine her hands' warmth had released into the air from the soft leather. She untied the strings of her *manteau*, pushed her veil farther back from her face, and held a glass out to Charles. "As Bon said, it's only local, from Suresnes, but it will serve to warm us."

When they had drunk in silence for a moment, she said, "I want to tell you something about Martine. Perhaps it doesn't matter, but it troubles me. And it may help you find her killer."

"The police are searching for the killer, *mademoiselle*," Charles said gently. "My rector has only ordered me to keep track of what is done, because of what is being said in the streets about Jesuits having a part in her death."

"But you care that justice is done for her. I see it in your face, I hear it in your voice when we speak of her."

"Yes. I care very much about justice for her. What is it that you want to tell me about her, *mademoiselle?*"

Isabel Brion set her glass down. "When her maid and I were caring for her body—" She bit her lip and picked up her gloves from her lap, smoothing their soft leather and sending more sweetness into the air. "When we had undressed her and started to wash her, I saw that the little necklace she always wore was gone. It was nothing valuable, just a little red enameled heart on a pretty embroidered ribbon. But it was the most precious thing in the world to Martine. I looked everywhere—where we were working, in her chamber, and at the foot of the stairs where she was found, but it wasn't there."

Trying to hide his disappointment that the great secret was only a lost keepsake, Charles said, "Perhaps the ribbon broke one day when she was in the street and the necklace dropped without her notice."

"No! She was so careful of it and she wore it under her clothes. It couldn't have fallen all the way to the ground, you know." She blushed suddenly. "No, I don't suppose you do."

Charles felt himself blush, too—ex-soldiers *did* know these things. "But if she wore it under her clothes, how can you be sure that she still had it?"

"She would have told me if she'd lost it. And when she came here with my father the day you met her, I untied her *manteau* for her and I saw the outline of the heart under the high neck of her bodice. Someone must have taken it; I think she would have parted with her life before she parted with that little heart!" Isabel Brion gasped and put her hand over her mouth, hearing what she'd said.

"Tell me about the necklace," Charles said, more because he saw that Isabel needed to talk than because he thought her story would be any help to him. He drank a little more of his wine, which was surprisingly good, and settled himself to listen.

"You can only understand if I tell you where the heart came from," she said. "I swore never to tell another soul. But now that both Mademoiselle Anne and Martine are gone, I will tell you, if you swear to tell no one else. Their memories must not be tarnished."

Charles nodded his acquiescence, with the mental reservation that should the story tell him something about the murders, he would have to use it.

Isabel Brion glanced at the open door and leaned toward him across the table. "Maître du Luc, everyone knows that Mademoiselle Anne Mynette adopted Martine after old Monsieur Simon Mynette died. But what no one but me knows now is that Martine was Mademoiselle Anne's own daughter."

Charles's eyes widened in surprise. No wonder Mademoiselle Anne had suddenly "adopted" a child. "But did Mademoiselle Martine resemble her mother? Would that not have given their secret away?"

"It would. But Martine somewhat resembled her father, her mother told her. Still, though Mademoiselle Anne's hair was reddish and her eyes were gray, she and Martine both carried themselves with the same elegance. They had truly identical airs. But that was easy enough for people to dismiss as simply how Martine had been raised. *Maître*, you must not think ill of Mademoiselle Anne Mynette. Her miserable old father refused to dower her, because she had a misshapen foot and limped badly, and he said that no man of quality would have her. The real reason was that he was too miserly to dower her." The girl lifted her chin and said defiantly, "I think that if she sinned, it was her father's fault, not hers."

Sidestepping that tangled question, Charles said feelingly, "She must have suffered."

Isabel Brion looked at him in surprise. Her brown eyes were full of questions, but when he said nothing more, she went on with her story. "There was a man Mademoiselle Anne had hoped to marry—so Martine told me—but he left Paris when he realized there would be no dowry. Then, when Mademoiselle Anne was about thirty, there was someone else. They met secretly and her maid helped her. Not that Renée, the maid Martine had—an older woman who died soon after. Mademoiselle Anne's father was ill by that time, too ill to know whether she was at home or not. And soon—well—Anne Mynette realized that she was with child."

"What did she do?" Charles said, absorbed in the unfolding tale.

"Until near the end, she was able to hide her condition. With her bodice more loosely laced and those little embroidered aprons some women wear—well, women know things can be hidden. For a time, anyway. Near the end, she arranged to go and stay with her maid's sister on the Île de la Cité, and the baby—Martine—was born there. While Anne Mynette's father lived, of course, she could not bring the baby home. So she found a wet nurse on the Île and left the baby with her. But first, she put a little red enameled heart on a ribbon around Martine's neck as a token of her love. Not long after, only about a month later, old Monsieur Mynette finally died. As soon as he was buried, Mademoiselle Anne went to get her daughter from the nurse, but Martine was gone and the house was in an uproar. The nurse had two children of her own, and they had fallen ill a few days before. The younger child had just died when Mademoiselle Anne arrived. A neighbor who was there told Mademoiselle Anne that the nurse had taken Martine to the Hôpital des Enfants Trouvé—the Foundling Hospital nearby, you know—hoping to keep the baby from falling ill, too. But the poor woman was so distraught over her own children that she hadn't sent Mademoiselle Anne any message. Well, Mademoiselle Anne was terrified, thinking that Martine might also be ill, or even dead, and she ran to the Foundling Hospital. When the nun there brought the baby, the ribbon with the little red heart was still around Martine's neck, so Mademoiselle Anne knew that Martine was her own." Isabel sighed deeply. "Then she took Martine in her arms and they went home, the mother and her beloved child. Mademoiselle Anne hung the heart on new ribbons as Martine grew up, and Martine wore it for the rest of her life, because it was a sign of how much her mother loved and watched over her. Is that not a wonderful story, *maître?*"

Charles nodded and smiled. He was touched and warmed by the tale of loving, losing, and finding. "I see how deeply Mademoiselle Anne Mynette loved her daughter." But the story was of no use in pointing him toward that daughter's killer. And, he reminded himself, drinking the last of his wine, he should probably not take the story as unadorned fact. As Isabel Brion had told her tale, her voice had taken on the ritual cadence of myth. He could easily imagine Martine's mother telling her this story. And he could almost hear Martine's high sweet voice telling her friend this tale of her beginnings as she grew up, telling it always in the same words, rejoicing that she was the cherished child of a beloved mother. And they all lived happily ever after . . .

"Though she was Mademoiselle Anne Mynette's natural daughter," Charles said, "she still needed the *donation* in order to have what her mother left, is that not so?"

"Yes. If Mademoiselle Anne had told the truth about her child, she and Martine would both have been socially ruined. Besides, illegitimate children cannot inherit like children born of legal marriage, you know. So Mademoiselle Anne told everyone that she hadn't wanted to live alone after her father died, and had adopted an orphan of respectable parents being cared for by a wet nurse on the Île. And then she used the *donation* to make sure Martine would get the Mynette *patrimoine.*"

"Did Mademoiselle Anne Mynette's lover know that she had a child? Did he ever see Mademoiselle Martine?"

"I don't know. Martine said her mother would never talk about him." She glanced over her shoulder at the open door. "Martine thought he was a great noble," she whispered, leaning closer to Charles. "A noble who dared not risk having his dalliance known!"

"I see," Charles said gravely. Well, the two girls must have had an exciting time whispering together as they grew this dazzling paternal family tree for Martine. But whatever his quality, a father there had certainly been. Charles gazed into his wineglass. Could Martine's father have known her? It didn't sound likely, but it was not impossible. After all, in some of the old tales—as in life—everyone did *not* live happily ever after, and fathers could be ogres. But those were tales, and how could a gentle girl like Martine have been a threat to her unknown father, especially after so many years? Charles abandoned that shadowy father for an all-too-real one.

"*Mademoiselle*, did your father often receive letters from abroad? Had he, perhaps, had letters from abroad recently? From the New World—Mexico, perhaps?"

She blinked at the abrupt change in the talk. "Not from Mexico, but he often had letters from New France. We have relatives there. He had a letter a few weeks before Christmas—an Ursuline sister returning from their mission there brought it." Mlle Brion smiled sadly. "After my mother died, my father put me with the Ursulines in the Faubourg St. Jacques for schooling. I loved it there. I still visit them sometimes, and they often bring us family letters when they come back from New France."

"Did you read the letter that came before Christmas?"

"No. My father always told us what they said, just family

matters—there was a betrothal under discussion, I think. And a cousin was safely delivered of a child. That sort of thing."

Another dead end, Charles told himself, New France being a wildly unlikely port of origin for a shipment of silver. But there was a much harder question he needed to ask.

"*Mademoiselle*, I must ask you a difficult question and I ask your pardon for it. On the day I met your brother, the day Mademoiselle Martine was killed, your great-uncle said angry things to your brother. You and your brother left the salon and went downstairs. You talked together there. Your uncle and I could hear your voices, but not your words."

Seeming to shrink into herself, Isabel Brion shook her head.

"You are telling me 'no,' *mademoiselle*? I have not yet put my question."

She stiffened and looked away. "Ask, then."

"When your brother left the house, you came back upstairs. You passed the *salon*, and Monsieur Callot and I both heard you crying. I want to know what your brother said that made you cry."

"Martine was dead," she said angrily, "of course I was crying."

Charles watched her and said nothing.

"I tell you, I was crying for Martine. I don't even remember what Gilles said. Or—" She smoothed her skirt. "Yes, I do remember. He said something kind, trying to comfort me, and my tears overflowed. As will happen, you must know that."

"Yes, *mademoiselle*, I know that. But I do not think that is what happened when you talked with your brother."

"I thought you were trying to help us, but now you talk as though you hate Gilles, too, just as my great-uncle does. You want to see him arrested for killing Martine! Well, he didn't, he wouldn't; Gilles is as timid as a doe, he couldn't kill anyone!"

"I do not think it likely that your brother killed her. But I need to know what he said to you."

Her tears were falling freely now, and she put both hands to her face. Gulping back sobs, she said, "You don't think Gilles did it? Truly?"

"Truly. I may be wrong, of course. But I do not think he killed her."

She dropped her hands into her lap. "Why not?"

"I think your brother has his faults, but not the faults of a man who kills."

She released her held breath and silently studied his face. "I have been so frightened," she said, almost whispering. "What Gilles told me when you heard us talking is that he'd gone to see Martine very early the morning she died. He'd spent Thursday night at the Capuchins, praying—he often does. He told me he went to her house when it was still dark and called up to her window. She went down to the garden gate—it opens from a little side street—and let him in. He said he'd been shown in prayer that he should ask her to tell my father that she would never marry him, so that my father would stop making him court her."

"And did she agree?"

Isabel Brion swallowed and looked down. "Gilles said she told him to stand up for himself and went back inside and left him there. Martine could be harsh when she thought someone was not acting honorably. But don't you see, he is terrified that if anyone knows he was there, before dawn, alone with her, and that they quarreled, he will be as good as hanged!"

Charles tried to keep his thoughts from showing on his face. Gilles Brion would certainly be arrested if the police learned of this early-morning meeting. It would have been so easy for him to follow Martine into the house, so easy to fall into a rage at her refusal and her disgust, so easy to kill her there at the foot of the staircase.

"*Maître?* You still don't think he did it, do you?"

"On the whole, I do not. But the police will surely think so, if they hear what you have told me."

She bristled. "And are you going to tell them?"

"As I said, I doubt he killed her," Charles said, hoping that would be answer enough. He could not make promises, and in truth, this new knowledge was damning. Gilles Brion had been desperate to have Martine out of his life. What was it La Reynie had said about him? *Even a would-be monk may strike back, if you push him too far.* With a sigh, Charles stood up.

"*Mademoiselle,* forgive my suddenness, but I must go back to the college. Thank you for your frankness." He wanted to say that if her brother was innocent, he had nothing to fear. But they both knew that innocent people were too often hanged. "Will you do one more thing for me? Will you ask your brother if he saw anyone else on the Place or in the side street that morning? Anyone at all."

Hope flared in her face. "Why?"

"If he saw anyone, that person may be able to help prove his innocence."

"Oh." It was a small chance, and her face showed that she knew it. "I will ask him. And Maître du Luc, please pray for us. For Gilles."

"Of course I will, *mademoiselle.* For all of you." He bowed and took his leave.

He was nearly at the rue St. Jacques when a new unwelcome truth hit him. Gilles Brion had probably known Martine all her life, which made it more than possible that he knew about her necklace. Though why he would have taken it, Charles couldn't imagine. But Gilles was much more likely to know about it than anyone else Charles could imagine as her killer. Unless his father was the killer. But if that was true, Henri Brion had been killed almost immediately after he himself had done murder. And how likely was that? Unless, of course, someone had seen her killed. But why would a witness not simply come forward and accuse Brion?

Chapter 13

With a heavy heart, Charles wrote an urgent note to Lieutenant-Général La Reynie after dinner, telling him that Gilles Brion had seen Martine Mynette on Friday morning. He gave the note to a lay brother to deliver, then caught the man before he reached the postern and tore up the note. He would tell La Reynie, he decided, but face-to-face so that more than the bare facts could be told. Gilles Brion deserved at least that.

Before the clock had chimed the beginning of Monday afternoon's classes, Charles was in the *salle des actes* trying to concentrate his thoughts on the first rehearsal of the February show. The students were not there yet, but Père Jouvancy and Maître Pierre Beauchamps, the college ballet master, were standing on the stage, arguing. Charles's resigned first thought was that nothing had changed since August's ballet and tragedy. The two men were standing toe-to-toe, not quite shouting at each other. Charles could not help but hear what they said, and his second thought was that this time Beauchamps was going to win.

"I tell you, you cannot do this, *maître!*" Jouvancy was swelling with fury. "We have a show in only six weeks!"

"At which time, I tell you, I will be in Rome." Beauchamps smiled down at him. The dance director of the Opera, former dancing master to King Louis, legendary dancer in his own right, was an elegant man in his fifties. His stylish shoes, heeled and high-tongued, made him look taller than he was, and his dark shoulder-length wig, which rose high on either side of its center part, added to the effect. His linen was embroidered, and his coat, waistcoat, and breeches were all of fine cinnamon broadcloth.

"Then who is going to teach and direct the dances in our musical tragedy?" Jouvancy hissed through his teeth. "We have engaged Monsieur Charpentier to write the score for *Celse*, and the man does not come cheap! Do we waste all this effort because you have a—*whim*—to go to Rome?"

"Not a whim, *mon père*, I assure you," Beauchamps said mildly, rearranging the ribbons on the inlaid silver head of his walking stick. "I have a magnificent opportunity to add to my collection of paintings. But I must be on the spot. As always, you make too much of a little difficulty." He smiled over his shoulder at Charles. "Your good Maître du Luc here could easily teach and direct the few dances." He brushed an imaginary speck from his wrist ruffles. "That is all that is required, after all. Since you have seen fit to have the music written by someone else."

Ah, Charles thought, *now the bone is laid bare*. For many years now, Beauchamps had not only created and taught the dances for college productions, he had also written much of the music. He and Jouvancy gazed furiously at each other.

"You are being childish," Jouvancy snapped. "After all, though I very often write our tragedies, this one is Père Pallu's work."

"You are a religious. *I* am an artist."

The air around Jouvancy fairly crackled, and Charles involuntarily shut his eyes.

Nothing happened, and he opened them in time to see Jouvancy arrange his face in a smile, put his head on one side, and widen his limpid blue eyes.

"We all know," the rhetoric master said, "how justly famous is your collection of paintings. It is known all over France."

"Europe."

"I beg your pardon?"

"Justly famous all over *Europe*."

"I was coming to that," Jouvancy snapped. He composed his face again. "But, *maître*, could you not give us the benefit of your inestimable skill and go to Rome *after* the tenth of February? Italy will be warmer then, you know."

"Italy is warmer now." Beauchamps made Jouvancy a flourished bow. "I take my leave, *mon père*, and wish you every success with your little show." With another bow to Charles and the triumphant lift of an eyebrow, he swept down the *salle des actes* and out the door.

Mentally girding his loins, Charles joined Jouvancy on the stage. The rhetoric master's face had gone purple.

"This is outrageous, *maître*. This is beyond anything, this is an unforgivable insult to the college. How dare he leave us like this? He is the ballet master and we have a performance! The man is always impossible, but who would have thought him capable of this? When Père Le Picart hears of it, that will be the end of Maître Beauchamps at Louis le Grand, I promise you!"

Charles doubted that, but had learned in the course of August's show to hold his tongue and let Jouvancy's indignation sputter itself out. The courtyard clock chimed and teenaged boys swarmed into the chamber, their *cubiculaire* escort waiting at the door until they were all inside. The midday recreation hour was supposed to be quiet, but in winter that rule was somewhat relaxed for the sake of warmth. The boys were red-faced and lively from running in the cold and wind, and more than one black scholar's gown was starred with wet patches, most likely from snowballs.

Jouvancy shook his head hopelessly and turned his back on the students. "And Monsieur Charpentier has not finished the music. He sent me a note just after dinner. What are we to do?" He dropped his head into his hands.

Charles gathered the boys with his eyes and, smiling, touched his finger to his lips. The students stood in a silent huddle, their bright eyes fixed on Jouvancy. Charles turned back to the senior rhetoric master and made the suggestion that had just leaped full-blown into his mind.

"*Mon père*, I think we can safely leave Maître Beauchamps to Père Le Picart. But allow me to suggest an excellent and honorable young dancing master who I'm sure would be only too glad of the chance to work for us. I have seen the results of his teaching and can wholeheartedly recommend him." Charles himself would, as usual, be the overall dance director. But since it was improper for a Jesuit to dance in public, even if only teaching, every show that included dancing needed a secular ballet master as well.

Jouvancy straightened and frowned at Charles. "Where have you seen these results, may I ask?"

"When I called on a member of our bourgeois Congregation of the Sainte Vierge, *mon père*. This young man was in the house, giving a lesson to one of the young people there. I was very impressed with him," Charles said, happily remembering his first sight of Mlle Isabel Brion, bouncing through her dancing lesson.

"His name?"

"Monsieur Germain Morel, *mon père*. He is at the beginning of his career and would not require high pay."

"That, at least, is to the good. Very well, tell him to be here tomorrow at this time, and I will see what he can do. I will speak to the bursar. He will certainly cost less than Maître Beauchamps, and we must have someone." Presenting his best profile, Jouvancy gazed tragically into the middle distance. "How it pains me to see these practitioners of dance act as though they are the center of every performance. How dare a mere practitioner like Maître Beauchamps treat a learned theoretician such as myself as he has just done? But that is increasingly the way; no one cares *why* a thing should be done. Or not done! They care only for doing it, as fast and as vulgarly as possible!" He lifted a graceful hand, as though inviting the ancients, those revered makers of art's eternal rules, to comment.

They did not, but Charles stood in for them, murmuring ambiguously as he always did when Jouvancy started the theoretician-versus-practitioner argument. The academic notion that theoreticians were superior to practitioners was a familiar one. But as he'd had occasion to think before now, calling the great dancer and dancing master Beauchamps "only a practitioner" was like calling the pope "only a priest."

Hearing the boys shifting impatiently behind him, and judging that Jouvancy's performance of the heroically long-suffering producer-director was nearly over, Charles said deferentially, "*Mon père*, today's rehearsal is not lost, you know."

Or wouldn't be, if they got to work soon. These rehearsals, shorter than those for the summer show, would last only two hours. At three o'clock, the boys would go on to the rhetoric classroom, where the remainder of class time was spent working under Père Pallu, another of Louis le Grand's rhetoric masters and author of the Latin script for *Celsus*, February's spoken tragedy. Jouvancy would go with them to share the rest of the afternoon's teaching. Charles, under Père Le Picart's order, was excused from assisting in the classroom while he followed the police inquiry into the murders.

"You have Père Pallu's tragedy script," Charles went on. "And

I can look at the dancers' particular skills to see who ought to be cast in what kind of dance."

Jouvancy suddenly abandoned his performance, clapped a hand to his forehead, and drew a folded paper from his cassock. "Forgive me, *maître*, this crisis drove everything from my mind. Monsieur Charpentier sent a list of dances." He handed the paper to Charles.

"Good. Then we have what we need, do we not?"

"Yes, of course we do!" As though Charles had been the one delaying him, Jouvancy turned in a whirl of cassock skirts and advanced on the waiting students. "So, *messieurs*. You already know which of you are in the tragedy and which in the musical *intermèdes*. We will begin. But first, let us pray."

Everyone bowed his head.

"Dear Lord of hosts," Jouvancy said, more militantly than was usual with him, "bless this work we begin today. Strengthen our voices and our bodies. And make each one *know his place*. And keep it with *humility*. Amen." Having thus further relieved his feelings, he took the actors onto the little stage while Charles gathered the dancers at the far end of the chamber and looked them over.

There were seven of them. Six were the best dancers in the senior rhetoric class: Armand Beauclaire, from Paris; Walter Connor, from Ireland; Michele Bertamelli, from Milan; Charles Lennox, natural son of the late Charles II of England; André Chenac, from Tours; and Olivier Thiers, from Paris. The seventh was Henri Montmorency, the oxlike eighteen-year-old scion of one of France's most noble families. His mother had "asked" that he be allowed to dance in the February show, which she and other Montmorencys would attend. Because they were Montmorencys, it went without saying that the boy would dance. No matter that the boy was one of Maître Beauchamps's few failures, having proved himself incapable of dancing. In Jesuit colleges, rank was less the arbiter of everything than it was elsewhere. All students were expected to treat each other courteously, and their success in the classroom depended solely on their own wits and achievements. Nonetheless, boys from great families got the classroom's best seats and the best chambers in the student living quarters, and nobility was—in Charles's opinion—too often a consideration in casting plays and ballets. Charles was not pleased at having to find something for M. Montmorency to do in *Celse.*

"Maître?" Armand Beauclaire, a pink, round-faced sixteen, with light brown hair as thick as thatch, was studying Charles. "Are you well?"

Charles looked up blankly. "What? Oh, yes, certainly!" He pulled himself together and tried not to hope that Montmorency would sprain an ankle. Or both ankles.

The other boys, though, were very good dancers. Several were good enough for strong solos, and together the six would make an impressive ensemble. He unfolded Charpentier's list of dances, and the students gathered around him. When Charles reached the end of the list, he was nodding happily. This composer knew what he was about. Of course, Charles knew of Charpentier's work for the noble Mlle de Guise and her household musicians, called The Guise Music. He had also heard one or two of the composer's pieces for the Jesuit church of St. Louis and looked forward now to hearing Charpentier's theatrical music.

He smiled at the boys. "Monsieur Charpentier has given us a fine list of dances and characters." His gaze traveled around the small circle. "Who knows the story of our hero, Celse? He is Celsus in Latin, but we will call him Celse, since our musical tragedy lyrics are in French."

The Italian boy, thirteen and in his first year in the senior rhetoric class, put up his hand. "He was Milanese, *maître*. Like me." Michele Bertamelli drew himself up, and his enormous black eyes glowed. "God made most of His saints in Italy."

Beauclaire retorted flatly, "He was French."

"One small moment, *messieurs*," Charles said, interrupting Bertamelli's protest. "Monsieur Bertamelli raises an interesting point. It is correct that many of our earliest saints are from the Italian cities. Why is that, do you suppose?"

"Because the Roman emperors killed so many Christians," Walter Connor said impatiently, as though that were obvious. Which it should have been to boys who had studied Latin classics for four or five years.

"*Habes.* Yet Monsieur Beauclaire is right that Celse was originally from Gaul."

Bertamelli's small fierce face became a tragedy mask.

Charles Lennox offered uncertainly, "And his mother was Saint Perpetua?"

"Close. Saint Perpetua was the mother of Celse's master, Saint Nazarius. The story goes like this. Nero was emperor—so it is said—when Nazarius was born. Saint Perpetua raised him as a Christian, though his father was a pagan. Nazarius gladly followed his mother's way and grew to be very devout. When he began his preaching journeys to convert pagans, he went to Milan. But the Roman soldiers there beat him and threw him out of the city. He then went to Gaul, where a woman asked him to take Celse, her nine-year-old son, and give him a Christian upbringing. So the two companions went on together, the little boy helping the man and at the same time learning to be Christian. They made many converts, but in Trier, they angered the Roman officials and were condemned to be drowned in a lake. When they were thrown overboard, a great storm came up and the terrified boatmen rescued them, realizing that God was angry at this attempt to harm them. They were set free and returned to Milan— where the Romans beheaded them. Many years later, Saint Ambrose found their bodies buried in a garden outside Milan. He also found a vial of blood beside the body of Saint Nazarius, and the blood was still bright red and liquid. So their holy remains were kept in honor and treated with the reverence they had earned in life."

Montmorency yawned widely, a very rude act in company, which Charles ignored for the deliberate provocation it was. Beauclaire put up his hand.

"Yes, Monsieur Beauclaire?"

"*Maître*, why was the blood already in a vial? Who put it there if no one had dug Saint Nazarius up before Saint Ambrose?"

"A very good question. Some tellings of the story say only that Saint Nazarius was bleeding when they dug him up, and that his blood was still liquid and bright red."

Beauclaire was shaking his head. "My brother told me dead bodies don't bleed. He saw a body dissected and it didn't bleed."

"No, no," Bertamelli cried, shaking a finger at Beauclaire. "They bleed! If they were murdered and the guilty one touches them, they bleed and that is how you know the murderer!"

"People used to believe that," Charles said. "But now—"

"No, no, I saw it, *maître*, I saw it myself, my uncle was murdered by his cousin and when his cousin turned the body over, it bled on his hands and made them as red as the devil's tongue to accuse him!"

Several of the boys were round-eyed with interest, but Beauclaire and Connor looked at each other and shrugged. Montmorency just looked confused.

To avoid another international dispute, Charles said firmly,

"There are many unexplained things in God's world. We must go on with our purpose here. Our dancing space today will be from the wall to where I am standing. Mark it out, please."

The boys took off their hats and began placing them to indicate a rectangle, deeper than it was wide. Montmorency haughtily handed his hat to little Bertamelli, who bowed ironically and added his own hat and Montmorency's to the rectangle.

Charles, watching, nodded thoughtfully. "Now, the first dance is a sarabande for Saint Perpetua." He let his gaze drift over the waiting dancers and come to rest on Montmorency. "Monsieur Montmorency, let me see your *demi-coupé*, two *pas marchés*, and a balance."

Montmorency stared in horror. "Saint Perpetua? Me?"

"Why not?"

"In a gown?"

"But of course."

The rest of the group was convulsed with silent laughter.

"I want to be a Roman soldier."

Charles raised his eyebrows.

"Please," Montmorency added grudgingly.

Charles waited.

"Please, *maître*."

Having extracted the required courtesy due a teacher, Charles graciously inclined his head. "Perhaps you are somewhat large for Saint Perpetua." He turned to the light and wiry Walter Connor. "Monsieur Connor, could you manage Saint Perpetua?"

Connor grinned all over his face. "With pleasure, *maître*. As long as she doesn't wear a clock." Charles had saved Connor from having to dance in the summer ballet while wearing a three-foot chiming clock on his head.

"My thanks, Monsieur Connor," Charles said, grinning back. "Show us your *demi-coupé*, two *pas marchés*, and a balance."

Connor took the female position for making a *reverence*, heels together, feet turned out, hands clasped palm up and palm down at his waist, bent both knees and straightened them. Then he stretched one leg back, the toe of his shoe on the floor, arranged his arms in the fourth position, and turned his head slightly toward the upraised arm. Charles drew his time-keeping stick from his cassock and set the tempo, beating a slow triple meter on the floor. Connor executed his steps and ended in an effortless balance on the ball of one foot.

"Excellent! You are our Saint Perpetua, Monsieur Connor." Charles looked at his list and then at the remaining six boys. "Monsieur Beauclaire, let me see your *pas de bourrée*, forward, backward, to both sides, and *emboité* with the heel beat. All at a slow tempo."

Again he set the tempo, and Beauclaire went effortlessly and beautifully through his steps. He was perhaps the school's best dancer, though he had bitter difficulty telling right from left.

"You are our Saint Nazarius," Charles said, smiling at him.

Beauclaire bowed. "I will write to my mother, *maître*, and tell her I have been made a saint," he said piously, laughter dancing in his eyes. The other boys groaned.

"Now we need a Celse." Charles would have liked to give the part to the quiet, anxious Charles Lennox, but Celse had to be small, and the English boy was as tall as Beauclaire. The Italian was the smallest and youngest of the group. Poised on his toes, Bertamelli was watching Charles with the eagerness of a fledgling hoping for a worm. Charles nodded at him. "Monsieur Bertamelli, show us all the hopping, jumping steps you know. I want to see how fast and light you are."

"Like the swallow skimming the clouds, like the eagle racing the wind, like—"

"Just show us, please, Monsieur Bertamelli."

The boy leaped to the center of the dancing space and, without waiting for Charles's stick, launched himself into a blur of aerial steps. His scholar's gown billowed and rippled through *pas de rigaudon, pas de sissonne, pas assemblé*, and some steps Charles suspected Bertamelli's feet of inventing on their own.

Laughing for sheer pleasure at the boy's exuberance—and raw talent—Charles called, "Thank you, Monsieur Bertamelli, well done." Bertamelli kept dancing. Charles clapped his hands. "*Mon brave*, come back to earth!"

Bertamelli stopped, panting and sweating, and waited anxiously.

"The part is yours; you will be our Celse, Monsieur Bertamelli."

Bertamelli flung out his arms, and for a moment Charles thought the boy was going to rush at him. "I thank you, *maître*! My mother will be so proud. All Milan will be so proud!"

He bowed and marched back to his *confrères*, a triumphal procession of one.

Cutting off Montmorency's scornful laughter with a look, Charles swallowed his own grin and consulted his list. St. Ambrose was to express his joy at finding the holy bodies by dancing a *forlane*, a fast dance only a little calmer than a *gigue*. Which Charles thought a little extreme for an elderly saint, but no doubt the miraculous discovery had renewed his youth.

"Monsieur Lennox."

The English boy flinched a little, his blue eyes anxiously fixed on Charles. He was of middle height, not as dark as his royal father and seemingly with none of Charles II's legendary self-assurance.

"I would like you to be our Saint Ambrose, Monsieur Lennox. If I remember correctly, you do not yet know the *forlane* steps, but your dancing is clean and clear, and you can learn it. I think you will do it well."

"Oh. Thank you, *maître*. No, I don't know that dance. I will try, but—I mean, I hope I can. If—" He broke off, red-faced and sweating in the cold room, though he'd only been standing still.

"You will do it admirably, I am sure, *monsieur*."

Which left André Chenac and Olivier Thiers. And Henri Montmorency.

"The rest of you," Charles said briskly, "will play a variety of roles as Roman soldiers, sailors, and so on. Everyone will dance in the final *chaconne*." He swept the group with a sober glance. "Now, hear me. Remember that this is our pre-Lenten show and its intent is to direct the thoughts of the audience toward keeping a holy Lent. The action of this lyrical tragedy is much the same as the action of the Latin tragedy. But lyrical tragedy is not simply action, it is also spiritual tragedy. You must make your characters' emotions—not only their good and devout feelings, but their other feelings, too—clear to your audience through your bodies. Do you understand?"

They all—including Montmorency—nodded somberly, and even with a certain eagerness, Charles was moved to see. He never stopped being surprised at the depth to be found in the souls of teenage boys. When he wasn't wanting to throttle them, he was often brought near tears by their innocent fervor. As he started to tell the boys what to do next, a lay brother opened the door.

"Maître du Luc? The rector asks you to pardon this interruption, but he needs you in the *grand salon*."

"Thank you, *mon frère*, I am coming." Wondering what had happened now, Charles told the dancers to wait and hurried to the stage, where Jouvancy was deep in excited planning with his actors. When a break came in the talk, Charles told Jouvancy that the rector had summoned him.

Jouvancy made an exasperated sound. "Very well, you must go, of course. Send your dancers up here. Each group should know something about what the other is doing."

With a stern command to avoid upsetting the rhetoric master, Charles sent his dancers to Jouvancy and hurried apprehensively downstairs.

When he reached the main building's grand salon, where outsiders were received, he found Père Le Picart waiting with M. Edmé Callot and M. Germain Morel. Callot was the color of old paper and looked ten years older than he had two days earlier. Morel looked not much better. Charles turned questioningly to the rector, but Morel, who seemed to have assumed the responsibilities of a son of the house, spoke first.

"They arrested Gilles an hour ago. He is in the Châtelet."

Charles's heart sank. "For Martine Mynette's murder?"

"And for his father's."

"Gilles is an idiot," Callot burst out, wringing his hands, "but he is not a killer. And, *mon Dieu*, he is not a parricide!" His voice shook. "My poor Isabel has cried herself sick."

Callot turned his head away and wiped furiously at his eyes. The rector guided him to an armchair by the wall and bade him sit.

"The worst thing," Morel said, "is that now they have arrested Gilles, the police think they have done their work."

Charles didn't know what new evidence La Reynie had found, but Isabel Brion would certainly blame Charles himself for Gilles's arrest, thinking he'd told La Reynie about her brother's visit to Martine on Friday morning. He sighed. "Why are the police so sure he killed them, Monsieur Morel?"

"As for his father's murder, we don't know. But some bedeviled woman has sworn to our *commissaire* that she was looking out her window before dawn on Friday morning and saw Gilles leaving the Mynette garden gate."

"She's probably half blind," Callot muttered. "Anyway, how could she tell who it was, before dawn in a side street, with the lanterns long out?"

"She claims there was light from the side door of the Mynette house, which, she says, was open," Morel answered unhappily. "She may be lying, but—"

"She isn't lying," Charles said reluctantly. "Monsieur Gilles Brion was there. Mademoiselle Brion told me herself this morning, when I saw her home after the funeral. Her brother confessed to her that he had gone to talk to Mademoiselle Mynette before it was light. She came down and spoke with him in the garden. He said that he left by the garden gate. And, of course, that he left Mademoiselle Mynette alive."

"The idiot!" M. Callot slapped his thin, veined hands on the arms of his chair. "Dear sweet Jesu, the turnip-balled idiot! I hope the Châtelet scares some sense into him. If being there doesn't kill him before he's even hanged. Or worse."

The Châtelet might well kill him, Charles thought. Jail fever raged in prisons and few, guilty or innocent, escaped it if they stayed long enough. "Is he in a common cell, Monsieur Callot?"

"Of course not," Callot growled. "Would I let him be thrown in with all the rabble of Paris?"

In the silence that fell, Charles saw that Morel was glancing furtively at the rector. The rector paid him no attention, standing serenely, hands folded at his waist, eyes cast down like a modest nun.

With the air of a man betting everything on a throw of the dice, Morel said, "Maître du Luc, you have followed the police inquiry since Mademoiselle Martine Mynette's death. You know Lieutenant-Général La Reynie. We want you to help us. If your rector permits. We want you to look for the real killer of both Martine Mynette and Henri Brion. The police think they have no more need to look, and if the matter is left there, Gilles will certainly die."

On the whole, Charles agreed. He looked at Le Picart. Le Picart raised his head, and his gaze hit Charles like gray lightning. Then he turned to study his guests. Neither they nor Charles moved a muscle.

"More than a man's life is at stake here," Le Picart said slowly. "Maître du Luc, I think you should go and see Monsieur Gilles Brion. Whether he is guilty or innocent, visiting the prisoner is certainly within our purview. And speak to Monsieur La Reynie, if you can. But first, come to my office." He turned to Callot and Morel. "*Messieurs*, I ask you to go to Mademoiselle Brion, who surely needs you, and wait patiently. I must think on what you have asked. We will send you a message saying what is decided. God go with you." He sketched a blessing in the air and withdrew.

"I will see Monsieur Gilles Brion and do everything I can for him," Charles said to Callot and Morel. "You can trust what Père Le Picart says. He will send you a message telling you what I learned in my visit, and very soon."

Accepting that they had no choice but to wait, the two men thanked him and started to take their leave.

"One moment, Monsieur Morel," Charles said, remembering other, lesser concerns. "Forgive me for intruding a very different matter, but we are in need of a dancing master for our Lenten show. Maître Beauchamps is unavailable. If you are free and will come tomorrow at one o'clock, Père Jouvancy would like to speak with you about replacing Monsieur Beauchamps for these weeks."

Morel gaped as though the sun had risen in black midnight.

"I am—I would be—more honored than I can say, *maître.* Certainly I will be here."

"Excellent." Charles smiled at him. "And, please, tell Mademoiselle Brion that she must not despair. The *bon Dieu* has her in His hand. And her brother, too."

As Charles went to the rector's office, though, he wondered if that was the happiest thing he could have said. It was the conventional thing to say and he believed it. But he'd rarely found God's hand a comfortable place to be.

When he opened Le Picart's office door in response to the command to enter, he found his superior rising from his prie-dieu. Charles was expecting a lengthy discussion, but Le Picart did not even ask him to sit down. Straight and unmoving, one hand still on the prie-dieu, he said, "Do you believe this young man is innocent of these murders?"

"On the whole, I do."

"Then I want you to do what our guests have asked, Maître du Luc."

"Yes, *mon père,* I will go to Monsieur Gilles Brion as soon as our rehearsal ends."

"No, not just that. You are already watching the police inquiry and keeping me informed. Now I want you to do more. I want you to help Monsieur La Reynie find the killers of Martine Mynette and Henri Brion."

Charles took a literal and metaphorical step backward and eyed his rector warily. Le Picart was ordering him to do what he wanted to do—what he had, in fact, already started to do. But . . . "Why, *mon père?* Why me?"

He flinched inwardly as Le Picart's eyebrows rose. The rector was all too familiar with Charles's struggles over obedience.

"In part, Maître du Luc, because the correct answer to my order is 'Yes, *mon père,*' but your answer is 'Why, *mon père?*' Even though I have told you to do what your heart is already driving you to do."

"'Why' is not 'No.'"

"True. I want you do to this because you have done it before and you did it well. Lieutenant-Général La Reynie knows you. I think he somewhat trusts you. And he is desperately understaffed. He cannot find these killers as quickly as we need them found. He does not have enough men. And as our friends have just said, he may have stopped looking. That is the plain truth, which I think he will acknowledge himself."

"*Mon père*, of course I want to do what you ask. But—just to take one doubt I have of my ability to do this—I know nothing about commerce or finance. And this silver scheme likely has a bearing on Henri Brion's death, at least."

"Père Damiot will help you there."

"And if I fail? To find either killer?"

"The Society of Jesus is being publicly accused of murder for wealth. That calumny has been painted on our doors. You—and we, and Lieutenant-Général La Reynie—have no choice but to make our best effort to find the real killers. If we fail, we fail, and God will have a reason for it. Will you do this?"

"I will, *mon père*." Charles returned Le Picart's level gaze. "For the dead as much as for the Society."

"And that is the most important reason why I ask you and not another to do this. Your heart is in it. So," Le Picart said briskly, "I will tell my own superior what I have set you to do. If he tells me I am wrong, then I will call you back. If any . . . difficulty arises from your task, I will take it wholly on myself. You are acting on my orders and you are acting as Ignatius said a Jesuit should: as the strong stick supporting your feeble superior."

"Feeble?" Charles snorted with unapologetic laughter.

Le Picart smiled slightly. "Our founder's words, not mine."

"*Mon père*, am I to tell the *lieutenant-général* what you have asked me to do?"

"Yes. As I said before, I have told Père Pallu that you will not, after all, be assisting in his morning classes for now. Also, I caution you again not to neglect your duties to Père Jouvancy and the February performance, unless—God and His saints forbid—a dire emergency arises. Furthermore, hear me well—you will use violence to no one."

"No, *mon père*. Unless—"

"No 'unless.' You have taken first vows—which you have renewed—and you are a Jesuit, if only a scholastic. But you have also been a soldier. And what you did and saw and learned as a soldier are not far under your skin. That is very clear to me and is another reason you are suited for what I have asked you to do. But you belong to the Society of Jesus now, you are one of ours, not the army's. Use what you know, but use violence to no one."

"And if it is a question of life or death? Mine or someone's whom I must protect?"

"Our Savior told us to turn the other cheek."

"My own cheek is my own to turn. Allowing someone else to die seems to me another thing altogether."

Le Picart looked long at Charles, who felt as though the man were seeing through his flesh and bone to his soul.

"That will have to be between you and God," Le Picart said.

Chapter 14

Gilles Brion sat hugging himself at his cell's battered table. He wore a black cloak over the same brownish-black coat and breeches Charles had seen him in before, and his elegant linen was still crisp and white. A single candle lit the small chamber and a tall brazier had been brought in for heat, but it did little to dispel the cold of the ancient stone walls. Still, it showed that M. Callot had laid out more than a little money to the jailor. Brion had started up when the thick-planked, iron-bound door opened, but slumped again into his chair when he saw Charles.

"What do you want?" he said listlessly.

"To know whether you've killed anyone."

"Don't mock me."

"I am not, I assure you. Did you kill Mademoiselle Mynette? Did you kill your father?"

"What does it matter? I am a dead man, anyway."

Charles turned abruptly and pounded on the cell door. "Jailor, I am through here," he shouted through the open grille.

Behind him, the chair scraped on the stones and Brion cried, "No, wait, please!"

Praying for patience, Charles turned around.

"Wait for what?" If harshness was the only thing that could penetrate this idiot's posturing, then harshness he would have.

"I didn't kill either of them. I own I wanted sometimes to kill my father. But I didn't. And I would never have killed Mademoiselle Mynette. I swear by all the saints, by my hope of heaven!"

"But you went to her house before dawn on Friday morning. The morning she died."

Gilles gasped and clutched the back of the chair. "Isabel betrayed me! Dear God, women are of the devil! Their tongues forge the chains of hell, they—"

Charles turned back to the door and raised a fist to pound on it.

"Don't go!" Gilles clutched Charles's arm. "Women are weak, I know that, Isabel surely didn't mean—forgive me—"

Charles shook off Brion's hand. The young man was swaying where he stood, his face was colorless.

"Have they fed you?"

"I don't want anything."

Charles sighed. "At least sit down before you fall." He pushed Gilles into the chair and picked up the cloak, which had fallen to the floor. "You were seen," he said, draping the cloak back around Brion's shoulders. "You were seen leaving the side gate to the Mynette's garden Friday morning. Why did you go there, Monsieur Brion? And why so early?"

Gilles froze as booted feet walked past the door. As the sound faded, he groaned and shook his head hopelessly. "I went to ask her to help us both out of the coil my father had made. I knew she would be awake. She always woke early to dress and say the early prayers." Haltingly, he told Charles the same story Isabel Brion had already given him.

"And when Mademoiselle Mynette refused to help you, what did you do?"

"I left. I went back to the Capuchins for Prime and Mass."

"They can confirm that you were there?"

"Yes."

Sitting now with his back turned to Charles, Gilles took something from his pocket. It caught the candlelight in a small red flash, and in one stride, Charles was at the table and wrenching open Brion's hand. But the thing was a rosary with reddish beads, not a red enamel heart.

"Forgive me," Charles said, laying it carefully on the table. "I thought this was something else. I was mistaken."

Brion, cowering away from him, snatched up the rosary and began to pray.

"Monsieur Brion, you most certainly need God's help. But you also need mine. Please listen to me. Your sister says you stayed at the Capuchin monastery on Thursday night. Is that true?"

"Yes," Brion said resentfully, opening his eyes. He glanced at Charles and ducked his head over the rosary again. "In a—a guest cell. I often stay there."

Charles watched him thoughtfully for a moment. "So you stayed the night in the monastery. Praying. Solitary. Celibate. Just as a future monk should be. Admirable. And regrettable, since there is no one who can swear you never left your guest chamber on Thursday night and the early hours of Friday morning. No one can swear for you that you were at the Capuchins during the hours when your father must have died."

Brion, clutching the rosary so tightly that his knuckles were bone white, seemed to stop breathing.

Charles decided to risk everything on one throw. "It is not unknown," he said, as though to himself, "for young men to decide to enter religious life together. Two heartfast friends sometimes vow to enter the same monastery, to live there chaste, but in each other's company."

Brion stared at him as though ensorcelled, his eyes like black pits in his white face.

"Do you have such a friend, Monsieur Brion?"

A silent sob convulsed the young man's body. He shook his head.

"I think you do, *mon ami*," Charles said gently.

Brion leaned his head on his folded arms and wept. "Don't tell them, I beg you, don't tell them. We've done no wrong. We are chaste, *maître*, I swear it!" Then, to Charles's surprise, he made an effort to pull himself together and took a square of linen from his pocket. He mopped his face and pushed back his lank brown hair. "It is not just for him that I want to be a monk," he said softly, running his fingers over a roughly formed rose some prisoner before him had carved into the table's surface. "But I want to spend my life serving and praying where he is. Is that wrong?"

Charles hesitated. The church, the law, and the world harshly condemned that kind of love between men, even when it was chaste. Sodomites were rarely burned alive now, but they could be—even though the king's brother and more than a few courtiers were notorious for "the Italian vice," as it was called. A century ago Henri III, who had piously inscribed and laid the cornerstone for Louis le Grand's chapel, had confounded his ministers by appearing at state functions in jeweled gowns, with purple powder in his hair and beard.

Charles knew that he, too, should condemn this kind of love, especially now, when Brion was frightened and maybe vulnerable enough to renounce his friend. But Charles also knew what it was like to be torn, albeit by the more usual kind of love, and had no taste for condemning.

"I don't think love itself is wrong," he said, walking away from the table to the brazier.

Brion twisted in his chair and stared in astonishment.

"Not love that wants the beloved's good more than it wants

fulfillment of its own desires. Though what we choose to do about love is often enough wrong, God knows. And in your case, you would do well to remember the punishment the law can exact for the act of love between men."

Brion laughed harshly. "As though I could ever forget."

"Monsieur Brion, there is already strong evidence against you in the Mynette murder. Mademoiselle Mynette was killed early on Friday morning. And it seems that your father was killed very shortly after that. If you cannot—or will not—provide proof of where you were on Thursday night and Friday morning, before you went to the Mynette house, no one will be able to save you from the other charge."

"What does it matter? I will hang for the girl's murder, anyway. And I will not put . . . anyone else . . . in peril."

Charles shut his ears to his conscience and used the weapons he had. "It is *you* who are in peril! How hard do you want your death to be? The penalty for parricide is worse than the penalty for homicide. Too many people know that your father was trying to force you into marriage. And that his death clears your way to the monastery."

"But it doesn't! Great-Uncle Callot will still stop me if he can. He wants me to marry and be a notary. And the Capuchin novice master says they prefer the consent of families when they take a novice."

Charles wondered if perhaps the Capuchins were looking for a graceful way out of coping with Gilles Brion. "Your great-uncle cares more for your happiness than you imagine, Monsieur Brion. Why do you think you were not flung into the filth and danger of the common cell?"

Gilles frowned and glanced around the chamber. "He did this?"

"He did." Charles let that sink in. Then he said, "Monsieur

Brion, did you know of your father's scheme to smuggle silver in barrels of chocolate seeds?"

A surprised smile appeared fleetingly on Brion's thin face. "No, I didn't. My poor father; his schemes for making money never worked. Did one of his angry investors kill him, then? I've always thought that was how he would end."

They both started as someone shot the door's outer bolt and Lieutenant-Général La Reynie came in.

"Bonjour, messieurs." He inclined his head to Charles. Then, leaning on his silver-headed stick, he gazed for a long moment at Gilles Brion. "I came to give you a little more to think about, Monsieur Brion. In spite of the fears you have confided to Maître du Luc—yes, I have been listening at the grille—we have determined that your father was not killed by the investors he was last seen with. Which leaves us once again with you as our man for that murder."

With more dignity than Charles had yet seen in him, Brion rose from his chair and faced La Reynie. "There must be other investors."

"Perhaps. But I usually find that men are quicker to kill their loved ones than their debtors and creditors. Especially since murderers so often face breaking on the rack instead of merely hanging. And occasionally, of course, there's burning. If other circumstances demand it."

Charles and Brion both flinched. La Reynie smiled genially at them.

"If I may have a moment of your time, *maître?*" he said to Charles. He gestured toward the door and they went out, leaving Brion crouched over his rosary.

"Will you at least see that he is fed?" Charles said, as they walked away from the cell.

"A little fasting will loosen his tongue."

Charles regarded the *lieutenant-général* with distaste. "He did not kill his father. I am certain of it. And I don't think he killed the girl."

"Oh? Who had a better motive than he to kill both of them?"

"I wish I knew." Charles stopped in the small light of a lantern beside the worn stone stairs. "Brion truly wants to be a monk." *And when*, Charles's mind said cynically, *did you decide his vocation is real? Just now in that cell*, he told it. *So please shut up.* "Monsieur La Reynie, no one with a real religious vocation would kill to get it."

"I agree that the sin of murder to gain monastic life would twist that life out of all rightness. But this Gilles Brion does not strike me as a humbly judging intellect. He strikes me as a weak young man floundering in tempests of emotion."

Lips pressed together to keep what he wanted to say behind his teeth, Charles hitched his cassock skirts impatiently out of the way and started down the stairs.

"That was well done to remind him of the penalty for sodomy," La Reynie said behind him.

"You cannot prosecute him for sodomy," Charles said curtly. "You have no evidence."

"No. I haven't. But threats about one thing have been known to elicit what I want to know about other things."

A wave of anger and disgust rose in Charles. Especially since he'd just done virtually the same thing in his talk with Gilles. "How you can bear your job, I cannot fathom." He turned abruptly toward where he thought the street door might be, suddenly unwilling to ask the way, or anything else, of La Reynie.

"Oh, I think you can fathom it." The ancient stone vaulting enlarged La Reynie's voice so that it seemed to come from everywhere at once. "There is little to choose between us. You and your brother Jesuits are accused every day of twisting questionable means to reach admirable ends. Come to my office. I have other things to tell you."

"No, thank you." Charles kept walking.

"Going back on your vow of obedience, are you?"

Charles stopped, but didn't turn around. "What does that mean?"

"Your rector told you to keep track of my inquiry into these deaths. So come to my office and keep track. Or are you simply another weak young man floundering in tempests of emotion?"

Speechless with fury, Charles turned slowly. He fixed the *lieutenant-général* with an unblinking stare, and then his eyes dropped to the sword at La Reynie's side.

"I could take it off, you know," the *lieutenant-général* said earnestly. "Then it would be just hand-to-hand combat. Will that do for a young man floundering—"

Charles's swelling anger deflated as suddenly as a punctured bladder in a boys' ball game. ". . . floundering in a tempest of emotion," he finished, with a snort of rueful laughter. "No, it won't do. Shall we go to your office?"

La Reynie made him a mock bow. "I am relieved that we're not dueling, because I have quite a lot to do today. And also because you are younger and would probably win."

"I would most certainly win."

Smiling, La Reynie led him into an office that proclaimed his exalted place in the realm. Wool hangings of the weaving called *moquette*, patterned in red and blue and yellow, softened the stone walls. A portrait of the king hung behind the wide walnut desk. A fire burned in a wide, stone-hooded fireplace, and a dark blue-and-yellow carpet with medallions representing Fame and Fortitude lay in front of it. The armchairs on either side of the fireplace were upholstered in garnet leather tacked with gilt nails and fringed in gold. La Reynie gestured Charles to one of the armchairs, spread his coat's thick skirts, and seated himself in the other one. He poured wine from a pewter pitcher standing on the table and held out a glass to Charles.

"I have first to thank you for the information about the silver smuggling. There was a report about it here when I returned, but it was useful to have it sooner. Monsieur Bizeul and a jeweler called Robert Cantel walked Brion out of the coffeehouse. Bizeul denies any part in either Brion's smuggling or death. I have not yet talked to Cantel for the good reason that I cannot find him."

"He's fled? Then there's your man! You can——"

"I know only that the man has disappeared. For all I know, he, too, is dead. Never fear, I am searching diligently for him. And looking closely into the financial affairs of both Bizeul and Cantel. I am nearly sure that Bizeul is involved in the smuggling. Which means that Cantel probably is, too. About Monsieur Brion, Bizeul says that he left Procope's with him and Cantel on Thursday night, all friends together, and stopped in a tavern. Then they apparently went on to Bizeul's house, because an *oublieur* finishing his rounds saw Brion and Cantel—who lives only a few streets from Bizeul—leave Bizeul's house together." *Oublieurs* were evening street vendors who sold their delicate pastry wafers, called *oublies*, for after-dinner treats at houses hosting parties. "The *oublieur* said they were arguing, but he couldn't say whether Brion went with Cantel willingly or not. Interestingly, I found a little room off Cantel's courtyard in which there was a pile of straw, blankets, half a loaf of bread, a pewter cup, and a length of rope, cut through. Madame Cantel says that she had a drunk, unruly servant put there overnight. I think that Monsieur Cantel put an unruly notary there. And meant to leave him there until Brion covered his and Bizeul's losses. I think a servant took a bribe and let him escape, probably shortly before he was killed. When we undressed him here at the Châtelet, there was straw under his cloak, on his coat. I think he was on his way home—your Monsieur Morel said that those streets were a back way to the Brion house."

Charles stared at La Reynie. "You've talked to one of the men who seem to be the last who saw Brion alive. You know that they abducted and imprisoned him. You know that the second man has fled! So why in the name of all hell's devils have you arrested Gilles Brion for that murder?"

"I don't think those two men killed Brion. Oh, I have not stopped making absolutely sure of that. But I think that they abducted him because they were furious over the failure of his smuggling scheme and the money they lost. I imagine that they thought they could force him to pay them some part of it. Which is a very good reason to think they didn't kill him. Dead, he would be able to pay them nothing. And I cannot see why they would follow and kill him after he escaped. He certainly would not have come to the police over his imprisonment; he was in far too much trouble himself. I agree that, of the two, Cantel has made himself far more suspect by disappearing. When I find him, he will find himself housed here until he explains himself to my satisfaction. But, again, why kill the man from whom you hope to get a large sum of money? So, until I know more, I am left with your devout friend upstairs."

"If Gilles Brion wanted to kill his father, why would he do it at that noisome ditch where his father was found? How could he know his father would be there? Why would *he* be there?"

"I have no idea."

"But you think he did it."

"On the whole, no."

Charles breathed slowly in and out, metaphorically clutching his temper with both hands. "Good. At least we agree about that. So what are you playing at?"

La Reynie rose from his chair, shaking his head in exasperation, and picked up the iron poker to stir the fire. "I am trying to shake loose from someone—him—anyone—what I need to know. Young Brion does not seem to me to have the stomach for killing either his father or the girl. But he is the only one we have clear evidence against, and I have to know for certain. The evidence against him in the girl's murder is damning enough. If he killed either of them, though, I would say he'd be more likely to kill his father. Sons so often seem to be, don't they, whether they really do or not." His voice was suddenly bleak and his shoulders rose and fell in a soundless sigh. "But I agree with you that both time and place speak against his guilt where his father is concerned. I heard what he told you about where he was on Thursday night and early Friday—before he went to the Mynette house—and I heard the conclusion you drew from what he said." He glanced over his shoulder at Charles. "This may shock you, *maître*, but if Gilles Brion did not kill his father—or the girl—I don't care what else he was doing, whether he was with his '*beau ami*' or the village goat or weeping the night through by himself in prayer. Though if you quote me, I will deny having said so."

"Paris doesn't have a village goat," Charles said mildly.

La Reynie turned and stared at him.

"Now that we've shocked each other, what are you going to do to find out who really killed Martine Mynette and Henri Brion so you can let Gilles go?"

"I wish I knew."

"I see. Well, you won't be glad to know that I have leave from Père Le Picart to give you another problem to solve. Louis le Grand was attacked on Friday night."

"What?"

"Yes, I thought perhaps you didn't know. Which in itself is interesting. Three men broke several of our windows on the rue St. Jacques and scrawled the word *murderers* on our doors. Père Le Picart assumed that the University was behind it, since they take any opportunity to stir up anti-Jesuit feeling. But he told me the next day that he talked privately with the University's rector—"

"And made a few threats of his own, I imagine," La Reynie said appreciatively. And added less appreciatively, "Instead of informing the police."

"As you say. He now thinks that it was not the University's doing. Some students returning from a tavern to a University house watched the fun and broke our door down, but it seems their presence was pure chance. I think the attackers were tavern drunks, maybe from the Place Maubert, where I first heard the song accusing us of conniving at Mademoiselle Mynette's death. Though, when I caught one man and talked to him, he wasn't very drunk. And he wasn't afraid, even when I threatened him with the police. At least, he wasn't as afraid as he should have been. He was just angry."

"Perhaps he was only exceptionally stupid."

"Perhaps. But news of the incident has been oddly slow to come to your ears. I imagine that the University rector has muzzled the students who saw it happen. But why wouldn't the men involved trumpet their exploit all over the *quartier*? Their *confrères* certainly wouldn't turn them in."

"Perhaps they did trumpet it, just not to me. If the man you caught wasn't just a tavern drunk, who do you think he was?"

"He was dressed like an ordinary workman and talked like one. But—" Charles threw up his hands. "I don't know. I suppose I'm seeing enemies everywhere. Perhaps he was a plotting

Jansenist. Or a Gallican." Charles grinned wryly. "Or a Jansenist Gallican."

"Or perhaps he was a Gallican Jansenist," La Reynie said, straight-faced. Jansenists, anti-Jesuit followers of a Dutchman called Jansenius, often seemed more straightlaced than Protestants. Gallicans were politicians who wanted no papal meddling in French government and sometimes allied themselves with Jansenists, since Jansenists were critical of the papacy. "I think, however, that we can leave France's political circles out of this, *maître*," La Reynie added.

"The hatred some people have for us frightens me, I admit. But, in spite of my fears, I have been given an order that directly affects you, Monsieur La Reynie." Briefly, Charles explained what the rector had asked him to do.

La Reynie listened without comment. "Unfortunately," he said, when Charles finished, "your rector is correct. I can use you. I have nothing like enough men to police Paris." He eyed Charles. "And I do recall telling you once that if you tired of your Jesuit vocation, I could find a place for you."

"You did." Charles returned his look unwaveringly. "But as I told you then, I am Père Le Picart's man, not yours."

La Reynie inclined his head with elaborate courtesy. "And I tell you now that if you break the law in the course of what you have been ordered to do, I will not protect you from the consequences. *Entendu?*"

"Understood."

The air between them crackled again with challenge, as it had in the corridor.

La Reynie glanced at the black-and-gold clock standing on a table against the wall. "Two things before we go our ways. First, I will see that the night watch pays more attention to Louis le Grand. Second, I have learned that your song is probably printed more or less under your nose. One of the vendors told me—after a little persuasion—that a stack of copies appears before dawn every day on the porch of St. Julien le Pauvre. Who puts them there, he doesn't know. Probably some street child, and never the same one twice. The child probably picks them up late at night from a Left Bank printer and leaves them on the church porch. I will have someone watch through the night, but all that will happen is that the child will see the watcher and the copies will turn up in some other place." The *lieutenant-général* rose to his feet and settled his coat skirts.

Charles rose, too, ready to take his leave. Instead, before he knew he was going to say it, he asked, "Who is Reine?"

La Reynie busied himself with pulling his wrist lace to hang straight below the wide cuffs of his coat. "She is Renée's mother, among many other things."

"I wondered," Charles said. "Green eyes like theirs are not common."

"Sometimes Reine is a *revendeuse*. But she cannot walk as far now, and old clothes are heavy to carry." Paris was full of *revendeuses*, women who sold secondhand clothes, the lucky ones in small shops, the others as street vendors. "Most of the time now, she simply begs." The *lieutenant-général* picked up his stick and faced Charles, who was also on his feet. His eyes were as cold as black ice. "Hear me well. Never, for any reason—*never*, do you understand?—cause harm to Reine." With a punctilious bow, and without another word, La Reynie walked out of the office.

Shaken, Charles found his way out into the cold air, which seemed a benison after the Châtelet's grimness and La Reynie's. The sky had cleared enough for the early sunset to splash streaks of orange down the western sky, and instead of taking the near way across the Pont au Change, Charles turned toward the sunset and set off along the Quay de la Megisserie, toward the Pont

Neuf. The bells began to ring for Vespers. As a scholastic, he wasn't yet required to say the daily office, but he knew most of it by heart and silently began the prayers.

"Oh, God, come to my assistance. Oh, Lord, make haste to help me . . ." Walking slowly, he reached the final "amen" with a deep sense of recovered peace, which shattered when he stepped on fresh, bloody cow guts and nearly slid into the Seine. Cawing laughter rang out behind him.

"Eh, Jean, did you see that? Praying and nearly drowned himself! Priests. Pah! Surprised they let the soft-wits out on their own."

Butchers working till the last light, Charles thought resignedly. He was glad—for once—of the cold, since it kept down the smell of the blood and entrails not yet disposed of in the river. Leaving the butcher stalls behind, Charles hurried toward the clatter of the Samaritaine pump. Working day and night in its little Dutch pump house at the Right Bank end of the Pont Neuf, it drew fresh drinking water from the river for the city. The color was nearly faded from the sky, and the lantern hanging on the elaborately gabled pump house was already lit. As he turned onto the bridge, a swarm of begging children appeared from nowhere and surrounded him, their small hands fluttering like birds as they patted his cloak, feeling for pockets or purse. Stricken that he had nothing to give them, he showed his empty hands and signed a cross over them.

"Come to the college of Louis le Grand on Friday," he said, pointing across the river. "We will give you food and clothes."

Their hands dropped and they stared at him with old eyes. Today was only Monday. One of them picked up a clod of frozen street filth and flung it at him, barely missing his face, and the whole flock ran back the way they'd come. Charles called out to them and then wrenched his cloak loose from his shoulders and ran after them.

"Here, take this, you can sell it, you can—"

But they were gone, expert, like all their kind, at vanishing. Charles slung his cloak around his shoulders, thinking how cold he'd grown without it even for a few moments, and how cold the children must be. *Why?* he demanded silently of God as he walked. *This is Christendom. Our Catholic church is supposed to be reformed now—at least the Protestants have done us that much good, making us look at ourselves. So why do we let children live in the streets?* The growing evening quiet of the street remained only quiet.

Most of the vendors in the small roofed stalls along the Pont Neuf were packing up their wares, but a few were still doing business by lantern light. At the weaponer's, three swaggering, posturing men were trying out swords. Charles barely jumped aside in time to avoid a stumbling experimental thrust, as two of them sparred, laughing.

"Your opponent could have killed you while you were spitting me by mistake," Charles said laconically to the man who'd nearly skewered him. "Keep track of where your real enemy is, or you'll be too dead to laugh."

The man's eyes narrowed and he moved toward Charles, but his companions roared with laughter and held him back.

At the end of the bridge, Charles headed for the Fossés St. Germain, thinking to go back to Louis le Grand along the old walls' embankment. Harsh voices behind him made him look over his shoulder and lengthen his stride. The men who'd been trying the swords were closing on him, not with any intent, it seemed, just arguing loudly about the virtues of Spanish steel. To escape their noise, he turned down a short street called Contrescarpe. To his relief, the men stopped, shouting into each other's faces, and he left them behind.

A coach turned into Contrescarpe at the street's other end, and he looked for a doorway to shelter in while it passed. But before the coach reached him, it turned right, through an archway, and disappeared. When Charles came to the archway, he saw that it led to an inn whose sign announced it as Le Cheval Blanc. The man begging at the arch held out a hand, and once again Charles had to say he had no coins to give. The White Horse was a rambling stone-built inn with three long-distance coaches standing in its busy yard. A group of beggars moved through the crowd of travelers as grooms changed the teams of horses. Bedraggled passengers clambered out of the newly arrived coach and new passengers boarded the other two. Long-distance coaches were more common now, though Charles himself had never used one. But he knew something from his soldiering days about the state of France's winter roads, and he pitied the boarding passengers.

As he walked on, another coach turned into Contrescarpe and lumbered toward the inn. Charles scrambled for a door to press his back against. By the time the coach had passed him and rumbled into the innyard, he realized that the door he was leaning against led to a tavern and that inside, people were happily shouting, *"Tu es riche? Tu es mort . . ."* The street was slowly filling with early-winter dusk, and a frisson of fear ran down his spine. He walked quickly away, just as the tavern door burst open behind him. Forcing himself not to run, Charles held to his brisk walk, tilting his wide hat slightly and hitching his cassock up a little under his cloak to make him harder to identify from the back as a cleric.

For a dozen steps, he thought he was going to get away with it. Then someone yelled, "There he is, take him!" and feet pounded over the cobbles. Hands grabbed his cloak. He pulled its ties loose, left it to the grabbing hands, and ran. The street was filling with darkness and shouts of "vultures, deathbirds, killers!" A lumbering man with a massive belly came at him from the side and he dodged. But he tripped over uneven cobbles, went down, and someone else jumped on his back. Charles's body, firmly convinced that alive and doing penance was preferable to dead and virtuous, took over. Flinging up an arm to block a kick to his head, he twisted half onto his side and smashed a fist into the face of the man who'd leaped on him. He scrambled to a crouch and set his back against a house wall. People were running toward him from the innyard, and the street was filling with people fighting each other. As Charles reached to arm himself with a loose cobble, someone swung a piece of wood at him. He ducked, kicking like a madman, and the attacker fell backward. Charles grabbed the piece of wood, swung it in a circle, and got his back against the wall again. A grinning man came at him from the side. Charles swung and the man went down, but the piece of wood hit the house wall, sending a numbing shock up his arms. Two women wrenched it away from him, shrieking with laughter, but other people grabbed them and pulled them back. Then light from the open tavern door glinted on steel and in the instant before the man with the knife lunged, Charles dropped to the ground, swung both legs from the hip, and scythed the man's feet from under him. A deep voice thundered curses, someone swung a club at the man with the knife, and he lay still on the cobbles.

"Get up," a pile of rags hissed at Charles. Past questions, he took the hand offered and stumbled to his feet. The pile of rags, also pulling someone along on its other side, hurried him to the end of the street and around the corner into a dark courtyard.

"Stay here!" the rags ordered the other person it had dragged to the courtyard, and turned to Charles. "Are you hurt?"

"No." After nearly being stabbed, bruises hardly counted.

"They wanted to kill you."

"Yes." Charles finally recognized the voice. "It's Reine, isn't it?"

"It is."

"How—where did you come from? And the others?"

She jerked her head at the man beside her, whom Charles could see only dimly in the near dark. "We were begging at the inn. I saw you pass." She paused and listened, her head on one side. "It's quieting down, the others will be coming. We have to be away from here. The man who came at you with the knife won't be getting up again and—"

The half-seen man beside her banged his heavy walking stick on the ground and roared, "By holy Saint Michel, he won't, the rotting son of a pig!"

It was the deep voice that had cursed so well in the street, and Charles recognized it now as the voice of the reliquary's attacker and the almsgiving coat snatcher.

"—and because of that, we must be away before the *guet* comes," Reine was saying fiercely. The *guet* was the nighttime police patrol.

A half dozen more beggars had drifted into the yard. Among them Charles spotted the old man's young keeper, who hurried to his charge's side. Reine started to lead them all away.

"Wait," Charles said. "You've saved my life. Come to the college and I will feed you, all of you, it's the least I can do."

No one spoke or moved. The old man roared out, "Mary's holy milk, of course we'll go! And if it's a trick, we'll kill him."

Chapter 15

"They can't come in here." Frère Tricot, the usually genial head cook in the lay brothers' kitchen, was blocking the kitchen doorway with his bulk. Firelight danced across the tonsure age had given him as he shook his head at the beggars. "They're verminous, see them scratching, even in the cold? You know how hard we work to keep the fleas down. Not to say the lice."

"*Bonsoir*, Guillaume." Reine moved into the light spilling from the doorway and stood beside Charles.

Tricot caught his breath and crossed himself. "Blessed Virgin," he whispered. "I thought you were dead."

"I've thought so myself, more than once. But never with you." Her smile widened.

The brother scowled, scarlet-faced, and pursed his lips. "Wait there. Stand away from the door. You." He pointed at Charles. "Come and help me."

Keeping his questions behind his teeth, Charles followed him into the kitchen. A thick soup simmered in a three-legged iron cauldron standing in the fireplace. A few tallow candles burning in wall sconces showed strings of onions and braids of garlic hanging from the ceiling beams. Muttering unhappily under his breath, Tricot handed Charles a knife and a basket and nodded toward the loaves on a table in the center of the room.

"Cut bread," he said curtly. "Two pieces for each one. I suppose you've counted them?"

Charles pulled several loaves toward him, mentally making the nine beggars waiting in the courtyard into eighteen and wondering if he could cut forty thick slices before Tricot caught him. Tricot banged a wire-handled copper pot down in front of the fireplace and ladled soup into it. Lentil, from the smell, Charles thought, and with bacon in it. Keeping himself between the lay brother and the bread, he shoved an uncut loaf into the bottom of the basket and covered it with a mound of cut slices.

"Here, then." Tricot held out the wire-handled pot. Two large spoons stood in it. "How am I supposed to account for all this food?"

"As a corporal act of mercy?"

Tricot grunted.

"Thank you, *mon frère*. If there are questions, I will take responsibility."

Charles took the pot, staggering a little at the weight, and led his flock of beggars past the well and through an archway into the tiny stable court. As he'd hoped, the lantern-lit stable was empty, except for the college's three horses.

He set the pot down and pulled the double doors closed. The beggars gathered eagerly around the pot. Reine surveyed the stable and then sat gracefully on a bale of straw. The old man sank down beside her and leaned back against the wooden wall. The thin, dark young man—boy, he almost seemed—who was his keeper saw him settled and then sat at his feet with his knees drawn up. The young man's eyes were shadowed and he was coughing harshly. Charles handed Reine the spoons, put the basket of bread beside the pot, and stepped back, wishing he had left the doors a little open to cut the beggars' fetid smell. A flurry of hands reached for the bread.

Reine looked at Charles. "A blessing?"

The hands stilled and Charles prayed. Reine gave a spoon to the old man's keeper at her feet and tossed the other to a young woman on the other side of the pot. Everyone fell on the food. Charles had expected them to be loud and rude, to grab for everything they could reach. But they ate in near silence, passing the spoon carefully from one to another, scooping the lentil and bacon soup from the pot without spilling a drop. When a boy of twelve or thirteen kept the spoon too long, a man cuffed him lightly, plucked it out of his hands, and offered it to the boy's neighbor. The beggars were indescribably filthy, and in the lantern light, Charles saw that many had some deformity. A young man had a twisted foot and there was a woman with a grossly swollen neck. A blind woman was so marked by smallpox that she seemed to have a webbed veil of white over her face and hands. A man who looked to be in his forties had what Charles thought was a withered cheek, but then saw it was a *fleur de lys*, the cruel identifying mark burned into the flesh of thieves.

When the soup was gone, the beggars clustered over the pot and wiped it nearly dry with hunks of the coarse brown bread.

The young man sitting with the old man leaned his head on Reine's knees and slowly ate the last of his bread. She leaned down and pulled his coat more tightly closed as a new fit of coughing took him. The old man absently stroked the young man's head. But the youth kept coughing, and Reine pulled a length of worn tawny velvet from her neck and wrapped it around his shoulders. He gave her a smile of such sweetness that Charles smiled as he watched. Reine looked at the old man half dozing beside her.

"Marin, will you eat more? There is more bread."

"Eh? Me, I will always eat more! Where is it?"

A young girl with greasy black braids wrapped around her

head brought him the basket. He took the last piece of bread, showing his few blackened teeth in a wide grin, and began chewing carefully. Reine looked up at Charles. Her eyes were like green flares in the dimness.

"Well?" she said challengingly. "Now you know my name and his."

Unsure what his response should be, Charles bowed. "Thank you." And added almost involuntarily, *"madame."*

Her eyebrows lifted. "Very pretty. But at my court, young man, the courteous thing is to give us your name in return. I have heard your name, but the rest of us have not."

"Gladly. I am Maître Charles Matthieu Beuvron du Luc." He bowed to the others. *"Mesdames et messieurs."*

They stared at him open-mouthed. No one bowed to beggars. Or addressed them with titles of courtesy. The girl with the braids stood up again and curtsied.

"I am Belle," she said gravely.

The man with the brand said, "I am Richard."

Then they were all speaking. "I am Matthieu—the same as you!" "I am Thérèse." "I am Alain." "I am Edouard, and the skinny one there who keeps Marin out of trouble is Jean." "I am Pasquier." "I am Raymond."

"Thank you," Charles said. "You saved my life tonight and I am deeply in your debt. But I cannot help asking why you risked yourselves for a stranger."

Richard stood up, moved a little aside, then cleared his throat and spat. "You gave Marin the new coat," he said. "And I saw those bastards standing at the corner when you turned down the street toward the tavern. I was at the innyard gate while we begged, it was my turn to keep an eye out for the archers." He narrowed his eyes and studied Charles. "You know about the archers?"

Charles said uncertainly, "From the Hôtel de Ville?"

"Yes." Richard spat again. "Them. They're not good for much except rounding us up and throwing us into the Hôtel Dieu or the Hôpital Général. You're let out after a while, but if they take you a second time, the men go to the galleys and the women are exiled from Paris. It's a terrible crime to be poor."

"It's not!" The blind woman turned her face toward Richard's voice. "If needing to eat's a crime, then Adam and Eve were criminals as much as us!"

"We know for sure Eve was," a man called out, laughing.

"Shut your mouth, Alain," the blind woman said. "If she was hungry as me most of the time, she'd eat a sour quince and not care who gave it to her."

"Well, your belly's full now," Richard said placatingly. "The thing is, *maître*, we knew those three bastards in the street. And when the fight started, we thought you'd need help." He scratched his ribs. "Though now I come to think of it, they faded away from the fight fast enough. So maybe they weren't following you. Anyway, you did need help."

"Indeed I did. And—which bastards do you mean exactly?"

Richard grinned appreciatively. "But yes, one must always be specific, there are so many bastards. We don't know their names." He looked at Marin, who was still chewing the last piece of bread. "They're archers from the Hôtel de Ville, all three of them. They took old Marin in the autumn. To kill him, but Marin got away."

Charles looked in surprise at the old man. "Why would anyone want to kill Marin?"

Richard grunted sardonically. "Remember when King Louis had the problem with his ass? The doctors were scared to cut on him. I mean, wouldn't you be? Think you'd be living long, if your cutting didn't work? So they wanted to practice. The archers started rounding up men and asking them if they had the same problem as the king. No women, just men. Sent them to Versailles and locked them up and the king's doctor tried out the surgery on them, one by one. A lot died and, when they did, they got dropped out a window, early in the morning, and taken away in a cart."

Horrified, Charles looked at Marin, who seemed not to be paying any attention to the story. "He told you this?"

"He did. Our Marin's old, and his ass hurts and his wits wander, but he's no fool. He got away before they cut him. Hid in the woods and walked all the way back to Paris."

Charles was speechless, thinking of the college's approaching celebration for the king's return to health. Pulling himself back to the need to preserve his own health, he said, "Were the three archers actually fighting outside the tavern?"

"They came down the street behind you, slow like, and they were in the beginning of it; that's why we came out after them. But then they disappeared and it was just the ones from of the tavern."

"Again, I am in your debt."

Old Marin grunted in satisfaction at Charles's words. Then he planted his stick and climbed slowly to his feet. "We thank you for our supper, *maître*."

His keeper, Jean, jumped up to help him and the others got up, too. On his way to the door, Marin stopped in front of Charles. He reached up and touched Charles's thickly curling blond hair.

"Almost like my Claire's," he murmured. "Kind, too, like her." He limped out into the courtyard, muttering to himself.

Jean wound Reine's velvet rag around his throat and smiled at her. "Don't worry," he said hoarsely, "I'll see to him." He followed the old man out.

The rest filed out, too, and Charles looked questioningly at Reine, who hadn't moved from her bale of straw.

"One more little moment of your time, if you please, *maître.*"

Charles nodded. "Certainly, but first I must bar the gate after them."

He let the beggars out into the lane behind the college, re-barred the gate, and went back to the stable, wondering why Reine had stayed and how he was going to explain her presence if anyone discovered her.

"*Madame?*" he said to Reine as he pulled the stable doors closed again.

She looked up from the piece of wood she had taken from somewhere in her garments and was busily carving. "How pleasant to be addressed so."

"It is obviously your right."

She put her head back and laughed until the stable seemed filled with bells. "You are a most courteous young *chevalier,*" she said, wiping her eyes. "And a most innocent one."

"Innocent?"

Her eyes warmed disconcertingly in their net of lines and her mouth curved in the most sensual smile Charles had ever seen. "The things I could tell you—but don't worry, I won't. Tell me, are you any nearer to finding Martine Mynette's killer?"

"Why ask me? I am not the police."

She bent over her carving again. "You came with Nicolas to The Procope. I saw that he trusts you."

Charles raised a skeptical eyebrow. Le Picart had said the same thing. But his own impression was that La Reynie trusted no one but himself. "Monsieur La Reynie has arrested Gilles Brion, Henri Brion's son, for both murders."

Reine made a dismissive sound. "That is unworthy of Nicolas."

"You don't think Monsieur Brion guilty?"

She held her piece of wood a little away and studied it in silence. A squarish shape was emerging, but Charles couldn't tell what it was meant to be.

Impatient with her silence, he said, "Did your daughter tell you that Mademoiselle Mynette's necklace was missing when she and Mademoiselle Brion undressed and washed the body? It was a little red enamel heart on an embroidered ribbon, not valuable, but I'm told that she always wore it. Now it's gone."

Reine gave him a narrow-eyed look. "Are you saying my daughter took it?"

"Did she?"

The old woman shrugged ruefully, rubbing the carving with her thumb. "Who knows, *maître*? Renée is weak." Taking the knife to the wood again, she said, "Renée told you a little about the servants who left the Mynette household. But she told you too little about Paul Saglio. The one who made indecent advances to Martine not long before her mother died. I was there when Martine turned him out, and I tell you, the man was savage with fury! Thank the Blessed Virgin he went, because he's dangerous. What Martine did not know is that Paul Saglio—Paolo as he was then—killed a man in Italy before he came to France."

"How do you know that?"

"His brother visited him one day when I was visiting Renée. I heard them talking." She smiled. "It's very easy to listen to people. Who pays attention to an old bundle of rags and the old woman dozing inside the bundle? So I heard everything. The two of them together had robbed a man on the road. He'd tried to fight back, and Saglio killed him. Knifed him. Find Paul Saglio, *maître*."

"Why did you not warn Mademoiselle Mynette about him?"

Reine shrugged in a wave of shifting colors. "Why would Mademoiselle Mynette listen to someone like me? I charged my daughter to tell her. But Renée was much taken with Saglio, and

I doubt she did. She was sure he had long repented, and she wouldn't hear a word against him. She only grew spiteful toward him when she saw that he preferred Martine."

"Is Saglio in Vaugirard? Was Renée telling the truth about that?"

"Oh, yes," Reine said dryly. "He has not come to see her, and she is very angry. Vaugirard is a small place, you should have no trouble finding him." She tucked the carving and the knife away under her skirts and pushed herself up from the straw bale. Her eyes slid sideways to Charles. "If, of course, he has not come back to Paris for his own reasons."

"What do you mean?"

"Nothing certain. I already told you he is handy with a knife."

"As are you, Reine," Charles said, on impulse. And watched her closely, waiting to see what she would say.

"Handier than you know. But it was not a bundle of rags that came at you in the street, was it?"

"No. Forgive me."

"*Maître*, a man tried to knife you tonight. You, who are looking for Martine Mynette's killer."

Taken aback, Charles stared at her, trying to tell if she was talking for her own reasons or giving him something he needed to know. "Do you mean that it was Saglio with the knife? I assumed the man tried to kill me only because I am a Jesuit."

She shrugged. "Perhaps. But the man was thin and agile like Paul Saglio. Even if you did not see him clearly, I did. And now I must go, *maître*."

Still unsure what to think, Charles went to the stable door and listened for a moment. He heard nothing outside, but before he opened the door, he said, "Tell me about Marin."

Reine's green eyes opened wide in surprise. Turning away, she went to the gray mare's stall and began to stroke the velvet nose.

"My poor Marin," she said softly. "Are you asking because of what he did on Christmas Eve?"

"Partly that."

"Marin is sometimes as sane as anyone, sometimes insane with rage and sorrow."

Charles hazarded, "Was he a soldier? Is that why he hates the old Condé?"

"No. He hates him because of how the man treated his wife, Claire Clemence, the Princess of Condé. Marin was a servant in her household." From somewhere in her layers of clothing, Reine took out a small piece of bread and fed it to the mare. "Claire Clemence lived mostly alone in Paris." She turned to face Charles. "The Condé despised her from the first, though the poor girl did everything she could for him. She brought him money when they married; she raised more money and saved him at least once during the Fronde wars; she gave him children, including a son. But he rarely acknowledged her existence, God rot him. And why? Because he had wanted to marry elsewhere, but his father—and Richelieu, who was Claire Clemence's uncle—forced her on him. No one said 'no' to Richelieu." Reine smiled bitterly. "It is too long a story for now, and you are wondering what it can be to me. That much I will tell you. Claire Clemence was only twelve years old when she married. Tiny as a dwarf but not one—she was very prettily shaped—and blond." She smiled a little. "As blond as you, that's what Marin meant just now when he touched your hair. He was fourteen, two years older than she, and he fell in love with her, beyond reason and deeper than the sea. He is in love with her yet. And I, great fool that I am, fell in love with Marin many years ago. Also beyond reason and deeper than the sea."

"How did you know him?"

"Blessed Sainte Marie Madeleine," she said impatiently, "are you truly that innocent?" Twitching her rags off the floor as though they were satin skirts, she gave the mare a last pat and crossed the stable floor to stand in front of him. "I was a whore, my handsome young cleric. When I was young, I was a very expensive whore."

Charles surprised both of them by replying with equal boldness. "I do not doubt for a moment that you were very expensive."

"Ah," she said with a pleased nod, "perhaps you are not so innocent after all. Good."

"I was a soldier, *madame*, before I was a Jesuit. There are no innocent soldiers. Is that how Monsieur La Reynie knows you? From your former life?"

Reine laughed softly. "Yes and no. That particular story is not mine to tell. If he wants to tell you, he will." She put a hand on Charles's arm. "Listen to me, *maître*. I think you do not know this, and Nicolas will never say it. He needs you. Remember that."

"You do me too much honor, *madame*. I came to Procope's café only because my rector ordered me to follow his inquiry on the college's behalf. I am sure you have heard the rumors about why these murders—Mademoiselle Mynette's and Henri Brion's—concern us."

Reine withdrew her hand. "Do you know that he is sixty-one years old?" she said, with seeming inconsequence. "We are the same age, Nicolas and I."

"He seems younger than that. As do you," he added courteously. *As do your eyes*, he really meant.

They both looked toward the stable doors as voices rose nearby and faded.

"I will go now," Reine said. "Can you let me out unseen?"

Charles opened the doors enough to look out. To his relief the little court was empty, and they went quickly to the gate.

"Are you going to——" Charles hesitated, not sure what to call the troupe of beggars. "To Marin?"

"Of course."

"Do you have enough for the night?"

"Enough."

Charles was suddenly reluctant to have her go. "The beggars seem to look to you as a mother."

She gave him a pleased glance, slipped into the lane, and walked briskly toward the small street that ran from the rue St. Jacques past the old college of Les Cholets. As Charles replaced the bar, making sure it was strongly set, her voice floated back to him.

"Even God needed a mother, *mon cher.*"

Chapter 16

The afternoon sunlight poured through the *salle des actes'* long row of south-facing windows, picking out the silver buttons on composer Marc-Antoine Charpentier's cloud-gray coat and gilding his wig's dark curls. It also plainly showed the growing panic on M. Germain Morel's face, as he and Charpentier and Charles stood together over the score. After today, they probably would not see much of Charpentier for several weeks, since he would be rehearsing the singers in the college calefactory, the warming room where there was always a fire. Looking at the composer, Charles was glad he would be warm. Charpentier, so Charles had heard, had never quite recovered from an illness several years ago, and his aquiline nose stood out like a hawk's beak from his thin face and hollow cheeks.

Morel had come well through Père Jouvancy's questioning at the beginning of the rehearsal, and Jouvancy had hired him on the spot as the new dancing master. But now, with Charpentier racing through the *tragédie lyrique*'s score, his dark eyes glowing as he sang and hummed dance music, Morel was clearly having second thoughts. He looked sideways at Charles in silent appeal. Not that the lyrical tragedy had many dances. Even half somnolent in the flood of sunshine, Charles was realizing that the piece was, in fact, a true opera, and that the singers would work far harder than the dancers. Charles decided to perjure himself a little for the sake of art and the new dancing master's sanity. He smiled apologetically at the composer and gathered his forces to make himself heard over the noise Jouvancy and his actors were making on the stage at the far end of the room.

"I beg your pardon, Monsieur Charpentier," Charles said. "But could you possibly help my confusion by going a little slower? I confess I am no musician."

Behind him, a student—Montmorency, he thought—sniggered audibly.

Charpentier looked at Charles in surprise. "Slower? Of course, *maître*, forgive me!"

To his credit, he really did slow down. Morel's shoulders dropped to where his tailor had meant them to be and he started breathing again. Charpentier had composed new dance music, and Morel would create new dances to go with it. A dance and its music were one entity and usually inseparable. Morel would then learn the music so that he could play the dances on his pocket violin at rehearsals. Charles's role was to be the overall dance director, matching dancers and dances, choosing costumes, and generally supervising the dance part of the production. As time went on, he would probably also direct some rehearsals himself to reduce the cost of the dancing master's hire. All of the above would, of course, be subject to Jouvancy's approval, since he was not only director of the spoken tragedy but overall director of the whole performance. Then beginning in February, the singers would move to the *salle des actes*, where everyone would rehearse and shiver together.

"There!" Charpentier handed Morel copies of the dance music. "A simple score, as you see. We will do excellently well together." The composer smiled benignly at the dancing master and Charles. "Now I must go to my singers." He nodded at Père Bretonneau, author of the sung tragedy's lyrics, who was waiting patiently beside the door to conduct him to the calefactory. "I will come from time to time to see how you progress," he said to Charles and Morel. "Or come and ask me anything you please. And get warm at the same time!" Charpentier bowed to them, gathered up the score's pages from the wide windowsill, bowed toward the busily oblivious Jouvancy on the stage, and inclined his head to the dancers. "I wish you all a *bonne année!*"

Somewhat belatedly, Charles joined Morel in wishing the composer a good year in return. Watching Charpentier's springy step as he left the room, Charles suspected that he might be nearly as good a dancer as he was a musician.

Startled that he'd forgotten about New Year's Day, Charles gazed absently at the bright fall of sunshine on the wide floorboards. A new year that Martine Mynette and Henri Brion would not see. While somewhere, their killer—or killers, supposing that two killers were still possible—might be wishing unsuspecting friends a good year and receiving good wishes in turn.

Morel's eyes on him called Charles back to himself. He sent the boys to mark out a stage with their hats.

"We begin," Charles said to Morel. "Are you ready?"

Morel swallowed, clutching the sheets of music to his chest. "With the help of Saint Genesius and Saint Guy." Genesius was the actors' patron who also spared a thought for dancers, and St. Guy—called St. Vitus in some places—cured the strange twitching sickness called St. Vitus's Dance.

"Don't forget the ancient goddess of dance, Terpsichore. We're classicists here, after all," Charles laughed.

"Terpsichore, by all means. It's just that I never dreamed of working with anyone as famous as Monsieur Charpentier. He was eighteen years composer for Mademoiselle de Guise, for her troupe of musicians, The Guise Music! Did you know that?"

"Yes, I did know. Well, into the fray, Monsieur Morel."

The dancers were arguing hotly on their marked-out stage.

"This Charpentier is nobody and he didn't bow to me," Montmorency said loudly, his left hand resting on his hip, where his sword would normally be.

Beauclaire, who prided himself on his wealthy bourgeois family's rise by its own wits, regarded the offended nobility in front of him. Seeing the look in Beauclaire's eyes, Charles had a good idea of what was coming and decided that Montmorency had earned it.

"Monsieur Charpentier is a most talented musician," Beauclaire said earnestly. "Is it not God who gives talent? And speaking of talent, would you be so good as to remind me exactly which talent of yours it was that got you born as a Montmorency?"

Crimson with mortal insult, Montmorency reached for him, but Charles got between them in time.

"Monsieur Charpentier has been many years in the Guise household, Monsieur Montmorency," he said crisply. "And the Guise household is in many ways the royal court of Lorraine. You may take it that our composer knows quite well how to conduct himself. Let me remind you that there is no fighting inside the college. I am sure you would never shame your illustrious house by forcing me to summon the college corrector." The college corrector was a lay brother charged with administering corporal punishment, professors being forbidden to lay hands on students for any reason.

Leaving Montmorency silenced but seething, Charles turned to the others. "Now that we have our music, we will review who dances what. But first, let me present Monsieur Germain Morel. Our Maître Beauchamps is not able to be with us for this production, and Monsieur Morel, a dancing master of great talent, is doing us the honor of taking his place."

Charles named the students to their new master and the boys bowed. Morel gave the group a nicely judged—but not overlow—bow in return and managed a few words of greeting. Charles went over the casting for Morel's benefit and then had the dancers shed their scholar's gowns and show a few steps in coat and breeches. Morel's anxiety fell away as he watched them. When Michele Bertamelli's turn came, the dancing master was open-mouthed in amazement.

"Opera material, that one," he whispered in Charles's ear, when Bertamelli had been enticed back to earth. "Where did you find him?"

"He comes from Milan. He told me that he has a cousin in the Comédie Italienne."

Charles nodded at Morel to proceed, and the dancing master consulted his score and addressed Walter Connor.

"Monsieur Charpentier has given Saint Perpetua a sung sarabande. Can you sing?"

"Yes, *maître*. All of us"——he glanced at Beauclaire——"most of us can sing."

"He means that I sing like a donkey, *maître*," Beauclaire said resignedly. "That is what Maître Beauchamps says."

"Unfortunately Monsieur Charpentier has not included a song for a donkey," Morel said regretfully.

Everyone laughed, and Charles mentally applauded Morel's effort to put the boys at ease. Morel riffled through the score and handed Charles several pages.

"Will you begin on the soldiers' first dance, Maître du Luc? And I will work here with the others."

Charles had not expected to be creating a dance. A Jesuit in his position was supposed to be a director, not a dancing master. But yes, this needed to be done. And he did love to dance. He took André Chenac, Olivier Thiers, and Henri Montmorency, went a little apart, and looked quickly at the music Morel had given him. The soldiers danced when they threw St. Nazarius out of Milan, and again toward the end, when St. Nazarius and Celse returned to Milan and were killed. The soldiers' first dance was an *Air Animé*, after a sung chorus asking the military trumpets to sound. Charles had once used an *Air Animé* at the Carpentras college, where he'd taught before coming to Paris, and remembering it now gave him an idea of what to do with Montmorency.

"We must imagine our stage, *messieurs*." He smiled at the trio of waiting boys. "The front of the stage and your audience are here, where I am standing. The back of the stage is there." He pointed to the wall. "There will be scenery, but no stage machines. Where the singers will be placed is, of course, up to Monsieur Charpentier. But we will worry about that later. Monsieur Montmorency, you are the captain of soldiers and will begin there, upstage near the wall and in the center."

Montmorency strutted to his place, assumed a dancer's fourth position, and expanded his not inconsiderable chest.

"Monsieur Chenac, on his left, please. Monsieur Thiers, on his right. Good." Charles counted the measures of music. "The melody goes like this." He sang the music's first two lines. "You begin with a *pas de bourrée*. Monsieur Thiers, yours goes to the left, and yours to the right, Monsieur Chenac. Yours moves straight forward, Monsieur Montmorency."

Chenac and Thiers quickly went through the step, then did it again in tandem, adjusting their spacing to leave room for Montmorency to move between them down the middle. But Montmorency didn't move.

"Like this, Monsieur Montmorency." Charles hitched up his cassock and demonstrated the step. "Now, the three of you together, just that step."

Ignoring Montmorency's stumbling, Charles nodded. "Now, the same step again. For you, it still travels forward, Monsieur Montmorency. For you others, it reverses to the opposite side."

Thiers and Chenac smoothly reversed their *pas de bourrées.* Montmorency's effort was at least in the right direction.

"Good," Charles said brightly. "Back to the beginning and do that much while I keep time." He picked up his time-keeping baton from the windowsill and took them through the short sequence three times. Montmorency was still stumbling. "Now, Monsieur Montmorency, when you reach the end of this sequence of steps, you will mount a small platform placed for you exactly center stage."

Montmorency looked interested for the first time. And, Charles thought, relieved.

"From there, you will use your gold baton of office to direct your soldiers through their steps. At the end of the dance, you will lead them away to capture Saint Nazarius and drive him out of Milan."

Thiers and Chenac, also relieved to have Montmorency safely confined, grinned at Charles and saluted their captain. Who tried so hard to look down his nose at them that his eyes nearly crossed.

The rest of the rehearsal went more smoothly. By the time three o'clock rang, the beginning of all the dances had been set. Morel gave the dancers a firm command to return on Thursday—tomorrow being the New Year's holiday—with their steps perfected. Jouvancy shepherded his actors down the room, the dancers put on their scholar's gowns and retrieved their hats, and all of them gathered at the door. Jouvancy joined Charles and Morel.

"Did all go well, Monsieur Morel?" he asked.

"Very well indeed, *mon père*. I congratulate you on your students."

"Do not compliment the rascals in their hearing," he said loudly, making sure they heard him. The boys swallowed grins and bowed to Morel.

Charles asked Jouvancy, "How is the play coming, *mon père*?"

"Well enough. I think it will all march together, now that we have the pieces in our hands."

He smiled happily at his subordinates and took the boys away to the rhetoric classroom. Charles turned to Morel.

"That was well done," Charles said, "Giving them something to practice between now and Thursday."

Morel laughed. "I confess, I feared that if I did not give the little Italian something to practice, he would be bouncing off the walls and ceilings." But as they left the *salle*, Morel sighed and his steps grew heavy. "It has been a relief to have something to think of these hours besides the Brion family's trouble. If working for the college were not such an honor, I would have stayed with Monsieur Callot and Mademoiselle Brion today."

"Forgive me," Charles said contritely, "I never asked you about Monsieur Brion's funeral this morning. Please believe me, I have been praying for all of them, and especially for Mademoiselle Brion."

"The funeral was well enough. They decided not to wait for elaborate decorations and so forth. They—well—they wanted to have it over, given how he died. Still, it was very decently done by Monsieur Callot and according to Monsieur Brion's station. But Mademoiselle Brion is nearly at the end of her strength. And now, with her brother arrested for the murders—how is she to support that?"

Charles let them out into the courtyard, where blue shadows were starting to gather on the snow. In spite of the cold, Charles stopped and glanced around the empty court.

"Monsieur Morel," he said quietly, "there is something I must ask you. How long have you known Mademoiselle Brion's brother?"

Morel eyed Charles warily. "A year, perhaps a little more. Why do you ask?"

"What do you think of him?"

"He is devout. Even overscrupulous. And easily upset. But he is not a murderer."

"What do you know of his friends? His male friends."

Morel drew back and shook his head vigorously. "I hope—someday—to marry Mademoiselle Brion. Though she is above me, I have hopes. I can say nothing more about her brother."

"Because what you could say would further hurt her?"

"No! It's just that—there is nothing to tell."

"I agree that he is not a murderer. But I think he is at heart a sodomite."

"No!" Morel's face flamed with embarrassment.

"I will tell you something," Charles said, "and, never fear, I will also tell my confessor. I do not care if Brion is a sodomite. Just now, other things matter more. I think he was with someone the night his father was killed, and if he will tell me who, it may save him."

Hugging himself against the cold, Morel looked anywhere but at Charles. Then, carefully studying the heaped snow beside the path, he said, "I only once saw him with a man who might—who—" He gulped and started over, speaking at a gallop as though to get his words out without hearing them. "One day last autumn I arrived at the house for Mademoiselle Brion's dancing lesson. I went upstairs and was crossing the landing to the *salon*, when I saw that Gilles was there with a man I didn't know, a young man. They were talking very softly, handfast and looking into each other's eyes. It was unmistakable."

"Did you hear what they said?"

"Only a little before they saw me." Morel frowned, trying to remember. "Gilles said, 'Thank God you are so close. If we could not meet there—' Then he stopped talking, because he saw me. They jumped apart and I pretended I'd noticed nothing."

"What did the other young man look like?"

"I hardly looked at him, I was so confused and embarrassed. He was ordinary enough. Lighter hair than Gilles. And only a little taller."

"Did you speak with him? Do you know his name?"

Morel shook his head. "We only had time to bow to each other before Gilles made an excuse and hurried him away."

"Does Mademoiselle Brion know what you saw?"

"Of course not!"

"Thank you for telling me, *monsieur*. Your frankness may go some way toward saving him."

They continued in silence to the street passage.

"I will be here at one o'clock on Thursday, *maître*," Morel said, as the porter opened the door. "I truly hope you can save Gilles. For his sister's sake."

After Morel had taken his leave, but before the porter could shut the door, a treble voice called out, "*Maître*, we are back! And look!"

Nine-year-old Marie-Ange LeClerc, daughter of the baker and his wife, whose shop was in the college façade, skidded to a stop in front of the postern, carrying what looked like a hairy melon. Her brown eyes sparkled as she peered into the dark street passage. The red hood of her oversize cloak had fallen back on her shoulders and Charles saw that cherry-colored ribbons were tied in her dark curls, on either side of her small coif.

Grinning, he went out into the street. "Welcome home, *mademoiselle!* We have missed you." He nodded toward the bakery. "Are your parents well?"

"They are very well, *maître,* thank you." Marie-Ange curtsied prettily. Then, social duties done, she thrust out the hairy melon. "Guess what this is!"

Charles bent to take a closer look. "Um—an ostrich egg with straw growing out of it?" There was an ostrich egg, though it wasn't growing straw, in the college's cabinet of curiosities.

Marie-Ange giggled. "You are not even close! Guess again."

"Mmm—let's see. A wig stand? With part of the wig still on it?"

She shrieked with laughter and shook her head so hard that her little white coif slipped sideways. "Only one more guess."

"Well, it looks a little like my uncle Edouard. But I hope it's not!"

This time her laughter brought Mme LeClerc hurrying from the shop. "Marie-Ange, hush, what will people—ah, Maître du Luc!" She started to embrace Charles, caught herself, and settled for beaming at him. "As you see, we are back. But are you well, *maître?* You are thinner. Surely they are not trying so hard to save money that they are making you fast through the holidays!" she said indignantly. "But there, the church has its own ways, and fortunately they are not those of the world," she added ambiguously. "Your mother, is she well? So far away there in the south, she must miss you terribly at Christmas. Though family is not always restful, is it?" She rolled her eyes and glanced over her shoulder at the bakery. "We had a very nice time in Gonesse, so many bakeries there, one end of the village to the other, but I assure you, Roger's brother does not make better bread than we do, even though he has the oh-so-famous Gonesse water! Our Seine water is just as good and better—*What*, Marie-Ange?"

The little girl was pulling at her mother's gray woolen sleeve. "Maman, I was trying to tell him about my coconut!"

"Is that what it is?" Charles said with real interest. He poked a tentative finger at the thing, which felt as rough as it looked. "Where did you get it?"

"That's the very best part, *maître*! A sailor brought it to me, just a little while ago. Antoine sent it!" Her eyes shone like brown stars. "He sent it to me all the way from Martinique!"

"Did he! What a magnificent present," Charles said, smiling. "Did the sailor who brought it give you news of Antoine and his father?"

Antoine Douté, the same age as Marie-Ange, had been a beginning student at Louis le Grand the year before and the two had become friends, in spite of the college rules.

"The sailor said he left them well," the little girl said. Her radiance dimmed a little. "He said that they are staying longer in Martinique. I wish they would come home. Because when they do, I am going to marry Antoine!"

Mme LeClerc shooed her daughter toward the bakery door. "Stop talking nonsense, Marie-Ange. You have shown your treasure, go in from the cold now. Go!" Marie-Ange huffed her way back to the bakery, cuddling her coconut, and Mme LeClerc wrapped her shawl more closely around her shoulders and moved nearer to Charles. "But, *maître*, what is this I hear about your college and a young girl dead? And her guardian dead, too? We heard such a terrible song on the way through the streets this morning. Young girls, now—and notaries, too, heaven knows—can cause anyone trouble enough, but why should Jesuits kill anyone, surely that cannot be!"

Notaries? Charles bit back an urge to swear. So now the song included Henri Brion. He started to ask Mme LeClerc what the song had said, but a familiar roaring voice rose over the noise of passersby, horses, carriages, and street criers.

"Dear blessed saints," Mme LeClerc cried, "what is that?"

Charles looked over her head, squinting at what looked like a procession coming down the slope of the street, and sighed. "That is old Marin, the beggar."

Marin was limping behind a string of mules being driven toward the river. The old man stumbled through their dung, his seamed face lifted to the sky, brandishing his stick and shouting, "Claire, blessed Claire, forgive me!"

"Ah, *ma foi*, it's that old man of Reine's," Mme LeClerc said. "The poor thing grows worse and worse; he should be shut up somewhere. Because you never know what they'll do, *maître*, when they get like that; why, it could have been someone like him who killed the Mynette girl!"

"You knew Martine Mynette? And you know Reine?"

"Everyone knows Reine. I didn't know the Mynette girl personally, of course, but I've seen her when I've gone visiting my friend Sybille, a baker's wife in the Place Maubert. Little Martine Mynette was so pretty, blond as an angel."

In silence, they watched Marin out of sight.

Mme LeClerc sighed. "His story is very sad, do you know it? But no, how could you, so new in Paris? I'll tell you, *maître*, but come into the shop, it's growing colder out here than the devil's—" She bit her lip, blushing, and hurried Charles through the door.

Shivering in the thinner cloak he'd been given to replace the good one snatched off his back in the street attack, Charles was glad enough to go. To his disappointment, though, the bakery's chill was only a little less than the street's, the oven having gone unlit while the family was away. Thumps from the workroom behind the shop, and Marie-Ange's steady stream of chatter, told him that M. LeClerc was there, building a new fire.

"Well," Mme LeClerc said, resting a hand on an empty counter, "the woman called Reine used to come around selling old clothes, and sometimes I gave her something to eat and we talked. Though I haven't seen her lately."

"I think she mostly begs now."

"Ah, so you know her, *maître?*"

"I've met her. And her daughter, Renée."

"That one I do not know. But Reine, well, she has a past one does not talk about—especially not to you—but that's men, isn't it? Anyway, one day she told me that many years ago she fell truly in love with that mad old man who just passed!" Mme LeClerc's plump shoulders climbed to her ears. "Who knows why women fall in love?" Her eyes grew vague for a moment and she glanced toward the back room and her husband's noise. "Dear Saint Anne, who knows indeed?" Seeing the expression on Charles's face, she laughed and said, "No, no, I am not regretting my Roger, not most of the time, but, dear God, how the man snores! I have been putting candle wax in my ears at night, but last night, in Gonesse, it fell too far in and it took three of us to get it out." She frowned. "Where was I? Yes, Reine. So she fell in love with—now what is his name, I have forgotten—"

"He's called Marin."

"Marin, then. Well, old Marin was not always so old. He was about forty, still very much a man, when Claire Clemence's tragedy happened. She was the Princess of Condé, and Marin was a servant in her house. Princess—how magnificent that sounds, but for her it was only sorrow. She lived alone with her servants in the Condé house here in Paris. Why alone? Because her ice-hearted husband hated her, poor thing. Well, one night, two men had a fight in her chamber. She tried to stop them, and Marin heard the shouting and ran in and threw himself between Claire Clemence and the men. He thought the two men were trying to kill her, but they were only trying to kill each other. I never learned what the fight was about, but it was certainly not about poor Claire Clemence, no matter what the thrice-damned Condé said after. She was more than forty by then, after all. And, so it was said, not quite right in her wits. What woman would be, treated as she was by the Condé! But the Condé used the fight as an excuse to accuse her of adultery. Almost overnight, she was gone from Paris, never to return. He shut her up in one of his chateaus, leagues from anywhere. With hardly the necessities of life, so they say. And never, not *once, maître,* did her husband ever visit her, nor does her son. So they say."

"She's still alive?"

"Oh, yes, the poor creature."

A gust of wind rattled the street door's latch and blew the door slightly open, but Mme LeClerc was shaking her head sadly over her story and didn't notice. Charles shuddered, as much from the story as from the chill.

"Marin's madness lies at the Condé's door, too," Mme LeClerc said. "Marin had been in love with Claire Clemence since he was a boy, though Reine said there was never anything improper between them, and she would know, because no man keeps a secret from Reine, they say! When they took Claire Clemence away, Marin tried to follow, he tried to hold on to her carriage, but the footmen pushed him off. The fall broke his foot badly, that's why he limps. He followed on his broken foot until he couldn't go farther, and finally a carter found him and brought him back to Paris. Well, when the Condé heard that Marin had tried to find her, he was furious and spread terrible rumors about Marin and Claire Clemence. He made sure Marin would never get another place in anyone's house, and he never did. By the time he got back to Paris, he was skin and bones, Reine said. They almost had to cut off his foot. The worst was that his sorrow over Claire Clemence being so reviled and taken away sent him mad." Mme LeClerc hunched her shoulders and shivered a little. "He's fearsome now, when the fit's on him. He used to go to doors asking alms, and people gave him what he needed. He was often around the Place Maubert, my friend Sybille said, but he doesn't go there now, they're afraid of him and drive him out. And who can blame them, the way he raves and shakes that stick of his when he doesn't get what he asks."

Charles was silent, thinking that Marin had very rarely gotten what he asked. And understanding now what blasphemy it must seem to the old man for the heart of the Prince of Condé to rest in a jeweled box, on an altar draped with cloth of gold. After hearing the story, Charles felt ready enough to call it blasphemy himself.

"At least Reine still loves him," Charles said, more to himself than to Mme LeClerc.

"Of course she does, she would do anything for him. As would I for my old Roger." She raised her voice. "Who snores like a pig!"

A grunt came from the workroom. "Close the street door, Beatrice! It's colder in here than the devil's cursed cock!"

$$\twemoji{flourish} \quad Chapter \ 17 \quad \twemoji{flourish}$$

NEW YEAR'S DAY, WEDNESDAY, JANUARY 1, 1687

The first morning of 1687 dawned clear and cold. Most people regarded New Year's Day as a holiday, and there were no college classes. After Mass and the briefest of breakfasts, Charles and Père Damiot, booted and cloaked and wearing breeches under their cassocks, went to the stables. Charles had told Père Le Picart about being nearly stabbed in Monday night's street brawl, and he was sending them to Vaugirard together, and on horseback for safety. To Charles's great relief, Le Picart had not only given him and Damiot permission to go to Vaugirard in search of Paul Saglio, he had excused them from the celebration of the king's return to health.

In the stable, a quiet gray horse stood saddled, bridled, and tethered to a post. The gray's dam, the placid dappled mare that had eaten Reine's bread on Monday night, was whickering softly from her stall, as though warning her offspring about the outside world. A young lay brother was trying to bridle the college's third horse, a restive black gelding Charles had been wanting to ride for months. Charles watched the gelding sidle and stamp and then stepped forward and put an arm over the glossy neck. He murmured in the pricked black ear, and the horse stood still and took the bit without further protest.

"What's his name?" Charles asked the brother.

"Flamme. Sure you can handle him?"

Charles nodded happily. "What's the other one's name?"

The brother laughed. "He's Boeuf. Anyone can handle that one, he's just like his mother. Agneau, she's called, the one in the stall there."

Lamb, Charles thought. Well, that seemed to suit her placid temper. Which she had apparently passed on to her son Ox. "Flame and Ox?" He laughed. "Well, between them, our speed should strike a happy medium."

Damiot was not laughing. "*Happy* is not the word I would use." He looked with distaste at both horses.

"Why? Don't you like horses?" Charles couldn't imagine anyone not liking horses.

"They're too big. And they bite."

The lay brother rolled his eyes at Charles. "If they were not so big, Père Damiot, how could they carry you?"

"They couldn't. I could just walk." Damiot looked at Charles with sudden hope. "We could easily walk to Vaugirard. It's only five or six miles."

Shuddering at the thought of a six-mile walk through the snow, Charles said earnestly, "But if we ran into trouble, which is the rector's fear, wouldn't we be much more vulnerable?"

Damiot glowered at the patiently waiting gray. "Not as vulnerable as I'll be on that thing."

"He's not even as tall as the gelding, and the gelding is only somewhat over average. Didn't you ride before you entered the Society?"

"My father has a coach. Or I walked."

"But you *have* ridden before." Charles looked at him in growing dismay. "Haven't you?"

"Yes," Damiot said sadly.

The brother finished tightening the black horse's girth, handed Charles the reins, and untethered the gray.

"Come on, *mon père*," he said kindly to Damiot, who trailed after the horse, looking like a Christian martyr on his way to the Roman arena. "I'll help you mount."

Charles led the gelding into the stable court, gathered his cassock out of the way, and sprang into the saddle. The horse shook his head and danced sideways and Charles let him, taking a moment to get a sense of the animal with his knees and hands, before pulling him back to good manners.

With the help of the brother and the stableyard *pas de mule*, the triangular iron mounting block, Damiot clambered astride the gray, which stood placidly. When Damiot was settled, the horse heaved a long-suffering sigh. The lay brother and Charles exchanged glances, shaking with smothered laughter.

"Have a good ride, *mon père*, *maître*," the brother said as he opened the gate. "And, *maître*, if you have a chance, a good run wouldn't come amiss to Flamme. God go with you."

"And God be with you," Charles returned, as he rode through.

The gray gelding, who had quickly assessed the situation, took charge of his rider and followed Charles. "Pray for me," Damiot muttered to the brother, clutching the pommel.

At a slow walk, they followed the lane and turned toward the rue St. Jacques on the side street that led past the old Les Cholets building. Charles recognized one of Reine's beggars sitting on what was left of Les Cholets' wall and raised a hand in greeting. He and Damiot turned south at the rue St. Jacques, and Charles reined in to ride beside Damiot and assessed his meager skills. Suddenly, the gray gelding stopped, spread his stance, and pissed mightily.

"Ah, *une très bonne année, mes bons Jésuites,*" the Necessity Man called from the street's edge. "I don't have a bucket big enough to offer your horse, that's sure!" Charles and Damiot laughed, and the Necessity Man walked ponderously across the cobbles toward them, wrapped in his enormous cloak and hefting his pair of buckets, with his string of old theatre masks hanging from his shoulder. "But if I did, which mask do you think he'd want to wear?" Avoiding the steaming river of piss running from under the horse, he put down the buckets, courteously doffed his battered black hat, and then held up a papier-mâché mask crowned with molting laurel leaves. "This one, maybe?" he chortled. "He pisses like a Hero!"

"See, *mon père?*" Charles laughed, "Your mount is a hero!"

"A hero named Ox?" But Damiot was laughing, too.

The Necessity Man moved a little closer. His fat, shining face grew serious. "Where are you going, if I may ask?"

"To Vaugirard," Charles said, wondering why the man had asked.

"Out of Paris, that's good. But be on your guard, that ugly song's doing its work. It's a holiday and Vaugirard's full of taverns. Last night, I heard new verses." He jerked his head vaguely toward the Place Maubert. "Want to know who you've killed now?" His eyes were mocking, but it was friendly mockery. "They've added in the poor girl's mother. Poisoned her, that verse says. Next thing you know, they'll be blaming Adam's death on you! But don't worry overmuch, *mes pères,* your Saint Ignatius was a soldier, he'll smite their balls off. When he gets around to it. Sooner the better, I say."

Rumbling with laughter, he picked up his buckets and started toward the river, scanning the mostly empty street for customers. New Year's Day being a holiday for visiting and eating, Charles thought that there would probably be no lack of men needing his services later in the day.

"So Père Le Picart was right to have us ride together," Charles said, as they started moving again.

"My least honorable parts hurt already."

"Our Savior rode. On a donkey, but still."

"I'd rather ride a donkey."

"Believe me, you wouldn't. I've ridden a donkey."

Damiot grunted. "Take my mind off my suffering. What are we going to do when we get to Vaugirard? All Père Le Picart told me was that you were working with Lieutenant-Général La Reynie to help him prove that the Society had no hand in these murders."

"I'm looking for a servant who worked in the Mynette household. An Italian named Paul Saglio. I've been told that he tried to seduce Martine Mynette when her mother was ill, and she turned him out of the house. He was furious, and there's some thought that he may have come back and killed her."

"How do you know he's in Vaugirard?"

"He may have a new situation there."

"May have?" Damiot groaned. "So this may be for nothing. If he is there, what are we going to do, knock on every door and ask politely whether they employ a servant who murdered his former mistress?"

"Something like that," Charles said vaguely, looking hungrily at the road stretching in front of them as they passed between the large houses built on the site of the massive old St. Jacques gate. Beyond the houses, the road was less hemmed with stone and begged for galloping hooves.

The lay brother had said that a good run wouldn't come amiss to Flamme, and it certainly wouldn't come amiss to Charles. But not yet, he decided, as a pair of cantering horses came from behind and passed them, their riders closely wrapped and squinting against the cold wind. In the distance, a line of laden mules was coming into view, and a cart lumbered out of a side road and turned toward the city.

He held the gelding to Boeuf's sedate speed and turned toward Damiot. "Here's how I'm hoping to find Saglio, without alarming him enough to make him run. If he's in Vaugirard, the parish priest has probably heard of him. We'll tell the priest that we've been ordered to find former Mynette servants, because there may be small legacies under Mademoiselle Martine Mynette's will."

"Are there legacies?"

"We're only saying there *may* be legacies. There aren't, because the girl died before her *donation* was found, but we have to say something."

Damiot snorted. "And if this priest has heard that the Society is being accused of her death?"

"I don't know," Charles said impatiently. "We'll know what our lines are when he says his."

"Nothing that sounds that simple ever is." Damiot looked glumly at the dome of the Val de Grace convent coming into sight above a line of trees. "We take the next right-hand turning. Between Val de Grace and the Port Royal convent."

They weren't in open country yet, but the religious enclosures were surrounded by large gardens and orchards and the private houses were fewer. The wind had grown blessedly quiet, and as the sun climbed, shortening the shadows following them along the western edge of the road, Charles could almost imagine that there was warmth in the light. Almost, but not quite. He shifted the reins to his right hand so he could warm his numb fingers under his cloak.

When they turned, just before Port Royal, the road became a dirt track with gentle vine-covered slopes on its right, and flatter fields on the south side. Beyond the fields, which would be planted with rye and barley in the spring, was a cluster of low hills.

"That's Mont Parnasse," Damiot said. "Quite a comedown from the Greek Mont Parnasse, home of Apollo and the Muses, wouldn't you say?"

"I hope the Muses and Apollo are wearing more than they normally seem to." Charles was studying the track underfoot and as far in front of them as he could see. "Père Damiot, the brother in our stable said that Flamme needs a good run. And so do I! We'll wait for you where the track crosses the rue Vaugirard."

"But what if this horse runs, too?" Damiot's eyes were wide with fright. "What do I do?"

"Wrap your arms around his neck and don't fall off," Charles said heartlessly. "But he won't; he knows you better than you know him."

Charles gathered Flamme's reins and shifted a little forward in the saddle. "Now for it, Flamme, *mon brave!*"

The horse leaped forward with no touch from Charles's heels. The track poured past them like a river in flood, and wind scoured Charles's face. The gelding's black ears were pricked happily toward the rapidly approaching distance. Charles realized that he was laughing aloud for sheer joy at the speed, the wind, the perfect body that carried him, and his own blood was pounding in answer. He wanted to go on riding like that till the world ended. Flamme wanted to go on running like that, too, and when they reached the fortunately clear crossroad, it took all Charles's strength and skill to pull the horse back to a canter, then a trot, and finally a stop.

Stroking Flamme's sweating neck, he looked back along the track, where Boeuf was carefully carrying Damiot to meet them. As he waited, Charles set his horse walking up and down the Vaugirard road to cool him off. The first of the village's hundred or so houses stood a little to the south, and the spire of the church, called St. Sauver, rose farther on, above a tight cluster of slate roofs on the left of the road. Vineyards spread out from the village in every direction, interrupted only by the little abbey of Notre Dame des Prez. Country quiet lay under the harsh cries of crows in the abbey trees, the soft lowing of village cows, and the thudding of hooves as Boeuf neared the end of the dirt track.

"You actually enjoyed that, didn't you?" Damiot said wonderingly, as he pulled Boeuf to a willing halt. "I was terrified you would break your neck and leave me stranded out here with *two* horses."

"Thank you for your pastoral concern, *mon père*. Yes, I enjoyed that with all my heart! And body. And soul, too, I think." He pointed at the houses. "And there is Vaugirard. Now we find the priest and ask for Paul Saglio."

Damiot's eyes went from the vineyards and fields to the crows. "How do we find the priest in this wasteland?"

Charles burst out laughing. "Do you see that big thing sticking up above the houses? Even in the country, that's called a church spire. Where there's a church, there's a priest. Anyone would think you'd never been out of Paris!"

"Why would I leave Paris? Why would anyone leave Paris?"

But Damiot managed to turn Boeuf toward the spire and they set off. The road became a slushy village street bordered by houses with snow-covered roofs and full of the sounds of morning chores that take no note of holidays. Doors banged, well pulleys squeaked, dogs barked, mistresses shouted at servants, and wooden shoes, the ubiquitous *sabots* of rural France, clacked sharply over courtyard cobbles. When they came to the church, they reined their horses in and dismounted. It was small and old, and stood in a large cemetery. Charles eyed its age-blackened walls and the statues of the apostles around its arched door, and Damiot told him that they were made from Vaugirard's own quarry stone, as were numberless houses and buildings in Paris. "And each apostle is framed in grapevines, as though they're all standing in a vineyard—a nice touch in a wine village."

Charles nodded, squinting at the foot-high figures and suddenly homesick on this day when families visited everyone they knew. "A very nice touch. We have churches decorated with vines at home, too."

They tied their horses to an iron ring in the church wall and went inside. For a moment there was nothing but darkness, and they had to stand still until the holy water font and the altar swam out of shadow. What light there was came through small windows of colored glass set high in the walls. As they dipped their fingers into the font's frigid water and crossed themselves, Charles saw that, unlike Louis le Grand's chapel, this church had no benches at all, only stone seats around the edge of the nave. Which meant that, as in the old days, the congregation still stood through Mass, or knelt—or sat—on the stone floor, or on cushions brought for the purpose.

The smell of incense hung in the air, evidence of an early Mass already said. Charles went to the vestry door, but it was locked and no one answered his knocking.

"The house beside the church looks too big for a single man," Charles said.

"He may live behind it."

Damiot led the way into the sunlight. They untied the horses and led them down a dirt lane along the church's north side and the cemetery wall. Where the wall turned, a black cat with a white feather stuck to its face sat on the angle, watching them, and beyond the cat stood a small stone house, its front bare to the lane.

Damiot stopped short and Boeuf, half asleep, nearly knocked him over. "Thatch?" Damiot stared in horror at the roof of a small lean-to wing built onto the side of the house. "Blessed Saint

Joseph, I don't think I've ever seen a thatched roof. Could a parish priest so close to Paris be this poor?"

"Well, the rest of the house is roofed in good slate tiles. But the church has a poor feel about it, too. I saw thatched roofs when I was in the army in the north." Charles grinned ruefully. "And slept under them. Do you know what lives in thatch?"

"No, and I don't want to. Did Père Le Picart tell you this priest's name?"

"No."

As they approached the house door, someone moved at one of the tiny windows, but the door stayed shut. Charles knocked, waited, and was about to knock again when the door flew open. A tall elderly man in a stained cassock stared unhappily at them.

"God's blessing," he said, without much conviction. "What do two Jesuits want of a simple priest?"

"God's blessing on you, *mon père*, and a good new year." Charles introduced himself and Damiot. "We are looking for a man who may be in your parish. His name is Paul Saglio."

"Saglio?" The parish priest laughed without mirth. "And why——" He broke off as wings beat over his bald head and a white dove landed on his scalp. "No, no, *ma petite* Fontange, that is agony to a bald man, how many times must I tell you?" He reached up and the bird walked onto his finger.

"What a superb dove, *mon père!*" Damiot's eyes were shining. He dropped Boeuf's reins and put out a tentative hand to stroke the bird. "And what a good name for her; that little tuft of feathers on her head looks exactly like a lady's headdress."

"Ah, you like doves?" The priest beamed at Damiot as though at a long-lost son. "Come in, come in!"

Damiot followed the priest into the house, leaving Charles to tether the horses loosely to a small tree beside the house, where they could crop the long grass. He went inside and found Damiot holding Fontange and the priest talking steadily about doves as he poured white wine into wooden cups.

"See?" Damiot said, as Charles peered at the bird, "see how perfect her eyes are, and how bright?"

"How do you know so much about doves? I thought you never left Paris."

"My father has a dovecote."

The priest turned, holding out two pottery cups. "Does he, *mon père?* What sort of doves has he? How many?"

The low-ceilinged, sparsely furnished room was marginally warmer than the outdoors. Charles leaned against the wall to listen to the bird talk, enjoying the wine and this new side of Damiot. And thinking that the parish priest would be more willing to answer their questions after he'd talked awhile. He let twenty minutes or so pass and was about to interrupt, when the church bell began to ring. The parish priest thrust Fontange at Damiot.

"Another Mass to say, but I will return as quickly as I can. Or perhaps you would like to come? And after, you are welcome to share my poor dinner."

"*Mon père,* you are most courteous," Charles said quickly, before Damiot could accept the invitation. "But we are here on the order of our rector and must be about doing what he has asked us to do."

The priest's face fell. "Oh. I see. And what is that?" Regretfully, he took the bird from Damiot, carried her to a window on the other side of the room, and let her fly. "To your cote, *ma petite,* I will come back to you very soon."

"We are looking for the man called Paul Saglio, *mon père.*"

The priest turned around with a sour expression. "He is at the big house on the right, almost at the end of the village. Anyone will tell you. But I warn you, the man is a rogue. I have tried to warn Madame Theriot, but she will hear nothing bad of him.

The idiot woman has made him her cook; he feeds her on Italian messes, and the other servants are saying he plans to poison her." He brushed uselessly at the bird stains on his cassock. "They say, too, that she will hardly let him out of the house. And that he purrs at her like a cat." He wandered across the room and opened the door. "You are welcome to my house at any time, *mes pères*, at any time." As he went out, he said over his shoulder to Damiot, "I need to rebuild my dovecote. Perhaps you can advise me, *mon père*, your esteemed father being such an authority . . ." They watched him go reluctantly up the lane, still talking.

Charles laughed and put his cup back on the sideboard. "Do you suppose the good man always leaves his guests the run of his house? Did he even tell you his name?"

Damiot shook his head as they went out into the lane. "I wish we could have stayed. That little Fontange is the prettiest dove I have ever seen. My father will be eaten up with envy when he hears about her."

"I had no idea men felt such passion for doves."

"I have tried to persuade the school bursar to build a dovecote in the fathers' garden, but he refuses to spend the money. Especially now." Damiot sighed. "Nothing is more beautiful in a garden than the cooing of doves."

They mounted Flamme and Boeuf and ambled along the village street until they came to closed wooden gates with a high expanse of slate roof showing beyond them.

"This looks likely." Charles swung his leg easily over Flamme's back and dismounted.

Damiot struggled out of his saddle and they walked the horses to the gate. The manservant who answered the bell was courteous enough and wished them a good year, but his uneasy glances and brief answers made Charles certain that he had heard the anti-Jesuit rumors. Yes, he told them, this was Mme Theriot's house. No, she was not at home. Yes, Paul Saglio worked here and could be found in the kitchen. He took them through the cobbled court, past a pretty girl drawing water from the well, and opened the rear door. He gestured them inside, called out to Saglio, and left them before anyone answered.

"What do Jesuits want with me?" a voice growled belatedly from the kitchen. "Tell them to go to hell."

Charles, with Damiot behind him, followed the voice into a large, high-ceilinged kitchen with two large fireplaces, a massive worktable in the center, and every sort of pot, pan, cooking fork, sieve, ladle, spice box, and kitchen cloth overflowing the shelves and cupboards crowded around the walls.

"Hell is a long journey, Monsieur Saglio," Charles said pleasantly. "Though the warmth might be all too appealing on a day like this."

The small lithe man with a white cloth tied around his head turned sharply from the oven set into the wall. He held a long flat wooden paddle for putting loaves in the oven. His lip curled and his eyes traveled slowly from their hats to their boots.

"Your Society already has the Mynette goods. So I hear. I am only a poor servant; you'll get no gold from me, my fine blackbirds." His face darkened. "How did you find me?"

"Someone knew you were here," Charles said vaguely, not wanting to set Saglio on the hapless priest. "So you have heard of Mademoiselle Mynette's murder."

"Who has not?" He began to softly beat the wooden paddle against his leg.

Charles decided not to waste time on subtlety. With an eye on the paddle, he said, "You tried to dishonor her and she turned you out of the house. Shortly before she was killed."

Saglio's black eyes flashed from Charles to Damiot. "What is that to you? "

"You were very angry with her."

"Fickle bitch." The Italian flung the paddle onto the work table. "Sweet as sugar and then acted like she was Blessed Mary herself. 'Ooooh, don't touch me, Paul Saglio!'"

Charles clasped his hands tightly together at his waist to keep himself from hitting the man. "She promised more than she gave?"

Nodding, Saglio widened his eyes and broke into a stream of furious Italian.

"Ah, *monsieur*," Damiot said, his voice full of spurious sympathy, "I see, she spurned your manhood. That has moved men to kill more times than can be told."

Saglio stared at him. "Kill her? Me? Do you think I am crazy? Why would I risk the gallows for the pleasure of strangling the little bitch?"

"Then tell us what you were doing before dawn on the Friday morning after Christmas."

"Why not? I was running all over the house like every other servant here, trying to get old Madame Theriot on her way to Paris." He rolled his eyes. "The old ones are worse than the young ones. But they have more money," he leered, "and money compensates trouble taken." Grinning at the expressionless faces of the two Jesuits, he slowly adjusted the well-filled front of his breeches. "Trouble of every kind, you understand."

Wanting to get out of Saglio's presence even more than he wanted to slam a fist into the man's face, Charles said curtly, "Who can swear you were here that morning?"

"Alain in the yard, the one who came to the door. The pretty maid who's been out at the well too long talking to Alain. My mistress herself, though she's already left on her round of New Year's visits."

Charles looked at Damiot. "*Mon père*, will you go and speak with the maidservant and Alain?"

"With pleasure." Damiot strode out of the kitchen, his boot heels striking like hammers on the stone tiles.

"If you want to know who killed Martine," Saglio said, watching Charles, "look for her ex-gardener. Tried to get into her bedroom, he did." He grinned. "Always saying she had something he wanted. Don't we kill the ones we love? Or lust for, anyway?"

"Do you mean Tito La Rue?"

"I mean Tito La Rue, indeed."

Charles gazed thoughtfully at a ham hanging from the ceiling, wondering if there might after all be reason to find the gardener and question him. "How old is this Tito? Describe him."

"I don't know his age, younger than me. Middle height, hair something like mine, not as black. Well fleshed, he liked his food."

"And where is he now?"

"Paris? Peru? Hell? Who knows?" Sniffing the air, Saglio whipped around and opened the oven. With the long paddle, he brought out four brown-crusted loaves and slid them onto the table. Charles's mouth watered at the rich, yeasty smell.

Saglio gazed with approval at his work. "Look, *mon ami*, I'm busy, I have to cook dinner for all the people *madame* is bringing back with her."

If the rest of the dinner measured up to the delicious-smelling bread, it would indeed be a feast. "Where did you learn to cook?" Charles couldn't help asking.

"From my mother, in Rome." He took a plucked chicken out of a cupboard, slapped it down on the table, and picked up a knife. "Like I said, ask my mistress where I was when Mademoiselle Mynette died. She'll tell you the same as I have."

"Shall I also ask her what you were doing in Paris on Monday?" Charles doubted now that Saglio was actually the man who'd tried to stab him outside the tavern that evening, but he had to put Reine's insinuation to rest.

The man stared at him. "I haven't been to Paris since Christmas. My dear mistress has kept me too busy here feeding her holidaying belly. What are you trying to make me guilty of now?"

"Of trying to stab me," Charles said conversationally, watching the knife in Saglio's hand.

"If I'd tried, you'd be dead." Saglio scowled, flourishing the knife, whether at the chicken or Charles, Charles wasn't sure. "Now go away and let me cook."

Chapter 18

Charles found Père Damiot chatting amiably with the two ser-vants at the well.

Charles nodded to the three of them. "Have you discussed Monsieur Saglio's whereabouts last Friday morning?"

"Oh, yes," Damiot said. "We have, and I've learned that he was here, though we've agreed that it is always preferable to have him elsewhere."

"That I agree with wholeheartedly," Charles said. "What about the day before yesterday, Monday?"

Both servants began to laugh.

"He was here, *mon père*," the maid said, with a glance at the manservant. "Very much here!"

"And why?" the manservant broke in gleefully. "Because some-times *madame* makes him wait at table as well as cook, so she can gaze at his pretty face—and on that Monday, at dinner, he poured hot cream sauce into her lap! By some terrible mistake, you un-derstand. He spent the rest of the day apologizing and making dainties to soothe her temper and make her love him again."

Charles gave them each a few coins and he and Damiot took their leave. As they rode away from the house, Charles told Da-miot what the cook had said about Tito La Rue.

"I think I need to find this gardener. To eliminate him, if

nothing else. And he's the only other name we have just now. What exactly did the servants say about what Saglio was doing on Friday morning?"

Damiot shifted uncomfortably in his saddle and reached under his cassock to pull at his breeches. "Dear God, it's sixteen hundred eighty-seven, why hasn't someone invented a comfortable saddle?" He stood up in his stirrups, twitched his cassock out from under him, and sat again. "They say he was here, up well before daylight, packing food for their mistress to take with her to Paris, and then cooking a five-course dinner for the friends she brought back that afternoon. I think it's true, because the maidservant said she spends her days running from his unwanted attentions. She'd be glad to help fork him into hell."

"Well, it seems that he's not a murderer—at least not lately—but based on what I saw and smelled in the kitchen, he's a good cook."

"I'm hungry."

"Me, too."

They left the village behind and turned onto the dirt track, back to the Faubourg St. Jacques. Tito La Rue, Charles thought glumly. With a description that could suit half the young men in Paris and a name as common.

"I want to stop at Procope's before we go back to the college," Charles said to Damiot. "Maybe the kitchen woman Renée knows more about this Tito than she said before."

"Then we should turn around and go up the rue Vaugirard to the old St. André gate. Otherwise we'll have to backtrack when we get to the city, and I'm not riding a step farther than I must."

Flamme shook the reins as Charles turned him, obviously hoping for another run, but Charles held him to Boeuf's slow pace. The road was full of traffic now, a steady stream of people and carriages heading from the city to Vaugirard, to celebrate the holiday in its taverns with cheap local wine. Charles heard angry murmurs from a few people who passed them, and ignored more than a few hostile glances, but that was all. They soon left the village's vineyards and fields behind, riding past country houses and gardens, which gave way to houses and shops built wall next to wall. When they reached what was left of the old city walls and the gate, Charles looked at Damiot, surprised by his silence. Judging from the man's pinched lips, he was in real pain.

"We'll have some coffee at Procope's before we talk to Renée," Charles said recklessly. "Père Le Picart gave me money, and I'll tell him that spending some of his coins was the only way to save you from death by horse."

"Which will be Gospel truth," Damiot muttered.

They reached Procope's back courtyard by the narrow lane that ran behind the café. As they were tethering the horses, Renée came out of the kitchen with a basin of apple peelings.

"*Bonjour, mademoiselle*, and a *bonne année* to you," Charles said, and jumped aside as she threw the peelings. Not at him, as he'd first thought, but at the waste pile behind him. Nonetheless, there was no welcome in her expression as she looked from him to Damiot.

"Madame won't let you into the coffeehouse. The customers are arguing about that song and some are saying Jesuits killed Mademoiselle Martine and her mother and the notary, too. If you go in there, there'll be a riot. So go away."

Renée turned back toward the kitchen and tried to close the door on them when they followed her. Charles grabbed the door's edge and held it open.

"The song is a lie; we have killed no one. But we *are* trying to find out who did, and we need your help."

"I have already helped you."

She struggled for a moment to shut the door, then shrugged

and let it go. Inside, the silent cook seemed not to have moved from his stool beside the fire where Charles had last seen him. He glanced at the Jesuits without interest and went on eating a piece of pungent cheese. Two glasses of wine stood on the floor beside him. Reine wasn't there.

Renée picked up one of the glasses and faced them. "What do you want of me?" Her eyes were as hard as green pebbles.

"Anything more you can tell us about Tito La Rue."

"Why?"

"We have seen Paul Saglio, and—"

Her eyes lit with hope. "Did he ask about me?"

"No," Charles said ruthlessly.

She looked away and drained her glass.

"Renée, it seems certain that Saglio did not kill Mademoiselle Martine Mynette. But he thinks this Tito may have killed her."

She made a sound like steam escaping from a pot. "Saglio is a spider. He is an animal. Tito had been gone a month and a half. He would never have come back to the house as long as I was there. He knew I'd make him regret it!"

Charles made a noncommittal sound and watched the cook by the fire pour white wine into a third glass for Damiot, who was eagerly holding out his hand. Renée took her glass to the cook to be refilled.

Charles said, "How long had you worked for Mademoiselle Anne Mynette?"

"About three years."

"And how long had Tito been there?"

Renée sighed and drank deeply. "Since he was a child, eight years old. It was like this. Thérèse, the cook in the Mynette house, the thief I told you about—she said that Mademoiselle Anne took him from the foundling home to be her servant. It was an act of charity. She gave him a way to earn his living and a better growing-up than he would have had." She shrugged. "But she soon discovered he was a liar, Thérèse said. Mademoiselle Martine was about four years old then, and she always wore around her neck a little red heart on an embroidered ribbon. And—"

"Mademoiselle Brion told me that this necklace was missing when you undressed Mademoiselle Martine for her coffin."

"Yes. Mademoiselle Brion was running everywhere, looking for it. I didn't see how a trinket could matter when my mistress was lying there dead. Well, as I was telling you, when Tito came to the Mynette house as a child and saw Martine's necklace, he grew very angry. He said it was his and tried to snatch it from her neck! Mademoiselle Anne beat him for it and almost sent him back to the foundling home. But she gave him another chance and he turned out to be a good worker, so she kept him. And finally the little liar stopped saying such foolish things."

"Do you know where he is now?"

"No."

"Paul Saglio described him as middling tall, dark haired, and well fleshed. Is that right?"

She shrugged. "I suppose so. Yes, that's—"

She broke off as the liquid-eyed waiter Charles had met when he was there with La Reynie burst into the kitchen. "Madonna says chicken pies," he yelled at the cook. "She says fruit pies! Cakes and cream, she says, maybe that will quiet them!" He gasped as his eyes fell on Charles and Damiot. "You! No! Go, go," he hissed, waving his arms at them. "If the *signores* in the café find you, they will kill you for murdering everyone! Go!"

Beyond the door, a surge of argument rose and chairs scraped across the floor. The counter woman screeched furious reprimands. Then, "Luigi what are you doing? Get out here!" Her voice was coming toward the kitchen. Casting dignity to the winds, Charles and Damiot ran for the courtyard and their horses.

"What a pleasant rest," Damiot said darkly, as they rode along the lane toward the Fossés St. Germain. "I hope we can get back to the college without more of that."

"We're not going back yet; we're going to the Foundling Hospital. Where is it?"

"We're going home."

"You go home. Where's the Foundling Hospital?"

"I cannot go back to the college without you; the rector will have my head."

"Then take us the quickest way to the Foundling Hospital."

"No. I am your superior. Going there is pointless. This Tito was there years ago; who will remember him? And what good would it do, if they did?"

"The rector is *your* superior, and he ordered me to find these killers."

Damiot breathed ominously and silently through pinched nostrils. "There are two Foundling Hospitals. Do you want infants or older children?"

"Older, I think."

"Then we go across Paris. *All* the way across Paris. Out the rue St. Antoine to the *faubourg*. Where I devoutly hope the populace is not starting its year arguing about how much better the world would be without Jesuits."

In a loud silence, they rode across the river and turned east. In spite of the cold, holidaymakers strolled along the rue St. Antoine in their best clothes. The *bourgeoises* wore sober black and gray and brown, but their inferiors were bright against the snow in reds and yellows and greens rarely seen on workdays. Fast-rolling carriages flashed by. Street peddlers bellowed the virtues of their hot coffee, chocolate, small pies and cakes, and smiled under a rain of small coins. Charles wanted to buy something to eat, but Damiot curtly refused and Charles decided not to argue. Most people ignored them, though as they rode past a snowball fight, a few angrily flung snowballs came their way; harmlessly, however, since the throwers' holiday drinking was influencing their aim.

Just past St. Catherine's well, at the Jesuit church of St. Louis, Charles put out a warning hand to Damiot and drew Flamme to a sudden halt. The beggar Marin, hatless but wearing his green almsgiving coat, already torn and dirty, was sitting on the church steps and holding out an insistent hand to passersby.

"Give alms, for love of the *Sacre Coeur!* Give alms for the Sacred Heart, have luck all year," he chanted, scowling blackly at anyone who ignored him. "Refuse, you'll have a year of tears! Give alms for love of the *Sacre Coeur.*"

Charles saw that tears were running down Marin's face. The people who dropped coins into his hand kept a tight eye on his massive walking stick, careful not to come too close. His long, tangled white hair and beard made him look like a prophet, and he seemed not only at the end of his patience, but nearly as distraught as when Charles and Mme LeClerc had seen him following the mules on the rue St. Jacques.

"Blessed Sacred Heart," he mourned, his voice rising in a wailing lament. "God and all the saints forgive me, blessed Claire, forgive me . . ." He began to beat his chest. "Sacred Heart, see my tears—" The words trailed off into keening and he rocked himself from side to side.

Charles got down from his horse. Leading Flamme, he went as close to Marin as he dared. "Marin, softly, hush, it's all right. God forgives you." He put a hand gently on the beggar's shoulder. "Claire forgives you, the Sacred Heart forgives you."

The old man's eyes flew open and he pulled away. His tears stopped and he stared wordlessly up at Charles, his eyes full of fear.

"What is it, Marin? You know I won't hurt you." Marin's eyes darted from Charles to the street. "Where is Jean, Marin? Is he here to take care of you?" There was no answer. Charles looked in vain for the beggar's keeper and then took money from the purse the rector had given him and put coins into Marin's gnarled hand. "For your supper and Jean's, too. Come now, get up, you can't stay here. You may not remember Christmas Eve, but if the Professed House rector sees you here, he'll surely remember and give you to the archers."

Charles was pulling Marin to his feet when the old man froze, staring past him. Then the beggar lurched upright, ducked away from Charles, and fled. Turning to see what had frightened him, Charles saw Lieutenant-Général La Reynie, imposing in a black-brown cloak and a wide beaver hat with a white plume, coming toward him. Behind him marched a solid phalanx of a dozen or more men in thick brown coats and breeches, with pistols in their belts.

Père Damiot, his back to the approaching police, said impatiently, "If we have to go to the Foundling House, let's go and get it over." Even the stolid Boeuf was shaking his reins, wanting to be gone.

Charles raised his eyebrows. "Turn around, *mon père*," he said quietly, "and you'll see why we can't leave just yet."

Damiot turned. "Oh, dear." He shifted miserably in his saddle.

"*Mon lieutenant-général*, a good New Year to you," Charles said courteously, as though they were in a *salon* and there were not a small army at La Reynie's back.

"And to you, Maître du Luc." La Reynie looked at Damiot.

"Monsieur La Reynie, may I present Père Thomas Damiot?"

La Reynie bowed slightly and Damiot acknowledged him.

"Damiot?" La Reynie studied the priest's face. "Your father is head of the Six Corps. A merchant goldsmith, I believe."

Damiot nodded. "I see that you know everything about the city you keep, Monsieur La Reynie."

La Reynie looked at Charles. "Unhappily, not everything." He said something to the officer standing just behind him and then to Charles, "A small word, *maître*."

Warning Damiot with a look to stay where he was, Charles led Flamme after La Reynie, a little way along the street and out of earshot of the other police.

"What has happened, Monsieur La Reynie?" he said, when the *lieutenant-général* stopped. "I doubt this is how you normally spend your New Year's Day."

"You doubt correctly. My spies told me last evening, and again this morning, that trouble is likely here at St. Louis. At your college and your novice house, too. I have put armed men at each place, nearly all the daytime men I have. At dark, the night patrol will replace them." La Reynie's head whipped around as shouts and loud laughter erupted from across the street. He watched a gesticulating knot of men in knee-length mantles, their broad hats askew as they argued. "Drunks." La Reynie sighed. "But it's drunks who generally start the trouble. Which they'll go on doing, until someone is charged with these murders." His gaze swept the length of the street. "Until someone confesses," he said flatly, refusing to meet Charles's eyes.

Charles's stomach turned over. La Reynie was talking about Gilles Brion. The Châtelet was notorious for its ways of making people "confess."

"I still have not found Monsieur Bizeul's friend Cantel. I did find three more investors in the smuggling scheme," La Reynie went on. "Two proved beyond doubt that they were elsewhere during the time when Brion must have been killed." La Reynie smiled sourly. "The third, on the other hand, has no proof. But he doesn't need any. He's seventy and frail, with only one foot. He lost the other forty years ago as one of Condé's men in the Fronde revolution." He stopped to watch his own men walking up and down the street in pairs, missing nothing, staying always within earshot of their fellows. "I can keep things quiet a while longer with shows of force in the street. And arrests, too, if it comes to it, though arrests may only stir the fires." He shook his head. "But the weather is growing colder, there's more and more sickness about, especially among the workers in the St. Victor quartier, prices are rising again—and we haven't even begun the worst of the winter! People are ready to take their fears out on whatever comes to hand."

"And Jesuits have come to hand."

The *lieutenant-général's* eyes held Charles's. "And therefore, I have to produce the Mynette girl's killer and Henri Brion's. Do you understand?"

"I understand," Charles said, colder inside than out, "that you have Gilles Brion in the Châtelet and will use him if you must."

La Reynie twitched his cloak angrily aside, as though his smoldering anger were heating him. "I will not 'use' him! I have never, to my knowledge, executed the wrong man and I never want to. But Brion seems more than likely as his father's killer, if not the girl's. And he had plenty of reason for her murder, as you well know." La Reynie sighed heavily. "There are other reasons for haste. On the thirtieth day of this month, the king is coming to a reception and dinner with the city worthies at the Hôtel de Ville. Do you know how rarely the king comes to Paris? He hates Paris. But you wouldn't know that, you're a foreigner. I cannot let him come into a city on the edge of riots." In Paris, a foreigner was anyone not from Paris.

"I may be a foreigner from darkest Languedoc," Charles said dryly, "but I can count. We have nearly all of January to find the killer."

"No. The king already knows of the unrest here. Have you forgotten that his confessor, Père La Chaise, is one of your own? I have been told that the king wants this affair concluded, and quickly. He is furious that his own confessor's order is being accused of murdering for gain. And furious at the thought of riots. I tell you, he hates unrest in Paris more than the pope hates the devil!" The *lieutenant-général*'s head whipped around again, as a roar of laughter rose by St. Catherine's well. Someone's hat, blown off in a gust of east wind, was rolling away down the street, chased by three skinny dogs.

La Reynie rubbed his tired face and turned back to Charles. "Do you have anything for me? Anything at all?"

With a pang of sympathy for the man's obvious exhaustion, Charles gave up arguing.

"Nothing you will like. Paul Saglio, the servant Martine Mynette dismissed for being too forward, is innocent. We talked to him and his fellow servants in Vaugirard this morning, and it seems certain that he was there when she was killed. But I learned more about the Mynettes' ex-gardener, Tito La Rue, the one Renée told us about, who was turned out in November for trying to get into Martine's bedchamber. It seems that, from a child, he claimed Martine's missing necklace as his own—God knows why. It seems unlikely that he'd come back and kill her over such a tiny thing. And I cannot imagine any reason for him to kill the notary. But since the necklace *is* missing, he ought to be questioned."

"Find him. Did Renée tell you where he went when he left the Mynette house?"

"No. All I know is his name and that he's in his midtwenties, middling tall and well fleshed, and that his hair is dark. And that he started life as a foundling."

La Reynie's face fell. "That's all?"

Charles nodded toward the east. "I'm going now to the Foundling Hospital to ask about him."

"The man was a foundling? And what—twenty years ago? Do you know how many thousands of children they care for? And their houses have been reformed and moved several times, so who knows what records they have?" The *lieutenant-général* looked ready to weep. "Oh, well, report to me what you find." He turned away, his face eloquent with exactly how much help he expected to come out of Charles's inquiries. Charles remounted and signaled to Damiot, and they rode toward the Faubourg St. Antoine.

"Old Marin looked more frightened than I've ever seen him," Damiot said, as they passed the stately redbrick houses of the Place Royale. "What was the matter?"

"You know Marin?"

"I've seen him often enough in the streets."

"I don't know why he was so afraid. Maybe he's getting crazier."

"I feel sorry for beggars, but Paris has too many. How can ordinary people go about their business?"

"Rich people, you mean. Why shouldn't they share what they have with God's poor?"

"Why should they be assaulted by stench and sickness and insanity and the demon possessed every time they leave their houses? All those people can be cared for in public institutions like the Hôpital Général."

Charles shook his head in disbelief. "*Mon ami*, haven't you heard what's said about places like the Hôpital? They're horrible. People who can't help being poor don't deserve that!"

Damiot sighed. "But there has to be something better than the street. Or that filthy mess those beggars have made out of the Louvre colonnade!"

"Well, think of something and make the Society of Jesus do it as a work of mercy."

A quarter mile or so outside the city, Damiot drew his horse to a halt beside a long high wall on the left of the road. "There it is."

A stone-shingled roof surmounted by a cross rose above the wall. Charles dismounted, leaving Damiot waiting in the dirt road, and led Flamme to the bell beside the stout wooden gate. Shivering in the wind that had risen, he rang the bell. In the last few minutes, the bright day had darkened, and as the grille slid open, Charles hoped for an invitation to talk inside.

"Yes?" The nun on the other side of the grille studied him and then glanced beyond his shoulder at Damiot. A small frown appeared between her black eyebrows. "A good year to you, *mes pères.*" Her voice was soft but there was no friendliness in her dark eyes. "How may I help you?"

"A good year to you, *ma soeur.* I am hoping to learn something about a foundling who may have been here fifteen years ago, perhaps a little more." Even as he said it, Charles realized what a hopeless question it was. "He was called Tito La Rue."

"We name many of them La Rue. The street is where we find them, after all. This Tito would not have been here. Our house for older children was in the Faubourg St. Denis then."

"Do you have records of the children?"

"Not here, not so far back. If he was brought as an infant to the Couche, near the Hôtel Dieu on the Île, someone there may remember. Go with God, *mes pères.*" She shut the grille and its bolt scraped across the iron.

Chapter 19

St. Basil's Day, Thursday, January 2

The night was quiet, but Charles's sleep was not. He dreamed of grilles and prisoners. Martine Mynette reached through the Foundling Hospital's grille to give him the little heart she wore around her neck, but when he reached out to take it, her hand was full of blood. Gilles Brion stared through the grille in his cell door until Reine, who had come to visit him, reached through and strangled him with his red-beaded rosary. Wearing a galley slave's iron collar and chain around his neck, La Reynie chased Marin through the church of St. Louis. Then a hand reached through the wall behind the altar and they both screamed in terror. The screaming turned into the rising bell and Charles sat up in bed, sweating in spite of the frigid air seeping through the temporary canvas over the window.

He dressed in a fever of haste and flung himself down at his prie-dieu. Fervently, he said the rising prayers, giving thanks for deliverance from night and darkness, and the Hours of Our Lady. He also gave thanks that the trouble La Reynie feared at the college had not come in the night, that the only troubles had been in his dreams.

In the chapel, kneeling on the icy stone floor and blowing on his clasped hands to warm them, he saw that a red chalk drawing of St. Ignatius's death mask was newly hung near the altar. Studying the saint's face comforted him a little, made him feel the littleness of his own fears and desires. Somewhat calmed, he prayed his way into the sacrament of communion, trying to open his heart to whatever the Silence had to say to him. Little by little, as the sacrament was celebrated and the Mass wound to its end, his heart filled with a terrible urgency. *Nothing is wasted,* the Silence had told him. *Unless you waste it.* If he wasted the chance he'd been given to find Martine Mynette's killer, and Henri Brion's, Gilles Brion was going to die as a double murderer. Isabel Brion and her great-uncle would be ostracized and indelibly marked by the scandal. Isabel would no doubt refuse to marry Germain Morel—for his own good, she would say. An innocent man would die horribly and at least three lives would be twisted past mending.

Gilles Brion's hopeless face seemed to follow Charles through the dark morning to the fathers' refectory. Dry-mouthed with fear that he would fail to prevent tragedy, Charles found he couldn't force the breakfast bread down his throat. He swallowed the icy watered wine and fled, thinking how to find out where the city's foundling records were kept, but the day's trouble found him before he reached the street passage.

"*Maître!*" Père Montville, the new principal, loomed out of the dark of the Cour d'honneur. "Our day boys are being attacked at the stable gate. Go and do what you can, I'm going for Frère Brunet!"

Charles sprinted across the courtyard's riffs of snow. Every morning, Louis le Grand's day boys poured in through several gates and doors opening on surrounding streets. The youngest used the stable gate. In the court where the student library was, a half dozen other breathless Jesuits caught up with Charles, all spilling together through the archway into the stable court, hindering each other in their haste. Charles felt the familiar momentary twist of his mind back into battle. Engulfed in the furious shouts ringing in the cold air, in shifting darkness and lantern light, in the cries for help, he threw himself at the gate into the lane, where a tangle of boys punched and kicked and shouted abuse. But these combatants were ten, twelve, fifteen years old, most wearing scholars' gowns and apprentices' aprons, and Charles was abruptly back in his present life. He reached into the tangle with both hands, grabbed two grappling boys by the backs of their clothing, and held them off the ground.

"Stop it," he said quietly, having learned from teaching that an ominously quiet voice did more than yelling. Both boys went limp. The boy in the long Louis le Grand scholar's gown looked about twelve and seemed to be bleeding from his eye. The other, perhaps fifteen and aproned like an apprentice, held his ribs as though they might collapse into fragments if he let them go. "Go for each other again, or for anyone else, and I'll throw you back into the fight and let the rest finish you off."

The student nodded, but the apprentice was too busy fighting tears as pain overcame his battle lust.

Charles set them on their feet. "Take your enemy here to Frère Brunet," he told the Louis le Grand boy. "He can have a look at you both."

The student pushed the apprentice none too gently toward the archway. When the apprentice stumbled and cried out, the student offered a reluctant arm, and they wobbled away together.

Other Jesuits had sorted out the rest of the gateway tangle, and Charles pushed his way into the lane, which was still full of shouts and wrestling and shoving. Ducking to avoid a rain of snowballs—laced with rocks, by the sound they made hitting the college wall—he was reaching for another pair of adversaries when a shadow running toward the end of the lane caught his eye. The shadow's shape told him it was a woman, and something about her seemed familiar. Charles went after her. As he knew to his cost from the brawl outside the tavern, it was not only men accusing the Jesuits of conniving at murder. Anyone running through the lane this morning needed to account for himself. Or herself. But before Charles caught up with the woman, he stumbled over a body.

Not a dead body, thank God. Charles bent closer and put his hand on the warm face. The boy was breathing, but he was ominously still. His scholar's gown was torn half off him, and Charles's hand came away wet with blood from the smooth cheek. He wiped the boy's face with his cloak, seeing in the slowly growing light that the blood was from a badly broken nose. Probably from snow packed around a stone, which had also knocked its victim out of his wits. As he picked the boy up, another hail of snowballs came at him, along with raucous singing from farther down the lane.

> *"Le notaire, il était fort,*
> *mais cette notaire est aussi mort!*
> *Il est perdue, pour ainsi dire,*
> *Les Jésuites pour enrichir!"*

The doggerel hammered at Charles as he carried the boy toward the gate. It was the first time he'd actually heard this verse. "The notary was strong, but he is dead, lost to enrich the Jesuits." Trying to shut his ears, he reached the courtyard, half running. Frère Brunet had set up a temporary infirmary in the lamplit stable. With the help of two other lay brothers, the infirmarian was tending boys injured on both sides of the melee. Père Montville, just inside the stable door, was grimly questioning two half-grown boys. One was a shame-faced Louis le Grand student, and the other, in a shorter scholar's gown, was a student from another college. Each had a rapidly blackening eye.

Brunet looked up from sponging blood off another boy's forehead. "Blessed saints, that one looks bad, bring him over here, *maître*."

Charles put the boy down beside the one Brunet was working on. "Do you need me in here, *mon frère*?"

Brunet shook his head, absorbed in checking his new patient for broken bones, and Charles hurried back to the lane. The brawl was mostly over, the last apprentices and alien students in rapid retreat, pursued by large lay brothers doing their best to lay hands on them. The more culprits Montville questioned—on both sides, Charles thought wryly, since the Louis le Grand day students were as likely as their adversaries to have started this—the more chance a coherent picture would emerge. Now that the way was clear, Charles went to the end of the lane, where it joined the side street near the old college of Les Cholets. The woman he'd glimpsed was no doubt long gone, but it wouldn't hurt to make sure.

As he reached the side street, his way was blocked by winter street cleaning—a plodding cart horse pulling a wide, heavy triangular drag that captured garbage and frozen horse and mule droppings, which workmen gathered into the cart alongside it. Waiting for drag and cart to pass, Charles eyed the ill-kept wall around Les Cholets and wondered if the shadow might have used the easy toeholds of missing stones to climb into the courtyard. He grabbed the wall's uneven top and pulled himself up, then wished he hadn't as pain shot through the old wound in his left shoulder. The price for striking useful fear into the hearts of the brawling boys he'd held off the ground, he realized ruefully. As far as he could tell in the poor light, Les Cholet's courtyard was empty, and he let himself carefully down again to the lane's snowy cobbles.

He hurried around to Louis le Grand's main doors. Père Le Picart was there, as Charles had thought he would be, talking to two of La Reynie's officers. The horse drag was toiling noisily up the rue St. Jacques, and the last day students were streaming into the college. These were the oldest day boys, fifteen to eighteen or so, and the only ones allowed to come and go by the main doors. From the look of the students, the fight here hadn't been as fierce, or it had at least been more equal. Some had black eyes, cuts, and bruises, but overall they seemed not much damaged.

". . . most likely to be last night, our informers told us," the older officer was saying unhappily to Le Picart. "Either they were in on it, or *their* informers were wrong." He smiled bleakly. "These bravos launched their attack just after the night patrol was gone, before we got here. That gap shouldn't have happened." With grim anticipation, he added, "And someone's head will roll for it. In any event, the *lieutenant-général* has assigned guards here all day, and you'll have the patrol again tonight."

Le Picart said, "And that song? What have you discovered?"

"Nothing. But as of today, we're confiscating all the copies we come across and arresting the sellers for inciting violence. That's all I know, *mon père.*"

Le Picart nodded and dismissed them to their places on either side of the doors. He turned to Charles. "Were any of the boys at the stable gate badly hurt? I have not yet been there."

"That's why I came to find you. One boy at least seems badly hurt. I found him unconscious in the lane. Frère Brunet took charge of him."

"May God forgive our enemies for attacking the youngest ones so savagely, because I am not sure that I can." The rector turned back through the double doors, toward the back door to the Cour d'honneur.

A carriage came rolling up from the Seine, its occupants leaning out the windows to stare at the police around the college door. Charles stood his ground and gazed back at them, wondering if they thought he was a killer.

Chapter 20

"ONE-two-three, ONE-two-three, sink-and-RISE, step-step." Banging his stick on the floor, Charles tried to ignore the competing counting from Morel's corner of the *salle des actes*, Jouvancy's shouts at his actors on the stage, and the mess Montmorency was making of the simple *pas de bourrée* Charles was counting in a misguided effort to help the boy. With equal lack of success, he tried to ignore the headache he had from banging the stick. And from the day in general, which had gotten steadily worse as it went on.

Lieutenant-Général La Reynie had come to the college to apologize to the rector for the failure of the police to keep the morning's attackers away, and Le Picart had called Charles to be part of the talk. La Reynie's mood had been as black as Charles had ever seen it, and the reason was quickly clear. The *lieutenant-général* had told them that the minister of war, Michel Louvois, had been informed of the attack on Louis le Grand and had come to the Châtelet just after dawn. Outraged by the burgeoning disorder in the city, Louvois had given La Reynie until Tuesday to announce that the murderers of Martine Mynette and Henri Brion were under arrest. Which meant that if new and compelling evidence had not turned up by Monday, Gilles Brion would be put to the question. Tortured into a confession, that meant.

Charles had pleaded. La Reynie had been implacable. The rector had been called to the *grand salon* to talk to the angry parents descending on the school and, left alone, Charles and La Reynie had been reduced to shouting at each other. The end result was that La Reynie had refused to let Charles go to visit Brion.

"Do you think I want this?" he had spat at Charles. "I have no choice. Let me remind you how the power goes in this matter. First, the king. Second, Monsieur Louvois. A poor third—me."

"You are head of policing, how can you be a poor third?" Charles had spat back.

"If you are that naive," the response had been, "you are no use to me. If you want to *be* of some use, go and find this thrice-damned Tito!"

"Before Monday," Charles had said bitterly.

At that, La Reynie's misery had shown briefly in his eyes. "Please God, before Monday."

As the day went on, the students had grown more frightened, angry, and distracted from their studies. The professors were angry and distracted, too. The lay brothers were simply angry, and secretly preparing for war. Charles heard two different groups of them fiercely planning to redeem the college honor, preferably tomorrow morning.

Now, wondering how he was going to get the dancers he was working with—and himself—through the rehearsal, he put a hand to his throbbing head and called a halt to the doomed dance. Montmorency was standing flat footed, scowling at the other two dancers.

"What is the matter, Monsieur Montmorency?"

"This is a stupid step."

"It's not the step that's stupid," Olivier Thiers said resignedly, but all too audibly.

Fortunately, André Chenac began laughing before Thiers finished his sentence and Montmorency did not hear. Charles gripped his time-keeping stick and prayed for patience.

"It is a simple *pas de bourrée*, Monsieur Montmorency," Charles said, smiling dangerously. "Or a simple *fleuret*, whichever you care to call it. Look. I will show you once more." He put the stick on a windowsill, hitched up his cassock, and spoke the step as he did it. "Bend your left knee as you put your right foot, cocked at the ankle, next to your left ankle. Like this. Then rise onto your left *demi-pointe* as you step forward onto your right *demi-pointe*, then step forward on your left *demi-pointe*, and forward again on your right *demi-pointe*, like this. Nothing could be simpler!"

"What about his arms?" André Chenac said.

"Perhaps," Charles said sweetly, "you would like to teach him the arm positions, Monsieur Chenac?"

Chenac took an involuntary step backward. "Me? No, *maître!*"

"Then shut up!" Thiers hissed in Chenac's ear.

A new thought made Charles's eyes light with sudden hope. Refusing to think about Madame Montmorency's wish to see her son dance at the February show, he said, "Monsieur Montmorency, I am going down to the scenery *cave* after this rehearsal. To bring up the gold block you will stand on as you direct your soldiers." He smiled. "I think we will have you in place there at the beginning of the scene. You will be a magnificent statue of a noble soldier, who comes to life to save the Romans from this Christian Nazarius. But, of course, it is really God bringing you to life, so that later Saint Nazarius and Celse can be gloriously martyred for our edification."

Montmorency looked blank, trying to work that out, but the other two boys nodded enthusiastically.

"That will be even more worthy of you!" Chenac gazed limpidly at Montmorency. "So much more noble!"

"Only a true courtier could bring to life the perfection of an ancient statue," Thiers said gravely.

"So tomorrow you will have your pedestal," Charles said. "Here is how you will stand on it, until you come to life." He took Montmorency into a corner and placed him firmly in a fourth position. "There. Excellent. Do not move even a muscle. I will tell you a very important secret, Monsieur Montmorency." Charles lowered his voice. "Not moving at all is far more difficult than moving. But I know you can do it."

With his right foot forward, his left arm raised in a curve, and his right arm curved long at his side, Montmorency went absolutely rigid and gazed with fierce concentration into the middle distance.

"Yes, excellent!" With a sigh of relief, Charles quickly set the rest of the dance on the other two boys, and by the end of the rehearsal their steps were nearly perfect.

The three o'clock bell was ringing, Père Jouvancy's actors were coming toward them down the room, and Morel had gathered the other dancers close around him, when a hoarse "*maître?*" made Charles turn. The noble statue was tottering but holding his pose like the last soldier defending a breached city gate.

With a pang of conscience, Charles said, "Come out of your pose, *mon ami*; well and nobly done, indeed!"

Gratefully, Montmorency dropped his quivering left arm to his side and shifted his feet. His big face was suffused with pride as he walked stiffly toward the door with his fellows.

"*Mon père?*" Charles stopped Jouvancy on his way to the door. "I need to go down to the scenery *cave*. Do you want me to look for anything while I'm down there?"

"Ah, yes!" Jouvancy included Morel, who was walking toward them, in his smile. "Find the street scene with houses and the

Temple of Mars. It's there somewhere. See how much retouching it needs. We'll also need the lakeshore with pine trees; that will be perfect for the near drowning. Even without an overstage for mounting stage effects, we should be able to put you somewhere with a bellows for wind. Don't bring them up from the *cave*, just place them at the front of the row of flats. But before you go, tell me how you're managing with young Montmorency."

"He looks somewhat happier," Morel put in.

Charles grinned. "Monsieur Montmorency is going to make an excellent statue of a soldier."

Jouvancy gave a bark of laughter. "Brilliant, absolutely brilliant! I shall remember that little idea. Wonderful! Come, then, you can go through the rhetoric classroom to the *cave*."

"Maître du Luc," Morel said diffidently, "if you would like help looking for the scenery, I would be glad to offer assistance."

Charles was ready to be quiet and alone. "I don't really need—" he began, but Jouvancy was beaming at the young man.

"Yes, good, very kind of you, Monsieur Morel. Come, both of you!"

Charles sighed inwardly and followed them down the stairs. Unless he was greatly mistaken, Morel wanted to talk about something, and Charles wanted nothing more to worry about.

"Where are the cellars?" Morel asked, as they emerged into the courtyard.

"Hmm?" Charles was looking up at the iron-gray clouds as he walked, hoping that whatever they had in store would hold off until he could put his evening plans into action. "The *caves*?" He pointed at the east side of the court, opposite the street passage and the rue St. Jacques. "We keep the scenery under the rhetoric classroom there. It's convenient, since we build the summer tragedy and ballet stage to back onto the rhetoric classroom windows. We have to haul what we use up the stairs, but at least we don't have to carry it far. I hope the lanterns are still beside the stairs. It's dark as sin down there, and open candle flames are too dangerous near the wood and canvas."

The dancers and actors had already taken their seats in the rhetoric room when Jouvancy, Charles, and Morel entered. Père Martin Pallu, pink and shy and round-faced, with almost comically big hands, had just called the students to order after a short break. When he saw Jouvancy, he stepped down from the master's dais and went to him for a hurried consultation. Watching Pallu, Charles marveled at the rank and fame the young Jesuit had already attained. Three years younger than Charles, he was through final vows and ordination, and already a rhetoric master. He had been charged with writing the Latin script for the *Celsus* tragedy because of his growing reputation as a writer.

Jouvancy answered Pallu's question, patted him encouragingly on the shoulder, and sent him back to the dais, where Pallu took his place behind the lectern and began to set the afternoon's Cicero translation.

"And when all have finished, each *decurion* is to hear his men's translations. All ten in a group will listen to each translation and will be prepared to say why a correction is made, if asked to do so by the *decurion*. *Habes?*" Pallu said.

"Yes, *mon père*," the students chorused, and set to work.

The *decurions*, newly designated each month, earned their rank by outstanding work in their rhetoric studies. Called by the ancient Roman army title for "officer," each was responsible for ten "soldiers." Now, before settling to his own work, each "officer" made sure that his "soldiers" were duly settled to theirs. Pallu sat down in the master's chair on the dais and watched them all closely, ready to offer help if he was needed.

Jouvancy opened the door to the cellar stairs, then went to join Pallu on the dais. Charles saw that the lanterns and the little flint and tinder box were still there on the top step, and set about making light. He handed Morel one softly glowing lantern, took the other, and led the way down the worn stone stairs.

"Close the door," he said quietly over his shoulder, "or the draft coming up from below will freeze the classroom. I hope we find what we need quickly, before we freeze down here ourselves."

The stairs ended in the dank lifeless cold of ancient cellars. The lantern light seemed as feeble as a single star in a black night sky, lighting patches of gray stone wall and picking out curved vaulting as Charles led the way toward the scenery, walking quickly to forestall talk. Beside one of the squat round pillars holding up the ceiling, he stopped, lifted his lantern, and hung it on an iron hook so that its light shone along a row of stage flats leaning face outward, against the wall. "Bring your lantern with you," he said to Morel, and started walking slowly along the line of flats. "The flats we want should be along here somewhere."

They quickly found the set of flats for the Roman town scene, with its tile-roofed houses, cedar trees with sharply pointed tops, an imposing Temple of Mars, and a severe-looking Roman family posing in the paved street. Morel set his lantern down and they pulled the flat away from the wall and carried it to the front of the line, so it would be easily found when they were ready to dress the stage. Finding the lake flats turned out to be another matter. They reached the end of the long line of scenery without seeing them, even though they stopped to pull out several flats that had been stacked with their blank sides outward. The clammy frigid air wrapped itself around them like a cloak, and their breath came in white clouds.

"They're not here," Charles said. "Well, let's get my lantern and Montmorency's box and get out of this underworld. Charon's river couldn't possibly be colder than this."

Squeaks and scufflings sent them hurrying toward the stairs, but not before an enormous rat waddled across their path, glancing at them with mild interest and not in the least afraid.

Morel shuddered as it disappeared beyond their lantern light. "I hate those things! Don't they eat your scenery?"

"Not the flats. The rest of the things we mostly keep in locked chests a little way beyond the stairs. That's where the box will be."

Morel stayed so close he kept treading on Charles's heels. They passed the foot of the stairs and walked along a line of low wooden chests. Charles knelt, dragged one of the chests aside, and pulled out a stout square box made of gold-painted wood.

"Voilà!" Charles stood up and handed Morel his lantern. Then he picked up the box, yelped in pain, and dropped it.

Morel jumped back. "What? Another rat?"

"No, no, it's my shoulder, I awoke an old wound this morning."

"In the attack? I heard about it."

"Everyone in Paris has probably heard about it. Yes, I pulled two combatants apart more eagerly than I should have, so my shoulder is telling me."

"I'll carry the box, *maître*," Morel said brightly, and hoisted it before Charles could object. "You want it in the *salle des actes*, don't you?"

"Yes," Charles said. "That's very kind of you. I'll carry both lanterns."

Feeling the young man's confidences closing in on him, Charles led the way back to the stairs, extinguished the candles, and left the lanterns where he'd found them. Morel followed him through the silent classroom where the boys were writing furiously, translating passages they'd been set. Bowing to Pallu and Jouvancy, Charles and Morel went out into the courtyard. Watching Morel stride across the snow-covered gravel with the box and climb the stairs to the *salle des actes* like a young goat, Charles felt suddenly old. *I'll be twenty-nine this year,* he told himself, *and then thirty, and thirty is certainly no longer young.* Morel, on the other hand, he thought drearily, was probably only twenty-one or twenty-two, not much older than some of the students.

In the *salle des actes,* Morel set the block down and turned to Charles. "*Maître*—I—may I—there is something—may I talk with you for a moment?"

"Of course." Forcing himself to look like he had all the time in the world, Charles backed up to a windowsill and leaned against it.

But Morel only stared dumbly at the floorboards.

"How is Mademoiselle Brion?" Charles asked, to start the stream flowing. Beyond the windows, the sky was growing steadily more leaden, and he had to get out of the college and across the river before the snow started.

Morel looked up in relief. "You are kind to ask, *maître.* But I have nothing good to tell you. She is more and more distraught, so distraught that she's thinking of entering a convent. She says that if her brother is convicted of these crimes, she will not allow anyone to marry into a family so shamed. She says she will join the Ursulines. She has even begun wondering if marriage is more sinful than being a nun." Morel flushed and looked down. "But I should not be talking about that to you; forgive me."

"Monsieur Morel, I do not disdain marriage. It is a sacrament, after all." Charles smiled suddenly. "Years ago now, our own Père Caussin wrote about marriage. He said that marriage is a mysterious sacrament. Precious in God's eyes and full of dignity."

"Did he really? She will like that! And so do I. No one could disagree with that."

"Anyone can disagree with anything, but I hope it will help." Charles straightened from the windowsill, but Morel stayed where he was.

"There is another problem, too, *maître*. I have only been certified as a dancing master very recently, and I am still building my reputation, as you know." He sighed and shook his head.

"You said once before that Mademoiselle Brion is above you. But you have never mentioned your own family," Charles prodded.

"They are respectable people. But artisans. My father was a violin maker. He did well, but I have three older brothers and a sister and must make my own way. Isabel—Mademoiselle Brion, I should say—is used to more than I can give her. She could marry far more to her advantage."

"Is that what she wants?"

"She doesn't say so. But—"

"And are you sure she is used to so much more?" Charles said, thinking of her father's hapless schemes and what she had confided about the family finances. "Even if she is, do you really want her to marry someone else just because he is rich? Or because he imagines that *she* is rich? I like what Père Caussin said about that, too. 'Away with these mercenary husbands, who are in love with money; they should marry the mines of Peru, not honorable girls.'"

Morel laughed in surprise. "Truly, he said that?"

"Truly. But more to the purpose than what Père Caussin thought, what does Monsieur Callot think about your suit?"

"Oh. I—I don't quite know. He teases us—me. But he doesn't stand in the way. With Monsieur Henri Brion gone, though, he may begin to feel he has a father's responsibility to Mademoiselle Brion, and perhaps that I am—well—good to tease, but not suitable as a husband for her."

"Is he behaving like that now?"

"No. But—"

"Then do not borrow trouble. The household is torn apart

just now, and the best thing you can do is what you are doing. Offer to help them, comfort them as you can. Stand by them. It is not yet time to do more than that. Which I think you already know." Charles moved firmly toward the door this time, and Morel trailed after him.

"Thank you, *maître*. Will you pray for us?"

"With all my heart."

A scouring wind was reaching into the Cour d'honneur as Charles walked the young man to the postern. Seeing that the porter, huddled inside two cloaks, was asleep in front of his little alcove's glowing brazier, Charles let Morel out into the street. Wishing him a good evening, he shut the postern and stood in the doorway of the porter's alcove, to have a little warmth from the brazier while he gave Morel time to be gone. As he stared at the small orange flames, he hardly knew whether to hope for success or failure in the coming night. There was danger for Gilles Brion either way. It all depended on what Lieutenant-Général La Reynie chose to do if Charles was successful. The rector had reacted with great distaste to this errand, as Charles had expected, but had reluctantly given permission. When the bells rang four o'clock, Charles pushed his broad-brimmed, flat-crowned hat tightly down onto his head and slipped quietly out into the rue St. Jacques on his way to the Capuchin house across the river.

Chapter 21

Sullen clouds hung over Paris. The day had grown so ominously dark that side streets were black tunnels pricked here
and there by candle flames in rooms otherwise as dark as the
streets. The street lantern lighters were not due out for an hour
or so, but shops were closing and most people walked quickly,
eyeing the ominous sky.

"Snow, for sure," Charles heard a Pont Neuf broom peddler
call to a bookseller packing up his stall. "Not a little snow, either.
I'm for home and the soup pot." She hefted her armload of
brooms and made off across the bridge. The first flakes started
to fall as Charles turned left from the bridge and cut up the rue
de L'arbre Sec toward the rue St. Honoré. By the time he reached
the Capuchin monastery's gate, north of the Tuilleries, he was
brushing snowflakes from his eyelashes, and he had dumped
snow off his hat twice.

He rang the bell and then waited so long that he wondered
if the friars, who rose at midnight like the Benedictines to sing
Matins and Lauds, had already gone to bed. The gate offered
little protection from the weather, and there were few buildings
across the street to block wind. Finally, footsteps slapped over
stone, the grille slid back, and a lantern was lifted to let the friar
see who was there.

"*Bonsoir, mon frère,*" Charles said through chattering teeth. "Forgive my intrusion, but I must speak with Père Michaut."

The grid closed, bolts were undone, and the gate opened narrowly. Charles went through and the silent friar, bearded and brown robed, closed and locked it behind him. With a gesture, he bid Charles follow and led the way across cobbles, the long point of his hood swinging at his back, and through a small door in a stone wall. Watching the man's sockless, sandaled feet flash in and out below his gown of raw wool, Charles thought how decadent he must seem to a brother of this deeply reformed Franciscan order. Even in leather shoes, stockings, shirt, and two layers of good, well-woven wool, he was shivering. They rounded the turn of the covered cloister walkway and the monk took him through another door, into a small, bare candlelit room. The monk signed to him to wait and left him there.

New-built a hundred years ago by Catherine de Medici, the monastery was more modern than some of the old monastic houses, but because it was Capuchin, Charles knew that it would be as austere as any ancient monk could have wished. The small room had no fireplace, and Charles walked briskly up and down, rubbing his hands together and working his cold-numbed face so that he could speak when the time came. He stopped before the lifelike crucifix on one wall and prayed for words to convince Père Michaut, the Capuchin superior, that what he'd come to do was necessary. Even if Michaut would not give permission, the heavy snow might work in his favor. If it went on as it had begun, returning across the river would be dangerously difficult, if not impossible. And any return would of necessity be on foot, since Capuchin houses kept no animals of any kind, not even horses or mules. Staying the night might well prove useful, even if the superior did not.

"God be with you, *mon père*," a deep voice said behind him.

Charles turned and saw an elderly, white-bearded Capuchin regarding him out of blue eyes sunk in a nest of wrinkles.

"And with you, Père Michaut." Charles bowed. "I am Maître Charles du Luc, come from Louis le Grand with the permission of my rector, Père Le Picart, to ask your help."

"You are welcome. How may I help you?"

With a last hurried inward prayer, Charles told him about Gilles Brion's danger, his own certainty that Brion was innocent, and the pressure on Lieutenant-Général La Reynie to extract a confession. Then he asked Michaut if he remembered Gilles Brion coming to the monastery as a guest a week earlier, on Thursday, December twenty-sixth.

Michaut nodded, but said nothing.

Nerving himself, Charles said, "Might young Monsieur Brion have spoken to someone else in your house during that night? Someone who could tell us for certain about his frame of mind?"

Michaut shook his head, his eyes never leaving Charles's face.

"A man may have need for spiritual counsel in the night hours, *mon père*," Charles said softly.

"We sleep early, we rise for the midnight offices, and we sleep again. We are a very silent fraternity, *maître*."

"Gilles Brion needs your help, *mon père*. I know that he wants to join your house."

"He is very young." Michaut smiled slightly. "Even for a young man."

"*Mon père*, are there other young men just now who mean to join you, young men Gilles Brion may have talked to that night about their mutual hope? Was there another young man staying as a guest that night?"

Michaut studied the plain stone tiles at his feet. In the utter silence of the monastery, the wind whining around the building was almost indecently loud.

"No one else was a guest here on the Thursday night after Christmas." He sighed and looked at Charles. "*Maître*, a Capuchin monastery is not for the faint of heart or spirit. Only a few find the vintage of our vineyard sweet. But God knows better than I who those few shall be. He brings them to us in His own time. Until then, judging is not my business. Nor is breaking my own peace over the matter. I will pray that if the young man is innocent, he will be delivered."

By which Charles understood that Michaut was not going to tell him anything about Gilles Brion or any friend of his. He made one last try.

"But if breaking your own peace might save his life, *mon père*? Is that not your business?"

Instead of answering, the Capuchin looked at the room's small window, which shook a little in its frame as the pitch of the wind rose.

"Let me offer you our hospitality tonight, Maître du Luc. I doubt you could see your way home safely. Even if the lanterns have been lit, they will not stay lit in this storm." He turned his gaze on Charles, his blue eyes suddenly sharp with intent. "You may have our guest cell, where Monsieur Brion sometimes stayed."

"You are very kind, *mon père*. I accept most gratefully," Charles said politely. He was grateful not to have to brave the weather. But he thought wryly that trying to find his way through blowing snow couldn't be any harder than trying to pierce this man's determined silence.

Because he counted as a monk, even if a sadly decadent one, Charles was invited to share the friars' meager supper. Seated at the bottom of a long table bare of cloth, he silently ate the dark bread, young cheese, and boiled vegetables. Outside the refectory windows, the storm had grown louder and drafts made the flames of the two tallow candles on the table jump and bow. When thanks had been said, the friars filed out of the rectory and Michaut gestured to Charles to follow.

They went to the church and into the candlelit choir for Compline, the last office of the day. Charles withdrew into the blackness of the nave. Not wanting to stumble over anything looking for a bench, he stood still and composed himself to pray with his hosts. Murmuring under their monotone chant, which was not quite singing and not quite speaking, he felt as though the Compline prayers washed through and over him, carrying away his worry and his fear. For the first time, he found himself wishing Jesuits did this, even wondering whether he should be a Capuchin, to have this vast healing silence as his home.

When the office ended, he moved toward the choir and followed the friars out into a passageway. The Capuchins turned toward their cloister. The friar who had brought Charles from the gate, now carrying a lit candle, made a sign and led him a different way. Stopping at a low door, the friar went into a tiny guest cell, lit a candle in an iron holder on the stone wall, bowed, and left Charles on the threshold.

Looking around the cell with a sense of shock that threatened to become shame, Charles's thoughts about becoming a Capuchin died a quick and permanent death. He could cross this cell in three strides. There was one narrow, shuttered window high up in the stone wall. There was no furniture whatever. The bed was a bare board with one rough blanket folded on it. *No wonder Capuchins get up at midnight and go to church,* an irreverent part of him said silently.

He sat down on the board. Did this austere nest have anything to tell him? His eyes went to the window. Gilles and his friend could not have come and gone that way. The window was too high to reach without something to stand on, and too narrow to go through, even if reached. He got to his feet, already glad to be off the bed, and took the candle from its iron ring. Huddling his cloak around him, Charles opened the low door and looked out. This guest cell was far away from the friars' cells, he guessed, nearer the front court and worldly comings and goings. But it wasn't far from the church. If the church was not only for the friars, but also a parish church, then it would have a door on or near the street. Germain Morel had heard Gilles thanking God that his friend lived "close to the house." The Capuchin house, Charles thought he'd probably meant. Perhaps Gilles had simply slipped out of the church door in the night and gone to visit his friend. Charles took the candle out of its holder and stole out of the cell into the dense silence and darkness of the house.

He found the door into the friars' choir and went from there down into the nave. Shielding his candle flame, which was writhing and dancing from the drafts under doors and around windows, he walked the length of the nave to the wide west door. It opened easily, into a courtyard smaller than the one he'd entered by. The falling snow was blinding, as heavy a snow as he'd ever seen, but as it swirled and shifted in the wind, he glimpsed a gate that had to lead to the rue St. Honoré.

Charles withdrew into the church again and leaned all his weight on the door to shut it against the wind. Now he knew for certain that leaving and returning to the enclave at night was possible. All Brion would have had to do was avoid coming and going during the midnight office. And if, by some chance, he was discovered in the passage between the church and his cell, he could easily claim prayer as his excuse. So going out to the friend who lived nearby was possible. And surely more pleasant than the bare, cold guest cell. How, though, to find out where the friend lived?

His candle was out now, but Charles found his way back to his cell with only one false turn and huddled on the straw-covered board, wrapped in his cloak and the blanket. He tried to think out what to do next. He was certain that the Capuchin superior knew who Brion's friend was. But he doubted he could make any more headway through the silence of these famously silent monks. He would have to scrutinize everyone who came to Prime and early Mass and afterward try to talk to any young men. Or at least follow the one who mostly closely fit the bare description Morel had given him of Brion's friend. Shivering and dissatisfied, Charles fell uneasily asleep.

He woke what seemed like hours later with his left shoulder aching with cold and shrieking its disapproval of the board. He sat up, looking for any sign of light around the cell's window, but there was only thick darkness. The wind seemed to be less, though. Telling himself that the cell was at least out of the weather and no worse than places he'd slept in the army, he thought about going again to the chapel to see if it was time for the midnight office, though he hadn't heard any bell. But before he could make up his mind, a bell's clanging split the night.

Thinking that such frantic clanging had to be more than the signal for prayer, Charles leaped up and went into the passage. He had no way to relight his candle and could see nothing. When the bell fell silent, he heard running feet and started toward the sound, feeling his way along the passage wall. Moving light sprang up ahead of him, and a line of silently hurrying friars carrying lanterns, a ladder, and enormous buckets crossed the passage and disappeared through the door he had entered when he first arrived. Charles ran to the door, but the friars were already pushing through the court's deep snow. The snow had nearly stopped falling and the big gates stood open. Beyond them and along the street to the left, an orange glow lit the night. Fire. And all too near.

Remembering that Lieutenant-Général La Reynie had once told him that the Capuchins were the city's firefighters, Charles made his way into the street to offer help. A gang of robed and hooded Capuchins had just come through a smaller monastery gate, pushing and pulling what looked like a monstrous wheeled pot toward the fire. Others with shovels were clearing snow as fast as they could in front of the wheels. Silhouetted against the blaze, people were gathering along the street. Charles grabbed part of a rope and threw his weight into dragging the wheeled water cistern. He could hear the roar of the flames now and saw that the fire was in the ground floor of a modest house standing alone, between two vacant lots. A weeping, wild-haired woman stood in the street, struggling in a man's hold.

When the cistern was close enough, the friars formed lines, filling buckets and passing them forward to the flames. Other friars waited to run the empty buckets back to the cistern. As Charles moved to take a place in the bucket-passing line, he passed the struggling woman, who held a mass of something white against her chest.

"But the new lace, the ribbons!" she sobbed. "Madame de Fiennes is coming tomorrow—" Then he heard an anguished shriek. "The mules, ah, *bon Dieu*, the mules!"

Charles spun around. Mules? Trapped in a burning stable behind the shop?

"No one is coming tomorrow!" the man shouted at the woman. "There will be nowhere to come to! Never mind the stupid pink mules; you are not supposed to sell them, anyway. No more than you are supposed to work by candlelight and burn the shop down!" He pulled her toward the gates of a townhouse farther down the street. "See, the Fiennes maidservants are at their gate. Come and let them salve your burns."

Ah, Charles thought, enlightened, *pink* mules. Thanks to his mother, he knew that mules were a woman's backless slipper. The sobbing woman was a *marchand de mode*, then, a seller of fashion accessories. Though why she wasn't supposed to sell mules, he had no idea.

A roar and a crash came from the burning shop, and one of the friars called from the front of the line, "A ceiling beam's come down!"

For a bizarre moment, Charles thought that burning white birds were fluttering toward him, but the birds were fragments of the shop's lace and linen carried on the fire's heat and vanishing into cinders as he watched.

A shrill, terrified cry above him made him stumble backward, craning his neck. A boy of eight or nine years was crouched on a window ledge above the shop door, weeping with terror and staring down into the maelstrom of smoke, water, and running people below him. At his back, a wall of flame reared itself where the beam had collapsed into the ground-floor room.

One of the friars came running with a ladder and tried to lean it against the building, but a sudden draft sent tongues of fire reaching through the shop door and he jumped back, cinders burning holes in his robe and catching in his hair.

"The boy must jump," Charles called to the friar with the ladder. He thrust his bucket at someone and hurried as close to the building as he could. *"Mon brave,"* he called up to the child, "hold on to the casement and stand up." He turned to the young and sturdy-looking friar. "Do you have rope?"

The friar looked wildly around, put his ladder on the ground, and ran. Within a few breaths, he was back with a coil of rope.

Charles took it and shouted up to the child, "Catch the rope and hold it as tightly as you can!"

But the little boy was clinging to the window casement with his eyes shut, too frozen with terror to move. Behind him, flames rose again from the ground floor, and tongues of flame licked out of the shop door.

"*Mon frère,*" Charles said to the Capuchin, "put your arm through the rope coil and climb onto my shoulders. Quickly, here, use my hands!"

Charles crouched. The friar took his proffered hands, put a foot on Charles's thigh, and scrambled onto his shoulders. Slowly, Charles stood up. They loosed hands, Charles gripped the monk's ankles, and the monk stood upright. Above them, the child was watching their acrobatics, momentarily distracted from his terror.

Charles said, "I will tell the child what to do. Then you will throw him the rope. Ready?"

"Ready."

"*Mon brave,*" Charles called to the boy, "we will throw you a rope. You must put it around your waist and tie it and then hold it with both hands as tightly as you can. Do you hear me?"

The child nodded.

"Throw it," Charles shouted to the friar.

To his relief, the man's aim was true and the child caught the rope and fumbled it around his waist. But before he could tie it, a gust of air sent new flames rising behind him.

"Hold it tight, *mon petit!*" Charles bellowed. And to the man on his shoulders, "Pull!"

The child flew toward them, the friar yanking with all his strength to pull the boy past the flames in the shop door, and Charles caught him as he fell. All three of them toppled backward into the fire-melted snow. Capuchins surrounded them. One of them took the child and began to comfort him. The others

pulled Charles and their brother to their feet, thanking and blessing them.

"Well done." Père Michaut, the Capuchin superior, bowed
slightly to Charles. His white beard was singed and streaked with
soot, and his gown was spattered with small holes from burning
cinders. Behind him, a young layman in coat and breeches, equally
singed and soot blackened, was smiling at Charles and the friar
who had helped him.

Charles said, "Who is the boy, *mon père?* Didn't the shopkeep-
ers know he was up there?"

"He is their servant."

Charles stared at Michaut, remembering the woman's grief for
her lace and pink mules. "And they left him to burn?"

"You have saved him." Michaut's eyes held Charles's for a long
moment. "I am reminded anew that God arranges all things." He
turned to the young man standing behind him, who looked to be
twenty years old or so. "Allow me to present Monsieur Fiennes.
He lives very near us." Michaut nodded toward the gates of the
townhouse where the shop owner had gone to have her burns
tended. His eyes sought Charles's again. "And he will soon be
among us as a novice." With that, Michaut turned away and took
the listening friars with him.

Fiennes bowed. *"Enchanté, mon père."*

"The pleasure is mine, Monsieur Fiennes. But I am only *maître.* Maître Charles du Luc. Our Jesuit formation is long, and I
am still a scholastic."

"I hope I will be as faithful in my own vocation." The young
man's smile was sweet. "I am Aubin d'Auteuil de Fiennes, but
Monsieur Fiennes is enough name to call me by."

"You do me honor. But after what I have seen tonight, my
choice seems a far easier one than yours."

"God puts us where our souls need to be," Fiennes said with

a little shrug, as though murderous fire, bare boards, scant food, and wicked cold were things of no account.

Charles studied the boy. "Will you speak with me for a moment, Monsieur Fiennes?"

"With pleasure." The youth looked back at the fire with a sigh. "At least the wind has died and it will not spread. Thank God the house stands by itself. There is not much more we can do. It is so often like that. If only God would show us some better way to fight fire." Fiennes looked down at his feet. "Shall we move farther away? The water is nearly over our shoes."

Charles's cloak and cassock were wet against his back, and his shoes squelched audibly as he went with the young man toward a townhouse where a knot of servants clustered beside the lantern-lit gate.

"You seem to know something about fires," Charles said, as they made their way into the courtyard.

"With God's help, I am going to be a Capuchin, and Capuchins are the firefighters of Paris. But I hear from your accent that you are not Parisian, so perhaps you didn't know."

"I did, but I had never seen them at it. I am much impressed by their bravery and effort."

"They impress devotion on my heart in every way. Please come inside, *maître*, you are welcome."

Inside the townhouse, a maid took them to a small *salon* where fire, reduced to the role of good servant, crackled welcomingly in the fireplace. A basin of warmed water and towels were brought, and when they had cleaned their soot-blackened faces and hands, Fiennes bade Charles sit beside the fire and served him wine and cakes from a side table. Charles looked at the *salon*'s sumptuous carpets and tapestry, at the rich red wine in his gold-veined Venetian glass, at the upholstered chairs fringed with gold. He, too, had given up some comfort, but nothing compared to what Fiennes was about to leave. Yet seeing him in the light, Charles realized that this son of wealth was dressed very differently from Gilles Brion, with his frothing lace and up-to-the-minute suit. Fiennes's coat and breeches were of plain, even rough, brown wool, with only a glimpse of coarse white linen at the throat and wrists.

Charles ate and drank gratefully, but also guiltily. If Fiennes was who Charles thought he must be, then God—or Michaut—or the fire—or all three together—had delivered him into Charles's hands. And what Charles needed to ask was not going to be easy.

But he was wrong. The youth was so radiantly happy that nothing seemed to trouble him.

"Yes, *maître*," he said simply, in response to Charles's question, "Gilles Brion is my dear friend. Dearer than life itself to me." His soft brown eyes were the most guileless Charles had ever seen. "I pray for him day and night. I have gone to the Châtelet, but the guards will not let me see him. He has done no murder, of that I am certain. Why God has put him into prison, I cannot understand."

"I think you may be able to help get him out, if you will answer what I have to ask."

"I will."

"Monsieur Henri Brion was killed early on the Friday morning after the Nativity. And Père Michaut says that on Thursday night, Gilles Brion was a guest at the Capuchin monastery."

"Yes."

"Did he come to this house during that night?"

Fiennes looked down. "Yes." He looked up again, and Charles was disconcerted to see his smile.

"How long did he stay with you?"

"He came just after Compline and he stayed until an hour or a little less before Prime. He left me then to go and do something we'd been praying about during the night."

"What was that?" Though Charles thought he knew, he wanted to be sure.

"We prayed that the young woman his father was forcing on him would agree to tell Monsieur Brion that she would not marry Gilles."

"And how long was he gone on this errand?"

"Perhaps three-quarters of an hour. It was still dark when I met him in the Capuchin church for Prime. We were there well before the Prime bell, so no one knew that Gilles had left the monastery."

Whether or not Père Michaut knew that Gilles had been out on that particular night, it was clear to Charles that the Capuchin superior was aware of the pair's mutual devotion. Though whatever doubts it may have given him about Brion, he seemed to have none about Fiennes. If only Gilles had not left Fiennes to go and plead with Martine. Because that three-quarters of an hour's absence was plenty of time to do murder. To do both murders, in fact, since Henri Brion's body had been found so near the Mynette house. And Fiennes's story also confirmed Gilles's presence at the Mynette house that morning. Still, though Gilles Brion seemed weak and self-regarding, he was not mad. Charles could not believe that he could pray all night with Fiennes, leave to go murder two people, and then return to Prime as though nothing had happened.

"How did Gilles seem when you joined him for Prime?"

Fiennes sighed. "Very upset. His errand had not sped. In spite of all our prayers."

Very upset. A detail that would not help convince La Reynie

that Gilles had done nothing but talk at Martine's house. Charles was staking everything on the hope that La Reynie would be swayed by Fiennes's guileless innocence and demeanor. "Is there anyone here in your house who saw Gilles Brion come and go?" Charles said. "And could swear to the times?"

"Oh, yes."

"Who?" Charles asked skeptically. It was not the answer he had expected.

"My mother's maid. She has been here for years and knows all about Gilles; she lets him in when he comes. And she's a very early riser and opened the door for him when he left to go across the river."

Charles blinked. "Well, what you've told me may help your friend. But if you agree to also tell the police, you will be risking hard questions about your connection to Monsieur Brion."

"There is nothing wrong in our connection, Maître du Luc. We love each other, yes. We consider ourselves spiritual brothers. Gilles has been tempted to a baser connection with me. But I have persuaded him that it would be grave sin. Now he wants only for us to be near one another and be truly brothers, Capuchin brothers, serving God together. We have nothing to hide."

"Still, it may not be easy to convince the police of that. They may well be merciless in asking what you did that night."

Fiennes's face shone. "We prayed for Gilles. And talked about God. What else would we do?"

Charles found himself speechless and rebuked. The young man's words rang with truth. He only hoped La Reynie would hear what he heard, and that it would weigh against that damning three-quarters of an hour's absence. "Will you go to the Châtelet with me when it's light? If we can get through the snow."

Fiennes jumped up and went to a window. "It's not snowing

anymore. Though the snow is deep. I will ask my father for horses."

"Thank you, *monsieur*. The sooner we get there, the better." Charles was hoping that Gilles Brion's long, dark night in the prison had been no more than lonely and uncomfortable, hoping that La Reynie was still holding out against Louvois.

Chapter 22

Without the horses, they would never have made it to the Châtelet. Even with them, a ride that should have taken a few minutes took nearly an hour. People wrapped in coats, cloaks, and shawls were wielding brooms and shovels to clear drifted snow from doors, gates, church porches, and streets. It was the Feast of St. Geneviève, the patron saint of Paris, a day full of processions through the city, coiling lines of laymen and clergy chanting and carrying relics and candles. Today, though, the saint's processions were going to be late beginning, because in most of the streets the snow was still deep and uncleared. As the Châtelet's white-blanketed roofs and towers rose before them, Charles realized belatedly that Lieutenant-Général La Reynie might well not be there. He might simply have decided to stay at home beside his fire in this weather.

The guards at the prison entrance were cold and irritable. The one Charles approached only shrugged and wiped his dripping nose on his sleeve. Cold and largely sleepless, Charles implied harm to the man's immortal soul if he refused. The guard finally left his fellow holding the entrance and conducted them to La Reynie's office. An even more irritable voice behind La Reynie's door called "Come!" when the guard knocked, and Charles released his held breath in a sigh of relief. The guard stalked away. Charles and Fiennes went in.

La Reynie stood in front of a dying fire, rubbing his face. His cloak was on the floor beside one of the armchairs and his wig lay on the other chair's seat. Startled at this state of undress, Charles wished him a good morning.

"It is not a good morning," La Reynie growled, raking a hand through his spiky gray hair. "What do you want?" He glanced unhappily at Fiennes. "And who is this?" His frown deepened as he looked more closely at Charles. "What's happened to you?" He reached out toward the burn holes in Charles's cloak.

Charles smiled. "Monsieur La Reynie, may I present Monsieur Fiennes? We have been helping the Capuchins fight a fire."

The two men bowed to each other.

"The Capuchins do well," La Reynie said, eyeing Fiennes. "I wish we had them all over Paris. And how did you come to be helping them, *monsieur?*"

"He is soon to be a Capuchin novice," Charles said, before Fiennes could answer.

La Reynie grunted, glowering at Charles. "And? Have you come to tell me you're joining the Capuchins, too?"

Charles bit back a reply, taking in the *lieutenant-général's* shadowed eyes and limp, wrinkled linen. La Reynie had apparently been up most of the night, too.

"I know now where Gilles Brion was the morning his father died. I have brought Monsieur Fiennes to tell you himself. And there is also another witness to confirm some of what he is going to say."

La Reynie closed his eyes and swore softly. Then, still without inviting his guests to sit, he went to the door, jerked it open, and bellowed into the passage. "Guillaume! Wine! Bread! Now!"

He turned back into the room, swore at the freezing air sweeping through the open door from the passage, went back and slammed the door shut, and dropped into an empty chair.

"Maître du Luc, put that wig somewhere—no, give it to me, at least it's warm." He jammed the wig on his head. "Forgive me, Monsieur Fiennes, please, sit down. I apologize for being somewhat *en déshabillé* this morning. *Maître*, bring a chair for yourself."

Charles went to pull a chair away from the wall and closer to the dead fire.

La Reynie was looking morosely at the cold hearth. "Who would have thought this day could get so much worse, so quickly?" he muttered. He scowled over his shoulder and bellowed "Fire!" at the closed door.

As Charles sat down in the chair he had brought, the door opened and a cheerful, middle-aged servant edged in, carrying a bucket of kindling and balancing a small pewter tray crowded with pitcher, glasses, and a loaf of bread.

"Here you are, *mon lieutenant-général.*" He put the tray on the table beside La Reynie and knelt in front of the fire. "And just so you know," he said, poking and prodding the ashes as he looked for live embers, "you're not here today."

"I am very glad to hear it," La Reynie said, sarcasm dripping from his words like melted butter. "Where am I? Am I enjoying myself, wherever it is?"

"I couldn't say where you are, *monsieur*, but I'm certain you're enjoying yourself more than you would be if I'd told Monsieur Louvois's man you're here."

"Blessed saints. Thank you, Guillaume. Every day I am so much deeper in your debt, I will never be able to repay you."

The man smiled to himself and fell to blowing on a live coal. La Reynie poured wine into the glasses Guillaume had brought, handed two to Charles and Fiennes, and took his own.

"Tell me then, Monsieur Fiennes," he said resignedly, "this tale that may help to release Monsieur Brion from his present accommodation."

Fiennes told him. As he talked, La Reynie's attention sharpened. By the end, he was gazing open-mouthed at the young man.

"You are very frank, *monsieur*," he said, when Fiennes had finished. "Either you are far too clever and devious an actor to waste yourself as a Capuchin, or you are so transparent that even the Capuchins may have difficulty coping with you."

Fiennes simply smiled like a small glowing sun. Watching him, Charles almost imagined that the air grew warm. The *lieutenant-général* drained his wineglass and reached for the pitcher.

"However, your rather startling story changes nothing." He glanced irritably at Charles. "You have confirmed for me that Gilles Brion was indeed at the Mynette house that morning. And in the three-quarters of an hour about which you are so certain, he had enough time to—"

"Oh," Fiennes interrupted, "I had forgotten, there is something else! Forgive me, Monsieur La Reynie—and you also, Maître du Luc. I forgot to tell you both that when Gilles returned that morning for Prime, he told me he had barely avoided encountering his father."

La Reynie was out of his chair and standing over Fiennes. "Saw his father where? Did they talk?"

Charles put a hand over his eyes, feeling like he'd just pushed Gilles Brion's head the rest of the way into the noose. How could Fiennes be so stupidly naive? That guilelessness was dangerous was a thought Charles hadn't had before.

Fiennes was looking earnestly up at La Reynie. "Gilles said that as he came out of the gate into the Mynette garden, he saw his father, hurrying across the Place Maubert."

"It wasn't light enough to recognize a face. How did he know it was his father?"

"Oh, he knew him from his shape and walk—it was his father, after all! But after what had just happened with Mademoiselle Mynette, Gilles didn't want to meet his father, so he turned and ran."

"So he told you."

"Gilles has never lied to me."

Charles hardly heard him, suddenly seeing Gilles's father walking toward the Mynette house that dark morning. Was that the answer after all? That Henri Brion had killed his ward to have her money? But Henri Brion was dead, and what mattered now was keeping his son alive.

"I see," La Reynie said to Fiennes. "Well, at least we know exactly how long he was gone from you. And that he was where both murder victims were. With time to kill them, since they were in the same place. Very valuable knowledge. Don't you agree, Maître du Luc?"

Charles got to his feet and said doggedly, "It will be valuable. When the whole truth comes out. But there's a bright side, even for me. Now that you've decided that you don't want any more truth, you have less reason to put Brion to the question."

Fiennes was looking in dismay from one to the other. "Put him to the question? Torture him, you mean? You must not do that, Monsieur La Reynie. Gilles is weak. He will lie to you to save himself pain. And his lie will be on your soul, surely you see that. It is for the good of your own soul that you must not torture him, *monsieur*." Fiennes walked closer to the *lieutenant-général*. Charles was almost embarrassed by the gentleness and sadness in the young man's face as he studied La Reynie. "Do not take your own unhappiness out on him. It will do no good."

La Reynie's face was like stone. Fiennes stepped away and sighed. "I will wait for you outside, *maître*."

In silence, Charles and La Reynie watched him leave.

"He may talk like a saint, but he's just handily convicted his friend." La Reynie laughed harshly. "Not what you intended, was it?"

"No. But you're still wrong. Gilles Brion didn't kill anyone."

"After what you just heard? You have more brains than that."

"You're not sure he's guilty, either. I see it in your face. So did Fiennes."

"What you don't see is that Monsieur Louvois was here again last night, in spite of the snow. He brought a delegation from the Hôtel de Ville. The good city worthies came to demand that I formally charge Gilles Brion with the murders of his father and Martine Mynette. Then the worthies left, and Monsieur Louvois stayed behind to tell me that if I do not charge him, and the people riot because they think I am protecting Jesuits and leaving these murders unavenged, my position is forfeit."

"But you cannot—"

"For God's sake, let me finish! Whether or not you and Monsieur Fiennes are right, I must keep Brion here. Having someone arrested for the murders—even if not yet formally charged—is preventing worse in the streets than has already happened. I cannot release him until I am certain he is not guilty—and, by the *bon Dieu*, that young man's wide-eyed statement has *made* me more certain that he is."

"Have you put him to the question yet?"

"No."

"Are you going to?"

"Are you going to find this ex-gardener?" La Reynie shot back. "This Tito you've been asking about? If by any chance Brion is proved innocent, I have to have someone to put in his place. Not that this Tito sounds likely. So, have you found him?"

"No."

"Well, keep looking."

With the slightest of bows, Charles left La Reynie and made his way to where Fiennes was waiting. Forcing himself to keep his anger and disappointment out of his face and voice, he said, "Can your father spare these horses a while longer, Monsieur Fiennes?"

"I imagine so."

"Then I beg the favor of riding to the Couche. On the Île."

Fiennes nodded. "I am sorry if I made things more difficult in there. But what I said was the truth and I had forgotten to tell you."

"I cannot but wish you had continued to forget, *mon ami.*"

"Gilles has killed no one, *maître.* I do not think God will let him be hanged. Or tortured. Perhaps if he were ready to be a saint—but my poor Gilles is not ready. So there is nothing to fear."

Charles could find nothing he trusted himself to say in response to that, so in silence they made their slow way across the Pont au Change, stopping while a belated procession in honor of St. Geneviève paced and chanted its slow way across their path. As Charles waited, he thought about the saint. Geneviève's story said that she'd saved Paris from Attila and his marauding Huns. Deciding that if she could handle Attila, she could probably handle Michel Louvois, he prayed to her to help him save Gilles, show him the real killer.

Keeping the horses to the edge of the narrow rue de la Juiverie on the Île, to avoid the impassible center where snow dug away from doors and gates had been flung, Charles and Fiennes finally reached rue Neuve Notre Dame. Charles drew rein and caught his breath, gazing at the cathedral's west front rising in front of him. He'd rarely seen it from this angle since coming to Paris. Its square towers rising into the clearing sky's icy blue, its crowding sculptures frosted in snow, washed the tiredness from his body and the worry and discouragement from his mind. Beside him, Fiennes also drank in the cathedral's wonders.

"How did they do it?" he said. "That's what I always wonder, *maître*. Wouldn't it have been glorious to help build it?"

In spite of his anger at himself and exasperation with Fiennes, Charles found himself smiling. "It would."

But his smile died quickly when they reached the Couche, the house where abandoned babies found alive were brought. As he stood at the gate, waiting for an answer to the bell, a booted man with a large cone-shaped basket on his back pushed past him with a muttered excuse. The man took a key as long as Charles's hand from his coat and forced it into the gate's frozen lock. Swearing under his breath, he worked to turn the key. Tiny cries came from the basket on his back. Charles's heart turned over as he realized that the man was a city worker paid to search for foundlings at doors, under bridges, in churches. The Couche was getting a new delivery of infants.

When the man finally opened the gate, Charles slipped through with him, leaving Fiennes to look after the horses. The baby finder slid in the courtyard's deep snow and Charles leaped forward, afraid the basket would upend. The cries coming from it grew frantic, but the carrier found his feet, and he and Charles reached the door together. The Sister of Charity watching the door allowed the baby finder to enter, but barred Charles's way.

"Yes, *mon père*?" she said, not so much unwelcoming as openly puzzled by the Jesuit standing before her with burn holes in his hat and cloak.

"Ma soeur," Charles began, but his voice died as he watched the man with the basket on his back disappear into a passageway. "What will happen to them?"

Her face softened and she beckoned him inside and shut the door. "They will go to wet nurses."

"And then?"

"Those who live will be returned to our house in the Faubourg St. Antoine. A few will be adopted. By common people, you understand. Most will be placed as servants and apprentices."

The terrified and forgotten child in the burning building's window rose in Charles's mind, and he nearly bit blood from his tongue to stop himself from demanding the basket and taking the infants with him.

"Ma soeur," he said, sighing, "I have urgent need of information. About a foundling who came to you as much as twenty years ago. All I know of him is that he was called Tito."

Her wimple and veil, so white and starched that light bounced off them, made it hard to tell her age. Charles guessed that she might be forty.

"I was not here that long ago." She smiled sadly. "I entered the order after my husband died." She paused, thinking. "But yes, there is a sister who was here then. Soeur Mariana, a Spanish woman."

"Please," Charles said eagerly, "may I speak with her?"

"No, *mon père.* She is old and has been ill."

His heart sank. "Is she expected to recover?"

"I think so. We are praying for her."

"If—when—she feels well enough, will you ask her about this boy Tito?"

"This is important?"

"Life and death may depend on it, *ma soeur.*"

"If she is well enough, I will ask her. Come back in a few days. I am Soeur Madeleine."

She inclined her head to Charles, who bowed and withdrew. The sky was cloudless now and Charles had to squint against the snow glare as he plodded across the court, trying to pray that Soeur Mariana would recover for her sake, not his.

Chapter 23

The lay brother in the clothing room was not pleased. Charles stood before the clothing counter in his cassock, watching the brother inspect the holes in his cloak. "Another cloak gone." The brother glared at Charles, demanded his hat, and turned it slowly in his hands. Charles realized that he was counting the singed places, perhaps to charge each one to Charles's purgatory account as so many extra years of penance. Charles unobtrusively clasped his hands behind his back to hide the tiny cinder burns in his cassock sleeves. As he moved, the brother sniffed the air.

"You smell like a peasant's fire. That cassock will probably have to be washed. Wool is never the same after washing, you know that. Let me see your shoes."

Charles held out one cold sodden foot and then the other.

The brother rolled his eyes and sighed. "Take them off. The cassock, too. Behind the curtain there."

Muttering and shaking his head, he left Charles shivering in shirt and stockings while he searched his stores for replacements. When he came back, he was still muttering.

"Frenchmen are short. Except, of course, you. At least your feet are smallish. Here."

He thrust a cassock, cloak, and shoes around the curtain. "The cassock hasn't been worn for I don't know how long. The smell will air out. Your hat you'll just have to keep for now," he added with satisfaction. "I don't have another one."

"Thank you, *mon frère*." Charles put on the ancient cassock and cincture, which smelled of moth remedies and looked as though they'd been in the clothing store since one of St. Ignatius's original companions turned them in. The shoes, for a miracle, came close to fitting him. And the cloak was heavier than the one he'd lost at the fire. Clothed again, he walked around the curtain and bowed to the clothing master. "Again, my apologies, *mon frère*, and my thanks."

"I trust your confessor will hear how much of my stores you have destroyed."

"He will, *mon frère*."

Charles bowed again and escaped. The bright sunshine was at its early January zenith, striking rainbows from ice crystals and glittering on the snow, but it had no more warmth than a painting of sunshine. Père Le Picart had received Charles's report before dinner with some alarm at the firefighting story, and disappointment that what Charles had discovered was not enough to confirm Brion's claims of innocence. Le Picart had also given Charles permission to return to the Couche when need be. For now, though, Charles had his usual duties to perform. He turned his steps toward the *grand salon* for the student confraternity's almsgiving, trying to ignore how little his wet stockings were doing for the comfort of the new shoes. He'd gone to the Capuchins wearing both his pairs of stockings for warmth and had not had the courage to ask anything more of the clothing brother.

Arriving early in the *grand salon*, he sat down in one of the armchairs to wait for the students. His eyes closed almost immediately and he slept till the jarring of his head falling forward woke him. He stared sleepily at the framed paintings of Jesuits on the *grand salon*'s walls, and the other paintings and engravings scattered among them. The nonportrait drawings were changed from time to time, and Charles got up to look more closely at one he hadn't seen before. It was an engraving of a heart—not the familiar symbol of Christ's Sacred Heart, but a liverish-red anatomical rendering that might have been drawn at an autopsy. It was pierced with a myriad of tiny black swords. Sins, the caption explained, damaging and deforming the heart of the sinner. Which should have made him consider the state of his own sinful heart, but instead made him wonder what the Condé's heart might look like under its silk wrappings.

"Here they are, *maître*," a tutor said from the street passage door.

The boys distributing the week's alms for the older *pensionnaires'* Congregation of the Ste. Vierge came in. Two carried a hip-high basket of loaves between them, and three others were nearly hidden behind the piles of garments in their arms. The remaining pair of boys brought the walnut table from the *grand salon* to the antechamber and placed it in front of the double doors.

Charles thanked and dismissed the tutors, helped the boys arrange the loaves and clothing, and gathered them for prayer. Then Armand Beauclaire and Walter Connor pushed open the great doors, the snow in front of them having been cleared aside by lay brothers. To Charles's surprise, Marin was already standing there. The old man hobbled forward.

"Have you medicine, *maître*?" He seemed much more himself than when he'd fled from Charles outside the church of St. Louis.

"Not here. Are you ill, Marin?"

"Not me. My boy Jean. He's coughing up his guts. Has been for a while, but it's worse now."

Charles grimaced in sympathy, remembering the young man's thinness and harsh cough. "I can ask our infirmarian for something to help him." Charles called Beauclaire to him. "Monsieur Beauclaire, go to Frère Brunet and ask for the remedy he uses for coughs. As many lozenges as he will give you. Quickly."

Beauclaire bowed, happily important at being trusted with the errand, and sped away. One of the other boys handed Marin a loaf, and the old man tore off a piece and moved aside, eating while he waited.

People were crowded around the doors now, narrow-eyed against the light. Charles stood back as the students distributed bread and clothes. Filthy hands reached for the round loaves, and pinched faces lightened at their solid weight. Charles smiled with satisfaction at the intensity of the boys' concentration, the effort they made to be courteous, in spite of the running noses, the breath stench, and the sores. In spite of wariness, and sometimes a little fear, they listened courteously to the grumbling, most of it merely sullen, some of it outright crazed.

The icicles hanging from the stonework above the doors were beginning to drip, lifting Charles's spirits somewhat to see that the thin sunshine had that much warmth. A man leaning against one of the open doors and trying on a pair of shoes cried out and leaped backward as a foot-long icicle fell to the snow beside him.

"Trying to kill you for your coins, are they?" a University of Paris student called merrily from the other side of the street. "Be on your guard!"

"Animals!" Old Marin began wading furiously through the snow toward the student, swinging his stick. "I don't see your kind giving anything, you pigs!"

The boy and his laughing fellow students hurled snowballs at him and darted down the rue des Poirees, which led off the rue

St. Jacques deeper into the University's territory. Cursing them and their fathers back to Adam, Marin brushed snow off his face and coat. Most of those receiving alms had prudently ignored the University students, but a few women cast frightened eyes at Charles, who sighed and stepped farther back into the antechamber's shadows. The almsgiving wore on. The last of several pairs of gloves (all worn and denuded of their trimming but still a rarity in the alms box) were given out, the man who'd dodged the icicles went away with his new shoes, and a student handed the last loaf to an old woman. Marin came back to the doors and looked anxiously into the antechamber, his face lighting with relief as Armand Beauclaire ran breathlessly in from the street passage.

"Here they are, *maître*, he just finished making them, that's what took me so long."

Thanking him, Charles took the little package wrapped in paper, told the boys to clear away the table, and went to Marin.

"These should help your Jean," Charles said. "I will pray for him."

Marin turned the little package over with his swollen, knotted fingers and glanced worriedly up at Charles. "Angels can't die, can they, *maître*?"

"Angels cannot, no."

"My Claire sent Jean to me." The old beggar's faded eyes shone with unshed tears. "I know, because he told me just how she looked. She won't let him die." Marin frowned suddenly. "Will Jean have to die for my sins?"

Charles was lost once more in Marin's crazy logic. Before he could answer, the tutors arrived to escort the boys to afternoon classes.

"Wait a little, Marin," Charles said, and called the boys together.

"Shall we close the doors, *maître?*" Beauclaire asked, but Charles shook his head.

"I will see to that. We will pray now."

He led them in giving thanks that they had alms to give, and asked that their giving be a means of grace, to themselves and to the beggars. As the boys left, the afternoon class bell began to ring. The bell also meant rehearsal, but Charles hesitated, feeling somehow reluctant to leave the old man. He went outside and pushed the double doors closed. Marin, standing in the street and murmuring to himself, didn't seem to notice.

"Marin, shall we go and stand by the postern door? I need to see someone as he comes in." Charles had decided to give Germain Morel a message for Jouvancy. "And then I will walk with you back to where you stay. And you can tell me about Claire."

For a moment, the old man's wandering wits were as clear as Charles's own. "No, no. You can't go with me." He shook his shaggy head until his ancient leather hat fell off. "Foxes have holes," he said sonorously. "But the Son of Man has no place. No son of man and no daughter of woman." He picked up his hat. "That's Scripture."

Glancing up and down the street for some sign of Morel, Charles led Marin to the postern. But before he could ask again about Claire, the dancing master arrived panting at the postern door.

"*Bonjour*, Monsieur Morel," Charles said. "I need to finish some business here and will be somewhat late to the rehearsal. Will you please tell Père Jouvancy I am detained on the rector's business?"

"Of course, *maître.*"

Morel bowed, glanced curiously at Marin, and went into the college. Charles turned to Marin, but he was interrupted again.

"Maître du Luc, look!" Marie-Ange LeClerc, in an old red

cloak trailing on the snow, burst out of the bakery and stopped breathlessly in front of Charles. "*Maman* made them!"

She held something wrapped in a white napkin out to Charles.

A strange sweet fragrance spread in the cold air. He bent closer, unwrapped the napkin, and peered at the two small golden cakes it held.

"What is it that smells so good, *ma petite*? I don't recognize the scent."

"Taste one and see if you can guess." She was almost quivering with excitement.

Charles obediently took a cake. Marie-Ange looked doubtfully at the old beggar, moved a little closer to Charles's side, and politely held out the napkin to Marin as well.

To Charles's surprise, Marin made her the ghost of a bow and held up the proffered cake in a kind of toast.

Charles bit into the cake's rich sweetness and his eyes widened in surprise. "It's wonderful! A taste I've never had before."

Marin nodded and muttered something around his mouthful.

"It's the inside of my coconut! *Maman* chopped it up and sprinkled it on the cakes."

"Tell her if she makes more, they will be the rage of all Paris! Thank you, *mademoiselle*, and our thanks to your mother."

Marie-Ange dimpled and curtsied. "I am going to Martinique, *maître*," she confided, "the very first minute I am old enough. I will marry Antoine and we will send *Maman* all the coconuts she wants and she will be rich from her cakes." With a confident smile that surprised Charles with a glimpse of the young woman she would be one day, Marie-Ange hauled up the tail of her cloak and went back to the bakery.

Marin, licking his fingers, watched her go. "That one is very pretty, but she is not Claire. I can tell by how brown her hair is. She is very kind. But not Claire. Sometimes I still find Claire."

He frowned suddenly and shook his head. "But sometimes demons steal her golden hair and when I ask for alms, they laugh at me."

Charles waited, baffled by the way the old man's mind twisted and turned among its phantasms.

"Fair as the moon. Sad like the moon." Marin sighed out a miasma of rotten teeth and garlic and clutched at Charles's cassock. "More fair than you," he said, looking hard at Charles's hair. "Do you know what they did to her? Do you?"

"No." Charles gently released himself from the clutching fingers.

"Twelve years old." Marin had turned half away and seemed to be watching the blue shadows creep across the snow in the street. "She was little, like a doll. Dwarf, some called her, but she wasn't; she was made as prettily as any girl. Her hair was like curled moonlight and they dressed her in jewels and satin for her betrothal. To that pig Condé. He was embarrassed because she was so little. He made them put heels on her like stilts. She could hardly walk. When all the show was over and it was time for her to dance with him, the actors wheeled a little bridge up to where she sat, raised up in a wooden stand with the rest of the nobility. She had to manage her skirts and walk across it to meet her bastard bridegroom. She did, and they started to dance, with everyone watching. My Claire did the best she could, but those devil's heels pitched her onto her face. Everyone laughed at her. The Condé was seventeen, he was nearly a man, but did he feel any pity, did he help her up? Not he; he turned red as a dog's behind and refused to look at her." Marin's eyes came back to Charles. "I tried to kill him," he said matter-of-factly.

"You—how?" *And how are you still alive if you tried*, Charles didn't say.

"I was a Condé page. They dressed us up and gave us boys'

swords and placed us around the dancing floor. The swords were sharp, and when she fell and he didn't help her, I ran at him, trying to draw, but my sword stuck in its scabbard. They only thought I was running to Claire's rescue. So they sent me to her household. So golden, so pretty . . ." His lucidity vanished in a long-drawn wail. "Claire, forgive me, Sacred Heart, forgive me . . ."

He lunged away from Charles and flailed his way through the tumbled snow up St. Geneviève's hill. With a sick sense of pity for the little princess and the boy the old man had been, Charles watched him go. Then, thinking uneasily about Marin's demons and the sword story, and remembering that Marin had struck down and probably killed the man who had tried to stab him in the tavern fight, Charles rang the postern bell.

Chapter 24

In the *salle des actes*, the familiar lunacy of rehearsal came as a relief. Germain Morel was shouting at Henri Montmorency, who was mounted on his golden plinth and pointing his baton at his two-soldier brigade with utter disregard for music, choreography, or the dancing master's exasperation. At the other end of the room, Jouvancy stalked back and forth in front of the stage like a displeased crow, listening to a scene from the Latin tragedy.

"No!" Jouvancy jumped onto the stage and grabbed the fledgling St. Nazarius by the back of his coat. "You are a saint! Have you never heard of humility? Dear God, are you *trying* to look like a fat merchant addressing his guild?" With both hands, he pushed the boy's shoulders forward, shoved his head lower, and stepped back. "Better."

St. Nazarius, looking now like a wild-eyed hunchback, quavered. "Yes, *mon père*. Shall I go on?"

"Yes. No! You're still not right."

"But, *mon père*," St. Nazarius ventured from his crouch, "the saints seem proud to be saints. At least, their statues do. I mean, not like this—"

"They're not proud till they're dead." Jouvancy glowered at his actor as though offering him that opportunity, then seemed to think better of it. "Watch." In a silken transformation, the rhetoric master softened his spine, bent his neck just enough, opened his hands, and became the perfect humble saint. "Like this, do you see?"

The other actors, recognizing the start of a long ordeal for the unfortunate Nazarius, faded silently into the background. Keeping his face carefully straight, Charles moved so that Jouvancy would see that he'd arrived. The rhetoric master gave him a vague glance, as though he'd forgotten quite who Charles was, and turned his attention back to his saint.

At the dance end of the room, Morel was now standing on Montmorency's plinth, directing the two soldiers through the steps of their *Air Animé* with authoritative grace and singing the music.

"Do I have to sing?" Montmorency asked in horror when he finished.

"No, Monsieur Montmorency," Charles cut in smoothly, to keep Morel from saying what he was all too obviously about to say. "No one is asking you to sing. Monsieur Morel, shall I work with the other dancers?"

"If you would be so kind, *maître*," Morel said through his teeth. "Now, Monsieur Montmorency, let me see you direct your soldiers." With the light of battle in his eye, he took up his small violin from a bench against the wall.

Smiling with satisfaction that Montmorency had met his match, Charles went to the other dancers. Most were going silently through their steps, though without the full execution the steps would have in performance. Marking the steps, dancers called it. Michele Bertamelli, though, was doing what he'd learned of his *canarie* as though the world were watching. *Canaries* were full of springing steps, and as Charles watched, Bertamelli nearly propelled himself through one of the south-facing windows.

"*Doucement*, Monsieur Bertamelli," Charles cried, running across the floor and pulling the boy to a halt. "You are a magnificent jumper, but that is not all you must be to perform this dance!"

"But, Maître du Luc, it only jumps, it jumps everywhere, what else does it do?" Bertamelli's shoulders were around his ears. "So what else can I do?"

"For your jumps to be as beautiful as they can be, you must also know how to go slow, Monsieur Bertamelli. Remember, dancing is not the same as doing tricks."

The little Italian stared at Charles in frank bewilderment.

"And jumping is like pulling a rabbit out of a hole," Charles improvised, miming his words. "If I only reach down a little way and pull out my rabbit, well, it's nice to see a rabbit, but it's not all that exciting. But if I pull my rabbit out of a very deep hole, it is another thing entirely." Charles extracted his imaginary rabbit.

Bertamelli's eyes widened. "I see, I see!" He clapped his hands. Then his face fell. "If my jumps are the rabbit, *maître*, where is the hole?"

"The hole is only a verbal figure, the kind you learn in the rhetoric classroom. You make your jumps more astonishing by being able to go slow as well as fast. So I am giving you a very very difficult exercise, *mon brave*," Charles said gravely. If Bertamelli thought the exercise was so difficult that doing it well enhanced his honor, he would give his life's blood to it.

"Watch now." Charles walked across the *salle* and faced the boy. He drew himself up and began to walk. With utter concentration, so slowly, so intentionally, that every smallest movement, every lightest touch of a part of his foot on the floor was a physical revelation. Hardly breathing, Bertamelli watched, his wide black eyes seeming to take up most of his face. Before Charles reached him, Bertamelli's body was moving as Charles was moving.

"You see, then," Charles said.

"Oh, I do, *maître*." The boy wiped his sweating face. "It is very hard indeed. How can that be?"

"Keep on doing it and you will understand. After you practice like that, you will understand much more where your jumps come from. You will pull astonishing and beautiful rabbits out of the very deepest holes, *mon brave*."

Thinking that this child's "rabbits" were going to be very astonishing and very beautiful indeed, Charles left him to it and called the shy Charles Lennox aside. They went to work on the majestic, but short, measured, and relatively simple *entrée grave* he'd persuaded Monsieur Charpentier to include for Lennox's St. Ambrose.

When the bell rang for three o'clock, Charles was sure it could not be so late. Lennox had turned out to be surprisingly good at making himself into a grave old man and putting the dignity of age into his steps.

"Well done, indeed, Monsieur Lennox," he said, as the boy made him a *reverence*.

"Thank you. I like dancing, Maître du Luc." Lennox's barely audible voice was presently wandering painfully up and down the scale. "I wish I could dance all the time. Or play cricket."

"Cricket? What is that?"

"It's just a game, *maître*. But I like it." Lennox's blue eyes lit with a rare smile and he bowed to Charles, picked up his hat, and moved with the other boys to the door.

Holding Montmorency's flaking gold baton and shaking it as he talked, Morel escorted the hapless noble soldier to join them. Jouvancy chivied his actors down the room, still talking intently to poor St. Nazarius, whose eyes looked as glazed as sugared figs. When Jouvancy saw Charles, he paused and Nazarius escaped.

"Ah, Maître du Luc, you are with us, good, good, it is all going very well. I think we must make these French operas a yearly thing, they are very good practice for the boys. Very beautiful. And you, Monsieur Morel, are heaven sent. Perhaps I will write to our usual dancing master—Maître Beauchamps, you know—that he may stay in Italy and buy pictures, for all we care! On, now, go on," he called to the students, "quickly, I am following. The ancients await us!"

With a bow to Charles, Morel moved toward the door also.

"Monsieur Morel," Charles said, "before you go, please, how is it with Mademoiselle Brion and Monsieur Callot?"

Morel shook his head. "Nearly as bad as it could be. She can think of nothing but her brother. Monsieur Callot tried to see him, but Lieutenant-Général La Reynie would not allow it. And he would not tell Monsieur Callot if he is going to charge Gilles with the murders. As for my own affairs, I fear more each day that Mademoiselle Brion will join the Ursulines. I must go back to them now. I try to keep them company in the evening."

Charles wanted quiet for thinking. When Morel's footsteps had faded on the stairs, he went out through the snow-covered courtyards, across the fathers' garden, and into the main college library. Built only a few years ago, the library was one of the quietest places in the crowded school. He would have liked to settle on a bench under Louis le Grand's ancient grapevine, said to be a relic from the Romans who had once settled St. Geneviève's hill, calling it Lutetia. But the vine was only bare sticks now and the library was relatively warm. Inside, he went quickly up to the second floor and along a gallery to the little chamber called the *cabinet* of natural history.

He'd often found it deserted and a good place to think. Though small, it had two large windows to throw ample light on the treasures ranged along its shelves and in its cupboards. Charles wandered past heaps of sparkling pink and purple quartz, nuggets of gold, ancient gold and silver coins, bronze and gold brooches for fastening cloaks, huge outlandish seashells, a stone head of Julius Caesar with a badly chipped eye (discovered when the foundations for the college chapel were dug), shelves of brilliant butterflies on boards, a tiny pair of embroidered Chinese shoes, and a grayish, uninviting bezoar stone from a Near Eastern goat's belly. There was also a waist-high globe, leather-surfaced and brightly painted, for those who wanted to see where all these things had come from.

Charles stopped at the end of the little room, in front of his favorite thing in the *cabinet*, and ran his fingers along it. The long, ornately twisted, ivory horn glimmered in a pool of sunlight. The fabulous unicorn's horn, some insisted, though Charles thought it was more likely the horn from a great fish sailors claimed to see—and sometimes catch—far out of sight of land. In truth, he didn't much care what it was; he loved it for its beauty. And for the way it drew to itself the human longing for miracles and wonders, for something good and beautiful beyond the everyday world. He rested his hand on the warmly glowing ivory, thinking unhappily about Marin.

The raving old man saw his lost Claire in every pretty, fair-haired girl. But some girls turned out to be demons, he'd said. They refused him alms, they laughed at him. Marin begged all over the *quartier*. What if he'd gone to the Mynette house for alms and Martine Mynette had been frightened by him, refused him, even tried to push him away? Marin had matter-of-factly told Charles that he'd tried to kill the Prince of Condé. And Charles had seen him strike down his would-be assassin outside the tavern. Even more disturbingly, Marin had suddenly taken to muttering about the Sacred Heart. Charles, like everyone else, heard it in capitals, Jesus' Sacred Heart of growing popular devotion. But what if Marin didn't mean it like that? What if he meant Martine Mynette's little red enamel heart on its embroidered ribbon? Involuntarily, Charles shook his head. He didn't want that to be true. But who else was there? So far, there was only the shadowy Tito, as hard to lay hands on as a unicorn. And there was Gilles Brion. Charles and Monsieur Fiennes could be wrong. Brion had had reason to kill both Martine and his father, better reasons, as sane men reckoned, than either of the others. But Charles simply could not imagine him doing it.

Loud whispers made Charles turn. A small boy, surely one of the college's youngest students, had come in with his tutor. Perhaps nine or ten years old, dressed in brown velvet under his scholar's gown, the boy stared wide-eyed around the *cabinet*.

"Where is it, *maître*?" he whispered hoarsely to his tutor, who smiled at Charles and led the child to the shelf with the horn.

But the boy was too short to examine what was on the shelf. Charles brought a stool for the child to stand on from the end of another set of shelves, and the tutor thanked him and helped his charge up onto it.

"Oooh." The boy touched the horn as though it might dissolve under his hand. "It really is here," he breathed, turning shining eyes on his tutor and then on Charles. "There really are unicorns, then," he said, with a great sigh of relief. "I was afraid there wouldn't be. Not here."

Charles left the two in possession of the *cabinet*. As he went out onto the gallery, he realized that he'd seen the child before, that he was the youngest of the three boys who'd gone to see if the holy water was frozen in the chapel on Christmas Eve. Smiling with pleasure at the boy's delight in the horn, Charles walked under the grand painted ceiling of the ground floor, past the paintings of St. Ignatius and Francis Xavier, and out into the frozen garden. Under the winter sunset's intense orange and red, he went slowly toward supper, thinking about the child's easy trust that the horn was what he wanted it to be. Charles told himself that he could do that; he could simply keep on believing that Marin would not have killed Martine Mynette, no matter what, and keep his mouth shut. But Marin did not just look wistfully at every pretty girl, hoping that she was his beloved Claire. He saw hateful demons when he failed to find her. *And I am not nine years old*, Charles sighed to himself as the supper bell began to ring.

Charles, whose table assignments paralleled Père Jouvancy's, was once again eating his meals in the older *pensionnaires'* refectory. The huge room was at least warmer with more students present, now that most classes had begun again. Charles took his place at the end of the faculty table on the dais, looking out over the vast room. Jouvancy sat a few places to his left, toward the center, and Père Damiot was beside Charles. Supper was beans again, but at least there was mutton in the pottage. Even so, Damiot was eyeing his bowl with distaste.

"Salt it," Charles recommended. "It's not bad with more salt."

"What's that?" Damiot lifted up a whitish chunk of something on his spoon. "Blessed Virgin, is that a—a potato? Or whatever they're called? Those things are cattle feed; surely we're not that badly off yet!"

"Whatever possessed a gourmet like you to become a Jesuit? It's not a potato, it's mutton fat." Charles passed Damiot the salt.

Outside the refectory windows, iron-grilled for protection against balls and flying shuttlecocks during courtyard recreation, dark had come. The refectory was lit with the bare minimum of tallow candles, and Charles supposed that Damiot could be forgiven for thinking that someone had put potatoes in the pottage. The feeble light picked out an occasional gleam of gold on the ceiling, but for once, the ceiling painted with the Virgin's stars failed to comfort him. He kept imagining Marin helpless in the Châtelet, a useless beggar whom no one cared for, the perfect scapegoat. But if Marin had killed Martine Mynette, there had to be two murderers. There was no reason for him to have killed Henri Brion. At least, no reason Charles could think of.

"Maître du Luc," Damiot said loudly, "have you heard anything I've said?"

"What?"

"Do you want to know what I've learned about the smuggling scheme or not?"

"Certainly," Charles said, pushing his fears away.

"Here is what I learned from my father this afternoon," Damiot said, pitching his voice under the beehive sound of talk in the refectory. "I've already told our rector. So far as my father has been able to find out, there were only three other investors in the smuggling scheme besides Monsieur Bizeul the goldsmith and his friend Cantel."

"Yes, Monsieur La Reynie already told me as much."

"Well, I don't think he's told you this! Cantel, according to his furious wife, left Paris—probably with his mistress—just before midnight on that same Thursday when Monsieur Henri Brion was last seen. Madame Cantel says he's fled his creditors, and my father thinks the same. Madame Cantel also told my father that it was she who found Henri Brion in a courtyard outbuilding, just before light on Friday morning, and let him out. So," Damiot finished brightly, "there were only five investors in all. Monsieur Brion kept the number small, you see, so that each could make more money out of the scheme. And very sound policy that is, remember that."

"Oh, I will," Charles said gravely. Beyond teasing his friend, he felt grave in truth. Madame Cantel had been much more forthcoming with Monsieur Damiot than with Lieutenant-Général La Reynie. Her evidence—if she was telling the truth—put Cantel out of the running as Henri Brion's killer. Which would only turn La Reynie's attention more determinedly to Gilles Brion.

The rector rose from his chair as the signal for the final grace, and all talk stopped. Then, as the Jesuits at the faculty table were filing out, the rector drew Charles aside.

"Have you learned anything more today?" Le Picart asked, nodding at Damiot to keep going.

Charles shook his head. He was not ready to tell anyone of his growing suspicion of Marin. "Nothing, *mon père*. Père Damiot has just told me what his father learned about the senior Brion's investors, but he said that he has told you, as well."

"Yes, he came to me before supper. So nothing has changed. We have nothing more to use to quiet the rumors. Or the song." His eyes ranged over the students leaving the refectory in the required silence. "If nothing has changed by Monday, I am going to order a general day of prayer and fasting." Humor sparkled briefly in his eyes. "Though, given our supper, perhaps that would not be such an unwelcome order. Meanwhile, I must tell you that you have an extra duty tomorrow after the rising bell and prayers. I began this morning having all our entrances guarded as the day students come and go, to prevent any repeat of Thursday morning's brawl. You will take your turn tomorrow morning at the stable gate, as the younger boys come in by the lane." The rector sighed and stifled a yawn. "Let us leave this day behind and hope for better tomorrow."

Dismissed, Charles crossed the court to the main building's back door, then went through the *salon* and up the front staircase to his chambers. He was suddenly so tired he could have sat down on the stairs and slept there. When he reached his sleeping chamber, he felt his way to his candle, took it to the passage lantern and lit it, and carried it back to his room. Hugging his cloak tightly around his body—there was still only canvas in his window frame—he looked at the candlelight dancing on the little black stone Pietà in its wall niche. Though his mother had sent it as his New Year's present, he would keep it only briefly, and then it would be placed where everyone could see it. At first, he hadn't much liked the carving's dark stone. But the longer he lived with it, the more its color moved him, as though the mourning Virgin and her Son's tortured body were dark with all the world's death and suffering since Adam.

Charles set his candle firmly in its holder beside the prie-dieu and knelt. Outside, bells began to ring, from the Carmelites, the Visitandines, the Jacobins, St. Germain des Pres, Port Royal, Cluny, calling the devout to end the day with prayer. When he finished his prayers, he stayed where he was—partly because he was almost too tired to get up, but also because his mind was still on the dark Pietà. In contrast, the little painting of the Virgin and Child hanging in front of his prie-dieu was full of light and soft, clear colors. The Virgin was young and round cheeked; the plump child was squirming and laughing. *Well, that's how beginnings are*, Charles thought. *That's how youth is.*

He pushed himself to his feet and took the Pietà from its niche. He brought it to the prie-dieu and knelt again, balancing the carving on the wooden ledge. His eyes went from the painting to the little statue, from the statue to the painting. Beginning and ending, the brightness of birth and the darkness of death. But that was hardly profound. Dead children had lain on their weeping mother's breasts since the Creation. Nonetheless, he found himself staring hungrily at the way the baby in the painting and the dead man of the statue both nestled against Mary's heart. Then, for an instant, he saw it, saw what was arcing back and forth between the painting and the statue like lightning. Truth, he thought, at first. No, not truth, only love. He shook his head.

"Only" love? Whatever he glimpsed was too bright to look at. And when it was gone, he was still unable to find words for what it had been.

All the weight of his body came suddenly back to him, and he stumbled as he got up from his knees and put the black statue back in its place. His eyes closing with exhaustion, he blew out the candle, clumsily kicked off his shoes, and got into bed, still wearing his cassock for warmth, and was asleep before he got his blankets drawn up.

He dreamed of a nun. He seemed to be standing in her cell, watching her as she slept. With a sigh, she turned over and was suddenly resting her head on a luminous figure he couldn't quite see—a man's figure, he thought uncomfortably. Then, in the way of dreams, her black habit became the black of the little Pietà, and then the nun was gone and the empty bed was glowing like a star. Slowly, inevitably, the light took the form of Pernelle's naked body, shining through her veil of black hair, and the bed she lay in was his. She opened her arms to him. With a great cry, he sank onto the bed, naked now himself, holding her warmth and fragrance, stroking her silken flesh, resting his head on her breast, listening to the beating of her heart. Then the chamber was full of people. A nun held out the Sacred Heart of Jesus to him, with cherubs fluttering around it like the natural history *cabinet's* butterflies restored to life. Martine Mynette took the nun's place, holding out her wounded heart and weeping. Then Charles, alone in his bed, was holding his own heart in his hands and seeing that it was full of tiny black swords buried to the hilt in his living flesh.

He woke with tears on his face and was still awake when the rising bell sounded.

Chapter 25

The night's darkness had thinned a little by the time the youngest day boys were pouring through the stable gate under Charles's watchful eye. At the ends of the lane, lanterns swung as the lay brothers there walked back and forth. So far there had been no trouble at all. But muted talk ran along the file of black-gowned boys, and they looked anxiously over their shoulders, still fearful that Thursday's attack would happen again.

"All is well," Charles said quietly. "And silence now, if you please, *messieurs*," the rule being that talk ceased at the gate. He held up his lantern and looked along the lane to see how many more boys were still to come. When all the students were inside the college, he would go out and look for Reine. Lying awake after his dreams, he'd settled with himself that before he took his suspicions of Marin to La Reynie, he had to talk with Reine.

Seeing that the line of boys was still long, he went back to thinking about his dreams. The nun had been the least disturbing of his phantoms. Perhaps Marin's talk of the Sacred Heart had summoned her, Soeur Marguerite Marie, the Visitandine who had revived the old Sacred Heart devotion after her vision of resting her head on Jesus' heart. It was Pernelle's visitation that had disturbed him, and profoundly. His famished sinking onto the bed, onto her body, his cheek on her warm naked breast . . .

"No!" he said desperately, loudly, shaking his head. The last boys in the line jumped and looked wide-eyed at him, and he managed a reassuring smile and waved them through the gate. Then he raised his lantern and signaled to the brothers at the ends of the lane that all the boys were safely inside the college. The brothers signaled back and went to report to the officers at the front doors, as Père Le Picart's plan for the morning demanded.

Charles was shutting the gate when the sound of quick footsteps at the end of the lane made him open it again and go out to see who was there. A woman, just visible in the slowly lightening morning, was passing the lane's end, walking toward the rue St. Jacques. By her shape, she was the same woman he'd seen yesterday morning. But this time he realized that what he recognized about her were the heavy braids coiled around her head. She was one of Reine's companions, one of the beggars in the stable the night he'd fed them. He called to a lay brother to lock the gate and ran down the lane, hoping that the woman could tell him where to find Reine.

When he reached the end of the lane, the woman wasn't in sight. Charles started down toward the rue St. Jacques, thinking he'd see her going in one direction or the other. But as he passed the old building that had belonged to the college of Les Cholets and was now part of Louis le Grand and undergoing renovation, the light of the lantern he still carried fell on the snow drifted and piled against the wall. Charles stopped, gazing at the little slope of snow. From the top of the old wall stones had fallen, and under the well-trampled snow they made a rough ramp to the top of the wall. Charles wondered if the woman in the lane had disappeared so quickly because she had gone over the wall. Looking, perhaps, for leavings from the workmen to steal and sell? Cautiously, Charles mounted the frozen slope and held up his lantern to light the court of the old building. The courtyard was empty, but its carpet of snow was full of crossing footprints. Not workmen's prints, because he knew that no work had been done on the building since Christmas Eve.

Charles jumped down into the court and followed the prints to the low, iron-bound door. The wood around the door's old lock was broken and the lock useless. Warily, holding his lantern high, he pushed the door open. When he was sure that the anteroom beyond was empty, he went in and promptly stumbled over a workman's bucket. The anteroom was cluttered with debris from the repair work, and a line of planks leaned against a wall. A strong draft was blowing from behind the planks. Curious, Charles shifted two of them where the current of air was strongest, put out a hand to feel the wall behind, and felt only emptiness. He let his lantern shine into the emptiness. Worn stone stairs opened at his feet. *Caves*, he thought. Cellars. Like Louis le Grand, Les Cholets would have cellars beneath it, cellars probably much older than the buildings themselves. Père Damiot had once told him that the city was honeycombed with *caves* built before anyone's memory, many of them connected, some leading all the way to the river. Rat squeaking echoed up the stairs, and Charles backed away. If the woman he'd seen was down in that rat-infested place, she could stay there. There were other ways to find Reine.

He was replacing the plank he'd moved when someone screamed in the *cave*, a harsh, guttural scream that shaded into the high pitch of terror and stopped abruptly. *Dear God*, Charles thought, *the woman from the lane!* He flung the plank to the floor, grabbed the lantern, and started down the stairs, telling himself how stupid he was being. He was alone, he was unarmed, he knew nothing at all about the cause of the scream. Except that it came from a human throat. Someone down in that ancient darkness was terrified of more than rats, terrified beyond reason, maybe beyond hope. With every step, he expected the scream to come again. It didn't, but when he reached the bottom of the stairs, he heard voices—distant, arguing, he thought, though he couldn't hear the words. The sounds whispered off the stone of the walls and ceiling, making him unsure which way to go. But if he went any way at all, how would he find his way back? He moved the lantern slowly, close to the floor, until he saw a loose fragment of stone. Marks on the wall would show him the way back—if the lantern's candle lasted that long.

Straining to make out words, he went slowly and quietly, giving himself at least those small protections. Only a fool would burst in on an argument after hearing a scream like the one still echoing in his head. Time seemed to melt into the darkness. Charles turned a corner. Now he could hear words. And he recognized one of the voices.

"You killed her," Marin was shouting. "My blessed Claire! You murdered all her sweetness and took her sacred heart, God damn you to the lowest hell!"

"No, I didn't. I didn't mean to. Not her! And it was for you, don't you—"

Marin howled with rage, the other voice cried out in pain, and then there was silence.

Charles froze, listening. Nothing. Only the rats. And then a sound that wasn't rats threaded its way toward him, a steady calm sound. He crept forward a few steps. A high, sweet voice was singing very softly. Charles felt his way around another corner and saw a faint glow, like fire. With the glow came the song's words.

*"Little white Paternoster, sent by God from paradise . . .
now I lie down——"*

Coughing stopped the voice, and the angle of another corner
cut off the glow. At nearly the same moment, the candle flame in
Charles's lantern guttered and died, leaving him in darkness thick
as Paris mud. The darkness seemed to pull at him and hold him
back. A desire not to see, not to know who or what was singing
beside the hidden fire, assailed him. The voice began again, crooning the garbled, ancient prayer every peasant knew, less prayer than
magic.

*"Now I lie down on my bed, an angel at the foot,
two angels at the head . . ."*

Charles forced himself forward and the cellar opened out.
Beyond a fire built on the stone floor, the singer leaned over
someone resting in his lap. Charles's breath caught in his throat,
and he put a hand on the *cave* wall to steady himself. Marin was
sprawled across the singer's lap—the singer was Jean, his keeper.
Blood streamed from the old man's chest and ran across the floor
into the fire. Smiling, carefully turning aside the long-bladed
knife he held, Jean gathered Marin more closely to him and began
singing again. Charles felt the hair rise on his scalp.

*"The Virgin Mary sweetly says, lie down now, do not be afraid.
The good God is my father, the good Virgin is my mother,
the three apostles are my brothers."*

A whimper began from the deep shadows veiling the *cave* walls
and was abruptly hushed. There were other people there, Charles
realized, motionless against the stone. Jean went on singing.

"The Virgin Mary walked in the meadows,
Madame the Virgin met Saint John.
Where is God, she begged to know.
On the cross tree, I tell you so,
His feet hang down, His hands are nailed,
a little white thorn cap on his head.
Who says this prayer, both morn and night,
shall surely go to Paradise."

Jean fell silent, stroking Marin's shaggy hair. A shuddering sob from one of the women huddled against the wall made Jean look up, and he saw Charles.

"Don't worry, *maître*," he said hoarsely. "Marin has ridden my Little White Paternoster straight to paradise; he is already walking in the meadows with the Blessed Virgin."

Charles moved slowly out under the stone-ribbed roof. "Give me the knife, Jean," he said quietly. If he could get the knife, at least there would be no more deaths. Not here, anyway. "You don't need it anymore."

"I do need it." Jean kissed Marin and smoothed the white hair back again. "Reine knows."

Charles stopped. "What does Reine know?"

"She saw. But she didn't tell Marin. That was good. But when he came to himself—he did sometimes—he remembered that she'd had it."

"Reine had it? Had what?"

"Not Reine." Jean held out his left hand and showed Charles the little heart resting on his palm. "Martine stole it." He closed his fist tight around the heart. "She stole it years and years ago, but now I have it back."

Charles gaped at him. "Martine? You knew Martine?"

Jean began to cough again, doubling over until his forehead

rested on Marin's body. Realization washed over Charles and nearly turned him sick. Understanding came, but not like light, only deeper and more mournful darkness.

"You killed Martine," Charles whispered. "You're Tito."

"I didn't mean to kill her! The heart was mine, not hers! They beat me when I tried to take it back. Then I wanted to give it to Marin. And God wanted it, too. I went to Martine's house and the angels unlocked the door and took the bar away. I went up to her chamber, but she wasn't there and I couldn't find my heart. Then I heard her outside, talking to someone. So I waited, and when she came in, I asked her for it. She said terrible things and hit me. I was only trying to cut the ribbon, but—" He shuddered and his fever-bright eyes pleaded with Charles to see the right of his complaint.

"Reine recognized the heart," Charles said relentlessly. "She knew you took it from Martine."

"It was *mine*! I took it for him, I loved him, he called me his son. He wore it around his wrist because the ribbon was too short for his neck. But when he remembered he'd seen it on Martine"—tears glistened in Jean's cavernous eyes—"he called me a murderer and beat me with his stick. I thought he was going to kill me. I won't let anyone take it away from me, not ever again!"

Keeping his eyes on the knife Jean still held, Charles moved a little nearer.

Jean brought the knife up, pointing at Charles. His eyes glittered, but with rage now, not tears. "I'll kill you if you try to take it. Like I had to kill the other man. I was sorry. But he saw her dead. I knew he'd tell someone and they'd take my heart again."

"Who saw you kill her?" Charles kept his tone quiet and even. He thought he heard a rustling sound in the passage to the *cave* but didn't dare take his eyes from Jean.

"He didn't see that. If he'd seen that, he would have known it was an accident, he only saw her fall down when I cut her. But he ran away. I had to chase him and it made me cough so hard I thought I would die, too." Jean began to cough again, and blood from his mouth spattered Marin's chest.

Charles moved almost quicker than sight, circling to come behind Jean and take the knife. But a new scream, one that might have risen from hell, filled the *cave* and spun him toward the entrance. Reine burst from the darkness, pulling her own small knife from the scarves wound around her waist, and flung herself on Marin's killer.

"He loved you, he loved you like a son!"

The man who had arrived with her tried to grab her, but he was too late. Jean lurched sideways and Reine's thrust went over his head, sending her off-balance. Jean sliced upward with his own blade and ripped through her layered clothes as she fell. Then he reared onto his knees, gripping his knife in both hands, ready to stab downward, but Charles and the other man caught his wrists. Charles jerked him backward, away from Reine, who was lying across Marin's legs, and twisted his arms until the knife dropped from his hand. Charles was pulling at the cincture around his cassock, thinking to restrain Jean with it, when the other man dropped to his knees beside Jean.

"See to Reine," he cried, "I'll manage this one."

Recognizing the man as Richard, the beggar with the *fleur de lys* branded on his cheek, Charles left Jean to him and went to Reine. She was struggling to sit up, feeling herself for wounds.

He knelt beside her. "Are you hurt, Reine? Can you walk?"

She shook her head. "I am not hurt. Not my body. He only tore my finery." Her face crumpled and she tenderly folded Marin's hands across his breast. "My poor Marin, my poor old darling." She bent and laid her cheek on his veined, dirty hands. "He loved his damned Jean, he called him his angel. God forgive me!" She straightened, crooning and rocking, lost in tears, stroking Marin's hands and smoothing his hair.

Leaving questions for later—or never—Charles said the prayers for the dead. The other beggars, still hanging back in the safety of the shadows, drew closer and joined him where they could, filling the *cave* with murmuring echoes. It seemed to Charles that he'd done little else these last days but pray for the dead and those in danger of death. But then, who was not in danger of death? And what was his business, if not to pray? When he finished, he went back to Jean. The beggar Richard was sitting beside him, and the boy was shaking with fever now, coughing and exhausted. Charles took off his cloak and covered him.

Richard said, "He's had the lung sickness awhile now. I think it won't be long until he goes where he's going."

Charles nodded and watched the other beggars slip away, glad to have them gone before he summoned La Reynie.

Reine wiped her face on her skirts. "Get Nicolas, Richard," she said, holding something out to him. "Take this, he'll know it. Bring him here. Only him, do you understand?"

Richard jumped up and took the square of wood she held out. He peered at it and shook his head in wonder. "It's exactly like Marin. It's your best, I think."

"He was my best. My mark is on the back. Give it only to Nicolas."

"No, Reine, I'll go," Charles said. "They won't let Richard in." He moved so that he could see what Reine had given the man and caught his breath. The face carved in a few inches of heavily grained wood was Marin to the life. "It's beautiful," he said, marveling at her skill.

Reine took a deep, steadying breath. "When they see my mark, they will let Richard in. I want you to stay here, *maître*; I have things to say before Nicolas comes."

Richard took a last look at Jean, who was shivering and murmuring to himself under Charles's cloak, and put the carving inside his jacket and went. Charles poked at the nearly dead fire with his foot and took refuge for the moment in the mundane.

"Where do you get wood?" he said. "From the workmen's store?"

Reine pointed to the place where Charles had entered the *cave*. "There is kindling there, beside the archway from the passage. And a few bigger pieces, too."

Charles went to the archway and returned with an armload of wood. "All from the workmen?" he said, putting the wood down near the makeshift hearth.

She smiled a little, one hand resting gently on Marin's still chest. "The workmen leave much that is useful. When things disappear, they accuse the apprentices of taking them to sell. When the apprentices swear that we are the thieves, the masters hit them for lying. But we usually stay here only when the men are not working. With fire, it's none too bad. They even leave buckets and there is water down at the Saint-Séverin fountain."

"I would guess, too, that there is another way out of here?"

"Of course."

The fire blazed up, crackling and spitting, and Charles settled beside her on the floor, but where he could see Jean, who seemed to be sleeping now.

"I am so sorry about Marin," he said. *And sorry for thinking he was a killer*, he added silently. "This Jean. He is really Tito? Martine Mynette's servant?" He shook his head, still hardly able to believe it.

Reine nodded.

"You knew who he was all along."

"Yes, but I didn't know until I was in the passage and heard him speak that he'd killed Martine. May heaven forgive me, I thought Marin had killed her." She bent and kissed the old man's cooling cheek. "I would see Jean when I visited Renée. And I'd seen Martine's little necklace once or twice—in summer, when she wore her bodices cut lower." She sighed. "My poor Marin had seen it, too. Marin and I used to beg there often enough, winter and summer, and the girl would bring us out clothes and food. She was very properly brought up. Most of the others who stay with us don't know whose the heart was. Beggars in Paris come and go, like birds. But Marin knew. At least, when he was himself, he knew."

"I begin to see," Charles said. "Jean gave Marin the heart. And this morning Marin remembered whose the heart was and accused him of killing Martine. Only Marin called her Claire and said Jean had taken her 'Sacred Heart.' Then Marin started beating Jean with his stick . . . and Jean killed him."

"Martine was so fair, so blond. Marin often confused blond girls with his Claire. Marin frightened Martine, though. Sometimes when we came begging and she brought out her alms, she shrank from him. Which made the poor man call her a demon and accuse her of having stolen his Claire's beautiful hair."

"Did Jean come to you in November?"

"Yes, when Martine's mother turned him out. He said his name was Jean, and I let him be Jean. I thought he would leave when he found a place to work, but he grew attached to Marin and stayed. He was coughing even then, and I saw that he was sicker than he knew. I also saw that he kept Marin safe, safer than Marin was able to keep himself. I never told Renée where he was. Then Martine was killed, and I saw her little heart on its ribbon around Marin's wrist, and I was terrified that Marin had killed her. I charged Jean to watch him every minute. God forgive me!"

"Did you know that he killed Henri Brion, too?"

Reine's old face crumpled in dismay. "Jean? Ah, no! But why?"

"It seems Henri Brion was on his way home after an unpleasant encounter with two men he'd involved in a smuggling scheme. I imagine that Brion saw the side door of the Mynette house open and heard a cry and went to see what was wrong. And saw Martine just after Jean had stabbed her. Jean told me he didn't mean to kill her and I believe him. He meant only to cut the ribbon and take the necklace, but he must have thrust too hard and opened the great vein in her neck. But he was afraid Brion would accuse him to the police, so he chased Brion and killed him and left him in the ditch. Where you found him."

Reine closed her eyes, twisting her neck as though she were in pain. "Jean was always timid, always afraid of what might happen to him." A sob rose in her throat and she covered her face. "If only I had asked Marin where the heart came from, if only I hadn't believed my worst fear, oh, blessed saints, Marin would be alive!"

If only I hadn't, if only I had . . . The universal litany of mourning, Charles thought, for which there was no comfort.

Charles got up and searched the *cave* floor where he and Reine had struggled with Jean. A gleam of red from the fire showed him what he sought, and he leaned down and picked up Martine's necklace. He held it out to Reine.

Reine shook her head and turned away, her hands busy again stroking Marin's face, resetting his hands on his breast.

Charles closed his fingers over the necklace, unsure what to do with it.

"Our poor hearts are so often stolen," Reine said softly, looking at the dead face in her lap.

Behind them, Jean tossed and moaned.

Reine looked at Charles. "We must decide what to do about him before Nicolas comes."

Chapter 26

Running feet struck thunder from the walls of the *cave*, and a swinging lantern sent shadows spinning crazily off the ceiling.

"Reine! Reine, where are you? Answer me, for God's sake!"

"I am here, Nicolas. I am well."

Silhouetted against lantern light, the beggar Richard appeared briefly in the *cave* entrance before Lieutenant-Général La Reynie shoved him aside.

"Here, Nicolas." Reine held out a shaking hand. La Reynie covered the space between them in two strides and knelt beside her.

"Truly, *ma chère*, you are not hurt?"

"Truly. I owe what is left of my life to Maître du Luc."

La Reynie looked at Charles with gratitude so naked in his face that Charles looked away in confusion. But not before he'd seen La Reynie wrap his arms around Reine and hold her against his chest, rocking on his knees, his lips tightly closed against whatever he was trying not to say to her.

Wondering anew what lay so deep between these two otherwise so far apart, Charles wondered if La Reynie had even noticed Marin's body. Slowly, the *lieutenant-général* released Reine and got to his feet. He took the little carving of Marin from his pocket and held it out to her.

"This is very like him, Reine."

She put it carefully away inside her garments. "Nicolas—"

"At least we have his killer." His face was hard with satisfaction. He went to where Jean lay tossing with fever and looked down at him.

"*I* have him, Nicolas. And I am keeping him. Maître du Luc and I are keeping him."

La Reynie stared at Reine. Instead of the anger Charles was waiting for, the *lieutenant-général's* face creased with worry. He glanced at Charles and said gently, "Grief makes you rave, Reine. Of course I must take him, he is a murderer. At least I have found one whose guilt is certain," he said, with an ironic look at Charles. "And I will see Marin decently buried."

"Nicolas, you do not understand—"

La Reynie tried to talk over her, but Charles stopped him.

"Jean is Tito. He killed Martine Mynette and Henri Brion."

La Reynie spun toward Jean, oblivious in his fever. "He is Tito? How do you know?"

Reine said, "I knew, Nicolas. I have known for a while that he killed Martine Mynette. But I did not know until this morning that he also killed Monsieur Brion."

Before La Reynie could find words, Charles said, "The servant called Tito left the Mynette house in November, and Reine says that he joined her group of beggars then, calling himself Jean. He told me himself this morning, after he killed Marin, that he had killed Mademoiselle Mynette and Monsieur Brion, though he did not even know Brion's name. He didn't mean to kill the girl; he was trying to cut the ribbon of her necklace. He thinks the necklace is his; I don't know why. As for Henri Brion, he was a victim of poor timing. He must have been on his way home that morning, after Madame Cantel let him out of his prison, when he saw a door open at the Mynette house and went to see if something was wrong. He saw Martine dying. Jean chased him down and stabbed him in fear that Brion would denounce him to the police. Remember that Monsieur Fiennes told us that Gilles Brion saw his father crossing the Place Maubert just at that time."

La Reynie looked as though someone had given him a chest of gold.

"Thank God and all the saints! Your Jean, Tito, whoever he is, goes to the Châtelet as soon as I can summon men to take him there. If these stories stand up, I can release Gilles Brion." He strode to Reine and stood looking down at her. "And from here on, I am going to see that you are cared for." His eyes swept the *cave*. "No more of this. And this street *crotte* who tried to kill you will die as he deserves."

"Listen to me, Nicolas! He is not street dung. It is partly my fault that he killed Marin. As Maître du Luc just told you, I knew who he was; I thought it was Marin who had killed the girl, but I said nothing. If I had, the truth would have come out. It is my fault it ended like this. If I had confronted Marin, or come to you—" Reine threw her head back and stared up into the darkness. "If I had done that, Marin would be alive." Then she sighed and bowed her head in defeat. "Instead, I gave Jean the chance to further damn himself. Unwittingly, but I gave it to him. Now I am not going to let him die in a prison cell, in worse misery than he's already in. He stays here. I will watch out his life with him. He has the lung sickness; he's had it a long time. I've seen the end drawing near him for days," Reine said, drowning out La Reynie's protest. "His fever will not abate now. I think he will be dead before another morning." She looked at Charles. "Maître du Luc agrees that he should stay here."

La Reynie rounded furiously on Charles, but Charles forestalled him.

"I agree with all my heart, *mon lieutenant-général.*"

"You are deranged, both of you, this is preposterous!" La Reynie went to the boy and nudged him with the toe of his boot. Jean's labored breathing didn't change. "He is a killer I'd almost despaired of finding and he is going to die where I put him. You," he said to Richard, who stood motionless and sharp-eyed at the entrance, listening intently. "Take this and go to the police *barrière.*" He held out a round token bearing the outline of the city's sign, the cathedral of Notre Dame. "Say that Monsieur La Reynie requires two men and bring them here to the *cave.*"

The beggar didn't move. "I am Reine's man, *mon lieutenant-général.*"

La Reynie reddened with anger. "You," he snapped at Charles. "Help me carry him."

"No, Monsieur La Reynie. I am not your man, either."

"You are a cleric. Where is your sense of justice, of sin?"

"Engaged in a fight to the death with my hope of mercy," Charles said dryly. He never after knew what made him add, "If you had a son, Monsieur La Reynie, would you not want mercy for him? No matter what he'd done?"

Behind him, Reine drew in a startled breath. La Reynie stood rigid, pressing his crossed arms against his chest as though against a wound. His eyes went to Jean, as the boy moved restlessly in his fever.

"Yes, Nicolas," Reine said, very softly, "which would you want for Gabriel?"

"Your clever question means nothing," La Reynie said harshly. "Gabriel is no killer. And he wants no help from me."

"But you want much from him. Give this dying boy mercy and perhaps the Virgin will give you mercy in return, you and Gabriel."

"Lieutenant-Général La Reynie," Charles said, appalled, "please believe that I did not know you had a son. I never intended—"

"Peace, *maître*," Reine said. "Perhaps God intended."

Chapter 27

The morning sun had risen high enough to fall greenly through the small window's old glass onto Père Le Picart's desk. The rector sat behind the desk, his long, sinewy fingers lying in the little pool of light, tapping softly and rapidly on the desk's scarred wood. La Reynie sat in one of the fireside chairs, which Charles had moved closer to the desk for him. Charles stood back, glad—for once—to let his superiors decide what happened next. His horror and astonishment at the morning's revelations had given way to quiet, and beneath its surface, his mind worked at making sense of what he'd seen and heard, especially at making sense of Jean.

"I will give out that I have the proven killer of Martine Mynette and Henri Brion," La Reynie was saying. "And then I will give out that he has died of fever."

Le Picart said nothing, and Charles saw that he was scrutinizing the police chief as he had often scrutinized Charles himself. Some part of him was glad to see that La Reynie was equally uncomfortable under that sharp gray gaze.

"Do you think I am wrong to let him die here?" La Reynie said, shifting in his chair.

"Have I said so?" The rector shook his head. "No, Monsieur La Reynie, I think you have chosen rightly. Why add more suffering to the world than there needs to be?" He looked at Charles. "Maître du Luc will see that he has a priest." His fingers continued to tap, as though knocking softly at some unseen door. "I suppose that your making it known that the killer has been found will release us from the recent accusations. And from that cursed song."

"Be assured that it will, in time. I will go on confiscating copies until the sellers and singers turn their attention to the next *scandale* in Paris."

"I trust," Le Picart said dryly, "that the Society of Jesus actually receiving the Mynette money will not be the next *scandale*."

La Reynie said grimly, "The closer we get to the end of January, and the king's visit to the city and grand dinner at the Hôtel de Ville, the faster disturbers of the city's peace for any reason will find themselves unpleasantly housed in the Châtelet."

Charles stepped forward. "*Mon père*, will you give me permission to watch tonight with the beggar woman and the dying boy? In the morning, if he dies as she predicts, I will see that . . . that all is attended to, and that the *cave* is empty." Charles glanced at La Reynie. "Monsieur La Reynie has offered to bury the young man, as well as the old beggar he killed."

Le Picart looked at La Reynie in surprise but said to Charles, "You have my permission, *maître*. See also that this dying boy and the beggar woman have what they need for their comfort."

"Thank you, *mon père*. I will see to it."

"When they are gone from the *cave*, I will send lay brothers to block the entrance." Le Picart's tapping fingers stilled. "Now that we will have money enough, repairs to the Les Cholets building can go forward, including a stout locked door where you say the beggars have been getting in."

Charles nodded, remembering what Reine had told him. It

was none so bad down there, she'd said. Not bad at all, with fire at hand and water nearby, especially when Paris was freezing or drowning in rain. What she hadn't told him was where the other entrance was, and how could he tell the rector what he didn't know?

La Reynie said, "If you will excuse me, *mon père*, I must send for men to take the beggar's body away." He rose from his chair.

Charles took another step forward. "Before I return to the *cave*, will you give me permission to go to the Couche, *mon père*? There is an old nun there who may know something about the killer."

"What does that matter now?" Le Picart and La Reynie said it nearly in concert, and Charles struggled to find an answer.

"I would like to know more about who he is."

"Curiosity is not a virtue in a Jesuit," Le Picart said mildly, eyeing him.

The silence stretched and Charles realized belatedly that the rector was waiting for a response to what he'd said.

"*Mon père*, it seems to me that the idle curiosity of distraction, which leads to meddling, is one thing. But the desire to know truth in order to see justice done and compassion given is another. It seems only right to know whom we are burying."

Le Picart still said nothing, his eyes boring into Charles.

"And to know why he killed," Charles made bold to say. "If we do not know why souls grow desperate, how can we help them?"

La Reynie was staring at him in open amazement. But the rector had relaxed into his chair and was regarding Charles with more than a little satisfaction.

"You may go to the Couche. But"—the satisfied look was replaced by one of unmistakable warning—"when you have asked your questions, whether or not you have your answers, the task I set you will be ended. You will then give your full and undivided attention to your duties here."

"Yes, *mon père.*"

Charles and La Reynie bowed and turned to leave. Before the door shut behind them, though, the rector called Charles back.

"I say this only to you, but I think you will want to know. It was one of our own from Louis Le Grand who spoke carelessly, outside the college, about the Mynette *patrimoine* coming to us."

Charles remembered his first walk to the Place with the dour Maître Richaud and the gossip Richaud had heard in the chandler's workshop. "And this Jesuit talked about the *patrimoine*?"

"Yes. But that is all that needs to be said. The rest is not your business."

The "rest" meaning consequences, including penance. *You should order him to go and see a comedy every day*, Charles thought irreverently, remembering Richaud's dislike of laughter.

"Before you go to the Couche," Le Picart said briskly, "take food to the *cave*. And blankets."

Charles bent his head in acquiescence.

"And Maître du Luc?"

Charles looked up.

"My thanks to you. You have done well what I ordered you to do." He gave Charles a small, wintry smile. "When I gave you this task, I said that a Jesuit's obedience should be his superior's supporting staff. You have upheld me, and also Louis le Grand."

Charles felt himself flushing with pleasure at the unexpected thanks. Jesuit obedience—no matter how hard he himself found it—was regarded as simply a given, not an occasion for thanks. "I only wish I could have prevented this morning's death," he said.

"I wish so, too. But that death and its sin are not yours to carry." Le Picart's smile reached his cool gray eyes this time.

"What would be the point of growing in obedience only to fall into overscrupulosity?"

Charles found himself smiling, too, and remembering the Christmas *Farce of Monks*. If the end of a scholastic was to be kicked, the frequent function of a superior was to douse the scholastic with cold water for the good of his soul. "Point taken, *mon père*."

Charles collected blankets from the central store of bedding, and soup and bread from the kitchen. With some difficulty, he made his way back into the Les Cholets courtyard and down to the cellar. Nothing had changed. Reine still held Marin's body on her lap, and Jean was still tossing and shivering with fever. Charles gently unwrapped his cloak from the boy and wrapped him instead in layers of blankets. He put another blanket around Reine's shoulders and set the soup and bread beside her.

"Where is Richard?" Charles asked, seeing that the beggar was gone.

"He went to tell the others not to return tonight."

"Where will they stay?"

"There are other places."

The sound of voices and footsteps announced La Reynie, followed by two *sergents* with a litter. Reine gathered Marin to her and kissed him.

"Good-bye, *mon coeur*, my heart, my life." She looked up at La Reynie, her eyes full of pleading. "Treat him gently, Nicolas," she whispered.

"You know I will." He called the two men forward with a look. "You will do this as though for your fathers," he said curtly, and stepped aside.

Obviously bewildered by so much care for a filthy beggar, but just as obviously flinching from the steel in La Reynie's voice, his men placed Marin on the litter with the care they might have given a marquis. They covered him with the blanket they'd brought, bowed to La Reynie, and bore the litter away to the Châtelet's mortuary chapel.

As their footsteps died away, Richard emerged from the passage and sat down beside Reine. "I will take care of her, Monsieur La Reynie."

"For now." The *lieutenant-général* strode out of the *cave* and Charles followed.

When they reached the front of the college, a red-and-black carriage drawn by a pair of black horses, standing in the little rue des Poirees across from Louis le Grand's main doors, came to meet them. A serving boy jumped down from his place between the high rear wheels and opened the door. Charles began his farewells, but La Reynie motioned him curtly into the carriage and climbed in behind him.

"La Couche," he barked at the boy, who told the driver, and they were off.

La Reynie crossed his arms on his chest and stared steadfastly out the window. That suited Charles, who settled back on the red cushioned seat, looking eagerly out his own window. He was so rarely in a carriage that the experience was still new. Beyond the window, people, horses, carriages, carts, mules, shops, dogs, courtyard gates flashed past in a flood of color. Watching the wheels throw waves of muddy snow and water against stone walls and swearing pedestrians, Charles realized that the day was steadily warming. Snow dripped from eaves and gargoyles, and people even leaned on the sills of open windows, airing their rooms. On the Petit Pont, a few well-wrapped women sat in west-facing doorways, their faces lifted to shafts of sunlight and long-absent warmth.

On the Île de la Cité, the carriage wound its way to the rue

Neuve Notre Dame and stopped in front of the gate to the long, stone-built Couche. La Reynie and Charles got out, still in silence, and La Reynie rang the bell. Charles waited silently behind him. A young, bright-eyed Sister of Charity hurried across the court and let them in.

"Our thanks, *ma soeur*," La Reynie said, lifting his hat, as Charles bowed. "We are seeking one of your sisters." He gestured to Charles to take over the asking.

"She is called Mariana," Charles said.

"Oh, you are in luck, come with me." The girl led them across the muddy court. "Soeur Mariana has been ill, but she is better now, and back with us." She ushered them through the door and into the anteroom. "Will you wait one little moment, please? I will see if she is busy." With another curtsy, she hurried away.

The dark, rambling old house smelled of babies. Dirty swaddling, sour milk, and strong soap scented air already rank with the closed-in smells of winter, while wailing cries, hurrying feet on stone floors, and sharply urgent commands smote their ears. The young nun returned, as serene as though they were all in a summer garden.

"Soeur Mariana will see you. Come."

She took them through the anteroom and along a dark, low-beamed passage to a small plaster-walled room where an elderly nun sat singing under her breath as she fed an eagerly sucking newborn with a rag soaked in milk. It was a common way of feeding babies, especially when there were several to feed at once. Wet nurses were sometimes accused of letting babies die, because the ones who got only the rag and not the breast often starved to death. Watching, Charles hoped this child—and the half dozen others in the cradles ranged around the room—would soon go to wet nurses of their own.

"*Ma soeur,*"La Reynie said, "I have questions to ask you, if you will be so kind."

The old woman's reedy singing stopped and she peered at him, blinking shortsightedly. Her aquiline nose was like a blade, and her starched white headdress stood away from her dark face in wide quivering wings.

"And who are you?"

"I am Nicolas de La Reynie, *ma soeur*, head of the Paris police. And this is Maître Charles du Luc, from the college of Louis le Grand."

Her black eyes flicked from La Reynie to Charles, and she pulled the rag from the infant's mouth, dipped it in the basin of milk on the table at her elbow, and wrung it out a little. "What do you want?" She gave the baby the rag tit again and resumed her singing.

La Reynie frowned impatiently. "Soeur Mariana, I beg the favor of your attention."

"You see me here, speak," the old woman said, and kept singing.

La Reynie shook his head in exasperation and looked at Charles.

Charles knelt beside her. "*Ma soeur*, did you have a child in your care, perhaps as many as twenty years ago, a boy called Tito? Also perhaps called Jean?"

"Tito?" She drew in a quick breath and looked up, seeming to see La Reynie and Charles for the first time. "My Tito? Where is he?"

Charles said softly, "When did you last see Tito?"

"Thirteen years ago. Only once. Soon after he went to be a servant, I was sent to see how he did. He was eight years old then." She sighed. "I missed him sorely. But it was best for him;

it was a place and a way into the world." The nun stared into the distance, her pale lips moving in prayer or memory, Charles couldn't tell. The child in her lap had sucked the rag dry and began to wail before she sighed and said, "Thirteen years ago he went to Madame Anne Mynette. Such a long time."

"*Madame* Anne Mynette?" Charles said mildly.

"So she called herself four years before, when she came looking for her own child. I doubted then she had a right to the title," the nun said acidly. "Women who come here to retrieve their babies—not that many ever come—hardly ever have a right to it."

La Reynie raised an eyebrow at Charles. "It seems a long time for you to remember the woman's name," he said skeptically, watching her soak the rag again and quiet the baby.

"Oh, no, when she came in search of a little servant, I remembered her. Why would I not, when I'd already given her one of our babies?"

Charles frowned in confusion. "But you just said that when she came earlier, it was to get her own child."

"Her own child had died."

"Died? But—"

Soeur Mariana bridled. "I remember quite well how it was. A wet nurse left the child, because her own children had fallen ill, and she feared the infant would too. The infant she brought to us did sicken, and when 'Madame' Mynette came, it had just died. But I saw a chance for another child." She made a derisive little sound. "Babies look much the same when they're very young. And 'Madame' Mynette had told me that she hadn't seen her child for some weeks. So I found a baby girl about the same age and with the same color eyes, though lighter hair. I wrapped her in a clean blanket, but then I was afraid the Mynette woman would see the difference and I would be in grave trouble. But

God used little Tito to show me what to do. Tito was with me that day—I often kept him with me, though he lived in the older children's house by then. Well, that day he was playing with the little trinket he had, a heart on an old ribbon. He'd always had it. It was around his neck when he was found in Notre Dame." The nun's face softened and she shook her head sadly. "His mother no doubt put it on him when she left him in the stone cradle that's been there time out of mind for leaving babies in. So I—"

"Wait, *ma soeur!* Tito's mother? But Martine Mynette told her friend that Mademoiselle Anne Mynette had put it on her when she was a baby!"

"Nothing of the kind." Soeur Mariana gave Charles a shrewd look. "The Mynette woman was desperate with guilt when she came searching for her infant. Guilt for leaving her with the wet nurse, I suppose. Well, she deserved guilt, if a woman has a child, she should feed it with the breasts God gave her. If she told the girl that *she'd* given her the heart, it was no doubt to make herself seem a better mother."

Charles's head was spinning. "Tito's mother," he murmured, trying to make sense out of what he was hearing. "So the baby Mademoiselle Anne Mynette took home was a foundling like Tito himself."

"Yes. Left on the Pont Neuf, if I remember rightly. Du Pont—from the bridge—we would have given her for a surname."

Charles's heart contracted as he tried to imagine young, desperate mothers, newborn children in their arms, watching to see that they were unobserved, putting their babies down somewhere that seemed safe. And walking away.

"The mothers often leave some trinket," the nun said. "They think they'll come and claim the baby, but they don't. They're whores, most of them."

"So you are saying, *ma soeur*, that you took Tito's necklace and put it on the baby who became Martine Mynette."

"I thought the Mynette woman would be more likely to accept the child as hers, if I said I'd put the little heart on her baby when the wet nurse left her, to be sure she wasn't mixed with the others and lost." Soeur Mariana smiled complacently. "'Madame' Mynette made us a very large gift for that." She rose and laid the sucking child in one of the beds, ignoring its cries when she pulled the rag from its mouth. Then she went to a different bed and busied herself with another infant.

Charles looked at La Reynie. The *lieutenant-général* looked like he was holding himself in the chair and in the room by main force.

Charles said, "What did Tito do, *ma soeur*? When you took his necklace?"

"Do?" Soeur Mariana sat down with the new child and soaked the rag again. "Oh, he cried. He even tried to kick me, but I beat him and he said he was sorry. It's the only way with them." She frowned, sucking her yellowed teeth. "I thought he would forget, as children do, but when I went to check on him after he was in the Mynette household, 'Madame' Mynette said she was going to send him back if he didn't stop trying to steal her adopted daughter's necklace. So I talked sharply to him and told him that if he didn't stop, she would throw him out in the street and no one would take care of him. Tito was bright enough, he took to heart what I said, and she kept him."

Charles swallowed hard. "Yes, she kept him."

"Is he there still, *maître*?"

"No. Anne Mynette is dead," Charles said. "And so is the little girl you gave her."

Soeur Mariana put the rag tit into the new baby's mouth and

stared beyond Charles and La Reynie, as though into the past, still saying nothing. Finally, with a faint sigh, she said, "Tito is dead, too, isn't he?"

Charles hesitated. "Yes," he said, and left it at that, because it seemed the kindest thing to do. "I am sorry."

"Before I joined the Sisters of Charity, I was a wife," the nun said, murmuring so that Charles had to lean closer to hear her. "We left Spain and came here. I had two children. They died, and my husband, also. So I became a nun. Little Tito came back to us from his wet nurse, and I had the charge of him at the house for the older children. But sometimes when I came here to work for a day, I brought him with me. He was like my son who died. Very like." Her voice trailed into silence.

"Was your son's name Tito?"

She shook her head. "They called my little foundling Jean Baptiste, because he was found on St. Jean Baptiste's day. In Spanish that is Juan Bautisto, and I called him that. But he couldn't say it, he could only say Tito, so that became what everyone called him."

Charles nodded, wondering if Tito had called himself Jean after he left the Mynette house because he wanted to be a man, called by a man's name, and not just little foundling Tito.

The nun was looking down at the child in her lap. "I only wanted to give another child a chance at life. So many die before we can even find them wet nurses."

"The baby you put Tito's necklace on had time to grow up, *ma soeur*. With a mother who loved her as her natural daughter."

She gave Charles a bleak smile. "That is something, then."

A sound from La Reynie made Charles turn to see him emptying his purse onto the table beside the basin of milk. "For the children," he said through stiff lips, and left the room.

Hurriedly, Charles thanked the nun and gave her the last of the coins from Le Picart's purse, made the sign of the cross over the babies, and caught up with La Reynie in the courtyard. When they reached the carriage, La Reynie dismissed it.

"Walk with me," he said.

Instead of turning toward the Right Bank and the Châtelet, the *lieutenant-général* walked toward the towers of Notre Dame at the tip of the island. Charles kept pace with him, watching him covertly and thinking about what the nun had told them. In the open square below the cathedral's west face, La Reynie stopped and looked up, past rank upon rank of stone saints wet with snowmelt, past the climbing towers, up at the brilliant blue sky.

"Sometimes," he said, staring at the soaring stones, "when I cannot face this city or myself any longer, I come here. I tell myself that no matter what happens, no matter the evil and suffering, day and night into day and night, the saints still stand there. So God must still be there, too. Still somewhere."

Too astonished to speak, Charles stood as motionless as the carvings, until the *lieutenant-général* began to walk again. They went around the side of the cathedral, along its line of buttresses.

"You want to know about Reine," La Reynie said abruptly. "Because you saved her life, I will tell you. She was the most beautiful woman I have ever seen. But her face and her body were the least of her beauty. Oh, not that I didn't appreciate them, I did, and fully." He glanced sideways at Charles. "You have known women, you will understand that. Though perhaps not the rest of it. I—I met Reine soon after coming to Paris and this impossible job. I think you know what she was then. A gloriously beautiful, royally expensive courtesan. I spent more and more time with her, time I didn't have, money I didn't have, but she kept me from losing my sanity. I would have married her, even with all I knew about her. But, of course, I could not, I was already married to my second wife. And Reine would not have had me, anyway. And why?" He laughed sadly. "Because she loved Marin. The beggar. Then, a few years later, when I was seeing her rarely, she was in great danger. I cannot tell you more than that, only that I was able to help her. And she has often helped me. For more than twenty years now, my heart has been more than half in her keeping."

They had reached the eastern tip of the *île* and turned to look at the cathedral again.

"And what of your own love?" La Reynie said roughly. "So far away in Geneva."

Charles caught his breath. La Reynie knew Pernelle, but this was the first time he had ever called her Charles's "love."

"As you say, she is in Geneva. I am here. That will not change."

"I see. And have you accepted your penance and done it?"

"Yes." Charles was shaken by how good it was to speak about her. "I did willing penance." He fell quiet, looking up at Notre Dame's great rose window. "I renewed my vows," he said finally. "God helping me, I will keep them." He caught La Reynie's glance and held it. "I did not do penance for loving."

"Is that an overfine Jesuit distinction?"

"I hope not."

Charles wanted to say something more, something to ease La Reynie's unhappiness, but before he found anything to say, the *lieutenant-général* faced him and held out his hand. Surprised, Charles took it. La Reynie nodded slightly, disengaged himself, and walked rapidly away.

Chapter 28

The early afternoon's blanket of clouds added to the mourning feeling of the Brion house, whose windows were still covered in black. To Charles's surprise, the manservant who answered his knock was wearing black, too, new breeches and a coat whose sleeves covered his wrists. The Sunday Mass and dinner—chicken stew today, to everyone's relief—were over, and Charles was on his way to the church of St. Louis. This stop was unauthorized, but he could not resist the chance to see how the Brions were faring, now that Gilles had been released from the Châtelet.

But when the servant showed him into the dark *salon*, he found only Monsieur Callot, Mademoiselle Brion, and Monsieur Morel. Callot smiled at Charles as he got to his feet, and so did Morel. But Isabel's face was unaccountably anxious as she made her *reverence*.

Charles bowed his greeting. "I came to congratulate you," he said, "that Monsieur Gilles Brion is with you again—at least, I trust he is?"

"Yes—that is, we've seen him." Isabel's tired face lit with a brief smile. "I know that it is you we have to thank for his freedom, *maître*. Though how we can ever thank you enough, I cannot imagine."

"Yes, you have given us more than you know," Morel said meaningly, and took Isabel's hand in his.

"As you see, though," Monsieur Callot said, "Gilles is not here." The words were sour as a lemon. "He deigned to give us a few minutes and then he went to his Capuchins. I have given him my permission, as the new head of the family." The sourness in his voice gave way to regret. "The best thing for him, perhaps. Though why a man would want to do it, I cannot fathom. I will say, though, that his narrow escape seems to have stiffened his spine a little. Ah, well, I wish the Capuchins joy of him." He backed closer to the small fire, whose light flickered over the black drapery at the windows. "And what of the real killer, Maître du Luc?"

"The Mynettes' former servant Tito—whose real name was Jean Baptiste—admitted that he'd killed them both, for his own tangled reasons. He was very ill and not altogether right in his wits. He died early this morning. Not alone, I was with him." Charles sighed, remembering the sudden silence when Jean's tortured breathing finally stilled, remembering Reine's gentle closing of the boy's eyes. "There will be no public execution."

Isabel said softly, "There have been enough deaths. I am glad there will be no public show of his." They were all quiet for a moment, and then she said, "Maître du Luc, we have something to show you." Biting her lip, she turned and took folded papers from a small table. "We found these hidden in my father's bedchamber yesterday. You must read them."

She held them out. Charles took them and realized immediately what the larger paper must be, with its seals and ribbons. He unfolded it. At the bottom of the page were Mademoiselle Anne Mynette's signature and Henri Brion's, as well as the signatures of witnesses, all to make certain that Martine Mynette would one day have the Mynette *patrimoine*. Slowly, he refolded the *donation entre vifs*.

"You found this hidden?"

Isabel nodded, red with shame. "Beneath his mattress. Read the letter, *maître*, and you will know why. It came the day after he died. An Ursuline returning from their New France mission brought it. But I did not have the heart to open it then. I read it yesterday and soon after, we found the *donation*. And . . ."

Callot growled, "Let him read it, Isabel."

The letter was from New France. It was about family matters, as Isabel had told Charles letters from there mostly were. This one was about a betrothal. Marc Brion, a young cousin of Henri Brion living in Quebec, wrote jubilantly that all was now concluded for his marriage to one Pauline Mynette.

"Mynette?" Charles shook his head in confusion. "But I thought there were no more Mynettes!"

"So did we all, *maître*," Callot said. "Keep reading, I beg you."

The letter went on, "My Pauline's father died soon after she was born, as I told you in an earlier letter, but I now have absolute proof that all is as she says. Her father was the nephew of the lawyer Simon Mynette on the Place Maubert. He was Simon's only remaining blood relative other than Simon's daughter. Who, as you tell me, is now dead. Thank God that this Martine Mynette is only adopted and that the *donation entre vifs* is lost. I trust, my dear cousin, that lost it will remain. I would, of course, love my Pauline without the Mynette *patrimoine*. but who would not love her even more with it?"

Feeling as though someone had knocked the air out of his lungs, Charles looked at the three watching him. "And this is true?" he said, when he could speak.

"I think it must be," Callot said. "I had heard years ago that

Simon Mynette quarreled badly with a nephew who then went to New France. Simon always claimed the boy died soon after arriving there—but it seems he had time to marry and father a child."

"According to this letter, it appears Monsieur Henri Brion had been getting letters for some time about this proposed betrothal," Charles said. "Which explains some things."

Callot nodded ruefully. "It explains the 'lost' *donation* quite nicely. No, Isabel, hold your peace, there is no other explanation. Your father knew that this betrothal was in progress, and he saw that his effort to get the Mynette money by making Gilles marry Martine was failing. But if Martine's *donation* disappeared, he could still secure the money for the Brion family by way of the New France marriage." Callot shrugged sadly. "And all his scheming was for nothing. Poor little Martine is gone, and so is he."

Charles let the hand holding the letter fall to his side and stood thinking about Père Le Picart's coming disappointment.

Isabel said diffidently, "Do you mind very much about the money?"

"Of course. The college needs money." He managed a smile for her. "But while a family lasts, no *patrimoine* should go elsewhere. This one goes where by law and right it should go. But I must confess I was hoping to be done with the eternal bean pottage in the refectory!"

That made them all laugh, as he'd meant it to.

"May I take the *donation* and the letter to my rector? He should see them, but I will make sure that you have them back."

Callot started to speak, but Isabel hushed him. "*Maître*, will my father's hiding the *donation* be made public? Please, I don't want his name blackened!"

"I don't see any need for it to be public, *mademoiselle*."

"Thank you," she whispered.

"Yes," Callot said, with an oddly amused glance at Charles. "We are grateful that his name will not be blackened." He hesitated, as though making up his mind about something. "Before you go, *maître*, will you come upstairs for a little moment?"

Curiosity got the best of Charles's knowing he should go if he meant to be at St. Louis on time. "By all means, *monsieur*."

Callot led him out onto the landing and up the stairs to what was obviously the old man's bedchamber. He held the door open for Charles and shut it carefully behind him. Then he went to the *ruelle*, the narrow space between the green-curtained bed and the wall, and took a key from his pocket. He opened the long heavy chest that stood in the *ruelle* and beckoned Charles to come and look.

The room's small window was shuttered, but even so, the chest was full of a silvery light. Dumbfounded, Charles picked up a small bar of silver. He looked up at Callot. Slow grins spread over both their faces and they began to laugh.

"I suppose I should have asked how you feel about taxes before I showed you this," Callot said.

"If you had, I would have told you that we in Languedoc are as French as anyone when it comes to paying taxes." Charles hefted the solid little bar of silver in his hand. "Was the smuggling your idea all along?"

"No, no. My good-for-nothing nephew, God keep his soul, did sometimes have a sound idea. I was merely an investor. And it was only this last shipment that was discovered, you know."

"I see. And do you also keep the chocolate?"

"Yes, of course. I enjoy a tall pot of it every morning. So does Isabel."

"She knows the—um—source of your wealth?"

"Oh, no. She does not need to know. When I am better acquainted with Monsieur Morel, perhaps I will tell him. Perhaps not. But if all goes as I think it will go and he asks me for her hand when the mourning for her father is over, they and their children will be provided for, no matter how well or otherwise our young dancing master does in his profession."

"So you support the match."

"His father was a fine craftsman. Her father was a smuggler." Callot's brows and shoulders climbed in the most Gallic of shrugs.

"Good," Charles said. "I like the match, too. And it means that you are provided with loving care in your old age."

"The *bon Dieu* orders all things."

As they went back down the stairs, the bells from the nearby Bernardins monastery began to ring for Nones. Charles went to the *salon* door and made his farewells.

"I am glad from my heart that Monsieur Gilles Brion is free and under no suspicion. I hope that more good news will come to you with the spring." He glanced at the ceiling and then at M. Callot. "And do not trouble about the money. No doubt the bean pottage is good for our souls."

Callot crowed with laughter. "You are invited for chocolate at any time, *maître*."

Charles bowed. "My thanks, *monsieur*. And I will see you Tuesday at our rehearsal, Monsieur Morel, tomorrow being the Feast of the Epiphany. May it be a blessed one for you."

Outside, Charles looked back at the Sign of Three Ducks over the house door, thinking that the fortunes of that house were changing for the better. And hoping that the fortunes of the college soon would. Entertaining himself by imagining a chest nicely full of silver bars hidden in the rector's austere chamber, he turned east to walk along the Quay de la Tournelle and across its bridge. The blanket of clouds had warmed the day somewhat and brought half the city out to enjoy the softer air. Wishing he had more time to enjoy this illusion of spring, he made his way to the rue St. Antoine and the Jesuit church to take up his ordinary Jesuit life again. One of his tasks from now till April would be fetching and carrying for Père Jouvancy and the great Jesuit creator of spectacle Père Menestrier, as they planned the decor for the interment of the Condé's heart in the church wall. The ceremony would be an elaborate funeral Mass, and Père Bourdaloue, the most famous Jesuit preacher, would preach. The new Condé had commissioned a new musical setting of the Mass and was paying for the sumptuous decor Jouvancy and Menestrier were beginning to plan today.

As Charles approached the church, he thought about Christmas Eve and his first sight of Marin and Jean-Tito. Only twelve days ago, but it seemed much longer. Inside, the church was chill, silent, and empty. Charles went past the gated altar where the Condé's jeweled box rested and knelt at the Virgin's altar. He prayed for Martine Mynette, and Henri Brion, and Marin, all violently cut off from life without a chance to make their last confessions. And for Jean, who had not come back to himself enough to make his final confession to a priest and also needed all the prayers he could get.

Charles also prayed for Reine and for La Reynie. When La Reynie came for Jean's body, Reine had refused all his offers of help, consenting only to go in his carriage to her daughter at Procope's.

Charles's prayers poured out like a silent river, flowing over the dead, over wounds, secrets, and revelations, over the fear and grief of these past holy days, even over the long-past tragedy of Claire Clemence, Princess of Condé, and her coldhearted husband. He prayed, too, for Pernelle and himself, for the healing of that grief and loneliness. When he had prayed himself dry, he stayed on his knees. The Silence closed around him and he felt, for once, no need to argue with It. *Nothing is wasted*, the Silence had said, that snowy day in a narrow alley. *Unless you waste it.*

The church door opened, bringing mild air and a burst of noise from the street. Charles rose stiffly from his knees and went to meet Père Jouvancy and the stately, white-haired Jesuit with him. Jouvancy made the introductions and Charles bowed deeply to Père Claude François Menestrier, who lived now in the Jesuit Professed House here beside the church. Menestrier was famous all over Europe for the glittering celebrations, ballets, and royal entries he created. Taking a key from his cassock, Menestrier led the way to the side altar where the Condé's heart rested and un-locked the gate. Giving silent thanks, because this was what he'd hoped for, Charles followed the two priests inside. Menestrier picked up the box, and he and Jouvancy discussed its colors, holding it up and turning it in their hands, while Charles stood back and waited.

"No, not black," Menestrier said judiciously. "Look at the sapphires. This is the church of St. Louis. His color is blue, and the Condé counted him an ancestor." He replaced the box back on the altar. "Blue, Père Jouvancy! We will start with blue velvet. Come."

The two priests went briskly to the high altar, the initially skeptical look on Jouvancy's face already flaming into enthusi-asm. Knowing that, for the moment, anyway, they wouldn't miss him, Charles stayed behind and picked up the box. He thought at first that it had been resealed since Christmas Eve, but the lid was only tight. He got it open and stared at the Condé's heart, resting on the blue velvet cushion in its swaddling of gold silk. Then he set the box on the altar and took Jean-Tito's necklace from his cassock. The red enamel heart glowed like a tiny flame as it rested in his palm. He thought of Tito's passion for this trinket that meant all he knew of love, of the unknown woman who had put it around her newborn son's neck in the hope of finding him again, of the nun putting it on another infant to give her a chance at life. He put the little heart on the cushion and coiled its frayed ribbon around it. Then he nudged it farther under the shadow of the Condé's heart so it was less likely to be seen if someone else opened the box.

Let both hearts rest here, he thought, replacing the jeweled lid. Both had brought suffering. But one, at least, had been given in love.

He put the box back on the altar and went to do his small part in surrounding its interment with beauty.

❧❦ *Epilogue* ❧❦

STE.-SCHOLASTIQUE'S DAY, MONDAY, FEBRUARY 10

With less than a half hour to go before the performance, Charles was in one of the small anterooms flanking the stage, overseeing the dancers and actors whose first entrance was from that side. Charles Lennox—St. Ambrose in the musical tragedy *Celse*—stood before him, wide-eyed and pale with stage fright. As Charles picked up the saint's mask and rubbed a smear of dirt off its faintly pink cheek, he half feared that the mask, too, would blanch when the boy put it on. But Lennox looked superb. The black-and-gold coat and breeches fit him perfectly, the coat's short stiff skirts standing well out from the breeches, and the heavy gold braid around the coat's edge matched the stockings and the gold plumes of the headdress. Wondering again at Jouvancy's ability to cajole college parents into paying for new costumes, Charles patted St. Ambrose reassuringly on the shoulder and turned his attention to the rest of the room. Michele Bertamelli, beside himself with excitement over his Louis le Grand debut as *Celse*'s star, was talking incessantly to anyone who would listen—in Italian, which he insisted was only more beautiful Latin.

From the anteroom on the other side of the stage, where

Jouvancy and the rest of both casts waited with the singers, Charles heard the singers' last-minute limbering of their voices. But only faintly, because the hum of talk in the *salle des actes* had swelled to a polite roar as the invited audience settled itself for the show's two o'clock beginning. From the courtyard, the tower clock struck the quarter before two. As though the chime were his cue, Bertamelli shot into the air between one of the Latin tragedy's Roman soldiers and the dancing master, Monsieur Germain Morel, and executed a jumping passage from his solo. Morel's startled oath made Charles grateful for the roar of talk in the *salle*. He grabbed the back of Bertamelli's shimmering green satin coat.

"*Doucement*, Monsieur Bertamelli! Softly, and still your tongue. This is the time for gathering yourself together."

"But I am gathered, *maître*, I am bursting, I am—"

Charles lifted an eyebrow at the actors glowering at Bertamelli and bent down till he was face-to-face with the boy. "Still your tongue, *signor*, or your *confrères* may cut it out. And I may help them."

"Oh, *no!*" Morel said despairingly, from somewhere behind Charles. "Not now, there's not time!"

Laughing, Charles turned around. "I was only joking—"

But Morel was peering anxiously through the slightly open door onto the stage.

"What is it?" Charles went to look over the dancing master's shoulder.

"Three candles have fallen out of the chandelier, the big one over the middle of the stage!"

"Never mind," Charles soothed, "one of the brothers will pick them up."

The small stage had no curtain and Charles could see the rector and Père Montville in the front row of the audience, seated on either side of Mme de Montmorency. Before coming back-stage, Charles had met Henri de Montmorency's redoubtable mother. Short, double-chinned, and solid in sea-green satin and a king's ransom of ice-white lace, she had eyed him severely.

"I trust that you have given my son a part worthy of his lineage," she'd said warningly.

"Ah, *madame*, be assured that he is a golden image of martial virtue on our stage, to whom all the others look up and whose commands direct his men," Charles had answered fulsomely, bowing—and earned himself a quelling frown from Père Le Picart. Now, watching the rector and Père Montville inclining their heads courteously toward Mme de Montmorency and her flow of talk, Charles grinned to himself. He could almost see them counting the coins of the gift she might give them if she was pleased with the show. The Mynette fortune being irretrievably lost to the college, a Montmorency gift would be very welcome, and he sent up a fervent prayer that she wouldn't realize why he'd cast her large, bumbling son as a magical statue and put him safely out of the way on a golden plinth.

He was about to tell Monsieur Morel to close the door when he saw Mademoiselle Isabel Brion sitting with her great-uncle Callot about halfway back. The mourning black they both wore did nothing to dim their obvious happiness. Callot was beaming. And Isabel, smiling at the stage, glowed like an earthbound star. Morel leaned farther out the door.

"I will tell the brothers about the candles, *mon ami*," Charles said, pulling him back and closing the door. "I, too, glimpsed Mademoiselle Brion," he said more softly. "She looks very lovely today."

"Ah, Maître du Luc, she is—I am—we—the first forty days of mourning for Monsieur Brion are over, you know," he finally managed, in a rush of words, and clasped his hands rapturously on his breast. "It still cannot be public, but—we are betrothed!"

Charles laughed for pleasure at the news. "I congratulate you both with all my heart!"

Wondering if Morel had been let into the secret of the contraband silver yet, Charles threaded his way through the crowded anteroom toward its other door, which led directly to a tiny backstage area where two lay brothers waited to change the minimal scenery.

"Done already, *maître*," a brother said, when Charles put his head around the door. "We picked up the candles. No time to replace them now, but the chandelier will do well enough."

As Charles turned away, the clock struck two. He braced himself for the beginning of the musical overture by Monsieur Charpentier and his musicians, positioned in the *salle* at the side of the stage. But nothing happened. Shrugging, Charles started to gather the boys for the customary prayer. Delays and theatre production were nearly synonymous, after all.

Then Père Montville hurried into the anteroom, hissing "*Maître, messieurs*, before you begin, a word!" His small dark eyes were bright with excitement. "We are unexpectedly honored with the presence of two *Legitimés* of France! A son and daughter of the king and Madame de Montespan have arrived, the Duc du Maine and Mademoiselle de Rouen." He eyed the performers sternly. "When you go out onto the stage, they will be directly in front of you. Do our college all the honor in your power by your dancing and acting today, *messieurs*. Let your eloquent voices and bodies speak feelingly of the teaching you have received in this college named for our king."

Charles seized the moment of quiet for the prayer. "And that we may do as Père Montville has bidden us, let us pray, *messieurs*."

The quiet in the little room deepened. Even Bertamelli was utterly still, his head so bowed on his clasped hands that the boy next to him reached out and steadied his slipping headdress of flowers and small birds.

"Our Father in heaven," Charles prayed, "let what we do today be a means of grace to those who watch and those who perform. Let us tell the story of your saints with reverence and joy. Grant us, we pray, a blessed Lenten season"—he hesitated, visited by the remembered taste of Lent's endless salt fish—"but first, grant us a happy Fat Tuesday tomorrow!"

That got a rousing "amen," everyone crossed himself, and the delayed musical overture sounded from the *salle*. Charles and Morel lined up their troops in order of appearance, eased open the stage door into the wings, and Charles walked between the flats to take a last look at the audience before the ordered mayhem of performance began.

From the chandelier hanging over the middle of the stage and the iron holders fixed to the side flats, candles cast a welcome yellow glow. But the gray light from the long room's windows was as somber as Lent itself. Charles reminded himself that nevertheless, the snow was gone, melted in the chill, dripping rain that had come with February. And that Lent brought spring as well as salt fish.

He feasted his color-starved eyes for a moment on the deep blue satin of the Duc du Maine's suit and his sister's rose brocade, bright among the more sober colors of their attendants. As he looked, though, he wondered whether the young woman, whose voice was more carrying than Bertamelli's, was going to chatter to her brother throughout the show. The overture was nearing its end. Charles's gaze swept one last time over the audience, and he smiled in surprise as he saw Lieutenant-Général La

Reynie standing at the back of the *salle des actes*, next to Père Damiot. Wondering if they'd found something to talk about before the music began, and hoping that they had, he went back through the wing to the stage door and pulled it all the way open.

Celse's overture was ending. Michele Bertamelli was waiting in the doorway in his spring-green coat and breeches, the wreath of flowers and birds—symbols of youth—nested in his dark curling hair, a branch of yellow silk flowers in his hand. Charles put a hand on his shoulder and guided him farther into the wing, ready for his entrance. In the pause between the overture and the first notes of *Celse*'s first act, Bertamelli lifted his radiant face to Charles and gave him a smile that made Charles's breath catch in his throat, a smile so joyous and young that winter and sorrow might never have existed. Then the music began again, and the little Italian filled his lungs and burst onto the stage like spring itself.

❧ Author's Note ❧

The poetry of history lies in the quasi-miraculous fact that once, on this earth, on this familiar spot of ground, walked men and women, as actual as we are today, thinking their own thoughts, swayed by their own passions, but now all gone . . . gone as utterly as we ourselves shall be gone, like ghosts at cockcrow.

—G. M. Trevelyan, *Autobiography of a Historian*

The Eloquence of Blood is fiction, but the story happens in real places and some of its characters are real seventeenth-century people. Charles du Luc is fictional, but his college of Louis le Grand still stands on the rue St. Jacques, in Paris's Left Bank University quarter. Its rhetoric teachers really did produce ballets, drama, and even opera, as part of teaching eloquence of body and voice. In 1687, the Latin tragedy *Celsus* and Marc-Antoine Charpentier's opera *Celse* (called a *tragédie en musique*) served as the annual pre-Lenten performance, celebrating the end of Carnival and ushering in the season of Lent, which began two days later, on Ash Wednesday.

As I was writing the book, people often asked me if a single woman could have adopted a child, as Anne Mynette does in the story. They could and did, even though in formal law, adoption had become illegal. But customary law—doing things as they'd always been done—was still strong in France. Anyone who wanted to adopt went to a notary and had papers drawn up detailing what they would do for the child. If they wanted money or property to go to the child after their own death, they drew up a *donation entre vifs*. Nothing could be willed to a child who was adopted or illegitimate. Also, people of the time made a harsh distinction between an orphan of married parents and a nameless foundling, and it is this distinction that worries Charles in relation to Martine. The concern for maintaining bloodlines—through children of one's own blood or children whose parentage, and therefore blood, was known—was growing in France and would eventually eliminate adoption altogether.

Nicolas de La Reynie, first head of the Paris police, is real, and so are Père Jacques Le Picart, Père Joseph Jouvancy, dancing master Pierre Beauchamps (a passionate collector of paintings), and composer Marc-Antoine Charpentier. The seventeen-year-old Duc du Maine, seen briefly at the February performance, was a legitimized son of Louis XIV. His sister is fictional, and I've given her the fictional title of Mademoiselle de Ronen. Père Claude François Menestrier, who appears at the end of the story, was a renowned creator of elaborate spectacles for European courts and public occasions. He wrote several books on dance and is regarded as the first European dance historian. He and Jouvancy planned the sumptuous decor for the April 26, 1687, interment of the Great Condé's heart in the altar wall of the Jesuit church of St. Louis. There is a drawing of the decorated church in the Carnavalet Museum in Paris, showing sweeping blue drapery and a myriad of skulls—whether real or of papier-mâché, it is hard to tell. The Great Condé was a Bourbon, a royal Prince of the Blood, and it had long been customary for royalty to leave their hearts, and sometimes their entrails, to religious institutions for separate burial. To receive a "relic" of this kind was considered a great honor for a religious house.

The sad story of Claire Clemence, wife of the Great Condé, is true, though her devoted servant Marin is imagined. Claire Clemence died in 1694, after many years of virtual imprisonment at the remote Condé castle of Chateauroux, in the province of Berry.

As for what else is real in the story, Louis XIV really did fear and dislike Paris, because of his experiences there as a child in the 1640s revolt against the monarchy. The war minister Louvois, who ranked above La Reynie, loathed any kind of disorder—especially in Paris and especially on the rare occasions when the king visited, as he did on January thirtieth 1687 for the dinner the city fathers gave him at the Hôtel de Ville. And the Capuchin friars really were the firefighters of Paris.

As for Henri Brion's smuggling scheme, it, too, happened—though the instance I know about happened in the eighteenth century, and that time, it was Jesuits who hid silver under the chocolate . . .

READERS GUIDE

The Eloquence of Blood

Discussion Questions

1. How does Charles struggle with his role as a man of the cloth versus that of being a man of worldly desires? How did he come into this position and how does his vocation both cause him to struggle (to give in to temptation) and provide him with direction?

2. Were you initially suspicious of the church in having a hand in the deaths of both Martine and the notary? Why? Who else had sufficient motivation to kill, especially as the *patrimoine* was surrounded by confusion?

3. Discuss the class structure (and the boundaries) of seventeenth-century Parisian society. How does social standing and parentage affect one's destiny? What might the future hold for an orphan, or young woman without a solid financial future?

4. Do you think the Jesuits did the right thing as tension against them began to mount—even as their silence began to put the students in jeopardy? How do you think they could have diffused the climate of violence?

5. What motivates Charles's commitment to the investigations? Why does he insist on clearing Gilles of the crime, even though it would not lift the veil of suspicion off the Jesuits?

6. Why does Gilles refuse to reveal the name of his companion? What might be the repercussions? What would be the sacrifices? Why do

you think Charles agrees to keep his investigation as discreet as possible?

7. How does the song allow the townspeople of Paris to deal with their outrage over the deaths of Martine and Brion? Is this a form of free speech or would you consider it intimidation or harassment? Do you think those who distributed the lyrics should have been punished?

8. Why did the beggars come to Charles's rescue against the attacking street mob, risking their safety to save him? How does Charles repay this kindness—and how is his behavior toward the poor different from the prevailing attitudes of the time?

9. Who is Reine and what was her life like before begging? What is her role in the streets—to both the Jesuits and the police? How does she work with all sides to create dialogue, to help keep a semblance of peace?

10. Were you shocked to learn the killer's true identity and motivations?

11. Where you surprised to learn who stole Anne and Martine's donation paper? Who was he ultimately trying to protect?

12. What is "the Sacred Heart" and how does it play a role in the novel? From Martine's necklace, the Prince of Condé's heart, and the symbol in Charles's dream—how are all these ideas united?

Would you like to have Judith Skype into your book club? Visit her website at www.judithrock.com for more information!

Turn the page for a sneak peek into Charles's next adventure . . .

A Plague of Lies

Coming soon from Berkley!

FEAST OF ST. CLOTHILDE, TUESDAY, JUNE 3, 1687

The storm-riding demons of the air were gathered over Paris, hurling thunder and lightning at the city's cowering mortals. Every bell ringer in the city was hauling on his ropes, turning the church bells—baptized like good Christians for just this purpose—into widemouthed roaring angels fighting off the storm with their own deafening noise. The terrifying spring thunderstorm had begun north of the river, but now it raged directly over the rue St. Jacques, sending thunder echoing off walls and stabbing roofs and cobbles with spears of rain. In the Jesuit college of Louis le Grand, teachers and students were praying to aid the clanging bells. But the prayers of the senior rhetoric class dissolved into gasps and cries when lightning struck nearly into the main courtyard.

The near miss made assistant rhetoric master Maître Charles du Luc's skin tingle. And startled him into wondering if the demons of the air, in whom he mostly didn't believe when the sun was shining, were bent on making this day his last on earth.

"*Messieurs*, I beg you, calm yourselves," he shouted over the noise to his students huddled together on the classroom benches. "All storms pass. The bells are winning, as they always do, because we baptize them to make them stronger than the demons of the air. Listen! The demons are fleeing toward the south now." By force of will and voice, he called the boys back to their unfinished praying.

When he looked up after the "amen," one of the students, Armand Beauclaire, was frowning thoughtfully at the oak-beamed ceiling. Beauclaire, a round-faced sixteen, with a thick straight thatch of brown hair, put up a hand and shifted his gaze to the teachers' dais at the front of the room.

"Yes, Monsieur Beauclaire?" Charles called over the storm's receding noise, girding his mental loins. Beauclaire's questions were always interesting and never easy to answer.

"Is it really demons, *maître*? If the demons of the air cause thunderstorms, why do the storms always end? Why don't the demons win sometimes?"

"An excellent question, *monsieur*." But not one Charles was going to discuss there and then. Though he mostly doubted the demon theory, many people—including many of the Jesuits at Louis le Grand—didn't. And he had to get the class through many more pages of Greek before the afternoon ended. He smiled at Beauclaire. "Perhaps the demons always lose because good is stronger than evil," he said. And hoped that his belief in the second half of his sentence was enough to justify his evasion. "But now, back to rhetoric!"

Though nearly eight years a member of the Society of Jesus, Charles was still in the "scholastic" phase of his long Jesuit training, with final vows and ordination as a priest still to come. His work assignment was as a teacher of rhetoric, the art of communication in both Latin and Greek, Greek being by far the most difficult. Now, as the storm receded outside, and he tried to find his place in the book open on the oak lectern in front of him, he wondered if he looked as unconfident as he felt. Behind the professor's dais where he stood was a tapestry showing the unfortunate philosopher Socrates drinking his fatal cup of hemlock. Its graphic showing of an unpopular academic's fate made an uncomfortable teaching backdrop, he'd always thought. But, no help for it, there were still two hours of class before the afternoon ended. He smoothed the book's pages open, pushed his black skullcap down on his curling, straw-blond hair, and twitched at his cassock sleeves. The long linen shirt under the black woolen cassock showed correctly as narrow bands of white at wrists and high-collared neck, and the cassock hung sleekly on his six feet and more of wide-shouldered height. With a deep breath and a prayer to St. Chrysostom, the only Greek saint he could think of at the moment, Charles tackled the Greek rules of rhetoric, sometimes reading from the book, sometimes explaining what he read.

But under all that, he was feeling overwhelmed by his responsibilities. He was assistant to Père Joseph Jouvancy, senior rhetoric master and famous for his teaching and writing, but Jouvancy was in the infirmary recovering from sickness, and the second senior master, Père Martin Pallu, had just fallen ill with the same unpleasant malady. Which left Charles in sole charge of the thirty senior rhetoric students.

He paused, giving the class time to write down what he'd said, and let his eyes wander over the benches. The boys bent over small boards braced on their laps, feathered quills scratching across their paper, and all he could see of them were the tops of their flat-crowned hats above their black scholar's gowns. Louis le Grand's students ranged in age from about ten to twenty. The youngest in this class was thirteen, a little Milanese named Michele Bertamelli, with a mass of curls as black as his hat. Most of the bent heads were French and every shade of brown, apparently God's favorite color for hair. But there were also boys from England, Ireland, and Poland—one with hair flaming like copper, others as blond as

Charles himself was, thanks to his Norman mother's Viking forbears.

Charles glanced out at the courtyard and saw that the rain had nearly stopped. The storm was south of the city now, and the bell ringers of Paris were letting their ropes go slack. Relieved at no longer having to shout over the noise, he went back to feeding his fledgling scholars Aristotle's rules for rhetoric. But even as he tried to make his dry morsels of knowledge tempting, his thoughts kept circling around all that he should have finished and hadn't. His biggest worry was the summer ballet and tragedy performance on August sixth. In Jesuit schools, both voice and body were trained for eloquence, which meant that part of Charles's job was directing the ballets that went with the school's grand tragedy performance every summer. This year, under Jouvancy's watchful eye, Charles was responsible for writing the ballet's *livret*, as well as directing the ballet itself. But because of Jouvancy's illness, the *livret* wasn't finished, and rehearsals were late starting. And what if Jouvancy's illness returned and worsened, as illness so often did? If that happened, Charles knew that he might end up directing the tragedy as well as the ballet, and the threat of having to direct both was almost enough to make him volunteer for the New World missions. But only almost.

He finished his lecture and told the class's three *decurions*—class leaders named for Roman army officers commanding ten men each—to collect the afternoon's written work and bring it to the dais. Then he set them to hear each of their "men" recite the assigned memory passage. Today it was from St. Basil's writings. Greek recitation was never popular. When the *decurions* delivered the bad news of recitation, thirteen-year-old Bertamelli sprang from his seat and flung his arms wide.

"But, *maître*," he wailed, "I cannot speak Greek, it hurts my tongue!"

Snorts of laughter erupted along the benches, Charles bit his lip to keep from laughing himself. Henri de Montmorency, the dull-witted scion of a noble house, turned on his bench and gaped at Bertamelli.

"You're mad. Words can't hurt anything!"

Charles called the class back to order, fixed Bertamelli with his eye, and schooled his face to stern disapproval. The boy's scholar's gown had slipped off one shoulder to reveal his crumpled and grayed linen shirt, and his huge black eyes were tragic with pleading. He was one of the most gifted dancers Charles had ever seen. He was also proving nearly impossible to contain within Louis le Grand's rules—and probably its walls, though Charles preferred not to think about that. He suspected that the little Italian would not be with them long, though who would crack first, Bertamelli or the Jesuits, he wouldn't have cared to predict.

"To put Monsieur de Montmorency's puzzlement more politely," Charles said, with a sideways frown at Montmorency, "how does Greek hurt your tongue, Monsieur Bertamelli?"

"It has hard edges, sharp edges, *cruel* edges, it bites me! My tongue is a tender Italian tongue!" To be sure Charles understood, he stuck the sensitive member in question out as far as it would go.

"No need for scientific demonstration, Monsieur Bertamelli, and please pull your gown closed over your shirt. And if at all possible, compose yourself."

Bertamelli yanked his gown onto his shoulder, pulled it straight, and clasped his thin brown hands together under his chin. His eyes grew even larger. "My tongue—"

"Let your tongue rest, *monsieur*, and make your ears work. Hear three things that I am going to tell you." Charles held up his thumb. "Number one: Learning Greek will strengthen the sinews of your tender Italian tongue." His first finger joined his thumb. "Two: Every educated man must learn Greek. While Latin is our international language of scholarship, what the Romans wrote in Latin is rooted in what the Greeks wrote first." Charles's second finger uncurled and his eyes swept the classroom and came to rest on Montmorency. "Three—and this is for each of you: You will observe the rules of classroom behavior. If you want to speak, put up your hand. As you very well know. Now, Monsieur Bertamelli, sit down and prepare yourself for your Greek recitation."

Bertamelli sat. Two tears spilled from his wounded black eyes. He wiped them with the edge of his gown, gazing at Charles like a martyr forgiving his tormentors. The room filled slowly with a quiet, dogged murmuring that Aristotle surely would not have recognized as Greek.

Charles left the lectern and opened one of the long windows, letting in a rush of chilly air the storm had brought. The rain had stopped, leaving behind the music of water dripping from the blue slate roofs and splashing into the courtyard gravel. He'd come to Louis le Grand from the south of France less than a year ago, but he'd quickly learned to love this sprawl of ill-matched buildings grouped around graveled courtyards. Some buildings were five stories of weather-blackened stone, the oldest were two stories and half-timbered, and a few were bright new stone with corners and windows trimmed in rosy brick. All the roofs bristled with chimneys and towers. Some of the courtyards had shade trees and benches, two had gardens, one had an old well, and one boasted an ancient grapevine on a sunny wall. Rounded stone arches led to passages between the courts and from the enormous main courtyard, called the Cour d'honneur, out to the rue St. Jacques.

It was in the Cour d'honneur, outside the rhetoric classroom windows, that the outdoor stage for the summer ballet and tragedy was built each year. As Charles stood at the window, he began imagining scenery to go with the final section of his ballet *livret*, called *La France Victorieuse sous Louis le Grand*. The title, like this school's name, honored King Louis XIV. The original *France Victorious Under Louis the Great* had been performed at the school in 1680, and Charles was only rewriting and updating it. Less work, to be sure, than creating an entirely new *livret*. But hard work still, and no easier because he so disliked Louis XIV—his passion for glory and his indifference to his people's suffering under the draconian taxes that paid for the glory-bringing wars. He particularly loathed the Most Christian King of France, as Louis styled himself, for hunting and slaughtering France's Protestants, called Huguenots, in God's name. Charles was a loyal son of Holy Mother Church, but he was utterly certain that God was Love. Demanding, relentless, even terrifying, but Love nonetheless. Which meant that cruelty in God's name was blasphemy, pure and simple. Which amounted to calling the king a blasphemer. Which was treason, pure and simple.

Even as he thought that, King Louis XIV was staring blindly back at him from the top of the Cour d'honneur's north wall. The recently installed bust was a copy of one shattered by a storm-felled tree the year before, and Charles had developed a teeth-gritting dislike of those sightless eyes overseeing his daily comings and goings. He turned away from Louis and watched dripping water dig a small pool in the gravel under the window. Small persistent forces often won in the end. He had the sudden thought that maybe he could slip something into the ballet *livret* that didn't praise Louis, some small piece of a different truth to raise disquiet in those with ears to hear . . . *Treason* again, the cool-eyed critic in him said sharply. *Kings are divinely anointed. Kings preserve order. Order allows good to flourish.* Just as sharply, Charles thought back on it—*Whose good?*—and turned from the window to his work.

The ending bell finally rang. The students filed out and were met by a *cubiculaire*, a Jesuit scholastic whose work was supervising students. As the *cubiculaire* chivied the boys toward their living quarters in the student courtyard, Charles went gratefully out into the watery, late-afternoon sunshine. But before he was half-way across the court, someone called his name, and he looked back to see the college rector, Père Jacques Le Picart, the head of Louis le Grand.

Bowing, Charles greeted him, noting his muddy riding boots and spattered cloak. "You've had a wet ride, *mon père.*"

"Wet enough, *maître.* The storm caught me on the way back from Versailles."

They walked together to the rear door of the main building where their rooms were, Le Picart asking Charles about his own afternoon and nodding in sympathy at his worry over the approaching rehearsals. But the rector seemed preoccupied and before they reached the door, he said, "Have you visited Père Jouvancy today, *maître?*"

Charles shook his head. "I've had no chance today, *mon père.* But Père Montville told me as we were leaving the student refectory after dinner that he's much better and able to eat now."

"Good. Will you come with me to the infirmary? I must speak with him, and the matter may concern you, as well."

"Of course, *mon père.*" Wondering uneasily what "the matter" was, Charles turned with Le Picart toward the infirmary court.

Most of May had been blessedly warm after the hard winter, and the physick garden in the infirmary courtyard was already blooming. The afternoon's rain had left the blossoms somewhat bedraggled, but the air was drenched in fresh sweet scents. Charles filled his lungs eagerly. Which was a good thing, because the fathers' infirmary, below the student infirmary and beside the ground-floor room for making medicines, smelled pungently of sickness. Frère Brunet, the lay brother infirmarian, turned from a bed at the room's far end and bustled toward them, his soft shoes whispering along the rush matting between the two short rows of beds. All but two beds were empty. Before he reached them, Père Jouvancy called out, "Ah, *mon père, maître*, welcome, come in, come in!"

His bed was in the left-hand row, between two windows, and he was sitting up among his gray blankets, the fitful sunshine warming the new color in his face.

"I would ask you how he is, Frère Brunet," Le Picart said to the infirmarian, "but I see for myself that he really is better." He smiled affectionately at Jouvancy. "You've had a hard time of it, *mon père*. But if you feel as much better as you look, you will soon be back among us."

"Oh, he will, certainly he will," Brunet said, surveying his patient with satisfaction.

"And Père Pallu?" Le Picart asked, looking toward the other bed.

Brunet shook his head. "Poor man, he seems to be in for the same hard time. Oh, he will no doubt do well enough, but for now he is suffering fever, chills, aches in his body, sore throat." Brunet glanced ruefully over his shoulder. "And he can keep nothing down."

Retching from the far end of the right-hand line of beds confirmed his words, and Charles swallowed hard. In his two years as a soldier, he'd helped care for bloody wounds without turning a hair. But spewing—his own or anyone else's—turned him weak-kneed.

"Sit, *mon père*, if you have the time," Jouvancy said hopefully, and Le Picart pulled a stool near the bed, gesturing Charles to bring a stool for himself.

"Visit then," Brunet said, laying a hand on Jouvancy's forehead and nodding approvingly. "But see you don't tire him." Behind him, the retching began again and he hurried away to Père Pallu.

Jouvancy beamed at Le Picart and Charles. "Thank you for coming, both of you! I only need to get my strength back now." He shook a finger at Charles. "So do not become too fond of your independence, *maître*, I will be back before you know it."

"Mon père," Charles said fervently, "I will give thanks on my knees when you are back! I fear I am a poor substitute."

Jouvancy eyed him shrewdly. "Greek today, was it?"

"Greek indeed."

"Yes, on Greek days, I often find myself moved to volunteer for the missions." His blue eyes grew dreamy. "Less use for Greek in the missions. And I understand they do theatrical pieces, operas, even."

Le Picart laughed. "That is as good an opening as any for what I have come to say. Because I do want to send you somewhere."

"I will, of course, go wherever you bid me, *mon père*. To Tibet, if you say so!"

"Somewhere much closer to home. As soon as you are well enough to travel, I want you to go to Versailles."

Jouvancy blinked. "What might a lowly rhetoric professor do at court?"

"You are a connection of the d'Aubigné family, I believe."

"D'Aubigné?" Charles looked in surprise at Jouvancy. That was Madame de Maintenon's name, the king's second wife, who was born Françoise d'Aubigné. "That makes you nearly a relation of King Louis, *mon père!*"

"Yes, I suppose it does. My father was a d'Aubigné connection, but a distant one, as distant as China from the trunk of the family tree," Jouvancy said. "For which I am thankful when I think of how worthless poor Madame de Maintenon's father was. She was born in prison, did you know that? Her poor mother had nowhere else to be, after the father was arrested for debt and dueling. Monsieur d'Aubigné was a charming scoundrel and no good to anyone. Though his daughter seems to be a pattern of uprightness. I have met her only once, you know, when she came here a few summers back, to see the tragedy and ballet. And the family connection was not mentioned."

"Still, that you have already met her is to the good. And what Maître du Luc has said is true. Consider, *mon père*," Le Picart said, leaning forward on his stool. "You are a distant relation of the king's wife, which, as Maître du Luc has said, makes you some sort of relation by marriage to Louis himself, and that is going to be useful. I am just returned from Versailles. The Comtesse de Rosaire asked me to come and talk to her about Louis le Grand. She wants to send her twin sons to us next autumn. Because she is recently widowed—and a comtesse—I went." He shrugged sheepishly. "And after, I knocked at Père La Chaise's door on the chance that he was there." The Jesuit Père François La Chaise was the king's confessor. "He was not, and as I turned from the door, I met Madame de Maintenon and her ladies in the corridor. I uncovered and made my *reverence*. She glared. At Père La Chaise's door and at me. Though she did acknowledge me with a '*mon père*,' just audibly and between her teeth, before she and her entourage swept on."

"Oh, dear," Jouvancy said. "I thought that after Père La Chaise made no objection to her marrying the king, she would think better of Jesuits." He looked questioningly at the rector. "I've even heard that our Père La Chaise conducted the ceremony that made her Louis's wife."

"Wife, yes," Le Picart said, ignoring the curiosity about Père La Chaise's role, "but not queen, because she's too lowly born.

And even as a wife, she is unacknowledged, which I suspect is part of her anger at Père La Chaise, who wants the marriage kept secret. Because of her rank, he fears the outcry there would be if the marriage were publicly proclaimed. Frenchmen expect glory to shimmer around everything connected to their king, and an aging lady of besmirched minor nobility is far from glorious."

Jouvancy's eyes danced with sudden laughter. "Well, at least she didn't mention the nickname when she saw you outside Père La Chaise's door."

Le Picart grinned. "No. But she was thinking it."

"What nickname?" Charles said.

"Forgive us, of course you wouldn't know," Jouvancy said. "I doubt it ever went as far as Languedoc. Long before the king married Madame de Maintenon, she was very angry at Père La Chaise's refusal to force the king to put away his mistress, Madame de Montespan. La Montespan and the king did part, finally—Père La Chaise had a hand in that—but then she came back to court, and the result was two more children. Madame de Maintenon was furious. She had been governess to their first set of children, which was how she met the king. But she refused to have anything to do with the second set of royal bastards. And she began calling our Père La Chaise *Père La Chaise de Commodité* for not stopping the liaison. As though he could have stopped it. But the nickname was the delight of the gossips, and all Versailles and Paris laughed themselves silly."

"She really called him that?" Charles was fighting laughter himself. The name La Chaise, of course, meant chair, so *Père La Chaise de Commodité*, to put it plainly and rudely, meant Père Toilet.

"Yes," Le Picart said. "Not that I think she'd call him that now—it would be below her new dignity. But I was alarmed by the ice in her manner this morning. I'm told the king does listen to her opinions, especially about the state of his soul. And anything that threatens Père La Chaise's tenure as royal confessor threatens the Society of Jesus. He is our Jesuit presence there, our conduit of knowledge about court affairs. Beyond that, I think he's a good director of the king's conscience because he knows how to influence without demanding. Who can *demand* anything of Louis and keep his position? It would only harm the king to lose a confessor who knows how to work for good within that constraint. So, Père Jouvancy, I want you to go to Versailles and sweeten your good cousin Madame de Maintenon."

"Cousin she is not. But I will do whatever you require and with a good will, *mon père*." Jouvancy drew himself up higher on his pillows and tugged his long white linen shirt straight, as though preparing to set out immediately. "But what exactly do you want me to do?"

"I thought we'd start with bribery."

The two priests exchanged a wryly knowing look.

"A time-honored method," Jouvancy said. "What are we bribing her with?"

"Saint Ursula's little finger. Given to us by your family and therefore, by extension, hers."

"If one makes a very long extension. But, yes, well thought." The rhetoric master's face lit slowly with enthusiasm as he pondered what the rector had said. "I do remember how much she admired Saint Ursula's reliquary when she came here."

"The lapis and gold cross in the chapel?" Charles said in disbelief. "You're giving that away?"

Le Picart gave him an admonishing look. "Why not? It is ours to give. Père Jouvancy's family gave it to us when he came here to teach. And as you have heard, Madame de Maintenon admired it when she brought some of the royal children to a summer performance here and afterward visited the chapel." The rector lifted a bushy gray eyebrow. "Though I don't think she admired the ballet." He turned back to Jouvancy. "So I want you to take the reliquary personally to Versailles, *mon père.* The gift will mean that much more, coming from the hands of a family connection."

"But why now?" Charles said. The other two frowned questioningly at him and he stammered, "I mean—do we have—um—a pretext, if I may put it that way—for giving it now?"

The rector's frown deepened. "Oh. No, we don't."

"I know!" Jouvancy said. "We can say it's because of the honor the Duc du Maine and his sister Mademoiselle de Rouen—Madame de Maintenon raised them both—did us in coming to our February performance and praising Monsieur Charpentier's little opera. We can say we are showing our gratitude to a fellow educator, the lady who brought them up to be such examples of kindness and piety."

Le Picart snorted. "Isn't that laying it on a bit thick? Considering Mademoiselle de Rouen's—um—reputation?"

"Is there any such thing as 'too thick' when speaking of Children of France?" Jouvancy shot back. And added acerbically, "Even Bastards of France?"

"Too true," Le Picart said. "Very well, then, we have our reason for the gift. We must contrive the presentation to take place in the presence of Père La Chaise—I will ask—"

"And in the king's presence?" Jouvancy asked eagerly.

"That may be too much to hope for. But I will ask Père La Chaise to see that as many courtiers as possible are there. The more witnesses, the better. It won't change her mind about us, but it should—for a while, at least—make her guard her tongue. Which will give Père La Chaise a breathing space to make Louis less vulnerable to her whispering in his ear about acknowledging the marriage." He looked down the room and called softly to the infirmarian. "Frère Brunet, a moment, please."

Brunet turned from bending over Père Pallu and hurried down the line of beds. "Yes, *mon père?*"

"When can Père Jouvancy travel safely? For a short distance?"

"How short?"

"To Versailles."

Brunet frowned at Jouvancy. "Riding?"

"Yes."

The infirmarian tsked disapprovingly. "Not for another week or two, if I had my way." He eyed Le Picart. "But since I am obviously not going to have my way, I suppose he could ride three or four days from now. *If* the weather is dry and warm. And *if* someone is with him. And when he gets there, he will go straight to bed and rest until the morrow. And no late nights, mind you," he said with mock severity to Jouvancy. "No court revels!"

"You are a terrible spoilsport, *mon frère*," Jouvancy said, with an aggrieved sigh. "I was only going for the revels!"

Le Picart nodded and turned to Charles. "Maître du Luc, you will go with Père Jouvancy. You will be his caretaker and companion, and you will save him from as much effort as possible. You have some medical knowledge from your soldiering and can help look after him, if need be." He paused thoughtfully. "You will also be able to go freely about the court. Some people will ignore you as beneath their notice, but some will be curious about a new young face and will talk to you. You will be an affable clerical courtier and listen to all the talk that comes your way and repeat it to Père Jouvancy and Père La Chaise." There was warning in his shrewd gray eyes as he watched Charles's increasingly dismayed face. "You will do all that for the good of the Society."

"That is sound sense," Jouvancy agreed.

"But who will teach the senior rhetoric class?" Charles tried, knowing it was useless. "And our rehearsals begin so soon——"

The rector raised a silencing hand. "You will be gone only a few days. Père Bretonneau has taught rhetoric in the past and could take the class."

"Père Bretonneau will do very well," Jouvancy said with satisfaction. "And so will Maître du Luc. The two of us can also work on the August performance while we are gone." He smiled happily at Charles. "Have you ever been at court, *maître*?"

"No, *mon père*." And never wanted to be, Charles didn't say, looking down to hide his face. He certainly saw the importance of supporting Père La Chaise, whom he'd met and liked. But the thought of playing the courtier, even briefly, to a king he detested, made him feel far from obedient. He looked up and saw that Le Picart's eyes were still on him, at once ironic and knowing. As usual, the rector saw more than Charles wanted seen. Charles forced the words his vows required across his tongue.

"I will do my best, *mon père*," he said. And added mulishly, "For Père Jouvancy."

"And for our king." Le Picart emphasized every word.

"With all our hearts," Jouvancy said, making the words sound like a liturgical response in the Mass.

Charles bowed his head, letting Le Picart take the gesture for submission—if he chose—and said nothing. Like it or not, he was off to Versailles to play the courtier.

NOTES